PRAISE FOR RACHEL LEE

"A magnificent presence in romantic fiction.
Rachel Lee is an author to treasure forever."
—*Romantic Times*

"The superb pen of Rachel Lee returns to
Conard County for *Cowboy Comes Home,* another
splendid novel of the healing power of love."
—*Romantic Times*

"Rachel Lee deserves much acclaim for her
exciting tales of romantic suspense."
—*Midwest Book Review*

RACHEL LEE

wrote her first play in the third grade for a
school assembly, and by the age of twelve she
was hooked on writing. She's lived all over the
United States, on both the east and the west
coasts, and now resides in Florida.

Having held jobs as a security officer, real-estate
agent and optician, Rachel uses these experiences,
as well as her natural flair for creativity, to write
stories that are undeniably romantic. "After all,"
she says, "life is the biggest romantic adventure
of all—things are just waiting to be discovered."

RACHEL LEE

A MATTER OF TRUST

Silhouette Books

Published by Silhouette Books

America's Publisher of Contemporary Romance

SILHOUETTE BOOKS

A MATTER OF TRUST

Copyright © 2004 by Harlequin Books S.A.

ISBN 0-373-28526-4

The publisher acknowledges the copyright holder of the individual works as follows:

COWBOY COMES HOME
Copyright © 1998 by Susan Civil-Brown

A QUESTION OF JUSTICE
Copyright © 1995 by Susan Civil

Visit Silhouette Books at www.eHarlequin.com

Printed in U.S.A.

COWBOY COMES HOME

For the little girls who taught me that home is not always the safe place it should be.
May you all find a home that is.

Chapter 1

Anna Fleming was sure no one could see her.

She stood in the back of Good Shepherd Church in a dimly lit corner and watched the wedding ceremony. It was everything she had ever dreamed of for herself and the embodiment of all the dreams she had lost. A sad little sigh escaped her, but almost at once she lifted her chin and reminded herself not to wallow. It was always wiser to count one's blessings.

She was a mousy woman, small and bland looking in a shapeless brown dress and sensible shoes. Her dark hair was drawn back severely, and her wide brown eyes peered at the world from behind gold-rimmed glasses. Those glasses were the most flamboyant part of her apparel, but they were nothing out of the ordinary.

And that was how she liked it, she told herself as she watched Sheriff Tate's daughter marry the policeman from Los Angeles. No one noticed her, no one at all, and in her invisibility and anonymity, she found the only safety she had ever known.

Reverend Fromberg, a gentle man in his late forties, read the vows in a sonorous voice that reached the back of the church without difficulty. Anna listened to the words and wondered what it would be like to trust someone enough to make those promises. She couldn't imagine it. Trust, she had long ago learned, was more likely to be betrayed than fulfilled.

Stifling a weary sigh, she turned quietly and slipped out the side door into the vestibule, where she descended the stairs into the church basement. The room was brightly lighted and decorated for the reception and supper to follow the wedding. Anna walked swiftly around, checking to be sure that everything was in order. The caterers were putting last-minute touches on everything, and it wasn't really her responsibility, but she checked anyway. This was her church, and she was secretary to Reverend Fromberg, as well as leader of the youth group. She couldn't help but feel that whatever happened on church property reflected on her employer, and upon herself.

Satisfied, she darted back toward the stairway, planning to vanish back into the shadows in the church above, but found her way blocked by the looming bulk of the man known to everyone as Cowboy. He wasn't a large man, but he was solidly built, with dark hair and dark eyes, and a face that looked as if it had seen a great deal of hardship and sorrow. Anna was scared of him for no other reason than that she didn't know him, or anything about him, really.

Being caught by him like this, all alone—she completely forgot the caterers at the other end of the basement—startled and unnerved her. She jumped back and stumbled.

His arm shot out as swiftly as a striking snake and caught her elbow, steadying her.

Anna froze, looking up at him, uncertain what would happen next. Part of her realized he had just saved her from falling, but mostly she was aware that he was touching her. She hated to be touched. Suddenly, freed from her paralysis, she shook off his hand.

"Sorry," he said, his voice slow, deep and steady. "I didn't mean to startle you."

"I…" Suddenly embarrassed by her reaction to him, she felt she needed to say something. But what?

He gave her a half smile. "It's okay. I saw you come down here and wondered if maybe you were sick or something. People don't usually run out in the middle of the wedding vows. I thought you might need help." He shrugged a shoulder. "I didn't know all these other folks were down here."

Before she could think of a single thing to say, Cowboy turned and climbed the stairs. Anna stared after him, her eyes full of unspoken fears and wishes.

Hugh Gallagher, known far and wide as Cowboy for some damn reason he'd never been able to figure out, took his place at the back of the church and watched Janet and Abel Pierce pose for photographs with the wedding party. A steady stream of guests began to make their way to the rear of the church, toward the stairs that led down to the church basement. There would be laughter and food and many more pictures taken before the day was over, but Cowboy turned toward the door, getting ready to leave.

He was invited to the reception—hell, the sheriff had invited damn near everyone in the county to one or another of the parties he was throwing to celebrate this event—but he wasn't a party person. Crowds still made him uneasy, and the basement itself was too confined a space to make him comfortable, even when it was empty.

He hesitated, though, thinking of mousy Miss Fleming, the church secretary, and how startled she'd been to run into him on the stairs. He didn't like it when people reacted to him that way. It reminded him of things better left forgotten.

If he made himself go down there, maybe he could talk to her a bit, get her over her fear. He didn't want her reacting that way when she saw him again. On the other hand, if he went down there he was going to have to deal with his damn claustrophobia and all the other phobias that he preferred to leave undisturbed as much as possible.

Hell.

He hesitated a few moments longer, then decided to head outside and smoke a cigarette. Forcing the issue wasn't going to make Anna Fleming any more comfortable with him. He would just have to bide his time until a better opportunity came along.

Outside, the October twilight was already fading into night. The air was chilly but still, not too uncomfortable. Besides, he was used to far worse after wintering in the mountains in lean-tos and tents. He stepped off the walk onto the grass and lit a cigarette, inhaling with real pleasure. He ought to quit, and knew he was going to have to if he ever got his dream of a youth ranch off the ground, but for now, he savored every puff.

He wasn't the only one who sneaked out for a smoke. A couple of minutes later the double doors opened to disgorge a group of laughing men. He recognized them all—with only five thousand people in this county, it was hard not to learn to recognize most of them—but he stepped around the corner so that he was out of sight. People tended to regard him uneasily, as if he were a time bomb, and while he didn't exactly blame them, he resented the hell out of it. Besides, he didn't much feel like being sociable. The only reason he was here was that he didn't want to offend the sheriff and his family. They'd been too good to him.

The group out front stayed where they were, and Hugh let the deepening night wrap comfortably around him. Unlike most people, he always felt safer at night. At night he could be invisible. At night he could vanish.

The basement was a madhouse. Everyone was drinking, laughing, talking. The noise level was almost deafening in the confined space, and the temperature was soaring, even with all the windows open to let in the fresh air.

Anna was beginning to feel claustrophobic, as well as far too hot in her wool dress. She had always hated large crowds and was able to tolerate Sunday worship only because everyone was so orderly. They were not at all orderly right now, and the champagne was making everyone a little bit raucous.

She was, she realized, afraid of being grabbed. It wasn't so much the crowding as the smell of champagne that was affecting her. The scent of alcohol had preceded some of the worst experiences of her life. As soon as she felt she decently could, she grabbed her jacket and slipped out the side door.

She was hurrying, not wanting to be stopped by anyone, and had her head bowed as usual. She didn't see Hugh Gallagher until she plowed right into him.

He reached out swiftly to keep her from falling to the cold, hard ground. She felt his arms close around her and heard him say laughingly, "We've got to stop meeting like this."

In an instant, panic flared in her. She flailed against his restraining arms, and as soon as he released her, she backed up quickly, nearly falling again in her haste to escape him.

Some portion of her mind was screaming, "No! No!" even while another part was recognizing that he wasn't coming after her. That in fact he had stepped back, as if recognizing her terror and wanting to soothe it.

She stood there staring at him with huge eyes, breathing in helpless gulps, and sanity hit her as suddenly as panic had, filling her with miserable humiliation.

The man called Cowboy stared at her, his mouth opening as if he wanted to ask but thought better of it. Finally he stuffed his hands into the pockets of his nylon jacket and took another backward step. "I didn't mean to frighten you," he said.

"It's not you," she managed to say shakily but honestly. "Not you..." Her voice trailed away, a forlorn sound like the whisper of the wind on a frigid night. "I was just startled," she added, afraid that he might ask her what had scared her so.

After a moment, he nodded. "You're running away, too?"

Her heart slammed. How had he known? "Running away?"

"From the party. Stupid as it is, that basement gives me claustrophobia, and with all those people in there, I'd probably lose it." He shrugged as if it were an unimportant thing, but Anna felt something inside her respond to his honesty.

"I know what you mean," she managed to say, and wondered why she suddenly felt as if some little patch of ice inside her had thawed.

"You, too, huh?" He waited, but when she failed to respond he continued. "Are you leaving?"

"I thought I'd just go home. No one will miss me." The

words admitted more than she wanted to, but it was too late to take them back.

He nodded as if he understood. "No one will miss me, either. I'll walk you to your car."

Another flare of panic. "I didn't bring a car."

"Then I'll walk you home." He hesitated. "You're safe with me, but with most of the sheriff's deputies at this shindig, I'm not sure you'd be safe on the streets."

She hadn't thought of that, and the night suddenly looked so big and empty. Frightening. Bad things happened at night. Weighing her options, she finally said, "Thank you."

They headed east down Front Street, past some of the town's most elegant homes. Anna's little house, rented from the church, was farther out, in a less prosperous neighborhood—although it was far better than some of the neighborhoods she had lived in.

"Do you always walk to the church?" Hugh asked her.

"When it's warm enough. It saves wear and tear on the car." She kept her head down, studying the sidewalk ahead of them. Some dried leaves stirred on a breath of breeze and for a moment danced ahead of them.

"I hear you," he said. "I walked myself."

"Oh. Where do you live?" She wished she hadn't asked. She didn't want to sound interested. But surely he would take it as a polite question.

"The other way, over toward Snider's Crossing."

Near the railroad tracks, she thought. One of the least pleasant neighborhoods in Conard City. But Sheriff Tate and Reverend Fromberg both liked this man, she reminded herself. They wouldn't feel that way if he was a bad person.

"Not a very good neighborhood," he said as if reading her mind. "But it's cheap. I'm saving every dime I can make to put into the ranch."

"The ranch?" She felt him glance down at her, but she didn't look up. It had been a very long time since she had felt comfortable meeting a man's gaze.

"I bought a piece of land out by Conard Creek, up near the Morrison spread. It's not much for raising cattle for profit, but it's good for what I want."

"And what's that?"

"Well, I really haven't discussed it all that much with anybody except Nate and Dan." Nate and Dan being the sheriff and the minister respectively. "But I'm hoping to open a ranch for troubled kids. A place where they can get out of their lousy homes and neighborhoods and start getting it together."

"That would be really nice." She meant it sincerely. It was not at all what she would have expected from this rough-looking man with his uncertain background. "Did you grow up in a bad neighborhood?"

"Oh, yeah." He gave a little laugh. "I just moved from one war zone to another when I joined the army."

"I never thought of joining the army." Once again she had spoken without thinking, and wished she could snatch the words back. They revealed far too much.

"You, too, huh?" He let it go. "Well, with all the work you do with kids, you probably see how much trouble at home affects them."

"I certainly do."

"So...well, I kinda figure that if I can give them a place away from those problems and influences, most of 'em would straighten themselves out."

"A lot of them just need an opportunity."

"Exactly."

"Would you take only children from around here?"

"Maybe at first. At first I wouldn't expect to be able to

take too many. I mean, there'd just be me, basically, and maybe a couple of other people. Gotta start slow.''

Anna nodded, her gaze still firmly fixed on the sidewalk. "I know of a few who could sure use a place like that."

A car beeped cheerfully as it drove by, and they both looked, waving when they recognized Emma and Gage Dalton.

"They're leaving early, too," Hugh remarked.

"Gage's back is giving him fits lately," Anna explained. "He says it's the change in the weather."

"Most likely. And boy, did it change fast. Here we were having this incredible Indian summer, and now it almost feels like winter is coming."

"It is."

He laughed quietly. "That it is, Miss Anna. That it is."

She flushed a little, realizing she had stated the obvious in response to his jesting remark. The tendency came from dealing with children so much of the time. In addition to her work with the church youth groups, she tended the church nursery during services. After a while with children, you got to taking everything literally. "I'm sorry. I get so used to talking with children."

"Don't sweat it. You're just so all-fired serious, it's hard not to pull your leg."

She didn't know how to respond to that. She didn't think of herself as being serious, but she supposed she was. There wasn't a whole lot in life worth laughing at or getting overjoyed about. Life was a serious business.

"Anyway, the sheriff thinks the ranch is a good idea. I figure maybe we'd start with a half-dozen kids and see how it goes. I'd like to be able to take girls, too."

"Really?"

"Sure. Everybody gets so concerned about all the crime

caused by boys that girls get overlooked. They don't commit as many crimes, but they have just as many problems at home and on the streets. Somebody needs to look out for them, too.''

"But won't making it coeducational cause problems?''

"Not if I do it right.''

They had reached Park Street and turned right, heading toward her house two blocks down. Most of the driveways were empty, since nearly everybody was partying.

Hugh spoke again. "I don't know how Nate is going to be able to afford to marry off so many daughters if he invites everybody in the county to the shindig.''

"It's amazing, isn't it? But he knows everybody. And he's not doing sit-down meals, so maybe it's not as bad as it could be.''

"Maybe.''

They reached her house at last, climbed the porch steps and stopped at her door.

"I'll just wait while you get inside, Miss Anna,'' he said. "You have a good evening, hear?''

She stepped inside, turned on the light and locked the door behind her. Then she ran into the darkened living room to look out the window to watch him walk away. He had a slow, easy stride, like a man who'd walked many miles and was in no hurry to get to his destination.

She envied him his calm confidence and steady determination. She wished that once, just once, she could feel as comfortable with herself as he seemed to feel. And it must be wonderful to be able to walk down a dark street and not feel a nagging need to look back over your shoulder.

She let the curtain fall over the window and turned on another light. She was home and she was lonely.

Nothing new. It was a fact of life. Loneliness kept her safe.

* * *

She had the nightmare again that night. It had been years since the last time, but it was still all too familiar when she woke up in a cold sweat, shaking with terror. The night-light she couldn't sleep without glowed softly in the wall socket, but suddenly it wasn't enough. Even the shadowy shapes of the furnishings refused to resolve into familiarity by its light.

Sitting up quickly, she reached for the switch on the bed-side lamp. It came instantly to life, then, with a flash, burned out. Shaking, shivering, breathing raggedly, she desperately fought her way out from beneath the blankets and ran as fast as she dared into the kitchen. There, the flick of a wall switch cast immediate normalcy over the night.

The refrigerator hummed softly, as it always did. She could smell the very faint odor of gas from the range and realized the pilot must have gone out. Searching for matches gave her something to do, something ordinary and real. Something to drag her out of the consuming depths of her dream.

The matches were where she always kept them, but she dropped the box twice just trying to get it out of the drawer. She waited a moment, taking deep, steadying breaths, then lit the pilot light under the range cover. The match slipped from between her fingers into the drip pan, but she left it. It could stay until she was steadier.

She poured herself a glass of milk and tried to ignore the phone on the wall, but it was as if her eyes were attached to it by rubber bands. No matter how many times she jerked her gaze away, it snapped back.

He might be dead by now. The thought was seductive and wouldn't go away. It had been years since she had called, and he would have to be in his sixties now, wouldn't he? So maybe he was dead. God, she hoped he was dead.

But she didn't want to hear his voice. What if he answered the phone? Then she would know for sure he wasn't dead, that he was still out there. It was better not to know.

She sipped her milk and shivered again, this time from a chill. It was four in the morning, and while the house wasn't cold, her body thought it ought to be in bed under the covers. But she couldn't go back to sleep. Not now. She would only have the dream again. Once it came, it just kept coming back.

She wandered through the house, turning on lights as she went, refusing to worry about the cost. She sat in the big, overstuffed chair she had bought secondhand last winter and tried to read a paperback crime novel. She turned the pages four times before she realized she hadn't absorbed a single word.

Giving up, she tried to turn her thoughts back to the wedding. Back to how nice Hugh Gallagher had been to her. And he *had* been nice. As threatened as most men made her feel, it was really surprising that he had managed to make her feel safe enough to let him walk her home.

There was a gentleness in his manner, she realized. Something that had reassured her. The slow way he talked, the easy way he held himself, the quick consideration of her feelings had all combined to make her feel she could trust him at least that far. Only Nate Tate and Dan Fromberg had been able to get so far past her defenses.

Deep inside her, she was astonished to realize, was a barely born hope that she would see Cowboy again.

As soon as she recognized it, she felt panic begin to build in her. No. No, she told herself. No. It was too dangerous.

There were too many secrets. Too many horrible things in her past. Even if she could trust him not to hurt her, she couldn't trust herself not to hurt *him*.

It wasn't just the fact that she was terrified of men that kept her away from them; she was terrified of what her past could do to her relationships, to her entire life, if anyone found out about it.

Solitude was her fortress, and she kept herself inside it of her own free will. She couldn't afford to lose sight of that.

But the phone kept beckoning her. He might be dead. It would be nice to know that he was.

The thought upset her, it seemed so evil, but the man had done evil things to her. She didn't exactly wish him dead, she assured herself. It was just that she knew she wouldn't be free of him until he was gone. Then she would have only the horrible things she'd done herself to be worried about. By comparison, her own deeds seemed paltry. She could handle that guilt.

She looked at the phone beside her chair and knew that she was going to call. She didn't want to. She couldn't stand the thought of hearing his voice again, but she had to know. Ever since she could remember, she had been doing things she didn't want to because of that man, and she longed to break his hold over her.

But she couldn't stop herself. As if watching from a distance, she saw her hand reach out for the receiver, watched her own fingers punch in a number she would never forget. Then, holding her breath, she waited while the phone rang. It was two hours later back there, and if he wasn't up already, he would be getting up soon.

On the sixth ring, a groggy male voice answered. "Hello?"

She slammed down the receiver immediately, disconnecting the call. Her heart hammered wildly, and she could scarcely catch her breath.

He was still alive. Still sleeping in her mother's bed as if he'd never done anything wrong. She would bet *he* never had nightmares about what he'd done to her. Never. He probably slept like a baby.

And suddenly, unable to help herself, Anna burst into tears and cried until she couldn't cry anymore.

Chapter 2

"Anna, you have to rescue me."

Anna looked up from her desk as Reverend Daniel Fromberg stepped in from the brisk day outside. She made a point of always getting to the office ahead of him, and he had to insist in order to get her to leave before him.

Daniel Fromberg was a pleasant-looking man in his late forties. Just average in height, he had a slight build that sometimes made people underestimate his backbone. As Anna had learned during the past five years, Daniel Fromberg had a backbone of steel when it came to what was right.

"What's wrong?" she asked, feeling a smile curve the corners of her mouth. With two teenage children and a pair of unexpected two-year-old twins, Dan Fromberg was often in need of her help. It usually involved finding him a babysitter so he could save his wife's sanity.

"The dogs!" he said with an exaggerated groan as he dropped into the chair facing her desk. Eight weeks ago, the Frombergs' Irish setter had given birth to four adorable little pups. "They're driving me nuts. They're driving Cheryl nuts. They're into everything! Piddling all over the place, making little piles behind the couch, the TV, the bed—you name it!"

"So get a gate and lock them into one small area of the house."

He shook his head. "I tried to. Clearly you do not know my children."

She laughed; she couldn't help it. "They let them out, huh?"

"All the time. The older ones finally got the message, but the twins…!" He shook his head. "They just love to release the catch. Cheryl tried using a twisty-tie to stop them, but Dan junior figured it out. Then we tried a padlock, but this morning Jolly—that's the momma dog—got fed up with being cooped up and knocked the darn thing down. I now have holes in the doorjamb and a broken gate. Cheryl's threatening to take the pups to the pound."

Anna felt a twinge of dismay. "You can't do that! Surely you can get someone to adopt them."

"That's what we thought. I mean, the whole reason we never got Jolly spayed was because the older kids wanted puppies, and Cheryl thought it would be a good experience for them. But now we've got too many puppies, and would you believe it? Nobody wants a dog, especially mongrels. Everybody already *has* a dog." He eyed her. "Except you."

"No, you can't do this to me."

"Do what to you? Give you a warm, furry little companion? Some soft-eyed little fuzzball that will curl up on your feet on cold winter evenings? A friend who will always be glad to see you and will lick your face when you get sad? How can that be construed as doing something to you?"

Anna felt herself weakening. It was true, she had been

thinking about a pet, but she had thought a cat would be better suited to her sometimes long work hours. "It wouldn't be fair to a puppy to leave it alone all day."

"So bring it here," he said. "I'll even get you a pet carrier to keep it in. I'll pay for all the shots. I'll help you housebreak it."

"Well..."

"Just a minute." He dashed back outside and moments later returned carrying a small auburn-colored puppy in his arms. "I call her Jazz, but you can call her whatever you want," he said, and dumped the puppy in her arms.

Anna was lost. She felt the warm little body quiver fearfully in her arms and instinctively began to pet it and coo gently to it. Jazz's ears were huge, so long that Anna imagined they must touch the floor when the puppy stood. It had a plump little pink tummy just like a baby. "Dan..."

"Adorable, isn't she? And I'll pay to have her spayed, too, so you don't develop a puppy problem. Trust me, she'll brighten your life."

Anna looked down into soft brown eyes and felt a tiny pink tongue lick her chin tentatively. "You are so sweet," she heard herself say to the dog. "This is extortion, Dan. You know I can't let her go to the pound."

"Certainly not. She's yours."

Anna looked at Jazz and smiled. "Thank you."

"I'll get the carrier out of the car."

By the time Dan returned, Anna had already figured out a bunch of benefits to having a dog. She would be able to take walks on dark winter evenings without feeling quite as afraid or alone. She would have a dog to keep her company in the dead of night when she couldn't sleep. In short, Jazz would go a long way toward easing her loneliness without forcing her to take risks.

Then the puppy licked her chin again, and none of the rest of it mattered. She was in love.

Dan set the carrier down in the corner with a stack of newspapers. "I figured the least I could do is provide the first batch of cage liners."

"Thanks."

He sat down facing her again. "You look awful, Anna. Exhausted. Have you been having trouble sleeping again?"

"Just a little." She really didn't want to get into it in any depth. She had never told him what had happened to her and never intended to. Still, she sometimes thought he suspected. His expression was so kind that she had to stop herself from blurting out the whole story. The impulse terrified her, and her heart slammed.

Dan regarded her gently for a while, then said, "If you ever want to talk about it, I'm here. I think I'm a pretty good friend."

"I'm sure you are." But she didn't want to talk about it. She tried her best not to even think about it. "At least, you are when you don't have puppies to get rid of. What are you going to do with the rest of them?"

"Oh, I already found homes for them. Jazz was the only one left."

"You stinker!"

He rose, laughing. "Hey, all I did was convince you to take a friend for life!" Still grinning, he went into his office.

Anna sat for a while longer, holding Jazz until the puppy's eyelids began to droop. Then she put the dog in the carrier and locked the door. Poor little thing, she thought as she returned to her desk. It might be the natural way of things, but eight weeks seemed awfully young to be taken from your mother.

Not that her own mother had been worth much, she

thought with a sudden burst of bitterness. The woman wasn't even fit for the title of mother. No question but that she herself would have been better off if she'd been taken away at eight weeks. At any time before she had turned twelve, in fact.

But she didn't want to think about that. With great effort, she forced her attention back to her work.

An hour later, Dan emerged from his office. "I have to go over to the hospital. Candy Burgess had a severe gall bladder attack last night, and they're doing surgery this morning. I promised to go by and sit with the family."

"All right. Are you taking your pager?"

He pointed to his belt. "Got it. Also, I asked a guy to come by and take a look at the church roof. Last winter we had some serious ice damming."

"I remember."

"I want to see if there's anything he can do to lessen it. He said he'd pop in when he had a minute and take a look, so if he gets here while I'm gone, will you show him where the damming was worst?"

"Sure."

"Okay, then. You and Jazz have fun." He headed for the door.

"Say hi to Candy for me."

He was halfway out the door as she spoke, but he leaned back in. "If you want my opinion, it's all that dieting she does that caused this. Remember all those news stories a few years back about liquid diets causing gall bladder disease? I don't think it's liquid diets in particular. I think it's starving yourself that does it."

"You might be right."

His eyes twinkled suddenly. "Of course. I'm always right. People should listen to me more often. Bottom line is,

God made some of us small and some of us tall, some of us skinny and some of us heavy, but we're all beautiful in His eyes. And just for the record, I think all this weight consciousness is a conspiracy on the part of men to starve women into submission.''

She burst out laughing and heard his answering laugh as he hurried to his car. What a character! He was such a joy to work for—even if he *had* foisted a puppy on her.

Jazz was still soundly sleeping, and she found herself wondering how often she should walk the puppy. Probably every time it awoke, until she learned its schedule. And she'd have to stop off at the store on the way home to get some puppy food and a leash and collar. The prospect gave her something interesting to look forward to.

In fact, she decided, Dan couldn't have done a nicer thing for her than dropping that pup into her arms so she couldn't resist.

She was thinking about doggie dishes and leashes, and wondering if she could take care of the shopping on her lunch hour, when a battered pickup pulled up out front. She watched with a suddenly pounding heart as Hugh Gallagher climbed out and walked up to the door. Her mouth went dry, and try as she might to tell herself she was overreacting, she couldn't stop it. Had he come to see *her?*

He stepped through the door and gave her a wide, warm smile. ''Miss Anna. How are you today?''

Before she could answer, Jazz, disturbed by the commotion, woke up and gave a squeaky bark. Hugh squatted immediately and looked into the cage. ''Who's this little fella?''

''That's…um…that's Jazz. Reverend Fromberg gave her to me.'' Anna sounded as breathless as she felt, and hated herself for it. She wondered why Hugh was here, and was afraid to ask.

"Jazz? What a cute pup. Irish setter?"

"Partly."

"A mutt, huh? Well, that just means she'll be really smart, won't you, girl? Can I take her out?"

"I guess."

She watched as Hugh unlatched the cage and reached in with large, strong hands to lift the little pup gently. Jazz decided she liked him and started licking his chin at once. Anna felt a sharp stab of jealousy, then castigated herself for it.

Hugh rose and faced her, still holding the squirming puppy. "Dan asked me to come take a look at the church roof. Something about ice damming?"

"Oh, yes! He asked me to show you where the worst problems were."

"Well, get your jacket on and let's take a stroll. This little gal would probably love to get outside."

"I don't have a leash for her yet."

"Just wait a minute. I can rig something with the rope in my truck that'll do in a pinch."

She rose to pull her jacket off the coat tree and found herself fascinated again by the sight of Cowboy walking away from her. He had such a nice...sway was the only word she could think of. Something that riveted her eyes to his flat backside and long legs. She felt a twinge deep inside that she hadn't felt in a long, long time. Embarrassed color flooded her cheeks.

Uh-uh, she told herself. You know better than that, girl.

She pulled on the jacket and stepped outside, taking care to lock the office door after her.

It took only a minute for Hugh to fashion a slipknot leash

for Jazz. The puppy was ecstatic to be outside and began to run this way and that, giving a squeaky bark of joy. Each time the loop around her neck started to tighten, she came to a swift halt.

"Smart little gal," Hugh said, giving Anna a smile. "She won't give you any trouble." He handed her the end of the rope. "Now, where exactly were the worst problems?"

They walked slowly around the church, with Anna pointing out the places where the ice had dammed the snow and caused leaking inside.

"It was terrible last year," she told him. "Reverend Fromberg went into the church one morning last winter, and he could hear water dripping everywhere. You couldn't see where it was dripping, but finally we noticed that it was running down the insides of the window frames."

"So it was coming down inside the walls."

"Apparently."

He nodded. "I'll have to go up on the roof and see if I can find out what's keeping the snow from sliding off. You'd think with that steep a pitch it wouldn't be a problem. I'll also want to get up under the eaves to try to see where the heat is escaping that's causing the ice to form. Can you leave the church open for a while?"

"Sure. Just let me know when you're done so I can lock it up again. I'll only open the side door, if that's okay."

He gave her a smile. "I only need one door."

Jazz had run off most of her energy and had squatted at four or five different points along the way, so Anna figured the puppy was ready to return to the cage for a nap. She unlocked the church's side door for Hugh, then hurried back to her office.

She loved this time of year, she found herself thinking as she and the puppy trotted along. The breeze was crisp, carrying a hint of the winter to come, and the light had a buttery color to it, the last golden glow of autumn. Any day now the snow would march down off the white-capped peaks to the west and sprinkle itself all over Conard City like powdered sugar.

Inside the office, she put Jazz in her cage, then hunted up a bowl and put some water in with the dog. The puppy lapped thirstily, then curled up into a little ball of fur and fell right to sleep.

Well, that wasn't too difficult, Anna thought as she settled back at her desk. She'd managed not to babble like a fool to Hugh Gallagher, she'd walked the dog successfully, remembered to give it a drink...hey, she was getting competent.

Chuckling at her own silliness, she reached for the next letter she needed to type, only to be interrupted by the phone.

"Anna, it's Dan. I'm going to be at the hospital a while. Candy had a bad reaction to the anesthetic, and we don't know what's going to happen. Say a prayer for her, will you? I don't know at this point if I'll be back to the office at all."

"I'll cancel your appointments."

"Thanks. Go ahead and take your lunch whenever you want. And close up early if you feel like it. You need some rest, my child."

Anna hung up the phone, wondering why she always felt like crying when Dan Fromberg got that gentle note in his voice and called her "my child." He called a lot of people "my child" when they were laid low by life and were calling on him in his ministerial capacity. Still, it affected her.

The phone rang again, just as she was getting ready to

call and cancel the first appointment. This time it was Sheriff Nate Tate.

"Hi, sweet pea," he said in his deep, gravelly voice. For some reason he always called her sweet pea. "Is the boss around?"

"He's at the hospital and probably won't be back in again today."

"Somebody get hurt?"

"A bad reaction to anesthesia."

"Not good." But he knew better than to ask who was involved. "Well, I got a leetle bit of a problem here. Maybe you can help."

"Me?"

He chuckled warmly. "Yes, you, sweet pea. Everyone knows how well you get on with the kids in the youth group, and you're the closest thing we have around here to a youth counselor."

Anna felt a pleasant blush fill her cheeks. "Don't exaggerate, Sheriff."

"I'm not. Do you think you can come over here to the office? I've got me a little gal you know in a cell who shouldn't be in the cell. I really need somebody to talk to her and figure out what's going on. I'll tell you more when you get here."

"I'll be right over, but I have to make a couple of phone calls first."

"It's not that big a rush," he assured her. "This little lady is going to be sitting here a while."

It took Anna ten minutes to make the calls and reschedule the appointments for another day. Then she grabbed her jacket again, hesitating briefly about leaving Jazz alone. After a moment she decided that the puppy was as safe as could be in the cage. Outside, she found Hugh up on the ladder, looking at the church roof. "Mr. Gallagher?"

He looked down at her. "Hugh. Just call me Hugh. Or Cowboy."

"Hugh." She repeated his name, feeling flattered that he'd asked her to use it. "I have to run up to the sheriff's office. I don't know how long I'll be."

"No problem. I'll be a while here. Probably most of the afternoon. There's a lot that needs to be checked out."

"Well, if you need to leave, just make sure the church door is closed tightly. I'll lock it when I get back."

"You got it."

The wind seemed to have gotten sharper, and some low clouds were moving in, concealing the sun. She hunkered deeper into her jacket and wished she'd worn slacks today.

The sheriff's office was only a block away, in a corner storefront overlooking the courthouse square. She'd come here often in the past when the youth group took tours of the office and the courthouse, and she knew most of the people who worked here from church, but she still felt uncomfortable walking into a place that was populated mostly by men. She stepped inside and hovered by the door for a few moments until Velma Jansen, the dispatcher, noticed her.

"Anna! Come on in. Sheriff's down the hall, first door on the left. He's expecting you."

Tate waved her in when she reached his office. He was a big man in his early fifties, with a rugged, permanently sunburned face.

"Come in, sweet pea," he said. "Close the door and grab a seat."

Closing the door proved difficult for her. Even after all this time, she couldn't be comfortable in a closed room with a man. But beside Nate's desk there was a window that overlooked the square, and the sight of people walking by eased her feeling of claustrophobia. She managed to take the chair facing him and folded her hands on her lap.

"What's up?" she asked.

"That's what I'm hoping you can find out. Lorna Lacey. You know her?"

Anna nodded. "She's in the youth group. A dear, sweet girl."

"Right. That's what everyone says. In fact, when I checked her school record, I found out she's never been in any kind of trouble."

"I'd be surprised if it said anything different. She's a natural peacemaker. Active, outgoing, popular—I'd say she's what every girl her age would like to be."

"Mmm." Nate rubbed his chin and swiveled his chair so he could look out the window. "Well, something's wrong. This dear, sweet girl set a fire in an empty classroom this morning."

"Good heavens!"

He nodded and glanced over at her. "She set the fire and was still in the room. If a teacher hadn't happened along the hallway just when he did, the school and the girl would both be gone."

Anna was appalled. She couldn't imagine anyone doing such a thing, but even less could she imagine Lorna Lacey doing it. That child was as close to an angel as a girl her age could be.

"You look chilled," Nate said abruptly. "Let me get you some tea or coffee."

"Tea. Please." Still stunned, she was hardly aware that he had left the office. Her gaze wandered out to the square, which looked bleak on this graying day. The flowers that usually filled the flower beds were gone, having died in the first frost nearly a month ago. Even the people who usually sat on the benches had vanished, driven away by the bitter wind.

Lorna Lacey. A petite girl of thirteen with soft blue eyes and long blond hair and an irregular face that saved her from being beautiful. But she was attractive, very attractive, because personality bubbled out of her, and she had an infectious smile. When Anna thought of Lorna, she thought of laughter.

But now she found herself remembering that Lorna hadn't been laughing as much lately and had missed quite a few youth group meetings in the past year. Anna had ascribed that to the changing interests of adolescence, but now she wondered.

What could be wrong? She hadn't heard stories of any kind of trouble either from Lorna or the other kids. The girl's parents, Bridget and Al Lacey, seemed like nice people. Bridget was a little restrained, but that didn't mean anything. Al greeted the whole world with a big smile, just like his daughter, and was well liked by everyone. He was active in the church, coaching youth soccer and basketball, and was always ready to lend a hand where it was needed.

Nate returned carrying a couple of mugs. He set the one with the tea bag in it in front of her, along with a couple of packets of sweetener and creamer, and a plastic stirrer. Anna reached for the mug gratefully and cupped her cold hands around it, soaking up the warmth.

"Thank you," she said.

"No problem." He sat back in his chair, holding his mug, and resumed his study of the square. "Sleet tonight, I hear. Make sure you get home before it starts."

"I will." Neither of them, she guessed, really knew what

to say about Lorna Lacey. "Are you sure Lorna started the fire?"

"She said she did. In fact, she seemed real eager to make sure we knew it."

Anna hardly knew what to say to that. "But why?"

Nate shrugged and looked at her. "That's why I want you to talk to her, Anna. I know people. You can't work with all kinds the way I do every day without getting an instinct. Now, most of the kids who get into trouble around here, I could pick 'em out by the time they were eight or nine. Sometimes even earlier. The troublemaking starts young. Some of 'em outgrow it. Those with rotten families are the ones least likely to outgrow it. But what I have never seen is a thoroughly good kid from a good home turn bad without a reason."

"Bad friends?"

He shook his head. "I'm a great believer in peer pressure, but most kids like Lorna, who are good through and through, withstand that kind of pressure and pick good friends. You know who she hangs out with. Any problems there?"

"I wouldn't have thought so."

"Me neither. So we got us a mystery, sweet pea. That child committed an act of arson, and all my warning bells are clanging that this isn't the act of a pain-in-the-butt kid. It's a cry for help."

Anna nodded, agreeing. It had to be. "But help from what?"

"God knows." Nate sighed and settled deeper into his chair. "I've gotta charge her with arson. No way around it. But what scares me more than arson is that I don't think she intended to leave that room even when the fire got really bad."

Anna gasped and nearly spilled her tea. She set it quickly on the desk. "Not Lorna!"

"That's the way it looks to me."

Even more appalled now, Anna looked blindly out the window. "She hasn't been coming to youth group meetings as often."

"No? Then maybe whatever this is wasn't sudden. Maybe something's been building for a long time. She could be depressed. That's not uncommon at her age, but maybe she doesn't know how to ask for help. Maybe she doesn't even guess what's wrong with her. Or maybe she got involved in drugs somehow. Or somebody just slipped her a mickey this morning and she's on a bad trip. I don't know."

He sipped his coffee, then turned to face her fully. "What I know is, I got a kid in one of my cells who shouldn't be there. It's not like the handwriting has been on the wall for years. And I'm not gonna be happy until we find the root of this little problem. I don't want that child to become an ugly statistic because we couldn't figure out how to help her."

"Certainly not!"

"So you'll talk to her?"

"Of course I will!"

He smiled. "I figured you would, sweet pea. I figured you would."

"Have you talked to her parents yet? Do they have any idea?"

"No idea at all."

"They're not going to leave her in jail overnight."

"They may not have any choice. Judge Williams has set a bond hearing at five o'clock to try to avoid that, but Lorna said she's just going to tell the judge she'll do it again if she gets out."

Anna drew a long breath. "I'll talk to her."

"Please. At the very least maybe you can find out why she thinks it's better to be in jail than out. I got my own ideas, and they ain't pretty."

Nor were the possibilities that were occurring to Anna, but she didn't want to give voice to them. At least, not until she knew what was going on.

"Anyway," Nate said, putting his mug down, "you've got a definite way with kids this age, especially the girls. I've noticed it. Hell, everybody's noticed it. The kids you work with trust and respect you. That gives you a big advantage from square one over some psychologist I might drag in from somewhere else. At least we can skip over the part about developing trust."

"Just don't forget that I'm *not* a psychologist. And speaking of psychologists, the school has one."

"But he's never dealt with Lorna before. How long do you think it would take him to get her to open up compared with you?"

"I can't venture a guess." And if Lorna had a guy problem of some kind, she might *never* open up to a man.

"I don't think we have that kind of time, whatever it is. I've known that girl since she was in diapers, and she won't talk to me. But I don't think I know her anywhere near as well as you do. So go talk to her, sweet pea. Find out what's wrong."

"If I can."

A few minutes later she climbed the stairs to the jail. Nate had buzzed the jail guard from his office, and she was taken directly to a consultation room. Lorna was brought in just a few minutes later.

"Hi, Lorna."

The girl didn't answer. She sat down at the table and kept her eyes averted.

Anna hesitated, trying to feel her way through this. "We've missed you at youth group. Don't you want to come anymore?"

Lorna gave a quick, negative shake of her head without looking at Anna.

"That's a shame. Everyone there likes you so much."

Lorna hunched her shoulders but didn't say anything.

Anna decided to take the bull by the horns. "Sheriff Tate tells me you set fire to a classroom at school this morning. He didn't want to put you in jail, but he had to."

Again no response.

"You've never done anything like this before, Lorna. Not even the little stuff that most kids do. So it seems to me that if you felt you had to start a fire, something must be hurting you terribly. If you tell me what's wrong, we'll do whatever we can to fix it."

Lorna looked up at her then, her gaze bleak, almost hollow. "Nobody can fix it."

"Nobody can fix what?"

But the girl didn't answer. She lowered her head again.

Anna wanted to reach out and touch her, but she wasn't sure that would be the right thing to do. Lorna had isolated herself emotionally, that much was apparent, and a touch might be truly unwelcome.

"When I was your age," she said finally, "something horrible was happening to me, and I couldn't figure out how to stop it. Finally I ran away from home for good, but that really didn't fix much. In fact, it made some things worse." She realized she had Lorna's attention now, so she continued. "Looking back at it now, I realized I should have trusted some of the adults in my life. I should have told them what was happening, because any one of them could have helped me. But I didn't. And that was a big mistake.''

Lorna glanced at her, then looked quickly away without saying anything.

"Just give us a chance, Lorna. The sheriff and I both really want to help you.''

"You can't. Nobody can.''

"You can't know that until you let us try.''

Lorna stood up so suddenly that her chair fell over backward. "I want to die! All I want to do is die! Nobody can help me. Nobody at all! Go away. Go away before you get hurt!''

Anna hesitated, but Lorna turned suddenly to the door and started beating on it, screaming, "Get me out of here! Get me out of here now!''

Shaken, Anna watched helplessly as the deputy took Lorna back to her cell. When she felt she could trust her legs to hold her, she went downstairs to Nate's office.

"Well?'' he said when he saw her.

She shook her head. "She won't talk to me. But she said something very strange. She told me to go away before I get hurt.''

"Was she threatening you?''

Anna shook her head. "Can I sit down a minute? My legs are still shaking.''

"Help yourself. So she wasn't threatening you?''

"I didn't get that feeling.'' She sank gratefully into the chair. "But something is terribly, terribly wrong, and I got the distinct feeling that someone has threatened *her*.''

He nodded, compressing his lips grimly. "Yup. That's about the only reason I can figure that she'd want to stay in a jail cell. Now we have to find out who and why. Damn!''

He passed his hand over his eyes, then drummed his fingers on the desktop.

"I'll talk to her friends," Anna offered. "The kids she always hung out with in the youth group. Maybe they can shed some light on this."

"You do that. I'd talk to 'em myself, but I don't want 'em to clam up for fear of getting Lorna into more trouble." He gave her a crooked smile. "That's the disadvantage of this uniform."

"I'll let you know if I find out anything. And will you let me know how the bail hearing goes? Maybe she won't make good on her threat."

"If she does, it's going to be a long night for her. God, I can't see leaving a young girl like that in a cell. We don't even have proper facilities for it. What if my men have to bring in some drunk tonight to sleep it off? Or worse?" He shook his head. "Hell, if it comes to that, I'll take her home with *me*. In custody. Maybe Marge and the girls can get to the root of it."

Anna nodded. "That might be a good idea. But no matter what, Nate, I wouldn't send her home."

He arched a brow at her and nodded slowly. "That's what I was thinking. I got a feeling there's something very wrong there. But I have to have something to go on, Anna. I can't just stick my snoot in without something."

"I know." Nor could she. But she could certainly call Lorna's friends.

A few minutes later she headed back to the church. The wind had grown cruel, and she had no trouble believing there would be sleet later on. The sky was leaden now, with no hint of the autumn sun left anywhere, and the last of the dead leaves were sailing across sidewalks and lawns. The town already looked deserted, as if it had settled down for its long winter sleep.

Dan Fromberg had returned, and greeted her the instant she stepped in the door. "Candy's okay," he told her, coming to stand in the doorway of his office.

"Wonderful!" She hung her jacket on the rack and rubbed her hands briskly together.

"I made fresh tea," he told her, pointing to the drip coffeemaker they used for brewing tea. "You look like you need to warm up."

"It's gotten really bitter out there. Oh, I forgot! I need to go lock the church door. I left it open for Hugh."

Dan shook his head. "He checked with me a minute ago, and I locked it."

Anna felt disappointed to realize she'd missed him. She immediately scolded herself for the feeling. "What did he say?"

"It looks like we're going to need some major work done. He says we need to replace the insulation in quite a few places, so escaping heat under the eaves doesn't cause the snow to melt, then turn into ice. He also pointed out some spots where the roof is concave, and it's trapping the snow rather than letting it slide off."

"That does sound expensive."

He grimaced. "I'm going to have to dip very deep into the building fund, but at least we can afford it now." Last spring, when they really should have had the work done, the fund had been nearly empty, having been used for repairs to the foundation. Good Shepherd Church was aging. "But first I'm going to get another estimate to compare."

Anna poured her tea and cradled the cup gratefully. "Did he mind?"

Dan shook his head. "He suggested it, actually. He's a very honest guy, you know."

She nodded and sank gratefully into her chair.

"So you went up to the sheriff's office? What happened?"

She outlined matters as briefly as she could and watched as his mouth drew into a thin line.

"This doesn't sound good," he said when she concluded.

"I'm going to call some of her friends tonight and see if any of them have any idea what might be wrong."

"Good idea."

Jazz whimpered just then, and Dan squatted down to take her out of her cage. "Hey, little one," he said softly. "How're you doing? Did you piddle on your paper?" He looked over his shoulder at Anna. "I can't believe anything's wrong at home," he said. "Bridget and Al are both the nicest people."

She nodded, and Dan looked down at the puppy he held.

"On the other hand," he said, "none of us ever really knows another person." Straightening, he turned to her. "So, have you had lunch?"

"No."

"Me neither. I'll go out and get us something from Maude's diner. In the meantime, why don't you see if any of Lorna's friends are home from school yet?"

He handed her the puppy and put fresh newspaper in Jazz's box before he left.

The pup seemed content to curl up on her lap while she sipped tea and dug out the roster for the youth group. One by one, she started calling the girls who seemed closest to Lorna. Only one of them was at home yet, and she said she hadn't really talked to Lorna in a while.

"She's gotten kind of quiet, Miss Anna, but I don't know why. She doesn't hang out like she used to. But I can't believe she actually started that fire at school. Everybody's talking about it. It just isn't like Lorna."

"So she hasn't found a different crowd of friends?"

"No. She doesn't have many friends at all anymore. I mean...well, we all still like her, but she doesn't want much to do with us. We ask her to go places with us, and she always says no. I always have a pajama party for my birthday, and Lorna always comes. Not this last time, though. She was the only one who didn't. When I asked her why not—I mean, I felt really hurt—she said she just didn't feel like it."

"So there's nobody at all she's close to anymore?"

"I don't think so. Debbie said she thinks Lorna's just getting snobby because her dad's a dentist. Mary Jo argued with her about that and said Lorna just isn't feeling good lately."

"Did Mary Jo say why?"

"No. And that's all I know, really. You want me to talk to the others?"

"Thank you, but I'll do that. If you think of anything, let me know?"

After she hung up, Anna found herself looking down at the puppy in her lap, thinking about how trusting young animals were, and how easy it was to shatter that trust. Something had shattered Lorna's trust.

Dan came through the door on a gust of cold wind, carrying a big brown bag from Maude's. "Steak sandwiches," he said. "I don't think either of us will want dinner. Which is okay with me, because Cheryl took the kids to Cheyenne this morning to visit their grandparents."

"So you're baching it?"

"Fine by me." He set the containers down on her desk and took his coat off. "I love those kids to death, but every once in a blue moon, it's nice to watch what *I* want on TV."

He pulled the chair closer to her desk while she cleared papers to one side, then set out containers full of food. Not only had he gotten the steak sandwiches, but he'd brought a salad, and brownies for dessert.

"Did you find out anything?" he asked while they ate.

"Nothing really useful. Apparently Lorna's even withdrawn from her friends."

He paused in the process of taking a bite of his sandwich. "Now that's really not good."

"That's what I think." She found she didn't feel hungry at all, but in order not to appear ungrateful, she nibbled at the salad.

"You know," Dan said presently, "I can think of a lot of things short of mental illness that could have caused this change in the child, and none of them are pretty."

"I know." That killed the last of her appetite. She absolutely didn't want to think about those things, but she couldn't avoid it. Experience had taught her that bad things could happen to people you knew, including yourself. For Anna, they weren't just newspaper stories.

"Anna?" Dan was looking at her with concern. "Would you like to quit early today and go home? You look really strung out."

"I'm okay. Just worried about Lorna. I think I'll go to her bond hearing at five."

"It's at five? I'll go, too. Maybe I can get something out of her parents."

"I hope you have better luck than Nate did."

"Nothing, huh?"

She shook her head. "And frankly, I don't expect anyone will get anything out of them."

"You seem awfully certain about that."

"I have my reasons." And more than that she would not say.

Chapter 3

Cowboy was disappointed when he finished inspecting the church roof and Anna still hadn't come back. Not that he had any business being disappointed. Anna Fleming was two or three cuts above the women who usually consented to spend time with him. And since deciding to clean up his act and get on with life, he was avoiding the women who didn't avoid him.

He was kind of ashamed of himself anyway, ashamed of the way he'd fallen apart. He knew as well as anybody that post-traumatic stress disorder wasn't something you opted to have, but he still felt weak for having had it. Nothing had happened to him in his life that didn't happen to a whole lot of people, but he'd come apart at the seams anyway, after the Gulf War. It had been one straw too many, so to speak.

Not that he was excusing himself. He never excused himself. And it wasn't that he felt he'd done anything wrong. He'd been a soldier doing a soldier's job. But nightmare images eventually gave rise to nightmares.

Still, he wasn't particularly interested in wandering down the paths of his own memory lane. Learning to look forward was one of the biggest hurdles he'd had to clear on his road to recovery, and he wasn't going to allow himself to backslide.

After he gave Dan Fromberg the roofing estimate, he made his way back to his one-room apartment on the second floor of a hotel that was almost as old as Conard City. Not that that was so godawful old, he supposed, but the building bordered on ancient.

It must have been a grand old hotel in its day, he often thought, near enough the train terminal to be convenient, but not so close that its patrons would have been breathing coal smoke and the aroma of cattle in the stockyard awaiting shipment. In fact, it was just about midway between the courthouse and the terminal. The way people were apt to lay things out in the days when your own two feet were the favored form of transportation.

What a person mainly noticed about the place now, though, was that the halls were dark and musty, the stairs and floors creaked and it looked like a firetrap.

His apartment was different, though. In the old days, they'd believed in building rooms big. He had a huge living room, an alcove for his bed, a tacked-on kitchenette and a bathroom with a claw-footed tub. His tall windows overlooked the street and faced south, so that sunlight poured in all winter long. All of this for less than anything else he could have rented in town.

If he hadn't been so fixed on his plan for a youth ranch, he could have turned this place into something spectacular.

But this afternoon, with the sky so leaden and a sleet storm getting ready to move in, he was finding it just a bit difficult to remember the potential he'd seen here. The hallway and stairs were as dark as if it had been night, and his apartment wasn't much better. He turned on a couple of lamps, but it didn't help much. The early-winter night would be falling soon, and all of a sudden he didn't want to be sitting here alone.

He decided his budget could handle dinner at Maude's, so he pulled on a warmer jacket and drove back up the street toward the church and Maude's place, which was right across the street from Good Shepherd. By the time he reached the diner, night had fallen.

Maude's was brightly lit but nearly empty. He slipped into a booth that let him look out the front window, and as he scanned the menu, he saw Anna and Dan leave the church together and get in their cars.

Anna's was an old vehicle, one that had seen all its better days long before it had come into her possession. It was big, built like a tank, and she backed up cautiously before pulling out of the parking lot and heading up the street. He realized she hadn't brought the dog, and he wondered if she was going to leave it in the office all night. That didn't seem right.

But then he noticed that she wasn't heading toward her home. Instead she turned up to the courthouse square. So did the reverend.

Shrugging, he went back to the menu. Maybe they had a meeting to go to.

"What'll it be, Cowboy?" Maude asked in her usual belligerent fashion as she slapped a mug of coffee down in front of him. She was a plump, older woman with grizzled gray hair and a no-nonsense face. "Eat hearty. They say it's gonna get damn cold tonight."

"Sleet's in the forecast."

"Yup. And don't skip the pie, neither. We got an elderberry pie that'll knock your socks off."

"Save a piece for me, then." He gave her a smile, but she didn't return it. He wondered if anyone had ever seen Maude smile. "Two bacon cheeseburgers with extra fries and a bowl of spinach, please."

"Spinach?" She looked surprised.

"If you have it."

"Oh, I have it, but most folks want salad."

"I like spinach." He shrugged.

"Why don't you have a side of onion rings instead of them extra fries? We got a shipment of some really good sweet onions."

"Sounds good." He'd never eaten here when Maude hadn't changed his order somehow. On the other hand, he'd never regretted following her suggestions.

She stomped away, leaving him to sip his coffee and stare out into the night. It was warm in here, he found himself thinking. Warm. Despite the threatening weather, people would come and go. He figured he might stay here a while.

He was certainly in no hurry to go back to his empty apartment.

The five-o'clock bail hearing for Lorna Lacey was a special session called for the child's benefit. The court's earlier business was finished, and no other prisoners stood in the dock.

The girl herself, hands handcuffed before her, sat with her head down at the defense table. Beside her sat an attorney Anna didn't recognize, apparently someone the Lacey family had brought in from another town. Sam Haversham, the prosecutor, was standing at his table skimming through a thin file. Probably Lorna's file, Anna thought. It was amazing how quickly you could develop a file when you got in trouble with the law.

Apart from herself and Dan, the only other observers were Bridget and Al Lacey, both of whom were sitting with Dan in the front row. Anna sat farther back, preferring to be unobtrusive. Besides, she hated courtrooms. They gave her the willies.

At the front of the room, the court clerk sat at her desk beside the judge's bench, and in front of the witness box sat a stenographer, feeding the leading edge of a fresh stack of fan-folded paper into her machine. Two bailiffs stood to the side, chatting quietly with Nate Tate.

The door to the judge's chamber opened, and one of the bailiffs called out, "All rise" as Judge Francine Williams walked to the bench. Lorna, Anna noticed, had to be encouraged to stand by a gentle tug on her elbow. When the judge sat, everyone followed suit.

Judge Williams sat and spent a moment glancing over some papers in front of her. "Good afternoon." She devoted a few minutes to reciting the case number and charges for the record, and having the attorneys identify themselves.

"Now," she continued, "let's get right to the point, shall we? We all know why we're here, and I'm willing to dispense with the usual formalities, if no one has any objection?"

"No objection, Your Honor," both lawyers answered immediately.

"Good. I'm sure everyone wants to get home for dinner. We have an unusual case here, unusual at least for Conard County. We have no facilities suitable for the keeping of a thirteen-year-old girl. Our limited juvenile facilities are set up only to handle boys, and I really don't want to see this child in the county jail overnight, so I'm going to ask the prosecutor to be reasonable in requesting bail. Mr. Haversham?''

''We're fully prepared to be reasonable, Your Honor. In fact, considering that Lorna Lacey has never been in trouble before, we were prepared to agree to have her released on her own recognizance. However, another fact has come to light, which I need to bring to the court's attention.''

''And that is?''

''Miss Lacey told Sheriff Tate that if she is released on bond she will start another fire.''

Anna's hands clenched in her lap.

Judge Williams looked at Nate. ''Is that true, Sheriff?''

''Yes, ma'am.''

She turned her attention to Lorna's attorney. ''Mr. Carlisle, what's going on here?''

The lawyer cleared his throat as he rose to his feet. ''A moment to confer with my client, Judge?''

''By all means,'' the judge said. ''Be advised that if your client made such a threat, I won't be able to release her from custody. Would you like to straighten that out for me?''

''Certainly, Judge.''

The lawyer sat back down and had a hurried, hushed conversation with Lorna. Anna found she was holding her breath, and her nails were digging in to her palms. Her heart squeezed when the man stood back up to speak.

''My client...is aware of the consequences of her statement,'' he said.

''Does that mean she's not taking it back?''

''I...for ethical reasons, Judge, I...ah...''

A sound passed through the courtroom then, a sound of muted dismay. Bridget Lacey looked as if she might cry.

Judge Williams sat back, a perplexed frown on her face. "You leave me no choice, young lady."

Sam Haversham stepped forward. "Your Honor, we have an alternative to propose. Sheriff Tate has offered to take Miss Lacey home to his family in custody so that she won't need to spend the night in jail."

"That's highly irregular." Francine Williams tapped a pencil on the bench, frowning down at the girl. Finally, she sat forward. "Off the record here."

The court reporter's hands dropped to her lap.

"Mr. Haversham, I'd like you to consider a grant of immunity here."

Anna leaned forward, holding her breath. What was happening?

Sam stepped forward. "I think I know what you have in mind, Your Honor. I'll offer immunity."

Williams looked over at the young girl. "Miss Lacey, you've been offered immunity for any answer you give to the questions I'm about to ask. That means whatever you say is off the record and can't be used against you in any legal proceeding. Do you understand that?"

Lorna's attorney added a quick, whispered explanation. Lorna nodded.

"Good," Judge Williams said. "Now, Miss Lacey, are you telling me you want to stay in jail?"

"Yes."

"But why?"

Lorna lifted her head then, looking straight at the judge, and the anguish in her voice caused Anna's heart to break. "Because I'm bad! I do bad things! And I'll keep on doing bad things! I tried to burn down the school! If you give me a chance, I'll try to burn it down again!"

When Lorna finished, she dropped her head to the table and sobbed.

The judge let out a heavy sigh. "I'd like to see counsel in chambers, please. Miss Lacey, I'd like you to come, too. And, Sheriff Tate, I think you're going to need to hear this, as well, if the defense has no objections?"

Mr. Carlisle hastened once again to his feet. "No objection, Judge. That's fine."

"And, counsel, I imagine her family hired you?"

"Yes, Judge."

"You know where your ethical duties lie here, right?"

The attorney put his hand on Lorna's shoulder. "*She's* my client, Judge. I made that clear to the family."

"Make sure you remember that. Let's go talk this over."

Anna had the feeling everyone in the courtroom knew what was coming. The type of thing you didn't say out loud, in public. The type of thing no one wanted to hear about someone they knew. The kind of thing Anna knew all too well.

As soon as the group had disappeared into the judge's chambers, Al Lacey rose and walked from the courtroom. He looked at no one as he left. Anna felt her stomach turn over in revulsion as she watched him go. Bridget followed a few moments later, her face set like stone.

Dan came to sit with Anna. "I'm praying I'm wrong, but the handwriting is about six feet high on the wall, isn't it?"

She nodded, battling a storm tide of emotions that all of this was raising in her. "That poor child," she managed to say finally. "That poor, poor child." Long-buried anger simmered in her stomach, making it hurt.

"It could be something else."

Anna didn't even bother to reply. She'd given up on vain

hopes a long time ago. "Why didn't somebody keep him from leaving?"

"Al? I don't think they can detain him without some kind of proof. That's probably why Judge Williams took Nate into chambers with them. If Lorna says anything about what's going on, Nate will take action."

Anna folded her hands tightly together. "I hope she tells the judge. Oh, God, I hope she tells."

Dan reached out and gently touched her shoulder. "She might not, Anna. There are an awful lot of people in that room, some of them strangers to her."

"I know." And she did, only too well. Some things just couldn't be spoken of, no matter how they tore you apart. There were some things just too awful to tell strangers. "If she doesn't tell them, Dan, I'm going to do everything in my power to find some proof, some evidence. We have to help her!"

"We could be wrong in our supposition," he reminded her gently. "The problem might not be her parents at all."

She looked him straight in the eye. "You don't really believe that."

He compressed his lips. "No, I don't. But I'm praying as hard as I can that this will be just a juvenile overreaction to something that isn't so terrible after all. God have mercy on that child if it isn't."

Twenty minutes later everyone traipsed back into the courtroom. The judge settled at the bench and spoke to the court reporter.

"On the record again, Mrs. Jubilo. All right. I'm denying bond. Lorna Lacey will remain in the custody of the sheriff's department until trial. Mr. Carlisle, what I said before holds. If Miss Lacey wishes to withdraw her threat at any time, or wishes to confide in you or anyone else the cause for her behavior, the matter of bail will be immediately reopened.''

"Yes, Judge.''

"I'm also recommending that Miss Lacey undergo psychological counseling. I realize we don't have psychologists growing on trees around here. In fact, I believe the only one we have is the school psychologist, and I'm not sure he'd be able to handle this situation. However, Sheriff Tate has kindly agreed to arrange for counseling in Laramie, and for a deputy to take Miss Lacey to appointments once a week. Any objections?''

None were voiced.

"Now,'' Judge Williams continued, "while it is highly irregular, I'm going to put Miss Lacey in the personal custody of Sheriff Tate. By that I mean that she will spend her days in jail and her nights at the sheriff's home with his family. This release will be contingent upon Miss Lacey promising to behave while in the sheriff's custody. No fires, no running away, no nonsense of any kind. Miss Lacey, will you give this court your promise?''

"Yes, ma'am.''

Anna heaved a huge sigh of relief. She couldn't think of anything better for Lorna than to be in the custody of a man who had raised six healthy, happy daughters, three of whom were still living at home.

"Now,'' the judge continued, leaning forward, "I'm going to take one more extraordinary step here. From now until this matter is settled, or until Miss Lacey explains her actions to my satisfaction, all of her contacts with any member of her family must and will be supervised by a member of this court or a member of the sheriff's department. Is that clear?''

Both lawyers answered that it was, but the judge was

more interested in Lorna's reaction. "Miss Lacey, do you understand what I've said? You can't see your family without someone from the court or the sheriff's department there. How do you feel about that?"

Lorna lifted her head and looked right at the judge. "Good," she said. "Except my sister. Can I see my sister?"

"How old is she?"

"Four."

The judge hesitated. "Not immediately," she finally said. "Let's see how it goes this way first. We wouldn't want to put your sister in a difficult situation, would we?"

To Anna's horror, Lorna's face drained of color.

"No," the girl said hoarsely. "No. I don't want to see her at all."

Francine Williams nodded slowly. "That might be best for a little while. Just one other thing, Miss Lacey. Every one of us in this courtroom wants to help you. Find one of us you can trust and give us the information we need to do just that. You are not alone."

Five minutes later, Anna was back in her car. She had left Jazz in her cage at the office so she wouldn't have to be left all alone in a cold car. It was, she decided, the perfect time to go get puppy chow and a collar and leash. Then she could pick up Jazz and take her straight home to a warm house.

But while she was thinking of Jazz, most of her attention was focused on what had just happened in court. Old wounds of her own had been torn open as she sat there, and she felt as if she were bleeding inside. Once upon a time, a judge had looked down from his bench at her and said almost exactly the same thing. He'd said, "We want to help you, but you have to trust us first." Finally she had.

And somehow she had to get Lorna to do the same thing: trust someone. The sheriff. Reverend Fromberg. The judge. Herself. It didn't matter so much who, as long as it was someone who was willing to go to bat for her.

Distracted as she was by worry and seething emotions from her own past, she spent more than was wise at the grocery, buying Jazz the fanciest blue collar and leash, a big bag of puppy chow, a box of puppy treats, a small bone and several squeaky toys. She picked up some carpet cleaner that was guaranteed to remove pet stains, but talked herself out of a flea collar. At this time of year, it would be a wasted expense. She also picked up a few groceries.

When she stepped back outside, the first spit of sleet was falling, fine, icy crystals that stung her cheeks. The pavement was wet, still warm enough to melt the sleet. That wouldn't last long. Hurrying, she emptied the shopping cart into her car and drove swiftly back to the office.

As soon as she opened the door, Jazz started barking, a high-pitched puppy yelp. Looking into the cage, she saw that the dog had had an accident. She cleaned it up swiftly and replaced the soiled paper with fresh newspaper. Then she put Jazz back into the cage and carried her out to the car.

The cage wouldn't fit into her car, though. Finally giving up, she put it in the trunk, then took the puppy into the passenger compartment with her. Jazz insisted on curling up on her lap, but she didn't think that would cause much trouble.

Then she tried to start the car. And tried again. The starter whined, but the engine wouldn't catch. What now? Sleet crystals were rattling against the windows of her car, warning her that the streets would soon be dangerous. Forcing herself to wait in case she had flooded the engine somehow, she counted seconds in the tick of ice on her windows.

The night was dark and empty. Funny, she thought as she drummed her fingers on the steering wheel, there had been a time when she had believed being out alone at night would protect her. Then she had discovered otherwise. The night was a time when predators stalked the young and weak. It was full of threat. At night she wanted to be safely within the walls of her snug little house.

She shivered as the night's chill began to find its way into her jacket. Jazz whimpered softly, suggesting that she was getting hungry. Anna patted her gently and tried to start the car again. And once again the engine refused to turn over.

A tap on her window startled her, and she gasped, turning her head swiftly. Hugh Gallagher stood there, bent over to look in her window. "Car trouble?" he asked through the glass.

She rolled her window down an inch. "It won't start."

"I heard. The engine's not catching. Let me lift the hood and see if the choke's stuck, okay?"

"Thank you."

Her gaze followed him as he walked around to the front of the car. Then the hood lifted with a protesting groan and he vanished from view.

He was a nice man, she told herself. He'd proved that already. She didn't have to be afraid to be in his debt.

He rattled around under the hood for a few minutes, then slammed it closed and came back to her window. "It's not the choke, Miss Anna, and I can't see well enough to check anything else out. How about I drive you home and take a look at it in the morning?"

She hesitated. It wasn't that she really had any option, but she hesitated anyway. It had been a long time since she had been comfortable getting into a car with a man. Any man. Even after all these years, she was still uneasy. But common sense won.

"If you wouldn't mind. I have the dog and all these groceries...."

"No problem. My truck's right across the street. Just let me bring it over."

A couple of minutes later, he had her groceries and the dog cage loaded in the back, and Anna and the puppy in the front seat with him.

"I'm glad I happened to be having dinner at Maude's," Hugh said as he pulled out onto the street.

"So am I. I really didn't want to call a tow truck. I can't afford that expense right now." Especially not now that she was going to have to get her car fixed. "I hope you didn't interrupt your dinner to help me."

"Naw. I was just finishing a piece of Maude's elderberry pie. You ever have any?"

Anna never ate out; her budget wouldn't allow it. "No, I'm afraid not."

"Well, let me take you over there for lunch tomorrow, before she runs out of elderberries."

Anna didn't know how to answer that, because she wasn't exactly sure what he intended by the invitation. Before she could think of anything to say, he went on.

"Did you hear about the fire at school today? They say the Lacey kid set it. Now, I don't know folks in the county as well as people who've lived here all their lives, but I did see that girl a lot around the church, and she always seemed like a good kid to me."

"She is. One of the best."

"Well, I just can't figure it. Now, if it'd been Bobby

Reilly, I would have thought it was just what you oughtta expect, but not that girl.''

''I know.'' She felt her heart accelerating as they edged near a topic she didn't want to discuss with him—or with anyone, for that matter. She didn't want to have to tell anyone what she suspected Lorna's problem was—at least, not unless she got some proof of it.

''You ask me,'' he said, ''there's something wrong there, and it isn't that girl.''

They eased to a careful stop at the corner, then turned onto Anna's street.

''Gettin' slippery,'' Hugh remarked. ''Guess I oughtta put the chains on after I drop you off.''

''That might be wise.'' God, how she hated this stilted conversation. How she hated being so uncomfortable with men that she couldn't think of anything to say to keep the ball rolling. How she hated being the prisoner of hurts that were so old they ought to be almost forgotten.

He turned into her driveway, and she felt the tires slip and spin on the icy pavement as he braked to a halt and switched off the ignition.

''You stay right where you are,'' he said. ''I'll come around and help you out. Those shoes you're wearing don't look like they'll give much traction.''

They wouldn't, she thought. They were a pair of cheap pumps she'd bought just because she had to keep up appearances at work.

Hugh climbed out and came around to her side. He opened the door and reached for her elbow to steady her. ''It's like a skating rink. Hang on to me.''

Even with all her caution, her feet slipped anyway, and he caught her around the waist. All of a sudden there was nothing between them but a squirming puppy and the layers of their clothing.

He smelled good, Anna realized with astonishment. He smelled really good, like freshly cut wood and soap. His arm around her felt powerful, but the way it held her was not at all frightening. She ought to feel trapped and terrified, but instead she felt...strange. As if the world had stopped between two heartbeats.

Then hc backed off a little, giving her space but keeping his arm around her waist. "Let's get you onto the porch. I'll bring your groceries in."

A few moments later she was safely inside her snug little house, watching Hugh Gallagher carry her groceries and the puppy cage inside. It took him two trips, and he insisted on putting everything in the kitchen while she stood there like a dolt, silent, clutching the puppy to her breast as if the poor little thing was a lifeline.

She ought to do something, say something. Make some gracious gesture to thank him. Instead she was feeling shell-shocked by today's events, and by the realization that she didn't want Hugh to go. She wanted him to stay. For the first time in her life, she actually wanted a man to stay. Was she losing her mind?

"Would you...would you like some coffee?" she asked in a rush as he prepared to leave.

He smiled, and she was struck by the warmth of that simple expression. "Thanks, but I drank four cups at Maude's. Tell you what. Promise to have lunch with me tomorrow. I'll bore you to death with my plans for the youth ranch, and we'll call it even, okay?"

She couldn't say no. The word absolutely refused to come to her lips. "All right," she heard herself say.

"One o'clock?"

"That's fine."

Then he walked out into the night and left Anna alone
with the realization that she had just made a date with a
man.

She, Anna Fleming, had made the first date of her entire
life. She should have been exhilarated, but instead she wondered if she'd just made another one of her gargantuan mistakes.

Jazz appeared to be pleased with her new environment.
As soon as Anna set out bowls of water and food, the puppy
dug in, in her eagerness making a minor mess that made
Anna smile.

But she couldn't smile for long. It was as if the shadows
in the corners of the room were whispering to her, trying to
call her back into the nightmares of her past. It was because
of Lorna, she decided. She was watching her own nightmare
unfold again through the child.

Remembering the roster she had put in her purse, she left
Jazz eagerly eating and went to get it. She had to call the
other girls from the youth group, to see if any of them had
a hint of what was wrong in Lorna's life. If she could find
a key, any key, she might get the girl to open up to her.

The first two girls had nothing new to offer, but then she
got through to Mary Jo Weeks.

"It's awful, Miss Anna," Mary Jo said. "I've been crying
on and off all day. I knew something was wrong, but I didn't
know how bad it was."

"What do you mean?"

"I mean, bad enough that she would set a fire. I heard
one of the teachers say he thought Lorna meant to stay in
the room until the fire killed her. It's terrible!"

Anna hesitated, aching for Mary Jo, but not wanting to

give the girl empty platitudes. Finally she said, "We can't know that, Mary Jo. That's just somebody's speculation."

"But what's going to happen to her now? Is she going to jail?"

Jail, Anna thought, could be better than some things, but not many. She couldn't say that to Mary Jo, though. "At present she's going to be staying with Sheriff Tate's family, until we find out what's going on."

"That's not so bad, then. But what do you think is wrong?"

"I don't know, not for sure. But I need you to help me, Mary Jo. I need every little thing you can remember that might give me a clue to what's wrong here."

"You're trying to help her?"

"Of course! There are a lot of people who want to help her. I don't know anyone who wants to see her go to jail. But unless we find out what the problem is, she may have to."

"Oh, no! I don't want that to happen to her—ever!" Mary Jo started crying again, and Anna waited patiently, making soothing sounds. There was never just one victim, she thought bitterly. There were always others.

When the young woman had her tears under control, Anna asked her if she remembered anything, anything at all, that seemed unusual.

"Well, I thought it was weird when her dad wouldn't let her come over to spend the night anymore. I mean, we'd always been best friends, and at least once a month I'd sleep at her place or she'd sleep at mine."

"When did that stop?"

"About a year ago, I guess. But what was so weird was that he'd let me come over there, but he wouldn't let her come to my house. I asked Lorna why, but she just shrugged and said nobody could explain parents. My mom and dad started to feel insulted by it and didn't want me to go over there anymore after a while.''

"I can understand that.''

"Well, it made me mad, so a couple of times I made 'em let me go anyway.''

"Did anything strike you as unusual?''

"Not really.''

Anna felt something brush against her leg and discovered the puppy had joined her and was looking up at her with hopeful eyes. Bending, she scooped Jazz onto her lap. "This is a harder question, Mary Jo, and I want you to think very carefully about it. When you spent the night with Lorna, did anything happen that made you feel uneasy? Did anything seem not quite right? Anything at all?''

"Hmm...'' Mary Jo was silent for a bit. "Well...it sounds silly, but her dad made us get ready for bed at eight o'clock. I mean, we always used to stay dressed until we went to bed, but the last few times he insisted we get ready before we watched TV. I thought that was kind of weird, but parents can be crazy sometimes, you know?''

"I know.''

"Anyway, that just seemed stupid to me, but...'' She hesitated. "This sounds awful, Miss Anna, and I don't want you to think poorly of me.''

"I won't. I promise.''

"Well...'' Mary Jo drew a long breath. "I don't have a sick mind or anything, but it just made me uncomfortable to see Lorna running around in front of her dad in those baby doll pajamas. She didn't put on a robe or anything. My dad would have a fit if I sat around in the living room dressed like that.''

It was now Anna's turn to draw a deep breath. Her heart accelerated. "But he didn't say anything or do anything?"

"Not about her running around like that. But then she was acting funny. I couldn't figure it out. It was like she didn't want to be dressed that way, either. She kept her arms all folded up and scrunched herself into a corner of the couch, like she wanted to hide. And she didn't say much after that. Her dad got on her about being so gloomy. She just kind of ignored him, and then he tried to tickle her out of it. Tried to tickle me, too, but not much. I figured that was because I wasn't one of his kids and he didn't think it would be right. But he tried to tickle her, and she said the weirdest thing."

"What was that?"

"She said, 'Don't touch me.' And then she looked at him like she was gonna kill him. It sort of scared me. I didn't know she hated her dad that much."

Anna drew a shaky breath. "Thanks, Mary Jo. You've been a great help."

"Really? I hope so. Oh! I just remembered one other thing. The last time I was over there, she had this big old pipe wrench under her bed. I asked her what it was doing there, and she told me she was afraid of burglars coming through the window. Did you ever hear anything so crazy?"

Anna had. Under her own bed she had kept a hammer. It required a lot of effort for her to find her voice. "Thanks, Mary Jo. This is what I needed."

"Good. If I think of anything else, I'll call you. But you know, Miss Anna, I haven't been over there since. When my dad heard that Mr. Lacey had tried to tickle me, he flat put his foot down about me ever going there again."

"Your dad is right, Mary Jo. Absolutely right. Don't go over there again."

When she hung up the phone, her hands were shaking. She looked down at the little puppy curled contentedly on her lap and tried to drag herself back to the present. But it was so difficult. Memories long buried were beating on the doors of her mind, demanding recognition.

Sleet rattled sharply against the window, and the wind moaned sorrowfully. A draft snaked across the floor and wrapped around her ankles, causing her to shiver. She needed to change. She needed to get into something warm and comfortable, and make herself some dinner. She needed to get busy so she could take control again and push the memories away. And she needed to figure out what she was going to do about Lorna.

It was going to be a long night.

Chapter 4

In the morning, the world was covered with a clear, sparkling glaze of ice. Anna looked out her window and wondered how she was going to get to work or to the sheriff's office. Not only did she not have a car, but it looked too treacherous even to walk.

She'd spent a disturbed night, sleeping fitfully, almost as if she were a child again, afraid that the bedroom door might open at any moment. Afraid that another night of fear and humiliation was about to begin.

She wondered if Lorna had slept any better at the sheriff's house. She hoped so.

Jazz was startled by the ice out back, slipping and sliding and looking at Anna with confused dismay. She finally managed to find purchase on some blades of grass that were poking up, and made a little puddle and a little pile. Anna praised her extravagantly, causing the puppy's tail to wag like a racing metronome.

While Jazz ate breakfast, Anna made herself some coffee and poached an egg. She was just getting ready to sit down when the phone rang.

"Anna? It's Dan. Listen, the roads are really bad this morning, so don't even try to come to work, okay? If it melts off later, we'll talk about whether it's worth going in, but for now, just stay put."

"You won't get any argument from me."

"Enjoy the break," he added. "I intend to. I've got this new computer game I've been dying to try. Talk to you later."

Anna ate her egg and a piece of whole wheat toast and wondered how she would fill her day, since she couldn't go anywhere. Plus there was the problem of Lorna, and she was really reluctant to let matters ride another day. What the child needed more than anything in the world right now was to know that someone was on her side and would protect her. She didn't need to spend even one more day alone in hell.

Making up her mind at last how she was going to handle the matter, she called the sheriff's office and was put straight through to Nate Tate.

"Lovely day, isn't it, sweet pea?" he asked in his deep, gravelly voice. "We've had a three-car pileup on the state highway, reports of cars in ditches all over the county, and half my men can't get to work. Velma managed to make it in, though, and she's teaching Lorna how to work the dispatch desk."

The image of wizened, chain-smoking, blunt-talking Velma Jansen working with a soft-spoken thirteen-year-old made Anna feel like smiling for the first time that day. "What's Lorna think of that?"

"Unless I miss my guess, she's thrilled. So what's up? Are you stuck in a ditch, too?"

"No, but probably only because my car died at the church last night."

"How'd you get home? Did you call a deputy?"

"Hugh Gallagher took me."

"Well, that's the next best thing. He's one fine man."

Anna knew she should come to the point, but she seized on Hugh as an excuse to avoid it just a little longer. "Is he?"

"You bet. He's a bona fide war hero, you know. Everybody knows he had some head problems after the Gulf War and hid up in the mountains with those vets for a few years, but that isn't the whole story. Anyway, for all that, he's got his head screwed on straight. But I don't gossip, so you'll just have to find out the rest for yourself."

Anna had to chuckle at that.

"Now, what's up, sweet pea? Not that I want to rush you or anything, but you never know when there might be another pileup on the state highway. Some of those damn truckers are pushing through like that pavement is dry."

"Well, it's about Lorna." She drew a deep breath and squeezed her eyes shut, reminding herself to keep her own feelings out of this. She had to speak to save the girl. "I'm convinced her father is sexually molesting her."

"So are all of us who were at that hearing yesterday. But there's not a whole lot I can do without proof. If she won't talk, my hands are tied."

"I talked to one of her friends last night, Nate. And she said some things…well, I think if I tell her what I know, I might be able to persuade her to confide in me."

He was silent for a moment. She could almost hear him ruminating. "All right. It's worth a stab. At least if she talks to you, I'll have something to start with. Okay, sweet pea, get into your outdoor gear. I'll have a deputy at your door in ten minutes."

"I'll be ready."

"Damn county's going to hell in a handbasket," he muttered. "See you in a few minutes, Anna."

Anna put Jazz in her cage, then dressed with trembling hands. She was about to do something she hadn't done in fifteen years: expose her past to another person. She didn't kid herself that she was going to get anywhere with Lorna if she didn't. God, she hoped she had the strength to go through with it.

The deputy took longer than ten minutes to get there. More like twenty, actually. Anna was just grateful that Nate had sent a woman. Sara Ironheart apologized profusely for the delay, but said she'd had to stop at an intersection to help get a car out of the way.

"Don't you live all the way out at the west end of the county?" Anna asked her. "How did you manage to get in this morning?"

Sara flashed her a smile. "I never got home last night. I've been on duty since three o'clock yesterday afternoon."

"You must be exhausted!"

Sara shrugged. "I caught a couple of catnaps at the office."

"Well, I hope the roads clear soon, so you can go home."

"I don't think that's going to happen. It looks like snow is moving in, and unless some of the other guys manage to find their way in, Nate's going to need every one of us still here to stick it out."

"It's been a long time since I've seen an ice storm like this."

"I don't recall us ever having one here. Usually it's just snow. Funny weather yesterday. Really funny."

The chains on the tires of the Blazer clanked loudly as they drove down the ice-coated streets. The trees looked like something out of a fairy tale, encased in ice and icicles. If the sun had been out, the world would have glittered and sparkled, but overhead, leaden clouds dulled the day.

"How's Joey doing?" Anna asked, referring to Sara's eighteen-year-old brother. When she had first moved here, Joey had been in the youth group and going through some hard times.

"Glad to be away at college, I think. I'm so glad my husband was able to talk him into at least trying it. I'd sure hate to see him miss the opportunity."

"Gideon seemed to have a good influence on him."

"He's been a good influence on all of us," Sara said. "And he's sure taken the load off my grandfather's shoulders."

"You board horses for people at your ranch, don't you?"

"Board some and raise some. Gideon's a wonder with those ponies." She shook her head and smiled. "The man is magic with horses. You ought to come up sometime and watch him work with them. It's well worth seeing."

"Some day I'd like to ride a horse."

Sara smiled at her. "We can arrange that, too. We have some really gentle ponies that are good for getting started on. Gideon's thinking about giving lessons to town kids who don't get the chance to ride like the ranch kids. I'm sure he'd love to practice on you."

"I'll think about it." But Gideon Ironheart, pleasant as he was, intimidated her. He was so big and muscular, and so exotic looking with his long black hair. She didn't think she would ever feel comfortable enough to take riding lessons from him.

They pulled up at last in front of the sheriff's office, and nervousness washed over Anna. It was no worse than stage fright, she told herself. Just do it. Just walk through it and do what needs doing.

Lorna was still sitting at the dispatcher's desk, working with Velma. When she looked up and saw Anna, she broke into a wide smile that nearly broke Anna's heart. This child looked so different today from yesterday. So much more alive and hopeful.

"Hi, Miss Anna!" Lorna said cheerfully. "Did you get stuck, too?"

"No, I just wanted to see you, so Sheriff Tate had Deputy Ironheart pick me up. Have you tried walking out there? You need ice skates!"

Lorna laughed and tossed her long blond hair. "I fell on my bottom this morning at the sheriff's house when I was helping put down salt on the driveway. And now it's going to snow. I hope it snows so deep that nobody can go anywhere." She looked suddenly wistful, and Anna identified with the feeling. How many times had she hoped her stepfather wouldn't be able to make it home from work?

"This child," said Velma, through a cloud of cigarette smoke, "just wants to be stuck here at this desk forever. Can you believe it? She actually likes talking to all these deputies and answering the phones. Next thing you know, they'll be retiring me and giving her my job."

Lorna grinned at her. "You shouldn't give them such a hard time."

"Child," said Velma, "giving deputies a hard time is my stock-in-trade. Somebody's got to keep them in line."

Nate Tate came down the hallway and greeted Anna. Then he turned to Velma. "Let Lorna go visit for a while with Miss Anna. We can't have you working the girl too hard. We'll run afoul of the child labor laws."

"Working her?" Velma snorted. "Boss, this child is having fun. Now scoot, Lorna, and go visit with Miss Anna."

Nate led Anna and Lorna to an empty office and left them

alone with the door closed. Anna sat on a creaky office chair, while Lorna went to the window to look out.

"Did you have a good time at Sheriff Tate's last night?"

Lorna nodded. "He has a nice family. He didn't even make me wear handcuffs like I thought he would. I just had to promise I wouldn't run away from him, so I did."

"That was a wise promise to make. And he does have a lovely family."

"They're all so happy," Lorna said wistfully. She kept on looking out the window. "We made popcorn after dinner and watched some funny movies. It was really fun." She paused. "I bet his daughters don't think about running away."

Anna drew a long breath to steady herself. "Do you think about running away?"

"All the time."

"Why?"

Lorna didn't answer.

Anna hesitated, wondering whether to keep beating around the bush or to just charge right in. For the first time in her life, she wished she had some formal training in psychology. At last she said, "I used to think about running away when I was your age. Finally I did."

Lorna turned from the window, looking at her with evident interest. "Did you make it?"

"That depends on what you mean by making it. I got away. But I paid a terrible price for it. There isn't much a fourteen-year-old girl can do on the streets. Nobody will hire you. I wound up having to do things I'm too ashamed to talk about."

Lorna came closer and sat, facing her. "I won't tell anybody. I promise."

Anna shook her head. "I don't like to talk about it. But

running away is never an answer, Lorna. I found that out
the hard way."

The girl nodded. "I kind of figured that out myself. Did
they catch you and make you go home?"

"They caught me. But no, they didn't make me go
home."

"How come?"

"Because I finally told them the truth about what was
going on. After that, they made sure I didn't have to go
home."

Lorna caught her breath but still didn't say anything. Her
look was one of painful yearning in the instant before she
averted her face. Silence reigned for several minutes.

Finally Anna spoke. "I talked to Mary Jo last night. She's
worried sick about you."

Lorna nodded but didn't reply.

"Killing yourself isn't the answer, either, Lorna. Honey,
you've got to trust one of us enough to tell us what's wrong.
We can't help you if you don't tell us."

"I can't. I *can't.*"

"Of course you can. Don't you see? Nobody can hurt
you anymore if you just tell us what's wrong. I'll protect
you. Sheriff Tate and the judge will protect you. Nobody
will ever lay another finger on you."

"You don't know. You can't promise that."

"Yes, I can. And I'm promising it right now. But we can't
do anything unless we know what's going on."

Lorna kept her head down and didn't answer.

Anna rose and went to the window, searching for the
courage to bare her soul. The words didn't want to come.
They lodged in her throat, stuck like glue. She dug her nails
into her palms, then forced the words out past lips that felt
like wood.

"Mary Jo said you sleep with a plumber's wrench under your bed."

"So?"

"I used to sleep with a hammer under mine."

She heard Lorna gasp, and part of her wanted to go to the girl and wrap her up in a tight hug. But she couldn't move. She kept staring out at the alley and the gray day. A solitary snowflake drifted down and vanished on the ice below.

"I know what's going on, Lorna. But I need you to tell me yourself. Nobody can do anything if you don't tell us yourself."

The girl sounded breathless. "You...you could be wrong."

"I'm not wrong. I slept with a hammer under my bed for too long to be wrong. I ran away from home and lived on the streets. I've been there, Lorna. I'm not wrong."

"You...you promise...you won't tell anybody?"

Anna hesitated. She needed Lorna to tell the sheriff or the judge about this. On the other hand, the first and most difficult step was getting Lorna to speak about it at all. One step at a time.

"I promise," she said, and turned to look at the girl. "I won't tell unless you say it's okay. But you'd better tell somebody fast, before that man leaves town and takes your sister with him."

Tears were running down Lorna's face now, huge drops, and she wrapped her arms around herself as if she were trying to hold in a pain too great to bear. "He said...he said he'd hurt Mindy if I told."

Anna crossed the room swiftly and stood before Lorna, taking the girl's shoulders gently in her hands. "Honey...honey, look at me. He can't hurt you *or* Mindy if you tell us.

Don't you see? He wouldn't dare, because we'll know about it.''

The sobs came then, huge racking sobs that shook the child's entire body. Anna drew her up, gathered her close and rocked her gently, murmuring softly as she stroked Lorna's hair. Her heart ached, and her throat was so tight she could barely force the reassuring murmurs out. Tears burned in her own eyes, and she felt the kindling of an old, old rage, a rage she thought she had buried.

Anna had no idea how much time passed before Lorna finally fell silent and grew still from exhaustion. Her back and neck ached from the way she was folded around the girl, but she hardly noticed.

"What will they do to me?" Lorna finally asked.

Anna stood back and gently dried the girl's eyes and face with the sleeve of her sweater. "Do to you?"

"If I tell."

"They'll make sure you never have to go home again. They'll find you a good foster home."

"And Mindy?"

Anna felt a sharp pang. "Has he hurt Mindy, too?"

Lorna shook her head and sniffled. "No."

"But he threatened to."

"He said—" Her voice caught and broke. "He said he'd do the same thing to her if I ever told anyone."

"They'll protect her, Lorna. But I can't tell you exactly what will happen, since he hasn't hurt her yet. I honestly don't know. But I think they're going to be all over him like white on rice, you know? They won't give him a chance to hurt her."

Lorna nodded and sighed shakily. "Will he go to jail?"

"I don't know. My stepfather got five years' probation, and he wasn't allowed to be around children anymore."

Lorna looked down at her hands, and a big tear squeezed from beneath her eyelid. "It's not fair."

"No, honey. It's not fair. It's the most unfair thing on the planet."

"What if nobody believes me?"

Anna touched the girl's cheek gently. "There was a courtroom full of people last night who figured out what was going on. Couldn't you tell? All of us are ready to believe you, honey."

"Do I have to tell the sheriff?"

Anna hesitated. "I don't know. Would you feel more comfortable telling Judge Williams? Because she's a woman?"

"Can she stop him?"

Anna felt a small smile curve her lips despite all the anguish she was feeling for this child. "Sweetie, Judge Williams is a powerful woman. I have a feeling she can do even more than Sheriff Tate about this."

Lorna sniffled again and looked down at her hands. They were knotted tightly together, so tightly that her knuckles were white. "Will you stay with me?"

"You can bet on it. Do you want to wait and just tell this to Judge Williams first?"

Lorna nodded slowly. "I guess so." She gave Anna a brave smile. "Once is enough."

"I agree."

"Did you have to tell more than once?"

"Unfortunately, yes. I told the lady at the runaway shelter the cops took me to, because she was trying to make me go home. Then I had to tell the cops. And then I had to tell a judge. Maybe we can cut a few steps out of it for you. Is that what you want?"

"I guess so." Another tear rolled down her cheek. "I don't know if I can talk about it, Miss Anna. I really don't."

"We'll all help you, honey. Believe me, we all know how hard it's going to be."

Nate called the judge and had a message taken to her in court. She asked him to bring Lorna and Anna to her chambers at twelve-thirty. When they arrived in the spacious room with a long conference table, a court reporter was there, setting up her equipment. For a minute Anna thought Lorna was going to bolt, but she touched the girl's shoulder reassuringly and guided her to a chair.

A few minutes later, the judge joined them. She'd cast off her black robe and sat at the head of the table in blue jeans and a sweater. She was an attractive woman of forty, with a trim figure, a brilliant smile and a no-nonsense reputation in the courtroom.

"Boy, isn't it cold today?" Francine Williams asked with a smile for Lorna. "All right, Miss Lacey. I realize this is going to be very difficult for you, but I need the court reporter here to take your sworn statement. It will save you having to go through this again unless there's a trial."

"Trial?" Lorna paled. "I don't think…"

"That's a long way down the road, if it even comes to that," the judge hastened to assure her. "And I'm going to do my darnedest to see that it doesn't. Okay?"

Lorna nodded hesitantly.

"So it's okay with you if Mrs. Jubilo stays?" the judge asked her.

Again Lorna nodded.

"From now on," the judge admonished her, "I'll need to hear you say yes or no in answer to my questions, so Mrs. Jubilo can record your answer, all right?"

"Yes, ma'am."

Mrs. Jubilo administered the oath. Then the judge spent a few minutes questioning her about whether she understood the oath and what it meant to lie under oath. Lorna was very clear on that.

"So now, Lorna," the judge said, "why don't you tell us why you set fire to the schoolroom yesterday?"

Lorna bit her lip and looked down. "I wanted to die." Her voice quavered, then steadied.

"Why did you want to die, Lorna?"

The story tumbled out then, spilling forth like water through a ruptured dam. She stumbled at times, cried at times, and at times was nearly incoherent, but the words just kept coming as she told them of the hell she had been living for the past year.

She told them how her father came to her room at night, after her mother went to sleep. She said that at first she wasn't even sure he was doing anything wrong but just knew she didn't like it. She spoke of the horrible, disgusting ways he touched her and made her touch him, of how he had told her he had a right to do anything he wanted with her, because she was his property. How, when she finally threatened to tell, he told her that he would hurt her little sister. That was when she realized for sure he was doing something wrong.

"He liked to make me cry," she said in a small, thin voice. "He liked me to fight him. So I stopped fighting."

And then she told them how she had decided to kill him. How she had put the plumber's wrench under her bed and was going to bash his brains out the very next time he came to her room. She told them how he found it and laughed at her, and told her that if she didn't do what he wanted from then on, he was going to hurt her sister. How he was going to do the same things to her little sister.

How she had finally decided that the only way out was to kill herself.

When the torrent finally stopped, Lorna put her head down on the table and wept. No one said a word. Anna put her arm around the girl's shoulders and blinked back her own tears. Dear God, she wondered, how could anyone do such things to a child?

Francine Williams waited until Lorna was calm again before asking, "Does your mother know about this?"

"No."

"Are you sure?"

Lorna shrugged. "I don't think so. I didn't tell her, because I was afraid he'd hurt Mindy."

"Would you like to live with your mother if we get your father out of the way?"

Lorna's answer was surprisingly swift in coming. "No. No! She didn't help me...she didn't *help* me...."

It made perfect emotional sense to Anna. Of course, in her case, her mother had refused to believe her.

But Judge Williams seemed to understand, too. "All right, then. I'd like to release you from custody on your own recognizance if you promise not to try to hurt yourself again, but for now I guess I can't do that. I'll have to look into a temporary foster home...."

"I'll take her," Anna said, closing her eyes against the difficulty of what she was about to admit. "I know I'm not a registered foster parent, but...well...I've been through it, too, Your Honor. My stepfather molested me when I was Lorna's age. At least I know some of the things she's feeling and experiencing. At least for now..." She opened her eyes and found Francine Williams regarding her kindly.

The judge nodded. "That might be a very good idea, at least temporarily. You realize I can't make you a permanent foster parent until you're approved, but as a temporary measure—well, you have an excellent reputation in this community, Miss Fleming, and everyone is aware of your wonderful work with the children in the Good Shepherd youth group. Lorna, how would you feel about living with Miss Fleming until we get this sorted out?"

Lorna lifted her tearstained face. "I'd like to stay with Miss Anna."

"All right, we'll do that, then. I'm granting Miss Fleming guardianship of Lorna Lacey until such time as this court chooses to make other arrangements. I'll have the order prepared by the end of the day, Miss Fleming. Until then, Lorna will remain in the sheriff's custody."

Then she leaned forward, looking at Lorna. "With regard to your father, Lorna, I'm going to issue a warrant for his immediate arrest. And I'm going to have the child protection people look into the matter of your sister. Trust me, I'm not going to let anyone hurt her. Or you. Ever again."

By one o'clock, the pavement in the downtown area of Conard City had cleared of ice. Sanding crews had been out, and the gradual increase of traffic had taken care of the rest.

Hugh Gallagher drove to Good Shepherd Church to pick up Anna for lunch. He figured they would have a nice meal together, and then he would take another look at her car. He hoped he could fix the problem for her, because he had a strong suspicion she couldn't really afford a repair bill.

He had mixed feelings about this lunch date, though. It had been a long time since he'd taken a woman out for any reason, even something as innocuous as lunch. He had an ulterior motive here in hoping that he could persuade Miss

Anna to help him with his youth ranch, but he was also uncomfortably aware that he was drawn to her. Something about her appealed to him, and that made him uneasy, primarily because it might mess up any business relationship he hoped to have with her.

Not that it probably mattered. Any way you sliced the pie, he figured she wouldn't reciprocate his attraction. There was no reason on earth why any woman would be attracted to a man like him. Any sensible woman would avoid an involvement with him like the plague, and Miss Anna struck him as a very sensible woman.

Which made him even more uncomfortable with his attraction to her. It could never be comfortable to be attracted to someone who wouldn't reciprocate.

But hell, he told himself, he was a grown man, and he could handle these things. So he would buy her lunch, talk about his youth ranch and see if he couldn't entice her into helping him.

He was acutely aware that his past, particularly the years he'd spent living in the mountains with the other vets who couldn't handle the world, was likely to make him a doubtful candidate for the trust of the people who would have to refer children to him. Sheriff Tate and Reverend Fromberg kept telling him not to worry about it, that they would stand beside him, but that didn't do much to reassure him. He'd gone out of his gourd up there in those hills, and the fact that he hadn't gone nuts in a long time now was no guarantee he would never do it again. Folks who looked into such things were apt to have serious doubts about him.

So he saw Anna, with her sterling reputation in Conard County and her much-lauded work with the youth group, as the perfect counter to his period of unsteadiness. He needed a woman, anyway, if he was to help out girls as well as boys, and Anna, with all her experience, looked like the perfect choice to be codirector of the ranch with him. He couldn't think of anybody in the county who would be better.

But first he had to get her to trust him and believe in him. That would be a whole lot easier if he didn't start panting after her.

But she was a cute little package, he thought anyway, as he drove to the church. He liked her bright brown eyes and her classically oval face. Her delicacy, as if her bones were not just small but tiny, made him feel protective. With all that, she had a cute little figure, too, to judge by what he could make out under those shapeless dresses and suits she preferred.

She hid all her assets as best she could behind glasses and ugly dresses, and kept her hair tightly bound, but he'd learned long ago to look past the superficial. That woman, he thought, would be beautiful if she ever relaxed.

He pulled in to the church parking lot and walked over to the office. Dan Fromberg was there, but no Anna.

"What can I do for you, Hugh?" Dan asked.

"I came to take Miss Anna to lunch."

Dan looked him up and down, and then a twinkle came to his eye. "Really? This is an interesting development."

Hugh opened his mouth to say it was purely business, then stopped himself. He didn't know what Anna thought it was, and he didn't want to embarrass her. "Yeah," he said, letting the unspoken question remain unanswered.

"Yes, indeed." Dan's twinkle faded. "Unfortunately Anna isn't here. I gave her the morning off, for the weather, and said to play it by ear this afternoon. Her car was here when I came in, but I haven't seen her. There's no answer at her house, either. If she doesn't turn up soon, I'm going to call the sheriff.''

"She left her car here last night," Hugh said. "It wouldn't start, and I drove her home."

"Then maybe I'd better call the sheriff right now. Grab a seat."

Hugh perched on the couch, resting his elbows on his thighs and letting his hands dangle between his knees. They were large, work-roughened hands, scarred from mishaps here and there, like the white line between his thumb and index finger where a saw had slipped. He tried to imagine a delicate little thing like Anna Fleming wanting those hands on her, and he just couldn't. Her hands were soft and white, graceful as birds. His thumb and forefinger would probably close easily around her tiny wrists. Naw. These weren't a lover's hands.

And he had to stop thinking of that, anyway. He had more important fish to fry when it came to Miss Anna Fleming.

Dan came out of his office. "Anna's in court. Something came up with the Lacey girl, and nobody seems to know when they'll be done."

Hugh nodded. He'd been stood up before. Rising, he reached to zip his jacket. "I'll just go on out and take a look at her car, then. I promised her I would."

He felt Dan's eyes on him as he turned toward the door. It was a whole lot easier to be stood up when nobody knew about it, he thought.

"Hugh?"

He paused and looked back at the minister.

"Do you think you can get the important work done on the roof before we get buried in snow?"

Hugh gave him a half smile. "You mean before tonight?"

Dan laughed. "It's only supposed to be a couple of

inches. I know, it would have been easier over the summer, but we didn't have the money then, because of the flood problem. So what are our chances now?''

"I can get right to work on the insulation under the eaves. That'll help stop the melting and refreezing that's causing a lot of the ice damming. The rest of the roof…well, if we get us a patch of good weather after this storm moves through, we might be able to get the whole job done.''

Dan nodded. ''Do what you can, then. After you see to Anna's car. The job is yours.''

Hugh stepped outside, half convinced he'd gotten the job because Dan Fromberg wanted him to be around Anna more. He thought about it, then shrugged. Not likely.

There was enough light for him to see his way around Anna's engine now. It was a 1976 Chevy, from the age when they still made cars a man could work on in his own driveway, back before all those computerized parts that needed special diagnostic equipment. Back when a man could still get his hands in there to work, before everything got shrunk to the point you had to drop the engine to do anything at all.

It didn't take him long to discover that the problem was in the distributor. The cap was cracked pretty badly, and some water must have gotten up in there last night when she was driving through the sleet. Easy and cheap to fix. She also had some bad-looking spark plug wires. Might as well take care of them and the plugs, too, while he was at it.

He hopped into his truck and headed for the auto parts store. It wasn't often that life gave you a simple fix.

It was two-thirty when Anna got out of the sheriff's car in front of the church. The day had warmed up a little, and water was dripping from the church roof. The sky was still dark gray, however, and occasional snowflakes drifted gently to the ground.

The first thing she noticed was that someone was bent over the engine of her car, presenting a rather nice view of a hard rump clad in denim. For all that she had sworn off men a long time ago, she still wasn't immune to such things. And there was definitely something about the male posterior and legs encased in well-worn denim that caught her eye every time.

Her reaction embarrassed her even as she had it, bringing a helpless bloom of color to her cheeks. She was just punchy from all the emotions of the past few hours, she told herself. Sharing Lorna's anguish had been as difficult as anything she had ever done.

But then she realized that the man bent over her engine was Hugh Gallagher, and that she had had a lunch date with him. Embarrassment swamped her. Never in her life had she missed an appointment, and this man had been kind enough to help her out. She wanted to sink.

He straightened and turned to look at her, a wrench in one hand. His hands were covered with black smudges, and there was even a smear on his cheek.

He smiled. "It's almost fixed, Miss Anna."

"L-lunch," she said, stammering. "I'm so sorry!"

He shrugged. "Some things are more important. Dan told me you were at the courthouse with the Lacey girl. It's okay. Can we do dinner instead?"

"Um...I'm getting guardianship of Lorna this afternoon at five. I really don't want to leave her alone her first night with me."

He nodded, and something in his face gentled. "You're a good woman, Miss Anna. Well, I'll take both of you out to Maude's for dinner. You just ask Lorna if that's okay with her and give me a call by six, all right?''

''I...thank you,'' she said. ''Thank you very much. And thank you for fixing my car.''

''Wasn't anything at all.'' He shrugged. ''That's what neighbors are for. Now go on inside before you get chilled.''

''You'll let me pay you, won't you?''

He looked at her standing there in her slacks and jacket and seemed to reach some kind of conclusion. ''Parts only,'' he said finally. ''You can pay for the parts.''

''Thank you.'' Feeling oddly flustered, she hurried inside and found Dan seated at her desk, talking on the telephone. He waved and indicated he would be out of her seat in just a minute.

Anna used the time to hang up her jacket and slip her over-the-shoe boots off. When she turned around, Dan was hanging up.

''What happened?'' he asked, standing. ''Did Lorna talk to the judge?''

Anna nodded. ''She told her everything. I'm getting temporary guardianship of her at five o'clock today.''

''That's good. That's really good. I was up most of the night praying for that child.''

So had Anna been, in her own way. ''Nate is going to try to collect her things from home, but he doesn't know how much luck he'll have. He's also going to arrest Al.''

''Good.''

It was one of the few times Anna had ever seen Dan's face grow hard. She watched as he looked down at the floor, rocking gently back and forth on his heels. When he looked at her again, his expression was still hard.

''You know, Anna, I believe in forgiveness, but I'm going to find this awfully hard to forgive. And you're going to

need some financial help with that child. Let me give you a
sum so you can buy her some things to wear and some extra
food. Take it from me, they eat an incredible amount at that
age. The church will help you out.''

Then he turned and went into his office, leaving Anna to
wonder if she'd made the right decision when she had offered to take Lorna. She might once have walked in the
girl's shoes, but that didn't mean she was a fit guardian for
her.

In fact, she was probably the most unfit person on the
face of the earth.

Chapter 5

Anna picked up Lorna from the sheriff's office at five-fifteen, just ten minutes after she'd received the call from Nate that all the paperwork had been received. When she arrived, he drew her into his office for a few quick words away from Lorna.

"I picked up Al Lacey," he told her, keeping his voice low so they couldn't be overheard. "You need to be aware of what's going on. Al will probably make bail in the next day or two. I can't see any legitimate reason for the judge to refuse it. So he may try to see Lorna, even though the judge is going to order him to keep clear of her."

Anna nodded. This was a complication she hadn't considered, and it made her distinctly uneasy.

"I don't think he'll try anything else," Nate went on, "but he sure is going to try to find some way to get Lorna to recant her story."

"I won't let her talk to him." Brave words. The thought of standing up to Al Lacey scared her to death. He was a man just like her stepfather, a child molester, and she was still terrified of her stepfather. Why else did she sometimes lie awake at night, feeling that she would never be safe until that man was dead? But for Lorna's sake, she was somehow going to have to find the courage to do what was necessary.

"Well, it gets worse yet," Nate said. "Bridget Lacey doesn't believe Al hurt the girl. She is absolutely convinced Lorna's lying. And what's more, she's being downright nasty about it. Some of the things she said weren't fit for my ears, let alone the ears of a girl that age." He gave Anna a wry smile. "I hope you don't have to hear that crap, but you probably will. Are you still sure you want to do this?"

Anna nodded, even as she felt nervous tension knot all her muscles and awaken butterflies in her stomach. "Somebody has to do it, Nate. And honestly, I don't think Lorna needs to live in a house with a man right now."

"I couldn't agree more. Lorna needs to sleep at night without wondering when the bedroom door is going to open. But, sweet pea, if you need anything, anything at all, I'm just a phone call away. I can be there in five minutes, any time, night or day."

"Thanks, Nate." She looked up at him, feeling a rush of warmth for this man who had never done anything except make her feel as safe and as welcome as possible in his county. Why couldn't there be more Nate Tates in the world? Why couldn't she have had a father like him? Life could just be so damned unfair at times.

Lorna was eager to go, smiling and cheerful, acting as if she'd just come out of a long nightmare and was sure there were only good things ahead. Anna hoped with all her heart that Lorna wouldn't be disappointed.

But she also feared that when the exhilaration wore off, Lorna was going to crash. Right now she was riding high on the relief of having escaped her demon, but sooner or later she was going to realize what that escape had cost her: her mother and her sister. Her family.

But for now, Lorna was focused on something of more immediate importance. As they drove toward Anna's house, she asked, "Miss Anna? Do you really want me to come live with you?"

"I certainly do. But I'd better warn you, I don't live in as nice a house as your family. Secretaries don't make as much money as dentists."

"That's okay." Lorna was silent for a moment before saying sadly, "Money isn't worth a whole lot if you're not happy."

"No, I guess it isn't." Anna hesitated, wondering if she should say any more or just let Lorna talk in her own way at her own pace. Better not to force a discussion of what had happened, she decided.

"My dad was always buying me pretty things," Lorna said after a moment. "I think maybe he felt bad."

Anna thought it far more likely that Al Lacey was trying to buy his daughter's silence, but she didn't say so. If Lorna wanted to believe the man was capable of shame and guilt, she couldn't see any reason to say otherwise. At least, not yet.

"I feel so bad for not making him stop."

Anna's hands jerked on the wheel, and she had to straighten the car out. "Lorna...Lorna, you're not responsible for what happened. And you weren't responsible for making him stop. There was nothing you could do to stop him, not when he was threatening your sister. The only thing you could have done was exactly what you did. You told people who could help you."

"I should have told you sooner."

"Maybe. But how were you to know we'd believe you?

Or that we'd do anything about it? And I can certainly understand you being afraid for your sister."

"I guess."

Lorna's euphoria was wearing off, Anna realized. She sought for a safe change of subject. "I'm afraid I don't have a bed for you yet, but we'll get one tomorrow." Dan had certainly given her enough to help with Lorna's expenses. "For tonight, we'll toss a coin to see who gets the sofa bed."

Lorna shook her head. "That's okay. I'll sleep on the sofa bed. You shouldn't give up your bed for me, Miss Anna. You're doing enough."

Anna reached out and gently touched the girl's shoulder. "You're a sweetheart, Lorna. Hey, I have a puppy now, you know."

"Really?" Lorna's expression brightened, and she turned to look at Anna. "When did you get it?"

"Yesterday. Her name is Jazz, and I'm sure she's going to love you to death."

"I always wanted a puppy, but Mom's allergic."

Anna glanced at her as she stopped at a stop sign, and saw something dark pass over the child's face, but it was gone so quickly she wasn't sure what she had seen.

"I can cook," Lorna said. "And I can help with the cleaning."

"That's wonderful!" She felt touched by the offer. "Hey, I'm getting the better end of this deal, you know. Someone to help with the cooking and cleaning. I hate cooking and cleaning."

"I think it's fun."

"Don't tell me that. I might take advantage of you."

Lorna laughed, and the shadows seemed to pass—for now.

Anna turned the car into her driveway and switched off the ignition before she turned to look at Lorna. "Do you know Hugh Gallagher?"

"The guy everybody calls Cowboy? Sure. He helped coach the girls' soccer team at church last year."

"Well, he wants to take us both out to dinner at Maude's tonight. Would you like to do that?"

"Sounds like fun."

There was not the least hesitation in the response, and Anna was both relieved and envious. Apparently Lorna hadn't translated her experience with her father into a reflection on all men. Anna unfortunately had...although, to be fair to herself, she had had some really nasty experiences with men when she was living on the streets.

What she knew for sure was that she wished she could regard this coming evening with Lorna's equanimity.

The instant Anna and Lorna stepped into the diner, Maude descended on them. Maude's usually annoyed expression melted into one of tenderness when she set eyes on Lorna. She stomped across the dining room to sweep the girl into a motherly embrace and tell her that she could have anything she wanted for dessert, on the house.

Lorna, far from being pleased by this announcement, appeared dismayed. Anna saw her look quickly around, as if she was wondering how many other faces in the room concealed knowledge of her dirty secret. Much to Anna's relief, no one else seemed particularly interested in them.

As soon as Maude moved away, returning to the business of running the diner, Lorna leaned close to Anna's ear and whispered, "She knows. Does everyone know about it?"

"By the time all of this is over, everybody's going to

know about it,'' Anna told her truthfully. ''But you don't
have anything to be ashamed of, honey. Not one thing.''

But Lorna looked at her sadly. ''Yes, I do, Miss Anna.''

''No, you most positively don't. But if you want to
leave…'' Now that they were here, Anna was reluctant to
let Lorna change her mind. If the child started hiding out
because people knew what had happened to her, she might
well wind up an isolated recluse. On the other hand, Lorna
might simply be feeling too raw to face it all right now—
something Anna could certainly identify with. So if Lorna
really wanted to leave, she would take her. This time.

But Lorna had already spied Cowboy sitting at a table
near the back. He had risen and was waving to them, and
Lorna smiled and returned his wave, heading back toward
him without hesitation.

Lorna had guts, thought Anna. More guts than *she* had
ever had. She'd spent her entire life trying to keep people
from knowing about her past.

Hugh held out their chairs for them, treating both Lorna
and Anna with equal gallantry. What struck Anna most,
though, was that he had exchanged his usual work shirt and
jeans for a nicely pressed pair of gray slacks and a white
shirt, and had gotten a haircut. He looked so nice that Anna
found herself tempted to stare.

His attention, though, was for Lorna. He told her he was
glad she had decided to come, then engaged her in conversation about last year's soccer team and his hopes for this
year's. Anna, who knew nothing about soccer, didn't have
to do anything except sit back, read the menu and pretend
to listen.

After they ordered, Hugh began to steer the conversation
back to areas that included Anna—the work on the church,

how her car was running and finally to the youth ranch he wanted to open.

As soon as the subject came around to that, Anna tensed. She had a strong feeling that he wanted more from her than a few suggestions from time to time. But she couldn't give him any more than that. Any deeper involvement with such a project might well open her past to scrutiny. It was bound to be more involved than being granted temporary guardianship of Lorna.

Her work with the church youth group was different. She had fallen into that gradually since she had started working for Reverend Fromberg. Dan was her reference, the only reference she needed to work with the children of Good Shepherd Church. She was not the only youth counselor at the church, although she volunteered considerably more time than anyone else. But even so, no one had ever thought to investigate her background.

It would be different with the kind of thing Hugh was proposing. He would be inspected by the state and probably the county, and all his counselors and helpers would be, too. Otherwise the state and county couldn't order children to be put in his care.

Anna's past couldn't stand up to that, she believed. She would be a detriment to his hopes and plans. But she didn't know how to tell him that, especially since so far he hadn't asked anything particular of her.

Watching him eat and talk with Lorna, she found herself wishing that just for once her life could be uncomplicated. That just for once she could sit with a man and not think about anything except how attractive she found him to be.

And she did find Hugh very attractive. It would have been nice, just once in her life, to look at a man with yearning and feel free to yearn. She'd missed all the normal stuff a

teenage girl was supposed to go through. She'd never had
a crush, and she'd never had a normal date.

And it didn't do any good to think about it, Anna reminded herself sternly. What was past was past, and all that
mattered was the kind of person she was *now*.

Much to her relief, Hugh avoided putting her on the spot
about the ranch. He kept the conversation general, talking
about the horses he hoped to have, and how he believed that
having a job to do and animals to care for could help build
self-esteem and responsibility in kids. It was clear to Anna
that he honestly believed environment was responsible for
a lot of the trouble kids got into.

"Now, I'm not saying there's no such thing as a sociopath
or a psychopath," he told Anna. "God knows I've seen 'em.
But I think the majority of kids who get into trouble do so
because they have too much freedom, not enough self-
respect and no real rewards for being good. That's all en-
vironmental. And those are the kids I want to help."

"You don't think anything can be done for sociopaths?"
Anna asked.

Hugh shook his head. "They either mature out of it eventually, or they wind up in jail for life. Those are people with
a serious screw missing in their characters, Anna. And I
don't think any head doctor can put it back in there. I'll be
the first to say that you can't always tell the sociopaths from
the troubled kids at these early ages, and I'm willing to give
'em all a chance—but I don't expect the sociopaths are going to improve much."

"I don't like to think that some people are just inherently
bad."

"Neither do I. But a small percentage of people simply
aren't interested in anything except their personal gratifica-
tion. God knows why."

"Like my dad," Lorna said suddenly. "He doesn't care about anything except what he wants."

Both Anna and Hugh looked at her, but neither of them seemed to know how to answer that bald statement.

"My dad knew what he was doing was wrong," Lorna continued flatly. "He knew. That's why he told me not to tell anyone. So what does it make you when you do something you know is wrong? Is that a sociopath?"

Anna and Hugh exchanged looks. "Not always," Anna said finally. "We all sometimes do things we know we shouldn't. Sometimes we just do bad things."

"Yeah." Lorna put down her fork and pushed her plate aside. She looked at neither Hugh nor Anna. "I did some bad things."

Anna leaned toward her, feeling an ache of sympathy. "That doesn't mean you're a sociopath, Lorna. In fact, I'm sure you're not."

"So am I," Hugh said gently. "Sometimes we have to do bad things to survive. I know I did."

Lorna looked swiftly at him, her eyes full of hope.

"It's true," Hugh said. "I did some pretty awful things to survive. I didn't have a choice at the time. But now that I have a choice, I'll never do those things again. Never."

"Neither will I," Lorna said.

"Well, then—" Hugh smiled "—you're not a sociopath. You're not even a bad person. You're someone who had to do some bad things to survive. It's what you do now that counts."

Anna watched as Lorna absorbed what he had said. Little by little the youngster's face lightened and relaxed. When Anna turned to Hugh, she found him watching the child, his face full of concern and genuine caring.

Hugh Gallagher, she decided, was a remarkable man. No

two ways about it. She was actually sorry when dinner was over and they went their separate ways.

In the morning, Anna drove Lorna to school. While Lorna went to her classroom, Anna went to see the principal with the guardianship papers.

John Kreusi invited her to be seated and scanned the papers at some length. When he finally looked up, the expression on his face was guarded. "I'll need to make a copy of these papers before you leave."

"Certainly."

"According to this, Lorna isn't allowed to see or talk to either of her parents."

"That's correct."

"That's a rather extreme, rather unusual order. Can you explain it to me?"

It seemed, Anna thought, that life was going to make her deal with this subject no matter how hard she tried not to. "Lorna was being sexually molested by her father. He's in jail right now, as a matter of fact, but he'll probably make bail shortly. For obvious reasons, Lorna isn't allowed to see him."

"And her mother? Why not her mother?"

"Bridget Lacey apparently doesn't believe her daughter's story."

"I see." John Kreusi looked out the window, as if the gray day held great fascination for him. "I'll have to decide what to do about the child."

"What to do?"

"Yes." He faced Anna again. "Two days ago, Lorna attempted to burn down this school building. Our usual reaction in these cases is to put the child on suspension."

"Suspension!" Anna could hardly believe her ears. "Didn't

you hear what I just told you? For the last year this child has been sexually abused by her father! The last thing she needs now is to be suspended from school.''

"I have to consider the other children here.''

"The whole reason she tried to burn the school down was because she couldn't escape her father. She's away from him now. There's no reason on earth to think she might try anything like that again.''

"I have only your word for it—''

"And Lorna's word! You weren't there. You didn't hear her tell her story. If you had, there wouldn't be a doubt in your mind!''

"But I wasn't there. And from what you tell me, her own mother doesn't believe her. Yet you're asking me to risk the lives of other children because Lorna Lacey has made an unsubstantiated claim against her father.''

Anna couldn't stand it. Rising to her feet, she let her anger come bubbling to the fore. "This kind of claim is almost always unsubstantiated, Mr. Kreusi. But the judge heard her, and I heard her, and we both know how hard it was to get her to tell us what was going on. You'll just have to take my word for it, and the judge's.''

"I'll have to follow the court order, to be sure, but I can't be forced to keep this child in school where she may be a danger to the other children.''

"She's not a danger! She's promised not to do anything like that again.''

"And I'm supposed to believe that? Girls this age get hysterical. They exaggerate things—''

"Exaggerate!" Anna glared furiously at him. "Mr. Kreusi, it is people like you who make it possible for fathers to do these things to their daughters!''

"I resent that! I know Al Lacey—''

"We all know Al Lacey. But not one of us except him and Lorna knows what he did to her in the middle of the night. And what about you and all your educators here? Where were you when the child became steadily more withdrawn? Didn't any of you ever think to investigate what might be upsetting her? For the love of God, you saw her every single day!''

"Children this age—''

"I don't want to hear about children this age. You will not treat this girl like a criminal! Enough harm has been done to her!''

"I have to consider the other children—''

"Fine, then I'll take Lorna home with me. You can discuss this matter with the judge.''

Turning, Anna strode out of his office to the front desk. "I want Lorna Lacey now,'' she told the woman at the counter. "I'm taking her home immediately.''

It was only later that she realized that for the first time in her life, she had stood up to a man and given him a piece of her mind.

She took Lorna with her to the office and left her sitting in the front room while she went back to Dan's office to explain what was going on. Dan looked as upset as she felt.

"Have Lorna come in here,'' he said. "I've got some books she can read while you call the judge. No point in her hearing that discussion.''

But the judge was in court, and the judicial assistant could only promise to have her call. Still furious, and all the more so because she couldn't get immediate action, Anna called Nate and told him what had happened.

"For the love of Pete,'' he said disgustedly. "That girl needs somebody to bend over backward for her right now.

I thought for sure the school would do it. Hell. All right, sweet pea, you sit tight while I see if I can't talk some sense into the man. Had to do it a few times with my girls. They were always up to some hijinks or other, seems like. Meantime, you wait for the judge to call. I got a feeling Francine Williams isn't going to like this, either.''

Anna sat at her desk for a few more minutes, staring out the window and fighting an urge to smash something. It had been a long time since she had felt this angry, and to be honest, she wasn't sure that all her anger had to do with John Kreusi's treatment of Lorna. No, some of it had to do with the way her own mother had refused to believe her when she had tried to tell her what was happening. Some of it had to do with the doubting responses from the cops in her own case, and the reluctance of the judge to give her stepfather anything stronger than probation.

Times were changing, but apparently they still hadn't changed enough.

But it *was* different for Lorna, she reminded herself. Lorna had the sheriff and a judge on her side. There *were* people who were prepared to believe a child when she told them that her father was molesting her. And that was an improvement.

And, to be fair to John Kreusi, he did have reason to wonder if he could trust Lorna. She *had* started the fire, after all. But his comments had gone beyond that, far beyond that. And that was what was making Anna so angry.

There was so little a child could do for herself. She couldn't leave home, move to another town and build a new life. A child had nothing and no one to depend on except her family and the authorities who were charged with protecting the welfare of children. If the people who could help didn't believe a child's complaints, the child was left absolutely helpless.

Anna, better than many people, could understand what it did to a child when the people she depended on either hurt her or didn't believe her. She understood the depth of those wounds, and the way they gutted a person's ability to trust. If she could do anything at all for Lorna, it would be to shield her from attitudes like John Kreusi's. If Lorna couldn't trust her own parents, the people she ought to be able to trust more than anyone else in the world, she at least ought to be able to trust the other authority figures in her life. And Anna was determined to see that she could.

Marge Tate, Nate Tate's wife, dropped in around two o'clock that afternoon. The judge still hadn't called, and Lorna was occupying herself reading a book from Dan Fromberg's bottomless library.

Marge was a beautiful woman in her late forties, with hair that was still a bright red, and dancing, laughing green eyes.

"I came to kidnap Lorna," she told Anna. "I'm going shopping and thought she might like to come along." She turned to Lorna. "If it's okay with Miss Anna, would you like to?"

"Oh, yes!" Lorna closed the book hurriedly and sent a pleading look to Anna. "Is it all right?"

"Of course." Anna couldn't imagine saying no to the child. In fact, she was going to have to figure out what Lorna could do with her time until this school issue was settled. The girl couldn't just spend her days sitting in this office reading books. Maybe she would have to look into home schooling.

For an instant Anna felt overwhelmed. She'd acted on impulse by offering to take Lorna, an impulse born of a strong protective feeling. But it was beginning to look as if she'd also taken on a whole bunch of complications she hadn't previously imagined.

Lorna was already pulling on her jacket.

"I think—if it's all right," Marge said, "I'll just take Lorna home to have dinner with us? The girls asked if she could come over again. I promise to have her home by eight."

"That would be fine," Anna replied with a smile, seeing the hopeful look on Lorna's face. "She had a great time when she stayed with you the other night."

"So did we." Marge smiled at Lorna. "Nothing fancy tonight, I'm afraid. Tonight's our night to eat chili dogs in front of a science fiction movie. You can help me pick out the film at the video store."

Then Marge turned back to Anna. "You're welcome, too, of course."

"Thank you, but I need to see about getting a bed for Lorna before the stores close."

"Oh! Well, I can help with that. We have a daybed the girls don't use anymore and all the linens for it. Come to think of it, we also have a dresser and a desk stored in the basement. I can have Nate bring them over later, if you like."

Anna had lived in this town for five years, but the generosity of her neighbors could still surprise her. She felt a trickle of warmth begin to thaw her anger. "That would be wonderful."

"Good. I'll talk to Nate about it when he gets home. Sure you don't want to come for dinner? I make a mean chili dog."

Anna had to laugh. "Really, thanks, but there are a bunch of things I need to do."

"Another time, then. Come on, Lorna. The stores are waiting."

Anna watched from the window as the two of them walked to Marge's car, a cherry red Fiero. There wasn't a doubt in her mind that Nate had asked his wife to come on this mission of mercy, to counteract the impression Lorna must have gotten from being yanked out of school this morning. The Tates were good people. But then, so were most of the folks in Conard County. She couldn't allow John Kreusi and the Laceys to blind her to that fact.

She managed to keep a positive view until she realized it was five-thirty and apparently the judge wasn't going to call her back. Of course, thinking about it, she wondered why she had ever thought the judge would want to get involved. Kreusi's decision about Lorna was a school administrative decision, not something a judge could get involved in.

So what now? What the hell was she supposed to do? But no answers came to her. None at all.

Chapter 6

Anna hadn't been using the room she was giving to Lorna for a bedroom, so she hadn't hung any curtains. As soon as she left the office, she went home to measure the windows. She wished she knew what color the linens for the daybed would be so she could coordinate. She thought about calling Marge Tate, then decided the easiest and safest thing to do would be to get white curtains. After all, she didn't know how long Lorna would be staying with her.

Night had fallen, and the streets were nearly empty. Freitag's was open until eight-thirty, but there were only two other cars parked in front of the store when Anna pulled up. The continuing threat of the season's first snowfall was apparently keeping people at home. Probably a good thing, since at the beginning of every winter everyone seemed to need to learn all over again how to drive on slushy roads.

Though it was just two days past Halloween, Freitag's was already sporting Christmas decorations. Thanksgiving somehow almost got forgotten in the extended Christmas shopping season, even here in this little town. At least they weren't playing Christmas carols on the piped-in music.

Freitag's was in a century-old building where the wood floors creaked beneath the patrons' feet and many of the display tables and racks were still built out of solid oak. Housewares was on the third floor, and Anna took an aging elevator up. There she found two bored, middle-aged sales clerks eager to help her choose curtains.

She settled finally on plain white ones with foam-insulated backs to keep down the drafts over the winter. They seemed so sterile to her, however, that she began to wander around and look for other things that might please Lorna. Nothing much, she warned herself, mindful of her limited budget and the church's charity. Just some little things.

She picked out some ceramic knickknacks to grace Lorna's dresser, and a lamp that was prettier than it was practical. She promised herself she would go downstairs and get a better desk lamp from the office supplies department, and once she made that decision, she bought a little fiber-board table and a white table skirt, figuring she could put the pretty lamp on it beside the bed. Later, if Lorna wanted, they could dye the skirt. She also picked out a big, fluffy white rug to put beside the bed.

Downstairs she purchased the desk lamp, but halted herself before she also bought a white blotter set with a delicate gold design on it. Lorna would want to pick out some of these things herself.

But Anna felt good, really good, about what she had done. She found herself smiling and humming, and feeling that in some small way she had been given a chance to right a terrible wrong. Lorna had been severely hurt, and she needed to know that someone cared about her enough to pay attention to the little things.

A boy of high school age helped her get everything into

her car, then went back inside the store. Snowflakes were
falling now, and before getting into her car Anna paused to
watch them twinkle in the streetlights as they spiraled downward. The year's first snowfall always made her feel different somehow, as if the coming hush of winter entered into
her with its promise of white magic and Christmas just
ahead. Later she would get as tired as anyone of needing to
shovel her driveway and of having to plan outings around
the weather, but right now, as the first snowflakes kissed the
ground, she felt full of hushed awe.

"She's lying, you know."

The harsh voice brought Anna whirling around to find
herself face-to-face with Bridget Lacey.

"That girl of mine is lying," Bridget said flatly, her face
twisted in anger. "The little bitch is a liar and always has
been. Her father didn't do a damn thing to her!"

Anna had no idea how to respond. All she knew was that
she was frightened by the way the other woman was looking
at her.

"Do you know why she tried to burn down the school?"
Bridget demanded. "Because her father wouldn't let her go
to Cheyenne to stay with her cousin. She got some wild
notion in her head that she had to go there to live, and there
was no talking her out of it. So finally Al flat-out told her
no, and this is how she gets even!"

"Mrs. Lacey—"

"Shut up. I don't want to hear anything you have to say,
Miss Goody Two-Shoes. You don't know what you're messing in. You and the judge and the sheriff—all holier than
thou. Taking a thirteen-year-old girl's word over the word
of a man who's been a pillar of this community for fifteen
years! Al is a good man. A *good* man! He's never hurt a
soul in his entire life!"

The woman pointed a finger at her. "It'll all come home to roost, just you watch. The little slut just wants the freedom to run around with boys, and her dad wouldn't let her do it. Well, she's your headache now. See how you like it when she doesn't come home till all hours of the night! See how you like it when she insists on dressing like a whore. But I tell you, Al is going to be vindicated, and when he is, both you and that girl are going to rue the day you started this mess!"

"I didn't start—"

"I know you and your kind, bitch. You think I don't know who it was planted all these evil ideas in Lorna's head? You go around pretending to be all perfect and then mix yourself up in things that are no concern of yours!"

By this point Anna was backed up against her car door, and there was no place to go to get away from Bridget Lacey. She was beginning to feel a little afraid, wondering what this woman might be capable of, but she couldn't think how in the world to defuse this problem. She stared up at Bridget, who was far larger, and wondered wildly if the woman was going to hit her.

But Bridget didn't hit her. Not yet. She just leaned closer and growled, "I'm going to get you, Miss Butter-won't-melt-in-your-mouth. I'm going to make you pay."

A male voice cut across Bridget's threat, and never had Anna heard a sound more welcome. "Is there a problem here, Miss Anna?"

Anna turned her head and nearly collapsed in relief when she saw Hugh Gallagher standing on the sidewalk. His posture was relaxed, his expression pleasant—except for his eyes. Those eyes held the promise of hell as they looked at Bridget Lacey.

The woman apparently got the message. She took one look at him and hurried away. Anna sagged against her car.

"You couldn't look any paler if you'd just been talking to a vampire," Hugh said gently. He slipped an arm around her and steadied her. "Are you okay?"

"I just need a minute...." Reaction was hitting her in a cresting wave of weakness that left her shaking. She found herself filled with the worst urge to just bury her face in Hugh's shoulder and burrow into his arms until she felt safe from the whole world.

"It's all right," he told her gently. "It's okay." With tender fingers, he brushed her cheek softly and tucked a strand of escaping hair back behind her ear.

"I heard what she said," he continued. "It sure wasn't pleasant. I'll be damned if I can understand how a woman could feel that way about her own child."

"It's not unusual," Anna said shakily. "She doesn't want to believe her husband cheated on her. She can't stand the thought that he might actually have done it with her daughter. Her whole life is falling apart, and it's just too much for her."

"It's still a poor excuse to dump all that vitriol on the child and you. You're a kind woman, Miss Anna. Not many folks would make excuses for someone who had just treated them like that."

Anna shook her head. "I'm not being kind, and I'm not making excuses for her. There aren't any excuses." She'd spent the better part of her life trying to find some forgiveness and understanding in her heart for her mother, and she'd managed to find some understanding. But understanding was a long way from forgiving or excusing.

She shivered again, feeling the cold that had seeped

through her jacket while they stood there. Hugh at once loosened his hold on her. "Are you okay?" he asked.

"I'm fine. Really."

"Ready to drive home?"

She couldn't help smiling at his concern. "I'm *fine.*"

"Okay, I'll follow you—just to be sure no one else does."

It had never occurred to Anna that Bridget Lacey might try to follow her home. She thought Hugh was being a little too apprehensive, but she had to admit she liked his concern.

The snow was falling thickly now, whirling into eddies on the wind as it whipped along the streets and around corners. As she drove forward, huge flakes flew at her windshield, almost giving her the feeling she was free-falling through stars.

Her tires skidded a little, then grabbed, as she turned into her driveway. Hugh pulled in right behind her and got out of his truck, coming to steady her as she stepped out of hers.

"Let me carry your packages in," he told her. "You just go inside and get warm."

Lorna had left a note saying that she had fed and walked Jazz, so Anna started a pot of coffee brewing while Hugh carried her purchases to the spare room. When he'd brought everything in, he paused in the doorway of the kitchen. "Where's Lorna?" he asked.

"She went over to the Tates' for dinner. She'll be back around eight."

"Well, you're going to need some help hanging those curtain rods and curtains. I've got the tools in my truck. Why don't you let me help?"

She hesitated, reluctant to accept any more help from this man. It was nothing about him personally, but it seemed he had done entirely too much for her in just a few days—

fixing her car, taking her and Lorna out to dinner, seeing her safely home, rescuing her from Bridget Lacey. She was reluctant to be beholden to anyone, and it was beginning to feel as if every time she turned around, Hugh Gallagher was doing something else for her.

"It'll only take a minute," he said, as if he sensed her reluctance. "And it's a whole lot easier if you have the right tools—which I do." The grin he gave her was engaging enough to ease her qualms. "Besides," he said, "I'm angling for a cup of that coffee. It sure does smell good."

She had to laugh and agree. He hadn't left her any other choice—and for once she didn't mind.

He went out to his truck to get the tools, while Anna put her other purchases in the closet so they'd be out of the way if Nate brought the furniture tonight, when he returned Lorna.

Watching Hugh hang the curtain rods was an experience in itself. He shucked his jacket, giving her a wonderful view of a work-hardened male body clad in denim and flannel as he stretched to measure, and climbed up and down a short stepladder.

Anna found herself leaning back against the wall and simply staring, letting her eyes look at a man the way she had steadfastly refused to for so long. What, she wondered, would it be like to want a man the way men seemed to want women? What would it be like to actually want to touch a man in love, rather than being forced to touch him in fear?

"There, that was easy," Hugh said, stepping down from the ladder. Both curtain rods were in place above the windows, more level than Anna would have made them. "Now, where are the curtains? We might as well get 'em up while we have the ladder."

She dug the bags out of the closet, and together they put the hooks on the curtains and hung them on the rods.

"Looks good," Hugh said when Anna stepped back to survey the effect.

"Yes, it does. But unfortunately, now I can tell how badly the walls need painting."

He laughed. "It's always that way, isn't it? Do one little thing, and you suddenly find a couple more that need doing that you'd never have noticed otherwise." He ran his hand over the wall. "Actually, I think you've got wallpaper under this coat of paint. You might want to think about stripping it before you try painting again."

"Not tonight," she said wryly. "Painting and stripping the walls will just have to wait."

He cracked another laugh and looked at her in a way that made her breath suddenly lock in her throat. He didn't move any closer, but she felt as if he were suddenly surrounding her. A combination of panic and excitement filled her, rooting her to the spot. For the first time in her life, she experienced the exhilaration of danger.

But then he looked away, releasing her, leaving her feeling somehow disappointed. He was going to leave, she realized, and she very much wanted him to stay.

"I was just about to make a quick supper," she heard herself say, her voice a bit unsteady and breathless. "Would you like to join me?"

His gaze came back to her, a little more cautious than a minute ago. "If it's not too much trouble."

"It's no trouble at all." He was afraid, too, she realized. Whatever she had felt a few moments ago, he had felt it, too, and it had made him uneasy. Somehow it was easier for her to handle, knowing that it had disturbed him, too.

Hugh offered to help with dinner, but there really wasn't

anything to do. "I cook large batches of things on weekends and then freeze individual servings. All I need to do is heat up some of the lasagna and toss a salad."

She gave him a fresh cup of coffee and pointed him to the table. He took his dismissal with smiling good grace and watched her as she bustled around. At first she felt nervous under his scrutiny, but she rapidly relaxed.

"What did you do before you came to Conard City?" he asked her.

She felt the uneasy quickening of her heart that always came whenever anyone questioned her about her past. But of course, he didn't know the whole story. He couldn't know it. "I worked as a secretary for a marketing firm in upstate New York."

"Why'd you ever come to a little out-of-the-way place like this? It must seem dull after the city."

She shook her head. "I didn't live in New York City." Except for a brief time as a kid on the streets. "The town I worked in was bigger than this, but not gigantic. Besides, it's the people who make a place, and the people here are nice and friendly. I got tired of cities, anyway. They're so crowded." So crowded with memories, she thought, hoping he wouldn't press further. She couldn't imagine that she would ever want to share her memories with anyone. Or that anyone would ever understand how she felt any time she saw a New York cop or a streetwalker on the corner, or heard certain street names.

"How about you?" she asked. "What made you come here?"

"Well, now, that's a long story. I left the army on a disability and wound up back home in Chicago. Trouble was, I couldn't hold a job for long because…" He hesitated. "Well, I just wasn't doing too well, you know? Some little thing would happen, and I'd suddenly feel like I was some-where else. I don't know if you know much about post-traumatic stress disorder?''

"Just a little. I've heard about it." And sometimes have it, but she didn't want to confide that to anyone.

"Well, some woman would speak Farsi to her kid, or I'd hear a particular shout—well, all of a sudden I was back in Iraq. Or wherever. Makes it kind of tough to hold a job.''

Anna nodded, turning to look at him as he spoke. She forgot about the tomato she was holding in her left hand and the knife in her right.

"Eventually I wound up living on the streets.''

She nodded again, feeling herself lean toward him, iden-tifying intensely with what he was saying, needing him to continue.

"Life on the streets is hard," he said after a moment.

"Oh, I know!" She was hardly aware that she spoke, and her words were barely more than a tense whisper. He heard them, though. She could tell by the way his gaze suddenly fixed on her. For a moment she feared he would question her, but he didn't. He just gave her a nod and went on.

"Anyway, it wasn't any kind of improvement over living in a fleabag hotel, or in an apartment. I still wasn't getting away from the things that were setting me off, and I was getting rousted from every warm place I could find to sleep. After a bit I started hearing about this place out west where some vets had a nice little community going in the moun-tains and the locals left them alone." He shrugged. "I hitch-hiked out here, and I've been here ever since.''

The oven timer dinged, jerking Anna sharply back into the here and now. She realized her hand was aching from gripping the knife so tightly, and it was a wonder she hadn't squashed the tomato.

Turning quickly, she sliced the tomato into the salad bowl, then dried her hands and pulled the casserole containing the lasagna from the oven. She wanted to know more about Hugh but found herself strangely reluctant to ask. It was almost as if she felt that hearing about his past would awaken memories of her own. Part of her wanted to have it all out in the open, and part of her shuddered at the very thought. She'd already let Hugh know too much, she told herself. If word of her past got around this little town, she would be out of a job and looking for somewhere else to live. People would never consider her fit for the role of church secretary and youth counselor. Never.

Hugh praised her lasagna generously and dug in to the salad like a man starved for vegetables. Anna found herself enjoying a rare bit of pride and pleasure in being able to give another person so much enjoyment. She couldn't remember the last time she had received a compliment that wasn't directly related to her work.

She even managed to get up enough nerve to ask Hugh a question. "Did living in the mountains help?"

"Yeah. It did." He gave her a smile with a little side-to-side movement of his head, as if to say, *It did and it didn't.* "It removed the stimuli that were most likely to set me off. I guess the best way I can explain it is that living in the city was like a constant rasping on my nerves. When I got to the mountains, the rasping was gone. Finally the flashbacks stopped entirely."

"And now that you're living in town again...?"

"It's still pretty much okay. I was one of the lucky ones, I guess. My problems started almost right away after Iraq, so I got over it quicker. The ones who have a delayed reaction go through it a lot worse and a lot longer."

He forked a tomato into his mouth and chewed it. "You're a damn fine cook, Miss Anna."

"Thank you. And just call me Anna, please."

He gave her a warm look. "Anyway, to finish a long and boring story, I stayed up in the mountains a lot longer than I really needed to, mainly because I felt some of the guys up there needed me. I still go up there from time to time to check on 'em, and Billy Joe Yuma and I take blankets and food up there whenever we can. But I don't need to hide out anymore. I need to do something useful with my life."

"I can sure understand that." It was the primary reason she had chosen to take a job with a church. It gave her something positive to contribute, to make up for all the negative things she had done with her life.

"And I guess that's why I need to do this youth ranch thing. I know what it's like to be out of control. I know what it's like to need help to get a handle on life before it steamrolls you. Kids are at an even bigger disadvantage than adults. A far bigger disadvantage. They don't have the emotional or intellectual maturity to deal with the tough stuff on their own."

"That's so very true." She looked down at her plate, thinking how different her life would have been if she had known at fourteen what she knew now. She would have made some very different decisions, with a very different outcome. "There's a tendency at that early age to take extreme measures."

"There sure is." Hugh looked down at his plate, then gave her a surprisingly shy smile. "You understand children very well."

She felt her cheeks warm. "Thank you."

"I was hoping you could help me with the ranch."

As rapidly as it had come, the color drained from her face.

No! The denial was like a thunderclap in her head. She felt herself start to tremble.

"Did I say something wrong?" he asked.

"I can't do it," she said shakily. "I mean…I'll be glad to make suggestions, but I can't actually be part of it. I *can't!*"

He looked as if he wanted to ask why, but after a moment he nodded and smiled. "I'll be grateful for your suggestions, Miss Anna. I really will. Thanks."

And as easily as that, the dangerous moment was gone. She didn't have to explain. The butterflies in her stomach didn't subside quite so easily, but then he changed the subject, letting her off the hot seat.

"About Lorna setting fire to the school." He pushed his plate aside and reached for his coffee cup. "Word is that the school isn't going to let her come back."

Anna looked up, distressed. "How did you hear that?"

"From somebody who knows somebody. You know how gossip goes. Apparently one of the school secretaries said something about it."

Anna shook her head and pushed her own plate away, losing her appetite. "I don't think that's settled yet. I know Nate was going to look into it. I called Judge Williams, but she hasn't called back. I guess that's because it's not really a legal matter. It probably *is* up to the school. But I don't want them to treat her like a criminal. She doesn't deserve it."

"Maybe not."

"Most certainly not!"

He smiled faintly. "Lorna's lucky to have you on her side, Anna. But consider this—don't get mad at me, just consider this possibility. The child did something very wrong. Admittedly, she had a lot of provocation. But maybe it wouldn't hurt her to realize there's a right way and a wrong way to deal with things. Burning down buildings isn't the right way.''

Anna looked at him. ''Are you saying she *should* be punished?''

''She may well be, by the courts. She *did* commit a crime. They may decide to give her detention, a suspended sentence, community control or just community service. But I think it's very unlikely the case is just going to go away. She's been charged and arraigned, and she's only out on bail.''

Anna looked down at the table, wishing she could argue with what he was saying but knowing he was right.

''I realize the child had extraordinary provocation, Anna. And the court, as near as I can tell, has been bending over backward to help her. But she committed a crime.''

''But she doesn't need to be treated like a criminal! She's been through enough!''

''I agree with you. To a point. But one thing society can't allow people to do is break the law with impunity. Even if she gets a not-guilty verdict because she was suffering from abuse syndrome, or whatever they call it, society is still going to exact its pound of flesh. And that's not necessarily a bad thing for Lorna. She made a choice, a poor choice, and there are consequences to that. It won't hurt her to realize that. The important thing is that we don't compound her problems by reacting in the wrong way to this. My guess is she's going to get some community service hours.''

''And the school? Should they be allowed to just throw her out?''

''For a few days, at least. Think about it. What would you want them to do if some other student had tried to burn down the building, and you had a child in that school?''

Anna couldn't argue with the justice of what he said, much as she wished she could. "Lorna's a special case."

"I think everyone will agree on that. But there's no reason to think she should get off entirely scot-free. It wouldn't be good for her."

"Maybe not. Maybe not."

Hugh reached out and covered her hand with his. "I know you feel very protective of her. Just like a mother should. But one of the lessons we all need to learn in life if we're ever to be responsible adults is that actions have consequences. The important thing here is to make sure that she understands that any punishment she receives is related directly to her decision to try to burn the school down, not to anything her father did. And she needs to be persuaded to accept the consequences as being just. It's an invaluable life lesson."

Anna sighed and nodded, and wondered why it didn't bother her that he was touching her. She usually hated to be touched by men, even briefly, and the way his hand was resting on hers was neither brief nor impersonal. But she liked it anyway. It was comforting, somehow, and reassuring.

And she was sorry when he drew his hand away.

"I'm not telling you what to do," he said. "It's not my place. Lorna's your responsibility now, and you should do what you think best."

"No, I see your point. It just seems unfair that on top of everything else she should be punished for crying out for help in the only way she could figure out."

"I hear you." With that, he rose and carried dishes to the sink. "Where's the soap?"

"Oh, just leave the dishes. Really. It's only a few things, and I can wash them up later without any trouble."

"You cooked. The least I can do is wash the dishes."

They wound up washing them together—he scrubbed, and she dried. And it was easy, she found herself thinking with something akin to wonder, to share the task with him. He didn't make her feel intimidated or uncomfortable.

Nate arrived with Lorna just as they were finishing up, and he had brought all the promised furniture with him in the van. Lorna was really excited about it, just thrilled with the white daybed and matching furnishings.

"You should see, Miss Anna," she said excitedly. "Everything matches!"

"How nice!" Although she couldn't help wondering why the child of a wealthy dentist hadn't had matching furniture all along.

"Lorna seems happy enough with it," Nate said. "Where do you want me to put it?"

They all helped move the furniture into the spare room. Lorna was thrilled by the curtains, thrilled by the white wicker furnishings given her by Nate, thrilled by everything. Anna couldn't imagine that she hadn't had things just as nice or nicer at home and wondered if Lorna's gratitude was more for being away from her dad than anything else.

Not that it really mattered. Lorna's gratitude clearly pleased Nate, and it certainly made Anna feel good about her purchases. After the bed was assembled and the royal blue dust ruffle was in place, they left Lorna to arrange her room as she saw fit.

Nate and Hugh both accepted an offer of coffee and joined Anna at the table in the kitchen.

"That child is a joy to have around," Nate said. "She tries so damn hard to please. You wouldn't believe she's the same girl I arrested just a couple of days ago."

"I hope it lasts," Anna remarked. She didn't expect it would.

Nate's look was at once wise and kind. "She'll be bound to crash sooner or later. By the way, it's been arranged for her to see a psychologist in Laramie every Friday afternoon. Sara Ironheart has been detailed to drive her up and back."

Anna felt a flicker of concern. "You're sure this psychologist can deal with these particular problems?"

"Her whole career is devoted to dealing with incest survivors, especially children. If anyone is suitable, she is. And she comes highly recommended."

"Okay, then. I don't mean to sound suspicious, but— well, Lorna's very vulnerable right now, and I wouldn't want somebody to make a mess of her."

Nate smiled at her. "I didn't take offense. You're the girl's guardian, after all."

"Temporarily. Just temporarily." Why did it upset her so to admit that? She let the pang go, however, because she didn't have time to analyze it just then. Later, she told herself. She would think about herself and Lorna later.

"Anyway," Nate said, "she'll be missing school on Friday afternoons until the judge decides otherwise."

"Speaking of school..." Anna looked at him.

"I talked to John Kreusi. He's thinking about it."

"The judge never called me back."

"I'll talk to her in the morning, then, but I don't think there's anything she can do. I think this one falls under the school regulations."

Anna nodded. "I was wondering about that."

"However, the girl needs schooling, and you sure can't do it yourself, sweet pea. You have a job. I'm sure I can get John to come to his senses, but it might take a day or two."

"A day or two out of school won't hurt her that much. I suppose I ought to see about getting her assignments from her teachers so she can at least make a stab at keeping up."

"That'd be a good idea. And now," Nate said, rising, "I've got to be getting back to my family. They think I'm a stranger who occasionally pretends to be one of them."

Anna had to laugh, but she didn't believe it for one minute. On many occasions she had seen how clearly Nate doted on his family.

"I guess I'd better be going, too," Hugh said. "Gotta get some serious work done on the church tomorrow."

It was still snowing when Anna said good-night to them at the front door. Snow was accumulating everywhere now, not quite enough yet to fully bury the grass, but she had a feeling that by morning the world would be a uniform white.

She closed the door on the chill and went to check on Lorna.

Chapter 7

Anna Fleming was becoming a nuisance, Hugh Gallagher decided a week later. Wearing nothing but the black briefs he'd slept in last night, he stood at the tall windows of his living room and looked down at the snow-covered streets through the white whirl of a blizzard.

A blizzard. An unexpected, unpredicted blizzard. What had been forecast as an inch or two was turning into one of those wild Wyoming storms for which he felt a great deal of respect. On a day like this, away from the security of town, you could get lost in the whiteout and not be found until spring. When he'd been living in the mountains, days like this had been life threatening.

According to the weather report, once the snow cleared out, the temperatures were going to fall to twenty below zero. Dangerous cold after a dangerous storm.

He ought to be feeling pretty good. He ought to be standing here grateful that he had to go out in this only to work on the insulation at the church, something he could do from the inside of the building.

Instead he was wondering why Anna Fleming was messing with his mind.

Not that she was actually *doing* anything to mess with his mind. Her mere existence seemed to be enough to do that. He'd dreamed of her last night, then first thing this morning. When he saw all that snow, all he could think about doing was heading over to her place to shovel her out.

Except there was no point in shoveling her out until the wind settled down some. The way it was right now, the damn stuff would blow right back as fast as he could move it.

Sighing, realizing he wasn't going to be able to put her from his mind, he went to the telephone and called the church. Nobody answered. Well, he couldn't very well work on the insulation if nobody was there to let him into the building.

He called Dan Fromberg's home next, and Cheryl answered. In the background he could hear the toddlers squealing and squawling. "Dan's not going in at all today," Cheryl said. "The schools are closed, and I'll kill him if he bails out on me." She laughed as she said it. "Besides, there's a huge drift across the foot of our driveway, and I don't want him giving himself a heart attack trying to move it."

"The streets don't look any too good here in town, either," Hugh told her. "I can tell the plows came through earlier, but everything's buried all over again."

"So it's a free holiday," Cheryl said, then added wryly, "at least for people who don't have kids."

"Are you sure you don't want me to come dig you out?"

She laughed. "Only if you can magically open up the schools! No, really, Hugh, this is a great chance for us just to be together. We don't get many of those opportunities."

After he hung up, he went to look out the window again. He could spend the day reading, something he hadn't been able to do enough of lately. Most folks liked to settle in with the TV to relax, but he never had. Since coming down from the mountains, he'd begun to build a paperback library for himself, and right now there were a couple of thrillers just sitting there on the bookcase, crying out for his attention. It had been a long time since he'd last taken an entire day to do nothing but read.

Except that Anna Fleming was driving him nuts. He kept thinking of her and that girl snowed in—admittedly, she was snowed in not twenty feet from the neighboring house, but snowed in nonetheless. Maybe she needed food or milk or something. Somebody ought to check up on her.

All he had to do was pick up the phone and call her. Except that he knew she wouldn't tell him the truth. If he called her, she would say everything was fine and not to worry. He'd noticed that stubborn streak in her. It was a mile wide, and only a blind fool would miss it.

But that was one of the things he liked about her. She had a stubborn independence to rival his own, and he suspected that she had things in her past every bit as dark as the things in his. There was no mistaking that look she got sometimes, as if she'd seen the worst and wasn't shocked by it anymore.

Except that she could still be shocked by people like Kreusi, who didn't put kindness before everything else. That was a quirk in Anna that really interested him. How could she know so much and be so unsurprised by the evil things people did, and then be so shocked by a simple act of unkindness?

Maybe he ought to ask her sometime. Maybe she would tell him it was really simple: that she expected ordinary, decent folk to be kind until they proved they weren't ordinary, decent folk. Maybe she had somehow managed to keep right on expecting the best when she had seen the worst.

She intrigued him, that little lady with her soft, frightened brown eyes. He noticed how jumpy she got around him, and initially there had been no mistaking how afraid of him she was. But that fear seemed to have settled down, and it made him feel good, somehow, that she was coming to trust him.

And he knew damn well that as soon as this blizzard let up he was going over to shovel her out, because he wouldn't be able to stop thinking about it until he did.

Boy, he was getting it bad.

The thought amused him. For years now he'd been pretty much immune to women on an emotional level. Even before he got sent to the Persian Gulf, he'd felt a distance between himself and other people that he couldn't quite bridge. It was a common feeling among special forces types who had actually seen action. You had to feel different when you knew exactly what you were capable of and you'd actually done it. Most people only suspected.

But after the Gulf War…well, something had been broken. He'd gone surreptitiously into Iraq, hiding out for weeks until it was time to do his job. He'd moved among the people, he'd talked to them and he'd seen what he'd done to them. They'd thought he was one of them, but he wasn't.

And that had ripped him up in some essential way. He still couldn't really deal with it. Oh, he knew he'd been a soldier on a soldier's mission, but it hadn't felt like it.

And then, when it had been time to pull out, he'd moved through that wasteland of burning oil wells and had felt sure he'd died and gone to hell for his sins.

Which he surely deserved to do.

Oh, hell, forget it! In disgust, he turned from the window and went to shower and dress. War made for intolerable moral dilemmas, and he knew it. Moaning about it wouldn't change anything. He'd done his duty, and now he damn well had to live with it. And someone sure as hell had to be willing to do the tough stuff, so why not him?

But he felt, in a very deep and important way, that his soul had been stained beyond redemption. And that meant he wasn't good enough for a woman like Anna Fleming.

So why the hell couldn't he keep her out of his head?

By noon the wind seemed to be letting up, so Hugh pulled on his winter gear and went down to his truck. It was parked in the alley beside the building, and he had to dig it out from the drift that had built up over it. It started right up, though, and soon he was grinding his way down the drifted streets on tire chains.

The plows were back out, he saw, working their way up the side streets toward Front and Main. The sheriff had evidently cleared out the area around the front of his office with the plow blades he mounted on the front of all his vehicles every October. The snow was still falling, but in the hiatus from the wind, signs of life were beginning to show everywhere. Shopkeepers were shoveling the walks in front of their stores. Kids were playing in the drifts in front of homes. More than one person was trying to clear his driveway. The whine of snowblowers could be heard from every direction.

He skidded as he rounded the corner onto Anna's street, but the chains caught quickly, and he straightened out. The plow had already been through here, leaving mounds two and three feet high on either side of the street.

Anna and Lorna were already out shoveling the driveway.

He parked in the street and climbed out, pulling his shovel from the back of the truck.

"Figured you might need a little help," he called to Anna. The smile she gave him made him glad he'd come. And for once she didn't try to talk him out of helping.

He dug in on the street side of the huge mound and began to sling the snow off to the side. The plow had packed it pretty well, making it heavy and hard to lift, but the strain on his back and shoulders felt good. He hadn't been getting enough hard physical labor lately, and his body, once tuned to the peak of physical conditioning, really missed it.

By the time he'd cleared away the mess left by the plow, Anna and Lorna had finished the rest of the driveway. They started together on the sidewalk, but that was easy by comparison, a very light six inches of snow that hadn't been compacted yet.

Then Lorna, apparently feeling both her oats and her youth, made a snowball and threw it at Hugh.

"You can't expect me to ignore that," he said, and reached for a handful of snow.

"Leave me out of this," Anna said hastily. Neither Lorna nor Hugh was willing to do that. They both threw snowballs at her. She ducked and twisted and got caught in the back.

"Now you're in for it," she said, and grabbed a handful of snow.

For a couple of minutes they lobbed snowballs at one another, laughing and running until they were breathless. But it was the sound of Anna's laughter that really grabbed Hugh. He'd heard her laugh softly before, always a quiet, restrained sound. But never before had he heard her laugh with complete abandon. The sound struck him somehow, working its way into the quiet places of his heart.

It also caused him to be inattentive, which left him wide

open for a snowball Lorna threw at him. It caught him on the side of the head and jarred him back to reality.

"I'm sorry," Lorna said, breathless and laughing. She backed away and held up her hands defensively. "Honest, I thought you were going to duck! I really didn't mean to hit you in the head."

He took a menacing step toward her, which caused her to shriek with laughter, but he didn't go any farther. He kind of felt as if he were walking on eggshells here, and the last thing he wanted to do was something that might upset either Lorna or Anna. Given his own background, he was all too well aware of how some innocent thing could trigger a reaction to a bad memory.

He brushed the snow off the side of his head, but some of it melted anyway, and icy water trickled down inside the collar of his jacket and shirt.

"Let's go inside," Anna said, still smiling. "It's time for hot chocolate and cookies."

"Cookies?" Hugh was definitely interested.

"Homemade," Lorna said. "Anna and I made dozens of chocolate chip cookies to take to the youth group meeting tomorrow night."

They went in through the side door, leaving their boots on some spread-out newspaper. Anna gave Hugh a towel to dry the side of his head, while Lorna ran to her room to change into dry clothes. Anna did the same, returning a few minutes later wearing a soft green sweater and matching corduroy slacks.

Sitting at the table with the towel around his neck and Jazz in his lap, Hugh watched Anna bustle about and found himself aching to go to her and wrap his arms around her. Stupid. It was really, really stupid to feel this way. It could only screw up his plans for getting her to help with the

ranch. But he wanted to hug her anyway. He couldn't remember ever having felt that way about a woman before,
and he didn't like it. Wanting sex was something he was
familiar with and could deal with. But wanting a hug?

"Is Lorna back in school?" he asked, trying to distract
himself.

"Tomorrow. John Kreusi settled on a one-week suspension. I thought about fighting it, but I remembered what you
said...." She looked over her shoulder at him and smiled,
giving him a little shrug. "I guess it doesn't hurt to learn
that actions have consequences."

"No, it sure doesn't."

"She's been keeping up with her work, though, and I
know she misses her friends. I also think she's a little nervous about going back."

"Hardly surprising. The whole damn town is talking
about her and her dad, and taking sides like you wouldn't
believe."

"I'd believe it, all right. I've been hearing some of it.
You wouldn't believe how many times I've been flat-out
asked if Lorna's telling the truth." Anna shook her head
and put mugs of steaming cocoa on the table. "Marshmallows?"

"Absolutely. It wouldn't be cocoa without them."

She brought a bag of marshmallows from the cupboard
and handed it to him. "Help yourself." Then she went to
get cookies from a big plastic container on the counter.

Hugh popped one of the big marshmallows into his mug
and watched it start to melt. "It's hard to believe that someone you know and like could be guilty of something so
awful."

Anna put a plate of cookies on the table. "Child molesters
aren't monsters with scaly skin and rotten breath. They're

ordinary, likable people. More likable than most, in my experience.''

He looked up at her. "How many have you known?"

Her hesitation was visible, and it got his radar going. What was she hiding?

"A few," she said after a beat. "I've known a few. And take it from me, everyone who knows them likes them and thinks they're incapable of such awful things.''

They both heard Lorna coming down the hall, and exchanged looks. By the time the girl entered the kitchen, the conversation had moved on to the upcoming holidays.

"I love Christmas," Anna was saying. "It's always been my favorite time of year. Still, I think the stores are starting the displays too early. I'm really not ready to think about it yet.''

"We have to have Thanksgiving first," Lorna added. "Are we going to have a turkey, Anna?"

"I...guess so. Usually I just do the Thanksgiving dinner at the church.''

"Me, too,'' said Hugh.

"Well, then, we ought to have our own here," Lorna said. "And Mr. Hugh can come, too, right?"

Anna and Hugh exchanged glances. He realized that Lorna was trying to construct a surrogate family for herself for the holidays, and he guessed Anna realized it, too.

"Sounds fine to me," Anna said.

"Sure does," Hugh agreed. He figured there would be plenty of time later for Anna to rearrange things to suit herself, and he intended to let her know that he wouldn't be wounded if she decided she didn't want to include him.

Although, truth to tell, he probably *would* be wounded, he realized wryly. Because he really liked the idea of having

Thanksgiving with a surrogate family rather than the large crowd at the church.

"Do you have parents, Mr. Hugh?" Lorna asked.

"They died a while back."

"That's too bad. No brothers or sisters, either?"

"Oh, I have a brother out in Arizona. Don't see him much anymore."

"Why not?"

"Lorna..." Anna said warningly. The girl flushed.

"Sorry," she said. "I guess that was a rude question."

Hugh sipped his cocoa, trying to decide how to handle it. "It was a natural question," he said finally. "It's just difficult for me to answer. We...just sort of drifted apart while I was in the army. I was always a long way away, you know? I stopped in once or twice, but we just didn't seem to have anything in common anymore." He shrugged. "People grow apart sometimes."

"I don't want to grow apart from my sister," Lorna said.

Hugh looked at Anna, but she didn't look as if she had any better idea how to handle that than he did. Just when he thought the silence had gotten so long that the child would probably burst into tears, Lorna shrugged and reached for another cookie.

"I guess we'll just have to see," she said.

For a moment Anna looked as if she might cry.

After finishing her cocoa, Lorna went to her room to finish her schoolwork. As soon as the bedroom door closed behind her, they could hear the radio come on, blasting some kind of cacophonous rock music.

Hugh sipped more cocoa and wondered if this was a good time for him to leave, but he felt reluctant to do so. Here he was sitting, across from this lady with mysteries in her eyes, and he found himself wanting to use the time to get to know her better. Problem was, he didn't know where to begin.

"Have you heard any more from Lorna's mother?" he asked her finally.

"Only indirectly." She gave him a humorless smile. "She's apparently talking all over town about what a lying slut Lorna is."

He shook his head, feeling anger grip him. "That woman's not fit to be anybody's mother. I heard what you said last week about her not being able to believe this. But whether she believes it or not, she shouldn't be going all over town talking about her daughter that way."

"I couldn't agree more."

"I think she knows exactly what she's doing. I think she figures if she can poison everyone's mind against the girl, they'll never get a jury to convict Al."

"It won't be easy anyway," Anna said. "It's her word against his, and people are surprisingly reluctant to convict with nothing more than that. They'll probably reach some kind of plea bargain, and a jury will never come into it."

Hugh looked at her. "You seem to know an awful lot about this stuff. Do you know somebody else who was molested by a parent?"

Anna looked away, drawing a deep shaky breath. And suddenly Hugh knew who had been molested. "God, Anna. I'm sorry. I didn't mean to pry...."

Not knowing what else to do, he pushed his way back from the table and reached for her, drawing her up from her seat. He felt her instant resistance and thought she was going to fight him like a cat. But just as he was about to let go of her, she sagged against him and burrowed her face into his shoulder as if she wanted to hide forever from everyone and everything.

He guessed he could understand that.

Holding her gently for fear of scaring her, he stroked her back softly and felt the quiver and quake of her slender form as she fought with whatever demons he'd just unleashed with his thoughtless question. Not that he felt particularly guilty. How was he supposed to know? And molestation *had* been the topic of conversation.

Damn, this all must be such a nightmare for her. He felt a strong surge of admiration at what it must have cost her to step in and help Lorna. This was definitely the kind of woman he wanted to help him with his ranch. This was exactly the kind of person he needed to make this thing go.

But he felt guilty for even thinking of that right now. Anna was hurting, and he wanted to console her—except that he didn't have a notion in hell how you could console somebody with a problem like this. It was almost too big to contemplate.

"I'm sorry," Anna said presently, her voice wispy. She stepped back a little and lifted her head from his shoulder. He didn't quite let go of her, and she didn't especially seem to want him to. "I keep it pretty well buried most of the time, but the last couple of weeks, what with all this about Lorna—well, it's gotten very close to the surface. I feel like my emotions are as fragile as glass."

"I can understand that." He wanted to squeeze her close and rock her like a child, telling her everything was going to be all right. But he couldn't tell her that. Nobody could. And he had a feeling she wasn't ready to be squeezed and rocked by anybody. "Was it your father?"

"My stepfather." She gave a little gasp that sounded like a bitter laugh. "Every now and then I call him to see if he's still alive."

As if she was shocked to have admitted so much, she

spun away from him and went to the sink, where she could stare out the window. The snow was blowing again, undoing all their earlier shoveling, but Hugh hardly noticed. He was as intensely focused on her as he had ever been on anything in his life.

"I won't feel safe until he's dead."

Hugh wasn't shocked. Not even hearing those words from Anna, whom he'd found to be unfailingly kind and gentle. "That's hardly surprising," he heard himself say.

She turned then, looking straight at him, and her eyes were wells of pain. "You don't think I'm despicable?"

"Of course not. Hell, Anna, I've killed men with my own bare hands. How could I be shocked that you feel that way about someone who hurt you worse than I can even imagine? If I were in your shoes, I would've killed the son of a bitch."

She almost smiled. It was a pale little expression, lifting just one corner of her mouth, and it didn't quite make it to her pained brown eyes. "I used to dream about it. I used to hope he'd get killed in a car accident, or shot by a mugger, or swept away on a tidal wave. It didn't matter, as long as he just didn't come home."

"But you got away finally, didn't you?"

"I *ran* away."

"Sounds wise to me." He hesitated, forcing himself to stay where he was for fear that if he touched her, he would terrify her. He was angry. He was so angry that he felt as if his blood were seething, but he didn't want his anger to frighten her.

She shrugged one shoulder but didn't reply directly to his comment. He wondered what had happened to her when she ran away, but he didn't ask. Instead he waited, giving her time to decide whether to trust him further.

She spoke. "When I saw what was happening to Lorna, I could hardly turn away."

He nodded.

Anna leaned back against the counter and wrapped her arms around herself, as if she were holding herself together. "I've spent a lot of time trying to forget all this, Hugh. But life seems determined to remind me."

"It goes that way sometimes." He hesitated, unsure whether to inject himself into this conversation. Then he decided that he might as well offer a piece of himself in exchange for the pieces of herself. "I felt that way after I left the army. I was determined I was going to forget everything that had happened, but I couldn't get through a single damn day without something reminding me. It was like I was just gonna keep reliving it until something snapped. Sometimes I felt if I could just let it run its course, the snap would come and set me free from all of it. It never did."

Her expression gentled. "Are you free from it now?"

"Mostly. But not completely. I'd be lying to you if I said I was all done with it. But these days it pretty much limits itself to my dreams. Or to odd moments. You know..." He hesitated, cocking his head to one side. "It's hard to describe. I'll get this little flash from a distance, something inside my head. It's kind of like an echo, or something you almost see from the corner of your eye."

She nodded encouragingly. "It's not really there."

"Yeah, sort of. It's not like the flashbacks used to be. I mean, man, those things were *real*. I was really there, doing it all over again, you know? This is more like...oh, I don't know. When you hear a snatch of a tune but can't quite place it, and you're not really sure you didn't just imagine it. It brings you feelings, maybe even memories, but it's not really there.''

"That happens to me, too. I never had flashbacks, though. Thank God. But I have all these little phobias now.'' She flushed faintly. "Like the way I reacted to you at the church.''

"I didn't think that was so out of line, Anna. Women have plenty of reasons to be uneasy when they run unexpectedly into a strange man.''

"You're not exactly a stranger. I've seen you around a lot. I know a lot of people have a high opinion of you.''

It was his turn to feel uncomfortable. "I'm nobody special,'' he said finally.

"Sure you are. And a lot of people think so.''

Something in her had apparently relaxed, because she stopped hugging herself so tightly and turned to point out the window. "Our efforts have been wasted.''

"Apparently.'' The world outside was once again a white swirl. "This sure isn't what they predicted.''

"No, but it's actually kind of nice. I always love days like this. It's so cozy, and so nice not to be able to go anywhere or do anything. Would you like some more hot chocolate?''

He hesitated. On the one hand, he felt it would be surprisingly easy to burrow in here for the day and play family. It had been the devil of a long time since he'd had a family of any sort, and Anna made it really attractive to just sit here and while away the time. On the other hand, it could be a real mistake to take her up on the offer and outstay his welcome. He didn't want her to feel as if he was moving in on her.

"You really don't want to go out in this if you don't have

to," Anna said. "Why don't you just stay a little longer and see if it lets up?"

It was an offer he couldn't refuse. "Thanks. Just a little longer. But then I've really got to get to the store. I always wait until I don't have a darn thing left in the fridge before I go to the grocery, but this time I guess I waited one day too long."

She smiled at that. "So eat some cookies while I make some more cocoa. Or would you like a ham sandwich? Lorna and I baked a ham last night. A really *good* ham."

"Are you trying to tempt me?"

"Am I doing a good job?"

He had to laugh. "You know you are. A ham sandwich would be wonderful. Can I help make it?"

She shook her head and pointed to the chair. "Just sit and let me do it."

First she went to ask Lorna if she wanted a sandwich. When she returned, she looked thoughtful. "She's not hungry."

"Is that a problem?"

"She looked—oh, I don't know. A little down. I keep waiting for the crash. It's been a week now, and sooner or later all of this is bound to hit her. But maybe I'm just being a worrywart."

Hugh shook his head. "Probably not. There's a whole bunch of stuff here she's going to have to deal with sooner or later. Did she see the counselor Friday?"

Anna nodded. "She didn't want to talk about it, though."

"That's probably understandable. Talking about some of this stuff just once has got to be hard enough."

Anna pulled the ham out of the fridge and a loaf of rye bread from the breadbox and began to make sandwiches. "Mustard, mayonnaise, lettuce?"

"All of the above."

The phone rang just as she finished slicing the ham. She wiped her hands on the towel and went to answer it. Hugh's gaze followed her, and he was suddenly uncomfortably aware that he liked looking at her. It was the strangest thing, and he couldn't remember ever having felt this way before, as if it was somehow enough just to look at somebody. Not even the long-stemmed beauties of his past had ever made him feel this way. He was like a kid with a crush.

But all thought of long-stemmed lovelies and adorable little brown-eyed ladies fled when Anna suddenly turned pale and slammed the phone down.

"Anna?" He was on his feet in an instant, prepared for anything. "Anna, what's wrong?"

She was hugging herself again, and this time the gesture actually frightened him.

"Anna?"

She turned her pale face toward him. "It was Al Lacey. I'm sure of it."

"Did he say so?"

She shook her head, and two spots of color appeared on her cheeks as she began to get angry. "No. No, he's too damn smart to do any such thing!"

"What did he say?"

"He said I was going to be sorry I ever persuaded Lorna to lie."

Chapter 8

When Hugh left Anna's house late that afternoon, he headed straight for the sheriff's office. Anna had flatly refused to call Nate about the phone call, feeling—perhaps justifiably—that Nate wouldn't be able to do anything about an anonymous call. But Hugh still felt it would be wise to let Nate know about it. And maybe he would have some suggestions about what to do.

For his own part, he was ready to camp on Anna's front lawn to make sure she was safe. The threat had been unspecific enough that it would be easy to dismiss, but he wasn't in a mood to dismiss it. Not when it came to Anna and Lorna. He felt a very strong surge of protectiveness for them, the kind of protectiveness he had once felt for his buddies in his squad. The kind of protectiveness you feel for people who depend on you completely.

Of course, neither Anna nor Lorna depended on him that way, but it didn't change what he felt.

Unfortunately, camping on her lawn would probably only make her miserable and embarrassed and make him damn cold. Not that he couldn't handle the cold. It sure didn't hold any terrors for him. But he couldn't follow her everywhere like a bodyguard, nor was he even certain it was necessary. Was Al Lacey the kind to take physical action on a threat like that?

Hugh doubted it. For God's sake, the man was a child molester, a cowardly son of a bitch who had apparently terrified Lorna into submission by threatening her baby sister. That kind of coward couldn't stand up to anybody who might fight back. It just wasn't in them.

The streets were calf-deep in snow again. He had no idea whether it was the same stuff that had fallen earlier that had just been blown all over again by the wind, or whether fresh stuff was still falling. Nor did it really matter. The driving was treacherous, and even his chains and the sandbags in the back end of his truck weren't keeping him from skidding every now and then.

When he reached the sheriff's office, he slid into a parking place and came to a jolting halt when his front tires hit the curb. The courthouse square looked as if it were inside one of those little glass globes that people liked to shake up to make the snow fall, except it was darn near invisible in the darkening afternoon. Wouldn't be long before night settled over the world, he thought, as he climbed out.

The wind snatched at him, snaking inside his jacket and nipping at his ears. He bent into it and walked around to the front door of the office. When he stepped inside, the warmth hit him like a blast. The wind grabbed at the door as he closed it, and it shut with a bang.

Velma was sitting at the dispatcher's desk, smoking a cigarette and looking for all the world like a wrinkled lady of leisure.

"No business, Velma?" he asked her.

She waved her cigarette. "Wouldn't make a damn bit of difference if there was, Cowboy. Ain't nobody going nowhere in this crud. At least, nobody intelligent. So what are you doing out?"

"I wanted to talk to Nate for a minute, if he's here."

"He's in his office. Go on back. He's been sitting around here all day wishing something would happen."

"Quit slandering me, Velma," Nate called from his office. "I've been praying all day that there won't be even one car accident. Seems pointless to risk a deputy's neck because some jerk didn't have the sense to stay home." He poked his head out and grinned at Hugh. "Present company excepted, of course. Grab a cup of coffee and come on back."

Hugh filled a ceramic mug from the coffeepot on a table near Velma's desk and went back to Nate's office.

"Pull up a chair, son. Take a load off."

Hugh sat, crossing his legs loosely and gesturing with his mug to the blizzard outside Nate's window. "Kind of early for this, isn't it?"

"I got a feeling deep in my bones that this is going to be one hell of a winter. We get one, every now and again. I can't help thinking of all the ranchers and all their cattle. This is going to hit 'em hard."

Hugh nodded. "I'm thinking about the guys up in the mountains. I don't think they were ready for this."

"Soon as it clears up a little, Billy Joe and I are going to take up some blankets and provisions. Want to come along?"

"Sure. I'd like that."

Nate swiveled his chair around and faced Hugh directly. "So what's up, son? You ought to be snug in your apartment right now."

"I still have to hit the supermarket."

"I think they're closed. You need something to get by until tomorrow?"

Hugh thought about it. "Nah. I guess I can make it. I've got a box of cereal and some milk. But I sure wasn't ready for this, either."

"None of us were. The weather service blew this forecast."

Hugh had to smile. "To say the least." He sipped his coffee and searched for a way to begin. "I was over at Miss Anna's a little while ago. I went over to help shovel her out during that lull we had earlier."

Nate chuckled. "Waste of time, wasn't it? A whole lot of people are looking out their windows right now at a whole lot of wasted effort."

"Actually, I think we made it worse. The wind's blowing the snow even deeper between the mounds we made. Anna's driveway is going to be a mess come morning."

"Mine, too. So what happened?"

"Well, she invited me in for a hot drink and a sandwich, and while I was there, somebody called her. She thinks it was Al Lacey."

"Damn it." Nate slapped his palm on the desk. "I was afraid he might try something."

"Well, he didn't identify himself, so it could be almost anybody, I reckon. A lot of folks in this town seem to think the girl is lying."

"I've heard." Nate frowned, shaking his head. "I guess it's understandable. Al Lacey has been practicing dentistry here for fifteen years. People feel like they know him. And Bridget grew up here. They don't want to believe Al could be capable of such a thing, and they don't want to believe that if he is, Bridget might have turned a blind eye to it. It's a whole lot easier to believe a child is lying.''

"Maybe." Hugh sipped his coffee and put the mug down. "On the other hand, it's dangerous to make that assumption.''

"Of course it is. Well, when all's said and done, we'll have more evidence than just the girl's say-so.''

"And if you don't?"

"Then Al may walk.''

"Can you get more evidence?''

Nate settled back in his chair. "I certainly mean to. I've considered Al Lacey a friend all these years, but I saw that little girl in court, and I've talked to her. I believe her, son. I believe her. So I'm going to do my damnedest to hang that son of a bitch.''

"Good." Hugh felt relieved. He didn't know a whole lot about what Lorna might have said, but he knew what Anna thought was going on, and he had a strong feeling that after what that woman had been through, she had X-ray vision when it came to a lie about being molested. Anna believed her, and that was good enough for him.

Nate spoke. "So what did this guy say when he called Miss Anna?''

"He said he was going to make her sorry she'd encouraged Lorna to lie.''

Nate unleashed a heavy sigh and rubbed his eyes. "Like that, huh? Hell.''

"I figure Al Lacey is too much of a coward to actually make good on that threat.''

"Maybe. Maybe not. There's a lot on the line here, you know. It might be enough to goad the man into something he wouldn't ordinarily do.''

"So how do we protect Anna?''

"Well, I can keep a close eye on her place, but there's ways he can get to her that don't involve physical intimidation."

Hugh arched a brow. "Gossip, you mean?"

"It'd be damn easy to start up gossip about a thirty-something spinster with no known past."

"But everyone has such respect for her!"

Nate shook his head. "Right now they do. But it wouldn't be hard to remind them that they didn't know squat about her until five years ago."

Hugh didn't at all like the sound of this. "That can't be allowed to happen."

"Trying to prevent gossip is like trying to hold back a flood with a broom, and the damage is usually done before you even know it's happening." He rubbed his chin with his hand. "Let me think on it. Meantime, you keep an eye on her, and I'll get my men to drive by regularly to make sure no one's bothering her."

"I'll sure keep my ear to the ground."

"You do that. Let me know if you hear anything at all. Now, what about you, son? How are you doing?"

"I'm doing just fine."

"No more flashbacks?"

"Not a one." Nor did Hugh mind Nate asking. Nate had been part of a Special Forces A Team in Vietnam. If anyone understood what Hugh had been through, it was Nate Tate. Nate had apparently never suffered from any post-traumatic stress syndrome, but that didn't make him insensitive to those who had. Far from it.

"That's great," Nate said. "That's really good news. Billy Joe's doing well, too." Billy Joe Yuma was Nate's son-in-law, a Vietnam vet who was closer to Nate's age than his wife's, but if that had ever caused Nate concern, he had never let anyone see it. "Maybe time really does take care of everything in the end."

If it was possible, the weather seemed to have worsened by the time Hugh left the sheriff's office. He dug his truck out once again, then, taking a chance, he drove out by Marshall's Quick Gas and Grocery. The gas-station-cum-truck-stop was right on the state highway, and miserable though the weather was, it was still open. There were a half-dozen eighteen-wheelers in the parking lot, holed up to ride out the storm.

"Hardly worth the electricity to stay open," Bud Marshall told him. "But I figured, what the hell. I mean, I live right upstairs, and you never know when somebody might get desperate for milk. Besides, those guys parked out there come in from time to time to use the john."

"Well, I'm desperate," Hugh told him. "I never keep much food on hand, but I'm down to next to nothing."

Bud chuckled and shook his head. "'Twasn't nobody expecting this storm. Listen, you want, I can cook you up a burger. I figure the guys in the lot will be coming in looking for some kind of dinner before long, and it wouldn't hurt to heat up the grill."

"Thanks, Bud, but I think I'll settle for a few odds and ends to take home with me. It's getting so bad out there, I don't want to be out any longer than necessary."

"Prob'ly wise. Well, poke around and see what takes your fancy."

He came up with a bag of chips, a loaf of bread, a jar of peanut butter and some cold cuts. He thought about getting some beer, then decided to pass on it. Alcohol had a tendency to lower the walls and let loose things he would rather keep locked up. Best to avoid it entirely.

As he was checking out, Bud said, "You hear about the Lacey girl?"

"I think everyone has."

"Terrible thing. Terrible thing. Can't imagine Al Lacey doing something like that to a child, let alone his own flesh and blood. My wife thinks the girl's lying, but I don't." He lifted his head from his task and looked Hugh straight in the eye. "Lacey used to be our dentist, but I stopped going there three years ago. Won't let my wife or girl go there, either."

"How come?"

"I didn't like the way he was looking at my daughter. I didn't like it at all. So I drive her over to Hansenville to see Charley Dukes."

Hugh nodded. "Think you could talk to Nate Tate about that?"

Bud looked surprised. "Why? Nothing happened."

"It just might help if you talked to him. Nate's gonna need all the help he can get to take this guy off the street."

Bud thought about it. "Don't see what good it'll do, but I reckon it can't cause much harm."

"It might keep Lacey from hurting some other kid."

Just then two of the truckers came through the door on a burst of cold air and swirling snow. Hugh took his change and left, while they joked with Bud about whether he could even thaw a hamburger enough for them to eat.

He figured he would mention his conversation with Bud to Nate before too long—just in case Bud forgot to.

The snow was still blowing and falling. Anna paused before she closed the front drapes against the night, loving the way the blizzard looked. In the past she would have left the curtains open to enjoy it, but since the phone call that afternoon, she felt uneasy. She didn't want anybody to be able to look in her windows and see what she and Lorna were doing.

Once the curtains were closed, she felt able to turn on the living-room lamps. Lorna was still in her room, studying, and the sounds of rock music were still audible through the house. Anna paused in the hallway, listening, and wondering if she should just leave the girl alone or check on her.

Check on her, she decided. It had been hours since Lorna had last emerged, and that didn't seem quite right to her.

She tapped on Lorna's door but got no response. Finally she opened the door a crack and peeked in. Lorna was lying prone on her bed with her face buried in her pillow.

Alarm gripped Anna, and she stepped into the room. "Lorna?"

The girl didn't answer. Anna hit the Off button on the tape player that Nate had brought from the Lacey house with Lorna's other possessions, and hurried to the bed.

"Lorna? Honey, are you all right?" Perching beside the child, she reached out and touched her shoulder. She could feel the tremors running through the girl's frail body. "Oh, Lorna, what's wrong? Tell me, sweetie."

Lorna rolled over, revealing a swollen, tear-streaked face and reddened, puffy eyes. "Nobody loves me, Anna. Nobody!"

"That's not true. *I* love you."

"But my mom doesn't! My dad doesn't! Even Mr. Kreusi hates me! He wouldn't let me come back to school."

Anna hardly knew where to begin. Reaching out, she gripped Lorna's hand and tried to draw her closer. The girl refused to budge and yanked her hand away. "In the first place, Mr. Kreusi doesn't hate you. He had to suspend you because you tried to burn the school down. You know that, Lorna. You know what you did was wrong, and you know you had to be punished for it, just like you're probably going to be punished by the court for doing it. People can't be allowed to start fires and then get away with it.''

"But he doesn't believe me, Anna! He doesn't believe me. Nobody believes me. And my mom is saying terrible things about me!"

Anna felt her heart clench. "Who told you that?"

"Mary Jo. When I called her this afternoon. She said everybody's talking about me, and my mom is saying I'm a liar and all kinds of terrible things. Why is she doing that, Anna? Why?"

Anna reached out to her, and this time Lorna came, sitting up and wrapping her arms around Anna as if she were hanging on for dear life.

Anna let her cry her heart out. There didn't seem to be much she could do except hold the child and wait for the storm to pass. But she was angry, furious at Bridget Lacey, and furious at Mary Jo for passing along gossip. Mary Jo had the excuse of youth, but Bridget had no excuse at all except willful stupidity and blindness.

A long time later, Lorna quieted, unable to cry anymore it seemed. She lay back on her pillow and stared blindly at the ceiling, looking for all the world as if something essential had been torn out of her soul. And finally she said one word. "Why?"

Anna sighed and shook her head, trying to find words that would both explain and comfort Lorna. The task seemed almost impossible.

"I know I did bad things," Lorna said dully. "I know they were bad. But my dad did bad things, too. How come everybody's ganging up on *me?*"

"I don't think they are, honey. I know it feels that way,

but I really don't think the whole world is ganging up on you. An awful lot of us are on your side.''

"And Mom? Doesn't she love me even a little bit?'' Lorna's voice cracked, and fresh tears ran down her face.

"Your mother—'' Anna broke off sharply, trying to choose her words very carefully. Finally she gave up trying to be diplomatic. "Frankly, Lorna, I think your mother's gone a little crazy.''

Lorna's wet blue eyes fixed on her. "Crazy?''

"Crazy. I think all this has pushed her over the edge. She's trying to make it all go away, but it's not going to go away.''

"How can she think it'll go away if she says terrible things about me?''

"Well, you see, if you're lying, that means everybody can forget about it. People would just shrug their shoulders and say how amazing it is that a kid can get mad enough to say things like that. But if you're telling the truth, your dad will probably go to jail. Even if he doesn't go to jail, they'll have to leave town, Lorna. They won't be able to stay here if everybody knows for sure that he hurt you. So your mom is trying, in a very bad way, to keep things from getting worse. What's more, she doesn't want to believe your dad could do those things to you. It hurts too much to even think about. It's easier to believe you're lying.''

"Did your mom act this way?''

"Not exactly. She said all those terrible things right to me. She wouldn't believe me at all. That's why I ran away.''

"Did she ever believe you?''

How Anna wished she could say otherwise. "No. Never. Not even to this day. She's convinced I just hated my stepfather.''

Lorna took a couple of shaky breaths. "What if my mom *never* believes me?"

There was nothing at all Anna could say to that, so she took the only other tack she could. "I think your mother still loves you, Lorna. I really do. I think that's why all this is hurting her so much and making her act crazy. Maybe someday she'll get over this enough that you can be friends with her."

Lorna looked as if she didn't believe it. "I can't ever go home again."

"It doesn't look that way."

"So can I stay with you until I grow up?"

Anna felt a burst of panic so strong that her heart seemed to stop. She wanted to say yes. Oh, God, she wanted to say yes! But with her past...there was no way on earth she would ever qualify as a foster parent. No way. Just as soon as all these matters were adjudicated, the child welfare authorities were going to start looking for a permanent home for Lorna, and they would never, ever, accept Anna Fleming as fit.

"D-don't you want me?" Lorna asked shakily.

"Of course I do!" The words burst out of Anna, carrying enough force that Lorna's face relaxed. "But it won't be my decision, honey. There are authorities who make these decisions. They'll be the ones who decide."

"I'll tell them I want *you* to be my foster mom."

"It may not be enough, sweetie. We'll just have to wait and see." Which was a cowardly way out of explaining the truth. But she couldn't possibly look at this child and say, I'll never be good enough to be your mother because I stole. Because I prostituted myself to get money to eat.

Her heart ached almost too much to bear, and she felt tears burning her eyes. There were times, like now, when she wanted to rail at the merciless fates for what they had done to her. If her stepfather hadn't molested her. If her mother had only believed her. If she had known there were people she could turn to. So many ifs. And not one of them could save her from her past now.

But she *could* save Lorna, she reminded herself. She *could* do something to ensure that this child didn't make the same dreadful mistakes that were made by so many children in this situation.

"You know, Lorna," she heard herself saying, "people who have been sexually abused as children often lose their self-esteem. We start to think we're worthless, that we don't matter, that other people can do what they want to us. Or worse yet, we start to think that if our daddies loved us for having sex with them, maybe other people will do the same."

Lorna's eyes widened, and she held her breath, listening intently.

"Don't ever, ever think you're worthless. And don't ever, ever allow anyone to use you the way your dad did, because that isn't love, and it never will be. Don't use your body to get love. People who really love you will love you even without sex."

Lorna nodded, her eyes still huge, as if she understood some of the subtext. But she didn't say anything.

"Now," Anna said briskly, "why don't we think about supper?"

Late that night, long after Lorna had fallen asleep, Anna sat up in the living room, listening to the wind blow its funereal tune. The snow had stopped falling at last, but the wind hadn't let up at all. It rattled the windowpanes and moaned around the corners of the house.

Anna curled up on the sofa with Jazz beside her and tried to read a book, but she couldn't concentrate. The phone was beckoning to her again, urging her to call her stepfather. She didn't usually get the urge this often, and it indicated to her just how much this business with Lorna was disturbing her equilibrium.

Her hard-won equilibrium. That careful balancing act she did that kept her safely on a tightrope over the abyss where her memories dwelt. Lately she felt as if the rope were bucking wildly and she was hanging on with both hands for dear life, knowing that if she slipped and fell into that abyss, her memories would come rushing back and drown her.

What she had wasn't amnesia. No, she knew what was buried in her past, but she'd somehow managed to distance it, until it took an effort to recall actual events. Most of the time, it even felt as if those things had happened to someone else.

But tonight the memories seemed awfully close, and her grip on the tightrope seemed perilously weak. Calling her stepfather would be the stupidest thing she could do. She was in entirely too fragile a state right now.

What was more, she seriously doubted he had dropped dead in the past couple of weeks. What she had to do was get over this ridiculous feeling that she would never be safe until he was dead and buried. After all, she had been safe from him for sixteen years now, ever since she had walked out of that house for the last time at the age of fourteen. He hadn't been able to touch her since, so why the heck couldn't she feel safe?

She sighed, and Jazz lifted her head, looking at her with sad puppy eyes. Anna reached out and scratched the dog's ears, saying, "It's okay, Jazz. It's okay."

Jazz licked her hand, then put her head back down on her paws.

The phone rang, and the sound jarred Anna, causing her for one horrifying instant to think her stepfather had found her. But he couldn't have. No way. Anna Fleming wasn't even her real name, and there was no way he could know that she had changed it the day she turned eighteen. Nor would he want to find her, she was sure.

But her heart was still hammering as she reached out for the receiver and lifted it. "Hello?" She sounded weak and frightened, even to her own ears.

"Anna?" Hugh's deep, warm voice came over the line. "Anna, is something wrong?"

"No...no, really. I was just...thinking about Lorna." It was a lie, and she felt guilty for it, but she couldn't possibly tell him the truth.

"Oh. Okay. I just had this weird feeling that something was wrong and I needed to call you."

"No, I'm fine, really." But she didn't want him to hang up, and she sought wildly for some subject of conversation. "It stopped snowing."

"So it did." She could hear his smile in his voice. "I'll be over first thing in the morning to dig you out. You and Lorna shouldn't have to do all that alone."

Her old stubborn pride reared its head, making her want to tell him not to come, that she could handle it. But the truth was, she wanted to see Hugh. She wanted very much to see him. So instead of arguing, she said, "Thank you. I'd really appreciate that."

"All I ask in return is another cup of that hot chocolate and a couple of those cookies. It's been a long time since I had anything so good."

A little laugh escaped her. "Are you trying the pity thing?"

"Absolutely. Here I am, a lost little waif with nobody to cook for me and no desire to do it for myself. Well, hell, Anna, I can't see the point of baking cookies just for me. So naturally I'm cadging them from somebody who's already baked them. Do I look stupid?"

She did laugh then, and the sound shivered pleasantly on the line between them. "In return for shoveling me out of this mess, you're entitled to *two* cups of hot chocolate and a half-dozen cookies, plus a breakfast of eggs and ham."

"You're on." He hesitated. "I take it you didn't get any more threatening phone calls."

"No, none." A little shiver of apprehension ran through her. "It's terrible, Hugh. Lorna was in tears tonight because she thinks everybody's against her and her mother doesn't love her anymore."

He swore, a word she wasn't used to hearing anymore, being associated with a church as she was. It was, however, a word she had once used frequently herself, during her street days. It certainly didn't shock her.

"Sorry," he said swiftly. "I shouldn't have said that."

"It's okay. It's a word I've wanted to use myself more than once in the last week."

"Yeah." He sighed; she could hear it clearly. "Look, Anna, I know you've got your hands full, but…maybe if you and Lorna together tried to help me with this youth ranch thing, we could get her mind off her problems. I know that sounds really crass of me, like I'm taking advantage of the two of you, but I'm honestly not. It just suddenly struck me that Lorna needs something constructive to distract her, something important and out of the ordinary. If you've got a better idea, I'll drop it."

Anna hesitated, wondering if he was manipulating her. But no, she'd already told him that she would be happy to offer ideas and discuss the ranch with him, even though she couldn't be part of it. This really wouldn't be anything she hadn't already agreed to, but it *would* include Lorna. And she could see a dozen ways it would benefit the child.

"I think that would be a great idea," she told him. "I really do. How can we start?"

"How about I take the two of you out to see the ranch one of these days soon? You can tell her about it, so she can look forward to it, and this weekend, assuming the roads are good enough and the weather has cleared, we'll go out and look the place over. I really *would* like her input on what she thinks kids her age need and would like."

"I know she'd love to help. Okay. Let's shoot for Saturday."

"Great."

He was silent for a few seconds, and so was she, but this time the silence between them didn't feel strained. It was nice, Anna thought, to be close to him this way. It would be even nicer if he were here, sitting beside her on the couch or across from her in the armchair. Nice if she could look into his craggy, weathered face and see the warmth she always found there. In fact, thinking about it now, she found it surprising how much warmth Hugh Gallagher showed. After all he'd been through, it wouldn't be surprising if he had developed a hard edge.

"I drove out to Marshall's truck stop after I left you," he said. "He was probably the only business in town that was open today. He had a half-dozen big trucks parked in his lot and was pretty much staying open to take care of the drivers. And in case anybody needed milk, he said."

"That was nice of him."

"I think he'd have been utterly bored if he hadn't opened," Hugh said on a chuckle. "For some folks, a snowy day isn't much of a blessing."

"I guess not."

"Anyway, he said something interesting about Al Lacey. He said that he stopped taking his daughter to Lacey for her teeth a couple of years ago because he didn't like the way Al was looking at her."

"Really?"

"Really. I told him he should talk to the sheriff. I'm not sure how much good it can do, but you never know. What I *do* know is that I can't imagine what makes men like that tick."

"Me, either." She hesitated. "Are *you* okay, Hugh?"

He was silent for a few seconds, then gave a small chuckle. "Does it show?"

"Does what show?"

"That it's a rough night. And I can't figure out why it should be."

"Maybe it's sitting all alone and listening to the wind moan."

"Could be." He hesitated. "Is it making you feel funky?"

"Just a little."

"Yeah."

She waited, feeling the seconds tick by, wondering if either of them had the gumption to take this conversation any further, or if they were both going to back quickly away from the unaccustomed intimacy. She knew *she* wanted to.

"It sounds a little like an incoming round," he said finally.

"What does?"

"The wind."

She felt her heart go out to him. She had some idea of what it was to wrestle with the past, after all. "I keep wanting to call my stepfather," she admitted.

He laughed briefly. "Aren't we a pair? How old is your stepfather now?"

She had to think about it. That surprised her, since the man had once been the main thing on her mind. "Sixty-four, I guess."

"Well, the old bastard could kick off any day now, then."

"Maybe." She felt awful for discussing such things out loud.

"Then again, seeing what a creep he is, he could live forever. I'm a great believer in that old saying that the good die young. I sure saw enough of 'em do it."

"I'm sorry."

"Hey, you've got nothing to be sorry for, Anna. Nothing at all. That's the risk a man takes when he puts on a uniform."

"It still isn't right."

"No, it isn't. It just *is*. So, did your stepfather go to jail?"

"He got five years' probation."

He swore. "That don't hardly seem right."

"It's actually quite common in cases like this. It's so hard to prove that anything really happened that prosecutors tend to work plea bargains. Plus, nobody wants the child to have to testify in court if it can be avoided."

"I guess I can understand that."

"*I* didn't want to testify," Anna admitted. "I just about panicked at the thought of having to face him and tell what he did to me. It was hard enough telling everyone else I had to tell."

"Lorna will probably feel the same."

"Probably. You know, I've often wondered about that. I

can't erase the memory of what he did to me. I have to live with it. So why did it seem so impossible to say it to his face? After all, he already knew it.''

"Ah, but you were terrified of him, Anna. Don't blame yourself for that. He'd hurt you and abused you, and had exercised total power and control over you. How could you not be terrified of having to face him? You're...what? Thirty now? You're a full-grown woman who's been standing on her own two feet for a long time. I'll bet you still wouldn't want to face him.''

Anna drew a shaky breath, surprised by how well he read her. "No, I wouldn't want to. Not even now.''

"And that's understandable. The man hurt you grievously, and it's hardly surprising that you're still afraid of him at a gut level. You can argue with yourself about it all you want, but the fear isn't going to go away. And that's why you wish he'd just drop dead. That's the only way you can be sure he'll never be able to hurt you again. Once burned, twice shy, as they say.''

Anna felt her throat tighten. Hugh's amazing understanding made her ache in the strangest way, as if she had suddenly found somebody who really cared about her, somebody she could turn to and trust. She couldn't remember the last time she had felt that way about anyone.

The feeling terrified her. It was full of danger and threat. It could lay her open to terrible wounds and disappointments. She couldn't afford to trust anyone that way. She just couldn't.

"I'm sorry,'' Hugh said suddenly. "This is probably the last thing you want to be talking about.''

"It seems to be all I can think about tonight,'' she admitted. "But you're right. I don't want to talk about it. I don't want to think about it. Until this thing with Lorna came up, I'd gotten to the point where I didn't really think about it for months at a time. Oh, I don't mean it never crossed my mind, but when it did it was one of those fleeting little things and was gone. It wasn't *possessing* me, if you know what I mean.''

"I know exactly what you mean, Anna. I wish I had some kind of remedy to offer, but I don't. I never found a way to keep myself from worrying over things that my mind was determined to worry over. It just goes on until it decides of its own accord to quit bugging you.''

"It seems that way.''

"I'd suggest getting out and doing something, but that's kind of hopeless right now.''

She had to laugh softly. "It sure is. I suppose I could go out and build a snowman in the front yard.''

"If the wind didn't blow you away.''

He stayed on the phone with her for another hour, talking about the work he was doing at the church, about the youth group's plans for a Christmas play and concert, about anything that occurred to either of them.

When she hung up, Anna felt more relaxed than she had all day. She didn't even think again about calling her step-father. Instead, she went to bed and slept soundly.

Chapter 9

Saturday dawned bright, clear and warm. The snow was beginning to melt away, leaving the streets and sidewalks slushy and wet. The unexpected warmth was welcome to Anna, who figured it would probably be the last they would see until spring. The weather forecasters were even now talking about another winter storm moving in across the Rockies, and predicting heavy snowfall beginning late on Sunday.

Lorna was excited about going out to Hugh's ranch, and was ready to go a full half hour before he came by to pick them up. Anna was glad to see that she had put aside her sorrow, at least for now. Going back to school had been good for her. She had discovered that her friends were still her friends, and that they were genuinely concerned about her. Anna had worried that their reactions might be very different and that some of their parents might want their daughters to stay away, but that hadn't happened. Nor had John Kreusi done anything to make the girl feel unwelcome.

When Lorna climbed into Hugh's truck to sit between him

and Anna, she was chatting cheerfully about everything that came into her head. Hugh smiled at her, then looked over her head at Anna and winked.

"My ranch is out east of here," he told them as they drove out of town. "About twenty miles. The land isn't useful for a ranching operation, but it'll sure provide a lot of room for teaching kids how to ride horses, how to camp out and hike, and maybe even how to raise a few head of livestock."

Lorna looked at him. "You'll teach the girls, too, won't you?"

"Absolutely."

"Good. I get sick of guys acting like they're the only ones who can do anything."

Hugh glanced down at her. "I figured out a long time ago that girls can do anything guys can do if they want to."

"Me, too," Lorna agreed, a satisfied smile on her face.

"Except when it comes to upper body strength," Anna said. "Guys will always be stronger in the arms and shoulders than girls."

"In general," he agreed. "But there are exceptions to the rule—which is a good reason not to make it a rule."

Anna decided she liked his attitude.

She didn't know what she had expected to find when they arrived at the ranch—maybe a run-down old house, a couple of sagging outbuildings and endless acres of snow-covered land. Instead she discovered a reasonably neat, large two-story ranch house; a barn in good condition, and what looked like a motel.

"This used to be a dude ranch," Hugh said as they bucked to a halt in the rutted driveway in front of the house. "The last owners had to close it about five years ago because it wasn't making any money, but they did their best to keep it in reasonably good condition so they could get a better price for it. Nobody but me wanted it, though, and after five years they were willing to come way down."

"It looks like you got a good deal," Anna ventured.

He flashed her a smile. "I got an *incredible* deal. Did you ever get the feeling that something was meant to be? That's the feeling I have with this. Like it's really meant to happen." He looked out at the house and outbuildings, his expression that of a man who saw his dream within his grasp.

He got out of the truck and came around to help Anna and Lorna down. "So," he asked, "do you want to go inside?"

"Of course," Anna said, then looked at Lorna. The girl was turning around slowly where she stood, taking everything in with an almost wistful expression.

"You'll have horses?" she asked.

"Count on it," he answered.

"My dad used to promise that we'd have horses someday, but then he started saying they were too expensive and too much work. He said I wouldn't be good about taking care of them."

"The kids who live here are going to *have* to take care of them," Hugh said. "I'll ride their butts to make sure they do."

Lorna suddenly giggled. "I bet you will."

"Believe it. I'm a great butt rider."

She giggled again, and they all moved toward the house. Anna loved the big, wide porch and had no trouble imagining it dotted with rocking chairs and maybe even a swing. She'd always wanted a front porch like this for long summer evenings. Her imagination filled it with people, with the kind of family she had been deprived of so long ago. Grandparents and parents and grandchildren lazing around in the evening breeze, maybe sipping lemonade or iced tea. It didn't matter to her that the image was clichéd. She needed some of those clichés in her life.

But snow covered the ground and had drifted on the porch, and she couldn't cling to the summery images for long. They stepped through the front door of the house and discovered a huge living room with a big fireplace.

"This was sort of the lodge for the dude ranch," Hugh said. "It'll be a great gathering place for the kids. And through there is a dining room big enough to seat thirty without any trouble. I'm figuring on putting in small tables, with four to a table. Make it cozier."

The walls in the living room were timbered, giving the feeling of a lodge, but the dining room had been wallpapered. The paper was coming loose in the cold and hung in forlorn strips.

"I don't much care for that paper," Hugh said. "It's too busy. I reckon I'll strip the walls and paint 'em white. It'll make the room seem bigger and brighter."

Anna nodded approvingly. Hugh then led them through to a huge kitchen that was equipped with restaurant-style appliances.

"Everything in here works," he said. "It's all ready to heat up and start serving the multitudes. I was concerned at first about the stove—a real restaurant stove can get as hot as six hundred degrees on the outside, but it's not the real thing. It's just an overlarge kitchen range that's insulated, so it'll be as safe as any stove around the kids."

Anna, who never would have thought of such a thing, was impressed that he had.

"The dishwasher is larger than standard, too, but it works pretty much like a home one, so the kids ought to be able to use it without any danger."

"That's good."

He smiled at her. "I figure they need to learn how to cook and clean up after themselves. Necessary life skills. I don't envision having a staff to do it for them. This isn't going to be a country resort."

"They'd have to do the dishes at home," Lorna commented.

"Exactly. And cooking is something everybody needs to know how to do. I've learned that one the hard way."

He showed them the bathrooms, one for ladies and one for gents. Anna thought that was a very useful thing to have in the common area, which would probably get a lot of use in the winter months.

"Now the best part," Hugh said. He led them up a wooden staircase to the upper floor. "The family living quarters."

Anna was delighted. There were three bedrooms, a sitting room, a bathroom and a kitchenette, and all of the rooms had tall windows with views of the surrounding countryside. "I love it up here!"

"It's perfect, isn't it?" he said proudly. "More than I really need just for myself, of course, but if I were to take on a partner who had a family, he or she could use it, and I could sleep in one of the rooms in the guest building."

"Or if you get a family," Anna said.

Hugh looked at her with a crooked smile. "Never going to happen. Nobody wants a formerly crazy vet like me."

Anna felt something inside her almost plummet. "Wendy Tate married Billy Joe Yuma," she reminded him.

"Wendy Tate was too young to know better," he said, then shook his head sharply. "That's not true. Wendy is one in a million, and the two of them are as happy as can be."

"That's right."

His smile grew wistful. "Some dreams aren't worth dreaming. They only make you sad."

"*I* think somebody would want you," Lorna said. "You're a very nice man."

He laughed then, and the shadows disappeared from his eyes. "Time will tell, missy. Time will tell."

They went out to look at the guest rooms next. Each was pretty much an ordinary motel-room arrangement with a full bath.

"I figure I can put four kids to a room in bunk beds," he said. "That means I can take on as many as forty kids— although I'm not planning to do it on such a big scale right off. Starting slow is the best way. Get all the bugs ironed out and figure out if we can handle a larger crowd."

"I agree," Anna said. "It's a lot to take on, even with a handful of kids. What kind of help are you thinking of having?"

"Mainly I want people who can help create a family atmosphere for these kids. I don't want to run a boot-camp type of operation where every minute is regimented. I see it as the kind of place where kids can learn to do new things with supportive teachers who'll take the time to listen to them and help them. I want these kids to learn self-confidence and self-reliance, and how to get along with people. I want them to learn the kind of pride that'll keep them out of trouble."

"Give them what they don't get at home, you mean."

"Exactly. I expect we'll have some behavior problems, so I'm thinking we'll need to have a psychologist on call, but I was kind of hoping for your help. I hear constantly about all the good things you do with the kids in the youth group, Anna. They trust you and like you, and they feel they can turn to you when they have a problem. We need somebody like you."

A bolt of panic shot through her, and she felt her mouth go dry. How could she possibly tell this man that she wouldn't be considered fit for such a role with children? That if he tried to draw her into his plan as a full participant, he was apt to find doors closing in his face at every turn? The only reason she was allowed to work with the youth group was that nobody had inquired that closely into her background. Her arrest record as a juvenile had been sealed, and there was nothing else that might turn up, but surely agencies thinking about sending children to a youth ranch would want to look more closely into the backgrounds of the people running it? And then they would find out. There were ways....

"Anna? Anna, are you all right?"

She blinked and realized she was standing stock-still in the middle of an empty motel room with her hands clenched so tightly into fists that her fingers ached. Through the open door of the room she could see Lorna outside gamboling in the snow. When had she gone outside?

"Anna?"

Moving her head stiffly, she looked at Hugh. Through wooden lips she managed to say, "I'm fine."

"Like hell. You turned white as a sheet a moment ago, and you're standing there looking like a horse that wants to bolt. What did I say?"

"Nothing. Really." She drew a deep breath and lied to Hugh for the second time. "I just felt…a little dizzy, I guess. I'm fine now."

"Are you sure?" His face mirrored concern. "Did you eat breakfast? Maybe I should get you back to town and feed you."

"No, really. I ate. I'm not at all hungry." She managed a smile. "I'm fine now. Honestly."

He looked at her for a moment, as if debating whether to take her at her word, then nodded. "Okay."

But she noticed he took her arm as they walked outside, as if he were afraid she might fall. The gesture touched her.

She insisted they go take a look at the barn. There she found stalls for horses and a loft for hay.

"They kept horses but no other livestock," he explained. "I figure we ought to have a few cows and sheep, though, just so the kids can learn about them and how to take care of them. Besides, they won't feel like they've lived on a ranch otherwise."

"I like cows," Lorna said. Her cheeks were flushed from the cold, and her eyes sparkled as if she were enjoying herself hugely. "Cows are just the sweetest things. A baby cow licked my arm once. I couldn't believe how long and big its tongue was. I like sheep a lot, too. I think that's a good idea."

"I'm glad you approve." Hugh spoke without a hint of patronization. When Lorna offered some more of her opinions, Hugh listened to her as seriously as if she were an expert on the subject.

Anna watched the two of them talking and felt a tug on her heart. The sight of them together filled her with a yearning she couldn't begin to name. Shaking her head, she tried to brush the feeling aside. It did no good to want things she couldn't have.

On the way home, Lorna asked if she could spend the night with Mary Jo. Anna hesitated, still uneasy about the gossip that Mary Jo had passed on to Lorna earlier in the week. Lorna, however, looked as if she wasn't the least bit concerned about such things, and regarded Anna with apparent hope and eagerness.

"When did Mary Jo ask you?"

"This morning, when she called."

"Why didn't you ask me right away?"

"Because I was afraid you'd say no."

Anna wanted to sigh, but she stifled it. "Waiting doesn't usually make it any likelier that I'll say yes."

Lorna smiled sheepishly. "I know. I just had to get up my nerve."

Anna could see Hugh behind Lorna, and saw that he was smiling. He thought it was amusing. Actually, so did she. "Well, all right, as long as she's cleared it with her parents."

"Oh, she did! She said her mom was the one who suggested it."

"Then okay. What time do you have to be there, and when will you be home?"

"She asked if I could come over at four, so I can have dinner with them. And I'll go to church with them in the morning and come home with you afterward, if that's okay."

"That'll be just fine. I need to talk to Mr. and Mrs. Weeks first, though."

"How come?"

"There's just a matter I need to discuss with them, okay?"

Lorna looked doubtful, but nodded. "All right."

Hugh dropped them off and turned down an offer of lunch. Anna watched him drive away and wondered if they had done something to make him want to get away from them. She couldn't imagine what it might have been and tried to tell herself she was being ridiculous, but a subtle sense of anxiety wouldn't leave her. She found herself playing back the morning's events over and over, trying to pick out what might have bothered him.

Maybe he was washing his hands of them because of her refusal to participate in his youth ranch in the way he wanted. But Hugh Gallagher didn't strike her as being that childish.

And maybe nothing at all had happened, she told herself sternly. Maybe he just had something else he needed to do. Or perhaps he felt he had taken enough of *their* time today. Either possibility was as likely as the things she was imagining.

After lunch she shooed Lorna off to her room to pack for her sleepover and took the opportunity to make the call to the Weeks family. Mary Jo's mother, Mildred, answered the phone.

"Hi, Mildred, this is Anna Fleming."

"Anna! How are you? And how is Lorna?"

"We're both doing fine. Lorna said Mary Jo asked her to come spend the night tonight, and I wanted to make sure that was all right with you."

"Of course it is." Mildred chuckled. "It took me years, but I've finally got Mary Jo trained to ask *me* before she asks her friends. We're looking forward to Lorna's visit."

"Lorna is certainly looking forward to visiting you. But there is a matter I needed to discuss with you. I don't know if you're aware that the court has forbidden Lorna's parents to have any contact at all with her?"

"Yes, I'd heard about that. Don't worry, Anna. Neither Bill nor I will let either one of those people near the child. Good Lord, I can't believe what that woman is saying about her own daughter! If one of my girls came to me with such a story, it'd kill me, but the first thing I'd do is move myself and the girls out, and I wouldn't come back unless I was absolutely sure nothing had happened. And either way, I wouldn't go around town telling everyone that my daughter was a lying slut!''

"Neither would I." Anna had always thought Mildred Weeks was a fine woman, but now she felt a strong burst of warmth toward her. The world needed more mothers like this, she thought. "There's another thing, too. There's an awful lot of nasty gossip going around—"

"Don't I know it! Don't you worry, Anna, Lorna won't hear a word of it here. I already scolded Mary Jo for telling Lorna some of it earlier this week. Mary Jo just thought it was all exciting. She never thought about how it would make Lorna feel. But don't worry. She won't hear another whisper of it from anyone in this family—or from anyone who happens to come around, either, if I have anything to say about it. That poor dear is going through quite enough without people saying ugly things about her.''

"Lorna's not lying," Anna felt compelled to say.

"We know she isn't," Mildred said firmly. "We've been uneasy about that man for some time now. It was nearly a year ago when we put our foot down and told Mary Jo she couldn't sleep over there anymore. It wasn't that he did anything terrible, but some of the goings-on just made us real uneasy." She fell silent a moment. "No, even looking back at it, I can't say he did anything *wrong*. It just didn't feel right, if you take my meaning.''

"I certainly do.''

"And I feel just awful now. I realize Bill and I didn't have anything we could really point a finger to at the time, but oh, how I wish we could've done something to save Lorna from the past year.''

"I think a lot of people are feeling that way, Mildred.''

"Possibly. Possibly." The woman sighed. "I wish foresight was as good as hindsight."

After she hung up, Anna felt a whole lot better about Lorna spending the night with Mary Jo. She was probably worrying too much, anyway. There was no way she could protect Lorna from the gossip. Not when the girl was back in school with dozens of children who were perfectly capable of keeping her clued in as to what their elders were saying about her. Poor Lorna!

Unable to do anything else useful, Anna went to walk Jazz.

That evening she received another threatening phone call. A man's muffled voice said, "I'm going to make you sorry you made that kid lie." Then, before she could do more than gasp, he hung up.

Anna sat on the couch, staring blindly, holding the receiver tightly in her hand, frozen by fear. She wanted to be angry. She wanted to be furious. She wanted to throw the phone and yell and scream and get even with her tormentor. But she was too afraid to do any of that.

She had too many secrets. Too many dark places in her past. And never, ever, had she been more aware of just how vulnerable she was. All it would take was one person digging deeply enough into her past and she would be ruined in this town.

Finally, with a trembling hand, she put the receiver down. There was no point in calling Nate, she thought. There was absolutely nothing he could do about an anonymous caller who made no threat other than that she would be sorry. She was convinced it had to be Al Lacey—who else would bother?—but she certainly couldn't swear to it. The voice was too muffled. Lacking an actual threat and a confirmation of identity, no one could help her.

Nor were they really likely to think she needed help. No one knew enough about her past to understand how easy it was to terrify her. No one would begin to imagine that what she most feared was the truth. Nor did she think this caller was threatening her physically. Lacey was in enough trouble. He would have to be the worst fool imaginable to get involved in another crime, one that would be a lot easier to prove.

Jazz nudged her leg, begging to be lifted onto the couch with her. She bent and took the puppy into her lap, marveling at how much she had grown in just a couple of weeks. Jazz curled up contentedly and closed her eyes, ready to nap.

Anna envied the dog. It had been a long time since she had last felt this helpless, and it was upsetting to realize that she was a prisoner of her own fear more than anything else. Her past *wasn't* in the past, the way she kept telling herself. Instead, it was very much in the here and now, influencing every decision she made. And she didn't know what to do about it.

Burying her hand in the dog's soft fur, she closed her eyes and tried to find a way out of a mess that was mostly of her own making. Unfortunately, every option that occurred to her had unacceptable risks. Every one of them would put her in exactly the position she was so desperately trying to avoid.

The phone rang again, and she almost didn't answer it. But then a spark of anger flared in her, and she grabbed the receiver, determined to tell her tormentor where to get off.

"Hello?"

There was a silence on the line, then Hugh's voice said, "Anna? Is something wrong?"

And without meaning to, Anna blurted, "I got another phone call."

"Threatening you?"

"Telling me I was going to be really sorry I encouraged Lorna to lie."

Hugh swore. "That does it," he said. "I'll be over there in ten minutes."

"But—" But he'd already disconnected, and she found herself listening to a dial tone.

And suddenly she felt better. For the next couple of hours, at least, she wasn't going to have to sit around and worry about this all by herself.

Hugh swore savagely after he hung up the phone, then went to get dressed. He'd been lounging around in sweatpants and a sweatshirt, feeling kind of blue and lonely, and wishing like hell he'd had the sense to have lunch with Anna and Lorna. Damned if he didn't miss the two of them not five minutes after dropping them off.

Then, sitting here listening to the old building creak and pop in the deepening cold, he'd found himself wondering what Anna was doing to fill the evening hours, and wondering if she was as lonely as he was. If she was at loose ends, too.

One thing had led to another, and finally he'd decided it wouldn't hurt to call, especially since his abrupt departure when he dropped her off had left Anna looking…well, surprised. He would have said hurt, except that he didn't think that highly of himself. No way he imagined he meant enough to that woman to hurt her by leaving abruptly. But he *had* been rude, and he figured he owed her a bit of an apology.

He hadn't had any idea how he was going to explain himself, but he wasn't all that worried about it. The apology was due, and he would make it. Knowing Anna, he thought she wouldn't press him enough to make him admit he'd been running from her like a bat out of hell because he was scared to death of the things she made him want. The dreams she made appear to be just within his grasp.

They weren't within his grasp, of course. No way. She would never be interested in a man like him, and given her past, it was entirely likely she wasn't ever going to be interested in any man at any time.

But now…now he was fighting mad. Apologies were forgotten. All he wanted to do was strangle the bastard who was frightening her. She didn't deserve this. In all his life, he'd never met a woman he thought was any more basically decent and kind than Anna Fleming. In fact, given the way her stepfather had treated her and the unwillingness of her mother to believe it was happening, it was wonderful that Anna had managed to become such a kindhearted and good woman.

He pulled on jeans and a Shaker sweater, shoved his feet into boots, grabbed his jacket and headed out. He didn't want to think about how frightened she must be, but it was all he could think about anyway. And if he could ever figure out for sure who the sorry so-and-so was who was calling, he would make sure the creep thought twice about doing it again.

Of course, it had to be Al Lacey. Who else could it possibly be? He didn't think anyone else in this town would think Anna was the root of the problem. Only Al Lacey was in a position to see things that way.

Damn!

His truck started easily enough, and soon he was zipping down streets that had frozen over again into ripples and ridges of ice. There had been enough traffic over the evening, though, to keep the meltwater from freezing into a smooth sheet that could be treacherous, so he didn't slow down much.

He reached Anna's in exactly the ten minutes he had promised. He saw her peek out the living-room window as he pulled up, and when he reached the door, he didn't even have to knock. She pulled it open immediately.

He stepped inside without waiting for an invitation and closed the door behind himself. Then, without thinking, he reached for her and drew her into his arms.

Her resistance was no more than a mere hesitation this time before she came willingly into his embrace. God, he thought, how good it felt to hold her! He closed his eyes with the pleasure of it, and lowered his head until his lips touched her silky hair. A warning bell sounded in his mind, but he ignored it. He needed this embrace entirely too much to give it up easily.

But finally even he realized they couldn't stand there that way indefinitely. He needed to let go of her, to talk to her, to ease her fear in whatever way he could. He needed to let her know that she didn't have to be alone.

Chapter 10

Anna laid three aces on the table and looked apologetically at Hugh. "The cards seem to be favoring me tonight." She'd already beaten him on three hands.

He smiled. "Lucky at cards, unlucky in love. I guess that makes me lucky."

"I'm not sure the reverse is true."

His smile broadened. "Are you telling me you don't think I'm lucky in love?"

She felt her cheeks heat. "I don't think I said that."

"No, but I inferred that from what you implied."

She hesitated. Her education hadn't been the best, and while she loved to read, there were still plenty of gaps in her knowledge. Never had she understood the difference between inferring and implying, although she had a sense of it from what he had just said. Trouble was, she didn't know exactly how to answer him. She wanted to keep things light and humorous, but there was no humorous way she could think of to answer him, especially when she had the feeling that she might just have insulted him.

"I'm sorry," he said suddenly. "I'm just teasing. I didn't really misunderstand you."

"Oh."

"Anyway, I've never had any luck at love, so these cards ought to be playing my way. And they're not."

He put his hand down so she could see it. "See? Nothing useful at all. Nothing that's likely to get useful."

"Would you like to play a different game?"

He shook his head, his smile returning. "Actually, I'm enjoying myself. The cards are just an excuse to sit here with you."

Her cheeks flamed. She was sure they were as red as the Christmas napkins in her linen closet. No man had ever said anything that sweet to her, and she didn't have the vaguest idea how to respond to him.

He looked at her as if he were perplexed. Finally, as if he didn't know what else to do, he said, "Would it be possible for me to have a cup of coffee?"

"Decaf?"

"That would be great."

She put her cards down and rose to make the coffee. Conscious of his gaze following her, she felt awkward. Her legs didn't even seem to want to move right, and she twice dropped the coffee filters she took out of the drawer. Finally, with trembling hands, she managed to fill the coffeemaker with water and the basket with the right number of scoops of coffee.

It was surprising, she found herself thinking, how difficult such a simple task could become when you were nervous. And she was definitely beginning to get nervous.

It wasn't that he had really done anything to make her feel that way. She just wasn't used to having a man around like this, and the longer he stayed, the more conscious of it she became.

She stood at the sink, rinsing the coffee scoop and taking as long at it as she could. Then she brought out mugs, milk and sugar, and all the while she was wondering if it would be wiser to ask him to leave.

But she didn't want him to leave. She didn't want to be alone. Not tonight. Not after that phone call. Not when a sense of unease just wouldn't leave her alone, reminding her that her life wasn't the placid pond she kept trying to turn it into.

Her memories were very near the surface tonight, she realized. Just below the level of consciousness, they were threatening to erupt in a maelstrom of pain and unwanted remembrance. Was just having a man in her house enough to cause that?

"Anna?" Hugh was suddenly behind her, close. Too close. She whirled around and looked up at him, uneasiness filling her almost past bearing. She wanted to run, escape, flee into the icy night and keep going until everything that worried and concerned her was so far away it couldn't touch her ever again.

He reached out and touched her shoulder, then her cheek, with a tenderness that deprived the gesture of any kind of sensuality. The last time anyone had touched her this way was childhood, and the last man to show her genuine tenderness had been her father. Her real father.

"I won't hurt you," he said. "I would never hurt you. If you want, I'll leave."

"No!" The word was out before she even realized she was going to say it.

He cocked his head a little to one side and let his hand fall. "I'm upsetting you."

"It's not...not you," she managed to say.

"So it's men in general?"

She was astonished that he was able to discern her problem so quickly and so easily. Was she transparent? Or was he just unusually sensitive?

"I know fear when I see it," he said. "In my line of work, you learn to recognize it." He sighed and stepped back. "So is it men in general?"

She managed a jerky nod.

He compressed his lips, looking almost sad. "Have you ever had a real boyfriend? A real lover?"

Shame suddenly flooded her, and she lowered her head.

"No, I guess not," he answered for her. He stepped even farther back. "I won't touch you, Miss Anna. I promise."

He turned his back, and she felt she was losing a chance for something precious, but she didn't know how to call him back. She didn't have any idea what it was she wanted from him, but she knew she didn't want the back of his head.

"Hugh..." She managed to speak his name in a hoarse whisper.

He turned and looked at her. "Yes?"

"I...I don't mean to hurt you."

He shook his head sadly. "You didn't hurt me, Anna. I'm hurting *for* you. I think it's just awful that you were wounded so badly by a man you should have been able to trust. Wounded so badly that you get skittish any time I step too close to you emotionally."

"Emotionally?" She didn't understand him.

He nodded. "I don't really scare you physically. I have a feeling you've dealt with that fear, whether you know it or not. You just don't want to be hurt emotionally again. And I can understand that. I'm not a good bet for anybody's trust."

Pain stabbed her heart, but this time it was for him, not her. "Oh, Hugh," she said, forgetting herself in her concern. "Hugh, that's not it at all! It's not *you!*"

He sat down at the table and spread his hands. "Then explain it to me, Anna. If I don't understand, I can't keep from doing things that bother you."

She looked away, staring blindly at the kitchen counter and cabinets, trying to find ways to express what was going on without talking about things she didn't want to talk about. Without raking up things she didn't want to think about.

"I'm...well, since this thing with Lorna started, I'm having trouble with my memories," she said finally. "Things I haven't thought about in a long time are trying to bubble up and make me think about them. It's making me uneasy and edgy."

He nodded reassuringly. She caught the movement from the corner of her eye and found the courage to look at him. "I'm not really comfortable with men, it's true. It usually takes a long time for me to get comfortable with men. I mean, I have to know them for a while before I don't automatically feel threatened every time I see them. I feel comfortable with Reverend Fromberg. I feel comfortable with Nate Tate. I feel comfortable with you."

"Not really."

"Well, more comfortable than I ordinarily would with someone I've just met." She sighed, unable to find the words she wanted in order to explain. "It's so hard...."

"Explaining feelings is always hard. But it's okay. Don't feel like you have to explain anything."

"But I want to," she argued. "Maybe I even need to. I'd like for us to be friends, but that's never going to happen if I keep getting all nervous on you."

"Hey, I've got news for you. We're already friends."

Struck, she thought about that and felt a soft smile gradually dawn on her face as she realized that he was right. They *were* already friends. Maybe not really close friends, but the friendship was definitely there.

"See?" he said as she smiled. "We're friends."

"Yes, I think so, too."

"But I still make you uncertain, don't I? Because you don't know quite what to expect from me."

She nodded slowly, agreeing. "That may be part of it."

"Well..." He paused thoughtfully. "Do you want me to promise that I won't touch you? Would that help?"

As soon as he made the offer, she realized that it wouldn't help, because she did want him to touch her. She actually *wanted* it! The thought astonished her so much that she froze, uncertain what to say or do about this unexpected feeling.

"Okay," he said, "I promise I won't touch you." He gave her a crooked smile. "And I think it's time for me to be going."

He turned and headed for the living room. He was going to get his coat and leave, she realized. Had she offended him somehow? But how? She hadn't said anything.

Except that she had frozen like a deer in headlights when he had mentioned touching her. Maybe he had interpreted her astonishment as fear.

The thought gave her a sharp pang, and she went after him, forgetting herself in her concern for him. Hugh had never been anything but nice to her. He didn't deserve to think she classified him with the men who had hurt her in the past. He didn't deserve her distrust or her fear.

"Hugh..."

He was standing at the coat closet, reaching for his jacket. He looked over his shoulder at her. "Yes?"

"I'm not afraid of you," she said in a rush. "I'm sorry I made you think I was."

He turned from the closet to face her, putting his hands on his hips in a way that made her acutely aware of his masculinity. Her breath nearly stopped in her throat.

"You know, Anna, I might find that a whole lot easier to believe if you didn't keep looking at me as if I were pointing a loaded shotgun at you."

"I don't! I mean...I don't mean to!"

He sighed and turned his head away for a moment. When he looked at her again, some of the exasperation had faded from his face. "I'm sorry. I ought to be more understanding. It's not like I never had a flashback, or never found myself suddenly remembering something unpleasant. But considering how often I seem to remind you of unpleasant things, maybe it would be best if I just keep clear as much as possible."

Her heart sank. She liked Hugh. She liked his easygoing companionship. She was even beginning to like that occasional tingle of sexual awareness he gave her. Considering that she hadn't felt sexually attracted to a man since...well, *ever*. All of her normal development in that regard had been truncated by her stepfather and the men she had sold herself to. For years now she had believed herself utterly *incapable* of feeling such things.

And all of a sudden she didn't want to go back to the numbness that she had once considered a blessing.

She looked at him, twisting her hands together and trying to find some way to tell him these things without dying of embarrassment. Trying to find some way to assure him that she didn't want him to withdraw from her life.

"I'm sorry," she said finally, at a loss. "I like being with you. I wish…I wish I didn't make you feel like you frighten me, because I don't…I don't want you to go away.''

Then, embarrassed by having admitted so much, and reluctant to watch him leave, she turned away to go back to the kitchen. There was no way she could ever tell him that the mere sight of him made her want things she had never wanted before. There was no way she could tell him that she had no idea how to deal with the feelings he evoked in her.

''Anna?''

She paused, her back still toward him.

''Come here.''

His voice was gentle, so gentle that the sound of it made her throat tighten. So gentle that it never occurred to her not to do as he said.

She turned and walked toward him, feeling her heart thud heavily with each step. Her awareness of everything except her own body and Hugh before her seemed to diminish with every step she took. There was nothing but her heartbeat, her breath, the unexpected but strangely welcome ache between her legs…and Hugh. Only Hugh.

She came to a stop right in front of him. They were close enough now that she could smell him faintly, the delicious aromas of soap and…man. For the first time since her twelfth birthday, the smell of a man didn't sicken her. It drew her, enticing her, and she wondered why.

''Anna…'' He murmured her name softly. ''Anna, this is killing me.…''

She tipped her head a little so she could look up into his face. ''What?'' Her voice was a choked whisper. There didn't seem to be any air in the room at all.

''I…want to touch you,'' he said. ''It's one of the reasons I think I ought to stay away. I want to touch you, and I'll terrify you if I do. Hell, I'm scared all the time that I'm going to say or do something that will frighten you. It's driving me nuts...."

Tears tightened her throat again, and she closed her eyes, seeking some kind of balance within herself. But there was no balance. She felt awful for making him feel that way, but she didn't know how to stop. Her reactions were so much a part of her that she couldn't even really remember when she *hadn't* been afraid of men. How could she possibly stop responses that were as much a part of her as the way she breathed?

"I'm not afraid of *you*," she said again. "Not you."

"I'm not really sure that makes any difference."

Her eyes opened, and she looked up at him again, reading the sorrow and longing on his face. He was going to leave, she realized, because he didn't know what to do about this situation. He didn't know how to go on wanting her when she was afraid, and he didn't know how to get past her fear.

But of course *he* couldn't get past it. She had to do that herself, and she didn't have any idea how.

There had been a time when she had been able to reach out and touch men because it hadn't mattered. From within the cocoon of numbness and indifference, she had been able to act boldly. Now that she wanted to reach out and touch, she found herself paralyzed by all the feelings that had once been unable to reach her through her cocoon.

She drew a long shaky breath and sought courage, real courage. Courage such as she had never needed before.

"I want..." Her voice broke, and she had to take another breath before she could continue. "I want...you...to t-touch me."

"Oh, God, Anna!" He turned from her and paced to the far side of the living room. "You don't, not really. You just don't want me to stop being your friend. I won't, I swear. You don't have to say things like that! You don't have to buy my friendship.''

She shook her head almost wildly and felt her hair begin to slip free of the pins. ''No. No. Really, I... Oh, it's so hard to say! I've never...this is the first time...I've ever felt this way. *Ever!*''

Hugh felt something inside him grow perfectly still. A hush seemed to settle over his mind and heart as her words sank home. He looked at her and saw the truth of what she said written on her face in an expression of yearning.

''Never?'' he asked hoarsely, hardly daring to believe what his ears, mind and heart were trying to tell him. Hardly daring to believe the evidence of his own eyes.

''Never,'' she said, her voice trembling. ''I never had a chance. Just about the time I started thinking about boys, my stepfather...well, you know. And since then, I've never wanted anybody to touch me. I even hate it when a doctor has to touch me. But you...'' She trailed off, unable to continue.

Hugh swallowed and felt his heart begin to beat heavily. She wanted him to touch her. But now he wondered if he dared. It was dangerous to cross that imaginary line, and he'd promised himself repeatedly that he wouldn't do it with Anna. It would screw up all his hopes that she might be willing to help with the youth ranch, especially if things didn't work out between them.

And they weren't likely to work out, not with her fears always ready to pop up. Not when she was likely to go into a tailspin over nothing at all.

But she deserved the same patience and understanding he had needed from other people when his own fears had swamped him. Not everyone had been understanding, but there were people to whom he owed a deep debt of gratitude he would never be able to repay—except by giving someone else what they had given him.

He tried to tell himself that the youth ranch was more important, but right now nothing seemed as important as the small woman facing him from across the room, awaiting his decision. If he walked out now, he would leave her wounded anew. She had revealed something very intimate, and if he responded wrongly to her trust, she might never be able to trust again.

Faced with her scared yet hopeful expression, he could hardly put the ranch first. Nor did he really want to. Anna had lately become his major preoccupation, and he had the feeling that if he didn't settle his relationship with her somehow, he was never going to have any peace of mind again.

But all those thoughts seemed to be drifting away on a tide of more important things, like his growing need to hold her close.

He crossed the distance between them and opened his arms, inviting her in. Everything else would just have to wait.

She looked at him for a moment, not moving, and he began to wonder if he had misunderstood everything up until now. Maybe she hadn't really said she wanted him to touch her. Maybe he was losing his mind once again, slipping into some place that had no relationship to reality....

But then she stepped forward, into his arms, and he felt wonderment as her arms wrapped around his waist. Then he closed his own arms around her and held her snugly against him.

Oh, God, it had never felt so right. A pang of fear pierced him, but he pushed it aside. He'd worried and wondered and puzzled enough things for one night. Right now all he wanted to do was give himself up to the absolutely joyous feeling of being held by a woman. By a woman he had been wanting to hold for what seemed like the longest time.

Lowering his head, he pressed his face to her silky brown hair and breathed deeply of her fragrance. Anna Fleming was in his arms, and nothing had ever seemed so right.

Anna listened to the steady beat of Hugh's heart beneath her ear, felt the softness of his sweater against her cheek but mostly felt the solidness of the man who held her. She was overwhelmed by a feeling of safety that she had thought she had lost forever until just a few hours ago, when Hugh had held her for the first time.

A man's arms could make her feel safe. She absorbed the feeling with every pore, storing it up against future nights when there would be no one to make her feel this way. She clung to the feeling, trying to memorize it so she could take it out on cold nights and close her eyes and remember in every detail what these moments had felt like.

But eventually it was not enough to feel safe. Eventually her body, young and healthy, began to remind her of other needs, needs she had never allowed herself to experience before. Needs that had been locked away in a dungeon so deep she had long since forgotten them.

She wanted more, and like a flower seeking the sun, she turned her face up. Her eyes were closed, so she couldn't see his face, but she heard his sharp intake of breath.

"Anna?" he asked on a whisper.

Then, before she could think what to say or do, his lips touched hers, gently. Oh, so very gently. At first she wasn't sure she felt the caress, but as her lips began to tingle she became aware of the heat of his mouth brushing ever so lightly against hers, as if he were afraid a stronger touch might shatter her into a thousand pieces.

"Hugh…" she heard herself murmur.

Maybe she meant it as an invitation. Maybe not. He took it as one anyway, and bowed his head lower until his mouth pressed firmly against hers. For a few seconds he just nestled there, leaving her to wonder if he would ever, ever, really kiss her. Because she wanted him to kiss her. The yearning was growing in her until she could think of nothing else except what it would be like to be kissed by a man she wanted to kiss her.

Then his lips moved, caressing hers gently. The ache between her thighs began to deepen, and she felt herself press closer to him, as if she wanted to melt right into him. His arms tightened around her, but the feeling didn't frighten her. It seemed right. So very right. She wanted him to hold her tighter still, to kiss her even more deeply.

As if he read her mind, his tongue began to tease along the seam of her lips, begging entry. Shivers of pleasure poured through her, and for an instant, just an instant, she thought of the other times she had kissed men this way and how she had never felt anything at all. But Hugh's kiss was special, the key to so many locked places inside her.

She let her head fall back farther so that she could give him what he asked. When his tongue slipped into her mouth and began to play teasingly with hers, a deep fire began to burn in her. More. She wanted more.

His hands moved against her back, stroking her gently, and it was as if that touch sensitized the rest of her body. She was suddenly achingly aware of her breasts pressed hard against his chest, of the bulge of his masculinity pressed hard against her belly.

For an instant, memories out of the past rose sharply, filling her with dread, but then they drifted away, carried on a stronger tide of the need he was waking in her.

Hugh lifted his head. Anna's eyes fluttered open, and she looked up at him, dismayed he had stopped kissing her. She didn't want him to stop. She wanted him to follow this miraculous journey to its end.

"Are you okay?" he asked huskily. "I felt you stiffen...."

"I'm okay," she managed to say, wondering why her voice sounded so thick. "I just had a memory...but it's gone now. Really."

He smiled, a sleepy, happy smile. "Yeah?"

"Yeah."

He hugged her tight, so tightly that her ribs felt the pressure, then loosened his hold just a little. "Can we move this to the couch? I don't know about you, but my legs are ready to give out."

Another spear of fear stabbed her, but she ignored it. A nod. She managed a nod.

He began to walk backward to the couch, drawing her with him. "I'd carry you, except I don't want you to feel you're not in control."

She was touched beyond words. And when he sat on the couch, he drew her onto his lap so that she straddled him, facing him.

"See?" he said. "You can get away at any time. I promise. Just say no, and I'll stop immediately, okay?"

She managed another nod and then sank against him with a sigh as he drew her close for another kiss. The fire already ignited grew even hotter, filling her with yearnings that didn't have names, needs and hungers she had never before known.

Gently, gently, she felt herself rocking against him. Part of her wanted to be embarrassed, but another part of her recognized that she couldn't stop. She needed him, needed to feel him between her legs, needed the pressure and release and rhythm of the movements of her hips.

Hugh's hips began to move, too, rising to meet hers in the most delicious way. When his hands slid down her back to grasp her hips, she was glad to feel them take charge, moving her even more deeply against him.

His mouth wandered from hers, following the contours of her cheeks, the hills and valleys of her chin and throat. The heat of his lips against the hollow of her throat made her gasp and arch against him in a way that filled her with new delight. He growled a sound of approval and licked her there with his tongue, fueling her passion.

She gasped and pressed harder against him. The ache between her legs was growing stronger, compelling her past all reason. She was a slave to it now, driven by needs as old as time, needs she had never before experienced.

Fear twinged sharply, disturbing her preoccupation. Not fear that Hugh might hurt her, but fear that she might not find what her body was so desperately seeking. For an instant she heard herself, heard the ragged pants of her breathing, the soft mewling sounds she was making, but before she could draw back in fear and embarrassment, Hugh spoke roughly.

"It's okay, Anna," he said raggedly. "It's okay.... Just let it...let it...."

Somehow she knew what he was trying to say, and the embarrassment faded away as she realized he was every bit as caught up in passion as she was.

There had been a time when she had thought passion to be an ugly, animalistic thing, but her body was teaching her otherwise now. It was showing her how wonderful she was able to feel, how strong the hunger was, how much she needed another human being to make her feel whole.

Higher and higher she climbed, afraid she might not be able to climb high enough, afraid she might fall, afraid she might suddenly freeze within reach of the pinnacle and never get there at all.

"Easy, sweetie," Hugh whispered. "Easy. There's plenty of time...."

She wanted to cry out, to wail that she couldn't, that she didn't know how to get there...and then his hands slipped from her hips to cup her breasts. Even through the layers of her sweater and bra she could feel the heat of his hands. He began to lightly rub his palms over the nubs of her swollen nipples. Electric sparks shot through her from her breasts to her womb and she felt everything inside her, everything, clench tightly.

And in one explosive instant, she reached the peak and tumbled over into completion.

Hugh felt her crest, and he gathered her trembling body close, holding her tightly while the aftershocks ripped through her. His own body was aching fiercely for the satisfaction he had just given her, but he ignored it.

Now was not the time, he told himself. It was plain as the warts on a toad that no one had ever given Anna anything sexually without demanding something in return—if anyone had ever given her anything at all—and he wanted to be different. He wanted her to know that it was possible for a man to *give* to her. He wanted her to know it was possible to be with a man who didn't use her to satisfy his own selfish needs.

But it was hard to resist the urge when she was so close. He could feel the heat of her through his jeans, and it would have been easy, so easy, to just press himself to her and find release. And it was hard, so hard, to be noble about this.

The thought made him smile wryly against her hair. It was such an odd word to apply to himself, *noble*. It didn't fit at all. No, he didn't want to be noble, he wanted to be *different*. He wanted to be the first man in her life who had given without taking. And he wanted her to feel safe with him.

Her tremors stopped finally, and she relaxed against him, making a soft sound of contentment when he ran his hand down her back. She was happy, and the realization filled him with joy and pride. It was such an easy thing to do for her—and such a sad thing that no one else in her life had done so.

Presently she lifted her head and looked shyly at him. "Did you…?" She trailed off, her cheeks turning red.

He shook his head and smiled. "Don't worry about it. This was for you."

"That's not fair."

He chuckled. "Making love isn't about being fair. It's about bringing pleasure to someone. I feel real good about what just happened, so let's leave it at that, okay?"

"But you said—"

"I needed to touch you. I did. And it was even nicer than I thought it would be." Afraid she might continue to press him when his willpower was at a phenomenally low ebb, he took her by the waist and swung her off his lap, setting her on the couch beside him.

"Well, will you look at that?" he said, touching the tip of her nose with his finger. "I fell down on the job."

"What?"

"I didn't even get your glasses off."

She laughed then, an easy, warm, delicious sound unlike any other laugh he had heard from her. It was also a sexy sound, and he found himself wanting to scoop her up and carry her away to bed with him so he could make love to her until they were both too weak to move.

Another time, he promised himself, even though he knew he wasn't going to let it happen. Even though he knew this was one woman he couldn't afford to get involved with.

He had to find a way to leave now, before he forgot his common sense and lost the last dregs of his self-control. But somehow he had to manage it without leaving her to wonder if she had done something wrong.

Damn it, he should have known better than to allow this to happen in the first place. Anna wasn't like other women. She didn't have enough self-esteem to deal with his departure right after the intimacy they had just shared. She would wonder what she had done to offend him or disappoint him.

So he had to hang around a while longer and ignore his own hunger as best he could. He had to sit within arm's reach of temptation and pretend he wasn't tempted at all. He needed his head examined.

"What I would really like right now," he said finally, "is another cup of coffee."

She hopped up off the couch as if she had been propelled by a spring. "I'll get it for you."

But he didn't let her bring it to him; he followed her into the kitchen. He feared that if he stayed on that couch, his mind was never going to stop suggesting ways to take advantage of it and her. After the intense moments just past, he had no trouble at all imagining what it would be like to make love completely to Anna Fleming, and he liked the images entirely too much for his own good.

They sat at the table again. Hugh absently picked up the cards they'd left scattered earlier and put them back in the box. Every time he glanced at Anna, he found her watching him with an expression between wonder and confusion. He didn't know which worried him more. The wonder, he decided. He didn't want her to fixate on him just because he was the first man in her life ever to give her an orgasm.

"Thank you," she said suddenly.

"For what?"

"For..." She paused, and color tinted her cheeks again. "I didn't know it could be like that, Hugh. I didn't know I could feel like that."

Oh, hell, he thought. Oh, hell. She was going to talk about it. He wanted to run before he could get sucked in any deeper. He already cared entirely too much about this woman, and listening to her say what he had already guessed was only going to make him care more.

"Almost everybody can feel like that," he heard himself say gruffly. "I didn't do anything special."

A shadow passed across her face. "Yes, you did," she argued quietly. "You most definitely *did* do something special. All the other men who've ever touched me did it for themselves. You did it for *me*."

"I did it for both of us," he said flatly. "You weren't the only one who enjoyed it."

She smiled shyly. "I hope not."

"Of course not." He took a swig of his coffee and tried to think of a way to end this conversation. He wasn't at all comfortable with what he'd started here, and now that his head was a little clearer, he was wondering why he hadn't managed to keep this relationship businesslike, the way he had originally intended. Anna Fleming had gone to his head in a dangerous way, and now she was turning him into a total idiot who couldn't even figure himself out.

"I need to be going," he said abruptly.

She looked surprised, then disappointed.

"It's late," he said. "You have to be in church early in

the morning, and you need your sleep.'' And I need some space to straighten out my own head. He rose from the table and watched as Anna rose with him. Something in her expression made him say, ''Anna, I just need some space to think. I didn't expect to take our relationship in this direction.''

She nodded her understanding, but her expression looked wooden in a way that told him he was hurting her, whether he intended to do so or not. And all of a sudden he could see that whatever he did now was going to hurt her. Stay or go, the price was wounding her. Hell's bells!

He went to get his jacket, aware that she trailed after him. He had to find something to say to her that would make it all right, but he was damned if he could think of a thing. He pulled his jacket on and zipped it up, pausing to look at her one more time before he left.

''I'm sorry,'' he said finally, because there didn't seem to be any other words to say to her. ''I'm sorry.'' Then he bent and brushed a light kiss on her lips.

''I'll call you.'' Then he stepped out into the frigid night, wondering if he was destined to hurt everyone he ever came in contact with.

Sometimes it sure as hell seemed like it.

Chapter 11

Anna woke in the morning feeling emotionally bruised. She didn't want to go to church. She didn't even want to get out of bed, but finally she padded into the kitchen and started a fresh pot of coffee. The pack of cards still lay on the table where Hugh had left them, and his coffee cup sat by the sink, waiting to be washed.

He hadn't meant to hurt her. At some deep level she knew that, but she felt hurt anyway. He had managed to get past some of her strongest barriers and awaken her to feelings she had never had before, and then he had taken flight as if it had all been a big mistake.

Which it had been, she admitted honestly. He wasn't wrong about that. He wanted her help with his ranch and nothing else. And she didn't want to get involved with either him or his ranch, because her past would eventually catch up with her and destroy the life she had built for herself.

Not that it was much of a life, she thought as she sat at her kitchen table and sipped coffee. She was barely making enough money to get by, she didn't have any real friends because she was afraid to let anyone get too close. Even her work with the church youth group, satisfying as it was, didn't give her any real ties to this community. She could pack up and move on at any time, if she had to.

Except for Lorna. Suddenly she thought of Lorna, and the idea of leaving that child behind hurt. Seriously hurt. As it was, she didn't know how she was going to handle it when the court ordered the girl to be put in a regular foster home, but at least if she stayed here she could keep in touch with Lorna.

Who did she think she was kidding? She didn't want to leave Conard City. For the first time in her life she had things she was truly afraid of losing. She didn't want to leave the church, or the youth group, or her job. Because even though she had tried so hard not to make any ties here, she had made them anyway. And if her past came out, she was going to lose everything that mattered to her: her job, Hugh, the respect of her employer…and most of all, Lorna.

She could have cried, except that she had long ago learned crying didn't help anything. She had cried when her stepfather raped her, but he hadn't stopped. She had cried when her real father had left, but he hadn't come back. She had cried when she had realized that she was either going to have to starve or sell her body to survive, but that hadn't changed the situation any. And she had cried after she'd slept with those men for money, but the hurt hadn't been mended.

So was she going to sit here and cry over something that hadn't happened yet? Hugh was right. Their relationship shouldn't take this direction. Absolutely not. It was too dangerous for her. She ought to be grateful to him for having the wisdom to see the problems, instead of moping because he hadn't wanted something more from her.

Her past hadn't been uncovered, nor was there any reason to think it would be, as long as she didn't get involved too deeply in Hugh's youth ranch project. As long as she stayed clear of that, no one would go digging around in her past.

That meant she couldn't keep Lorna, but surely she could live with having Lorna nearby. She would just be a sort of aunt to the girl, rather than a foster mother.

She could live with that. Yes, she could. It would hurt, but she was used to that kind of pain. Her whole life had been filled with it.

The phone rang, and she jumped. She almost decided not to answer it, but then she remembered Lorna was with Mary Jo Weeks. What if something had happened?

Tensing in expectation that it would be Al Lacey with yet another threat, she picked up the receiver.

"Anna?" It was Lorna, her voice full of warmth and laughter. "Anna, would it be all right if we meet you after the eleven-o'clock service instead of the nine-o'clock? We're just having so much fun that Mrs. Weeks said it would be okay with her if it's okay with you."

"That'll be fine, honey. I'll see you then."

Anna hung up the phone, feeling at once relieved and disappointed. She was missing Lorna, but on the other hand, this would give her time to get her own head together before she had to face the child.

She was walking down the hallway to her bedroom to get dressed when she heard a knock at the front door. She froze, wondering who it could possibly be, fearing that it might be Al Lacey come to create some new unpleasantness. But that was ridiculous, she told herself. There was no reason to believe the man would do anything at all except make nasty phone calls.

She went to peek out the front window and felt her heart leap when she saw Hugh standing out there on her front step. Without even thinking about the fact that she was still in her robe, she hurried to open the door.

"This is ridiculous," he said, and stepped inside. Never taking his eyes from her, he kicked the door closed. "I've been up all night thinking about you."

Something inside her quivered, and she felt suddenly breathless. "Good morning to you, too," she managed to say.

"Don't get difficult on me, Anna. This is difficult enough."

"What is?"

He glared. "I don't want to get involved with you. It'll mess up my plans to get your help with the ranch."

"I can't help you with the ranch. I told you that."

"Well, I didn't believe you. I still don't believe you. But you know what? I don't give a damn. I may be losing my mind, but nothing seems to matter except that I want you. I'm going out of my mind with wanting you."

A shiver passed through her, a shiver of delight and fear. On the one hand, she was thrilled that he wanted her enough to put everything else aside. On the other, she was scared to death of what that might mean. Despite what had happened last night, she still dreaded sex. The men she had been with before—only a few, she reminded herself honestly—had left her feeling raw and dirty and so very cold. She didn't ever want to feel that way again.

Hugh had given her hope last night, hope that it didn't always have to be a dirty, disgusting act. That it might be something in which she could find joy and delight. Going any further with him would be taking the risk that that frail hope would shatter. What if he left her feeling the way the others had? What if he left her feeling that she was nothing but a used husk?

"You're scared," he said.

She nodded jerkily. "I've had... My experiences have been...bad."

He stepped closer. "But last night wasn't bad, was it?"

She shook her head.

"It can all be that way, Anna. All of it. Give me a chance to show you."

Torn between desire and fear, she looked away, trying to make up her mind one way or the other. Remembering how bruised she had felt this morning, she wondered if she would feel bruised in a couple of hours when he left. It was such a risk!

"I'm sorry," he said abruptly. "I shouldn't have come."

He turned and reached for the doorknob, and Anna suddenly knew that the only thing worse than taking this risk would be not taking it.

"Hugh! Wait."

He paused, then turned slowly to face her. In his eyes she could see his yearning. "It's crazy," he said. "It's really crazy. I figured out a long time ago that I'd be smart to stay away from women. I mean...look at me. A down-at-the-heels handyman with a bad past and overinflated dreams of building a youth ranch. I freaked out, Anna. For all everybody in this town is acting like it never happened, I know it did, and so does everyone else. So what woman in her right mind would want anything to do with me?"

"Hugh..." Anna reached out to him, forgetting all her own fears as sympathy and concern for him rose in her. She wasn't the only one with a past or problems, and it was high time she started remembering that.

He shook his head. "Let me finish. I figured it would be

crazy to get involved. And it is. But…well, ever since the night of the wedding, I've been thinking about you more and more.''

Anna listened, uncertain what to make of this, fearing the worst and hoping for the best.

He sighed heavily. ''I see secrets in your eyes, Anna Fleming. I see pain and fear, and shadows from the past. I guess maybe you can understand that the past haunts me, too.''

She nodded. That was indeed something she could connect with.

''The thing about the past,'' he continued, ''is that it has only as much power as you give it. You have to face it straight on. Quit hiding from it. Accept it.''

She caught her breath and held it, trying to understand what he meant. Did he mean she should confront her own past? She couldn't do that. It would ruin her!

''I've been hiding,'' he went on. ''Plain and simple. I've turned my back on where I've been and how I came to be here, and I've been acting like a damn turtle with my head stuck in my shell, avoiding anything that might make me face all that.

''But I'm facing it anyway, sweetie. I'm facing it because I can't get you out of my mind. I'm facing it because I want you so damn much I can't stay in hiding anymore. I've got to accept who I am and what I've done, or I'll never be able to ask anybody else to accept me.''

She nodded, understanding, but terrified of where this was leading. Had he somehow found out about her past?

''I was a soldier,'' he said. ''I hurt people. Some of the people I hurt thought I was a friend. But I wasn't. I was an enemy soldier behind enemy lines who was pretending to be one of them. And because of me, some of them died. I have to live with that. Tell me, Anna, can a woman want somebody like me?''

Her heart went out to him, and she instinctively held out her hands. "Of course a woman could want you, Hugh! Of course she could."

He gave her a crooked smile. "What about the woman who's standing in front of me?"

"You don't know me...."

"Then tell me, Anna. Tell me what it is that puts those shadows in your eyes."

"I can't. I can't!"

"Did you kill anybody? Maim anybody?"

"No!"

"Are the cops looking for you?"

"No."

"Then you don't have any secrets worth hiding at all." He took one of her hands and squeezed it gently.

He didn't understand, she thought. He didn't understand at all.

"I want to make love to you, Anna. Will you let me?"

After what he had just told her, she couldn't possibly say no. She couldn't hurt him that way. And it suddenly struck her that she had once given herself for money. How could it possibly be as bad to give herself to a friend out of compassion?

"Hugh..." She whispered his name and stepped toward him.

He lowered his voice. "When do you have to be at church?"

"At eleven."

"Not enough time, but it'll have to do." Holding her hand, he tugged her gently down the hallway toward her bedroom. "You try so hard to hide yourself," he said quietly as he led the way. "You pin up your hair, and wear glasses and those shapeless dresses. But you know what, Anna? I've never seen a more beautiful woman, especially now, with your hair down."

Her bed was still rumpled from her difficult night. He pulled back the covers, then faced her. "Take off your robe for me?"

She couldn't do it. Men had made her undress for them before. Her stepfather had demanded it. She couldn't do it now. It was too much like before. Was she out of her mind? She couldn't possibly do this…and yet she couldn't possibly stop.

"Can I help?" he asked finally.

She nodded shakily.

He reached for the belt of her terry-cloth robe and untied it. With gentle hands, he pushed it from her shoulders and let it fall to the floor. She shivered, even though she wore a warm flannel nightgown.

"I like this," he said, gently touching her sleeve. "Soft, warm and cuddly."

Then, as if he sensed she was verging on flight or collapse, he guided her to the bed and helped her lie down.

Standing beside the bed, he reached for his own clothing. His jacket flew across the room to land on a chair. His shirt followed, revealing his muscled chest and broad shoulders. The pale light of the winter day that filtered through the drawn curtains was just enough to let her see how powerful he was. How beautiful he was.

He reached for the buckle of his belt and dropped his jeans, revealing olive drab boxer shorts. He sat on the bed beside her, yanked off his boots and kicked his jeans away. Then, still wearing his shorts, he stretched out beside her.

Her heart was hammering so hard, she felt as if she

couldn't get enough air. Turning her head, she looked at him.

He propped himself up on his elbow and smiled down at her. "This is your show, lady," he said softly. "If I do anything you don't like, anything that frightens you, just say so."

She managed another nod.

"God," he said, "you look so frightened." Reaching out, he gently stroked her cheek with a fingertip. "Don't be afraid. I swear I won't hurt you."

She didn't see how this could do anything *except* hurt her, but she didn't say so. Hugh wanted this so much that he'd come back here this morning and laid himself bare to her. How could she possibly deny him?

Bending, he kissed her, and almost from the instant his mouth met hers, she felt something inside her softening and opening to him. Part of her wanted to keep her distance, to remain cold and unmoved as she had once done to protect herself. But somehow she knew that wasn't going to be possible this time. Hugh had already gotten within her defenses, and it was too late to protect herself. What happened now was going to affect her as strongly as anything in her life ever had.

He sprinkled soft kisses on her face, then trailed his mouth down her throat. Before she even knew he was doing it, the buttons on the neck of her gown fell open, and his mouth began trailing hot kisses over her chest. No one had ever kissed her this way before, as if he was trying to give rather than take, and she felt herself grow even softer.

He didn't ask anything of her. He allowed her to lie there, and he asked not a thing as his hands began to roam her gentle curves through the flannel.

A slow heat began to build in her as he explored her.

Gentle tongues of flame seemed to leap from his hands everywhere he touched her. Even the caress of the flannel against her skin began to arouse her, sensitizing nerve endings she had never before been aware of.

Across her breasts and down to her belly his hand roamed. She had been touched in these places before, but never like this. Never with such dedication to pleasing her, never with concern that she like what was being done to her.

But Hugh cared. She could feel it in every kiss and caress, and it began to thaw something long frozen inside her. She felt her arms move of their own accord, felt her hands grip his shoulders, felt that wonderful deep pulsing begin again between her legs.

"You're so sweet," he whispered to her, and dropped a gentle, questing kiss on her mouth. "Open for me, Anna. Let me in."

Her mouth opened to receive him, and at the same instant his hand slipped up under her gown, turning the gentle glow of passion into a conflagration that burned through her and burned away every preconception about this act that she'd ever had.

Nothing and no one had ever made her feel this way before.

"Want me, Anna," he whispered raggedly. "Oh, sweetheart, want me, too!"

"I want you," she said huskily, hardly recognizing her own voice. "Oh, Hugh, I want you, too."

"Thank heaven," he whispered, and buried his face in the side of her neck. His hand, rough and callused from hard labor, found her naked breast and closed on it. A ribbon of sheer delight ran from her breast to her core, causing her womb to clench in reaction, and for the first time in her life she felt herself grow damp with passion.

"So sweet," he murmured again.

Somehow her nightgown was up around her shoulders and his mouth had closed on her breast, sucking gently at first, then more strongly, as her hips began a helpless undulation in response. When his hand trailed down to her dewy center, she clamped her thighs around it, holding him there, wanting him never to stop touching her there, wanting answers to all the mysteries.

Her own hands began to wander restlessly over his back and shoulders, trying to draw him closer. She needed him now, she realized dizzily. She needed his weight on her and his heat within her. His mouth and hand would never be enough to assuage the roaring hunger he had built in her.

"Hugh...oh, please..."

"In a minute...just a minute...."

His finger slipped between her dewy folds and gave her a touch so exquisite that it was almost painful. She cried out, and he swallowed the sound with another kiss. Relentlessly he stroked her, teaching her that pleasure and pain were indistinguishable, carrying her higher and higher with each movement of his hand.

And then he took his hand away. She made a sound of protest, but before it fully left her lips, he was back, moving over her, between her legs. Instinctively she lifted herself to him and felt him slide home.

Nothing had ever felt so right.

With each thrust, he answered the need deep inside her, taking her higher and higher on a tide she was helpless to resist. Then, just when she thought she could take no more, he lowered his head and took her breast in his mouth, sending yet another blinding shaft of pleasure zinging to her core.

She shattered then, into a thousand flaming pieces of pleasure. Moments later, she felt the shudder rip through him, heard him groan, and knew he had joined her.

He coaxed her into the shower with him. "Trust me," he said, "you don't want to go to church smelling like a woman who's just been loved."

She blushed and tried to draw the covers higher, but he tugged them insistently away and let his eyes feast on her.

"You're gorgeous," he said, and smiled right into her eyes. "And now I've seen it all, so you don't have to be shy anymore."

When he tugged her hand, she rose and went with him to the bathroom. She had been naked with men before, but only this time seemed to matter. Her attitude toward her body had changed, she realized suddenly. It was no longer an object that had once been used against her will. Now it was an integral part of her, not simply a possession she felt detached from. That detachment had protected her in the past, and now she worried that its absence had left her vulnerable.

But that didn't seem to matter, at least not right now as Hugh stood with her in the tub and soaped her gently while hot water sprayed on them. His touches were gentle and arousing, and when she realized that her body was awakening once again, color stained her cheeks.

He saw the blush and correctly interpreted it. "It's okay," he said gently. "It's all right." His soapy hand slipped between her legs and caressed her gently. "It's supposed to feel like this."

She found herself clinging desperately to his shoulders, afraid that at any moment her legs were going to give out. And suddenly, twisting out of the depths of her mind came an image of herself and what she was doing. She was behaving like a wanton, something she had long ago sworn she would never do.

"I can't," she gasped. "I can't!"

"It's okay...."

"No!" She shoved him away and grabbed the shower curtain, yanking it open. Nearly stumbling, she climbed out of the tub, grabbed a towel and ran for her bedroom. Once there, she closed the door and leaned against it, shaking and weeping all at once.

How could she have done this to herself again? How could she carry on like this when she had sworn she would never again let a man touch her that way? Oh, God, was she losing her mind?

A gentle rap on the door caught her attention and caused her heart to leap into her throat. She didn't want to face him. She couldn't face him. Not now!

"Anna? Anna, did I hurt you?"

"No...no..."

He was silent for a moment. "I guess I made a mistake," he said finally. "I'm sorry. I'll leave now."

Part of her desperately wanted him to stay, but the part of her that was terrified of what she was becoming kept her silent.

"Anna? I'm going now. But...maybe it's high time you faced your past, because you're sure as hell not going to have a future until you do. I'll see you around."

Her past. Why did he keep referring to her past? Oh, God, what if he knew about it? What if he had found out? What if that was why he had wanted a fling with her, because he figured she was cheap?

The thought filled her with even more shame, and finally she collapsed on her bed, weeping silently for things lost and things that could never be.

* * *

Hugh left Anna's house feeling bruised and angry, though he wasn't quite sure why he felt angry. Maybe because he had let himself down. He'd promised himself that he wouldn't get involved with a woman, and then he'd made the supremely stupid move of getting involved with a woman he needed to have a business relationship with. For all Anna protested that she wouldn't help him with his ranch, he had persisted in believing that he would find the right key to unlock her resistance. Now he had gone and made it all but impossible by getting sexually involved with her. He couldn't imagine any way on earth that she would now consent to a business relationship with him.

That made him furious at himself.

Then there was Anna and what had happened between them. He had honestly thought he'd carried her past her very natural reluctance to let a man make love to her. Instead, he apparently hadn't done anything of the sort. As far as he could tell, he had simply added to her injuries.

And it didn't matter a drop of water in the Sahara that he hadn't meant to hurt her at all.

Nor did he feel qualified to figure out her emotional state or to try to help her with it. Apparently matters were worse than he'd suspected, and simply enjoying making love wasn't going to get her past her problem.

So, he told himself, the only thing he could do now was stay clear. In time she would realize that he wasn't going to make a move on her, and then maybe they could get back to discussing a business relationship. He needed her for the ranch. People who could work well with children, who could inspire in them the kind of affection and trust Anna did in them didn't exactly grow on trees around here, and in dealing with a troubled child her ability was worth far more than a slew of professional degrees. She just naturally loved kids, and they just naturally loved her back. He needed her to be the foster mother to all the children he hoped to help. Professional expertise he could hire, but a mom was something else altogether.

But he'd gone and done all the wrong things, and had probably blown it for good.

Cursing his stupidity and his sex drive, he drove back to his apartment. If there was any mending that could be done, only time could do it. He had to keep clear of her and bide his time. There weren't any other options.

Not now. He'd blown all the other ones.

Chapter 12

A week later, Anna and Lorna went to court together to hear Judge Williams announce that with the prosecutor's agreement, she was going to withhold adjudication on the arson charge. If Lorna completed a year's worth of the psychological treatment she had already begun, then the charge would be dismissed. If she failed to complete treatment, the matter would be reopened.

Then the judge turned to another matter. "Miss Lacey, your father has decided to plead to the charges against him in exchange for receiving probation rather than a jail sentence. He would be required to move to another city and to stay away from you, and social services will investigate his fitness to parent your sister. However, I'm not going to agree to this plea bargain if you aren't happy with it. As I see it, taking the deal will prevent you from having to testify in open court against your father. But if you want him to go to jail, you're going to have to testify. No one can make that decision for you. Do you understand?"

Lorna nodded. Anna looked at her, feeling anger and dismay on the child's behalf. It seemed so unfair that a girl of thirteen should have to make decisions like this.

"I guess what it comes down to," the judge went on, "is how badly you want your father to go to jail right now. If that's important to you, then you'll have to testify. On the other hand, taking the plea will require him to move a long way away from you and forbid him from ever seeing you again. I can give you a few days to think this over, but I'll need your answer by Monday. All right?"

Lorna nodded again. "Yes, ma'am."

"And now we come to the question of a permanent foster home for you."

"I want to stay with Miss Anna, Your Honor."

Anna felt a bubble of panic begin to rise in the pit of her stomach. How was she going to handle this? She would love to have Lorna live with her, but there was no way she could take the risk.

The judge looked at her. "Miss Fleming, how do you feel about that?"

"I...um..." She looked at Lorna and wondered how she could possibly say no, even though there wasn't a chance in hell that she would get permanent custody of Anna.

"I could just give you guardianship," the judge said, "but I'd prefer it if you would apply to become a permanent foster parent. By doing so, the state will be able to pay you something toward Miss Lacey's upkeep. In my experience, church secretaries rarely get paid enough to support themselves, let alone another person. Now, I'm planning to require Dr. Lacey pay child support, but given that you have no official standing unless you become an approved foster parent, I'm not sure that he couldn't make things difficult for you somewhere down the road. If this is something you want to do, if you do indeed wish to keep Miss Lacey per-

manently, then you'll have to apply to become approved.
And I'll need your answer on that Monday, as well.''

"Yes, Your Honor."

Two minutes later, she and Lorna stepped out of the
courthouse into a bright, cold afternoon. Sun glared off the
snow that covered the square, and Anna squinted.

"Anna?"

"Yes?" she turned to look at Lorna.

"Don't you want to keep me?" The child's lower lip
quivered.

"Yes, of course I do! I'm just not sure it's possible. Look,
could we talk about this at home?"

"No! I don't want to talk about it at home! You don't
want me. Nobody wants me."

"Lorna…" But the girl was already turning and running.
Anna started to go after her, but she slipped on a patch of
ice and fell into a snowbank. Before she could regain her
feet, Lorna had disappeared around the corner of a building
and vanished from sight.

Shivering, shaking from the emotions that buffeted her,
Anna stood on the icy walk for a long time, wondering what
the hell she was going to do now.

"I'll have my men keep an eye out for her," Nate Tate
told her when she called him an hour later and told him
what had happened. "She's just upset, sweet pea. She'll
come home."

"I hope so. I can't imagine where she might have gone,
Nate. All her friends are in school for another hour and a
half."

"She's probably just walking around in the cold, feeling
sorry for herself." He sighed. "I don't mean to sound harsh
here, sweet pea, but kids that age are a royal pain in the

butt. Everything is so damn cataclysmic to them. Now, I'm
not saying that little girl hasn't been through an awful lot,
and she's got as much right to drown in self-pity as anybody, but all she's doing right now is getting colder and
lonelier. Eventually she'll turn up. They almost always do.''

But Anna, who had once run away, knew exactly how far
a child that age could go, knew exactly what could happen
to kids who didn't come home.

She didn't share any of that with Nate, though. It would
open too many doors that she wanted to keep closed.

Then she had to call Dan and tell him that she wouldn't
be back to work that afternoon, because Lorna had run
away.

''No, of course you have to stay at home in case she
shows up,'' he said. ''I know exactly how you feel. My
Ginny ran away last year.''

''Really? I didn't know that.''

''Of course not. I didn't tell anybody. Thank God she
came home before I finally called the sheriff. But I was
about out of my mind with worry.''

''Why did she run away?''

''Because I grounded her for a week for being out past
her curfew.'' He sighed. ''Teenagers are the devil to raise.
I'll be glad when mine are safely grown up. Call me if you
hear anything, and I'll do likewise.''

Anna found it impossible to hold still, so she paced her
house from one end to the other. At first Jazz trotted after
her, right at her heels, but finally the puppy grew weary and
curled up on Lorna's bed and fell asleep.

She wasn't used to the house being this quiet anymore,
Anna suddenly realized. These days, whenever she was
home, Lorna was usually here, too, and there was music in
the background, or the sounds of her talking on the phone

with one of her friends, or the sounds of her friends who
had come to visit. Now there were no sounds at all except
the whoosh of the central heat and the whine of the refrigerator compressor. And right now the only sound on earth
Anna wanted to hear was the sound of Lorna's voice.

She had the worst urge to call Hugh and tell him what
had happened, but she didn't dare. Since they had made
love, he'd stayed away from her. On the rare occasions
when they happened to run into one another, he always gave
her a pleasant greeting, but he didn't linger to talk.

He must know about her past, she decided. He must have
heard about it from somewhere—maybe from Al Lacey,
who had made those threats. Her heart slammed as she considered the possibility.

Her juvenile records had been sealed, but sealing them
didn't mean they were totally inaccessible. Someone with
money—and Al Lacey certainly had money—could probably hire someone who knew how to get hold of those things.
What if he had? What if it was already being whispered
around town that she had been arrested for prostitution?
What if Hugh had heard about it, and that was why he had
dropped her so suddenly and so completely? What if that
was why he no longer wanted her help with his ranch?

Her heart climbed into her throat again and lodged there,
threatening to choke her as she faced all the possibilities.
But no, she told herself, if gossip was going around the
community about her, she certainly would have caught wind
of it. At the very least, some people would be treating her
differently, and she had seen none of that.

But the fact that the story wasn't in common circulation
didn't mean Hugh hadn't heard it somehow. The more she
thought about it, the more convinced she was that he *did*
know, and that was why he was avoiding her. In fact, that

was probably why he had come on to her in the first place. Because he knew she was cheap.

But what did it matter what he thought? It was nothing but what she would have expected from someone who learned what she had done. They would all turn their backs on her, all these nice people who were so kind to her now. None of them would want to admit that they knew her.

But none of that really seemed to matter right now. The only thing that mattered to her was Lorna, and whether the girl was all right. Closing her eyes, Anna prayed that the phone would ring and someone would tell her where Lorna was. It didn't matter if it was a deputy sheriff, a schoolteacher, or the parent of one of her friends. Just someone, anyone, with the news that Lorna was all right.

A half hour after school let out, Anna started calling Lorna's friends. None of them had seen her since earlier in the day. Anna's worry mounted with every passing minute, until she felt as if she were going to crawl right out of her skin.

The early-winter night fell and brought with it a whole new surge of anxiety. In the dark Lorna would be harder to find. In the dark there was a lot more danger to a young girl on her own.

She fed Jazz her evening meal, then stepped out back with the puppy, leaving the door open so she would hear the phone ring. No one called. By nine she began to fear the worst. Lorna had hitched a ride with someone and was miles away. Lorna had been kidnapped. Lorna was lying dead in a ditch somewhere....

Just after nine, someone rapped loudly at the door. The knock wasn't Lorna's gentle tap, and fear clutched at Anna. Her heart in her throat, she ran to answer it.

Lorna was standing there, with Hugh right behind her. The child's expression was sullen. Hugh looked frazzled.

"I believe you were looking for someone," Hugh said. "She's here, but she doesn't want to be here, so...if you don't mind, Miss Anna, I'll just step inside to keep an eye on her until the two of you settle the problem."

Anna hardly heard him. Before he had even finished speaking, she stepped forward and threw her arms around Lorna, hugging her as tightly as she could. "I was so worried," she said shakily. "I was so afraid something bad had happened to you...."

Lorna refused to hug her back. She stood stiff and unresponsive. When Anna finally let go of her, she walked inside like a condemned prisoner.

Anna looked after her, then looked up at Hugh. She hardly noticed the frigid air that was making her shiver. "Inside," he said. "It's cold out here. You'll get frostbite."

She turned and went into the living room. Lorna stood there with her shoulders hunched and her head bowed. Her expression was downright mutinous. Figuring she wouldn't learn anything there, Anna looked at Hugh. "Where did you find her?"

"She came to me, actually. I had no idea she'd run away. Along about eight-thirty, there she was, knocking on my door. She wanted to know if she could come live at the ranch with me."

Anna nodded and drew a deep breath, trying to calm the storm of emotions that was buffeting her, so she could think.

"For some damn reason," Hugh continued, "Lorna thinks you don't want her. Me, I don't exactly think that's true, but maybe I'm wrong. Anyway, I got her to agree to come here and talk to you about it."

"She doesn't want me," Lorna said stonily. "Every time I ask her, she has an excuse."

Hugh didn't say anything. Anna felt her heart squeeze and begin to ache anew. She didn't see any good way out of this, for either her or the child. What purpose would it serve to open her past to scrutiny when it would only disqualify her anyway?

But that seemed like a lame excuse now. By refusing to explain the reasons for her hesitation, maybe she was hurting Lorna even more than she would be hurt if Anna couldn't be approved as her foster parent. Maybe, for Lorna's sake, she had to explain her hesitation. She didn't have to go into detail, after all. The mere existence of a police record ought to be enough to make Lorna understand the problem.

"I *do* want you," Anna said.

"Yeah. Right. Like my parents want me." Lorna's voice cracked. "You heard the judge. He's willing to go away and never see me again. And you know what? So's my mom. They didn't even try to fight it."

Anna caught her breath as understanding hit her. Lorna didn't see how the offered plea bargain would protect her. She saw it as her parents giving her up without even a fight.

"Lorna—"

The girl shook her head sharply. "The counselor said my dad doesn't really love me. If he really loved me, he wouldn't have hurt me like this. She said he would have put me first, before his urges. So he doesn't really love me."

Feeling helpless, Anna could only listen.

"So okay," Lorna said with a little shrug of her shoulder. She still wouldn't look at them. "I can handle that. He's sick, you know? That's what everyone says, that he has to be really sick to do what he did to me. And maybe sick people can't really love. But what about my mom? Why doesn't *she* love me? What's wrong with me?''

"Honey, there's nothing wrong with you at all," Anna said fiercely. "Absolutely nothing."

"Then why don't you want me?"

The question cut Anna to her soul. Tears burned in her eyes, and her throat tightened as she faced just how seriously she had hurt this child with her hesitations. "Lorna, I *do* want you. I love you very much. The problem isn't you at all. It's *me*. They'll never let me be your foster mother. Not even if I beg and plead."

For the first time, Lorna looked at her. "Why not?"

"Remember when I told you what a mistake it is to run away when you're only fourteen? How there's no way to live on the streets when you're too young to even get a job?"

Lorna nodded.

"Well…I did some things that were wrong so I could get by. I stole food…and other things. And I have a police record. They'll never let me be your foster mother when I have a police record."

Hugh cleared his throat. "I guess I'll be going now. You two have a lot to talk about." Without pausing, he opened the door and left.

Lorna and Anna looked at one another across the gulf, and at the same instant closed the distance between them. This time, when Anna hugged Lorna, the girl hugged her back. And both of them burst into tears.

After she called the sheriff's office and Dan to tell them Lorna had come home, Anna cooked them a simple dinner of hamburgers and French fries. For the moment, Lorna seemed content to let things rest where they were. But after dinner, when they were washing the dishes, she brought the subject up again.

"I don't want to go live with strangers, Anna."

"Maybe they wouldn't be strangers."

"They probably will be. I might not even be able to stay here in Conard City."

"Who told you that?"

"The psychologist. She said that sometimes, because there aren't any places available in a town, kids get sent to other towns. I don't want to leave all my friends."

"I can certainly understand that." In fact, it seemed unbearably cruel to uproot the child that way after all that had happened.

"She tried to tell me it could be a good thing to go somewhere nobody would know what had happened to me, but I like it better here. My friends know what happened, and they don't hate me. Some of the grown-ups probably do, but I don't care about them."

Anna nodded as she finished drying a bowl and put it away. That was the last of the dishes, so she joined Lorna at the table.

"I don't think it's fair," Lorna said. "People keep telling me I didn't do anything wrong, but I keep getting punished anyway."

"I don't think you're being punished, honey."

"It feels like I am." Lorna found a crumb on the table and pushed it around with her forefinger. "Sometimes it's just plain awful being a kid."

"Yes, it is."

Lorna gave her a wan smile. "I still want you to be my foster mother. Are you really sure they wouldn't let you?"

"Pretty sure."

"So I'm supposed to go live with somebody who doesn't

know me and doesn't care about me. Somebody who is maybe doing it because they want the money."

"I don't think anybody becomes a foster parent because they want the money," Anna said, stifling a qualm. "I don't think it's very much money, anyway. I think most people do it because they like children and want to have children in the house."

"Maybe. But that doesn't mean they'll like *me*. Or even really care about me. Why should they? I'll be a stranger."

"But that would change, honey. Anybody who gets to know you will love you."

Lorna shook her head. "Maybe not. But you already love me, so why should I have to give you up? It's not right!"

It didn't seem right to Anna, either, but she didn't know what to say to Lorna. If she agreed, she might be encouraging the girl to nurture false hopes, and that would only hurt more in the long run.

On the other hand, maybe she was just being too cowardly.

As if she had read her mind, Lorna looked at her and said, "How can you know they won't let you if you don't try?"

Anna drew a long breath, facing the stark reality of her situation. She had always been a runner, someone who fled when things got tough. Maybe that was what she was doing now. And maybe she owed it to herself and Lorna to quit running.

"I'll think about it," she finally said to Lorna. "I need to think about it, all right? Give me a few days. Not because I don't want to keep you, Lorna, but because I'm going to be opening up a real can of worms here. Regardless of the decision the authorities make about you, it's going to change my life forever."

Lorna nodded, her eyes suddenly shining with hope. "Okay," she said. "The judge said until Monday. I can wait that long."

Anna couldn't sleep that night. The past was a bear growling at the door of her mind, demanding to be let in. Long after Lorna had fallen asleep, she paced the house, listening to the night wind moan around the corners and wondering if she could live with a big mistake. Because whether she applied to be Lorna's permanent guardian or refused to do so, she was going to have to live with consequences of major proportions.

The famous rock and a hard place, she thought wearily at one point. Either one was apt to injure her seriously.

But not applying to be Lorna's guardian was also apt to injure Lorna. The weight of that rested heavily on her heart.

Finally, weary of pacing, she sat on the couch with Jazz, cuddling the puppy close in her lap.

Seeing Hugh tonight had added to her miseries, she realized. She was missing him with an ache that went to her very soul, and seeing him again had only made her more aware of it. But the quick way he had left when she mentioned she had a police record had only convinced her that he already knew all the details. Otherwise he surely would have been curious enough to stay, wanting to know more, wouldn't he?

At some point she dozed off without even being aware of it. She heard her stepfather's voice as he came into the room in the middle of the night, calling her name softly, telling her that he wanted to play their "little game." He'd always tried to make it seem like a game, but she had never believed it was.

And suddenly she was a child again, lying beneath her

blankets with her eyes squeezed shut, trying to convince him that she was asleep, too heavily asleep to be awakened by his whispers and his touches. She could feel him sitting on her bed, could feel the blankets being pulled away, could feel her heart hammering wildly as she tried to control her breathing so he wouldn't guess she was awake and feeling as if she was going to suffocate because her fear made her need air and more air....

Anna jerked awake, bathed in a cold sweat of terror, the events as vivid in her mind as if they had happened just yesterday. Jazz sensed her fear and whimpered.

With a trembling hand, she petted the dog, then lifted her to the floor. Jazz stretched and yawned, then headed for the kitchen to find water.

Anna stayed where she was, staring blindly at her familiar living room, trying to shake the terror that sleep had brought her. He couldn't hurt her anymore, she told herself. The man couldn't touch her or hurt her ever again.

But he was still controlling her life. Even at a distance and over all these years, he was still affecting every decision she made. His control was an evil thing, causing her to make choices she would not have otherwise made.

And so it had been since the first time he had come to her room. Except for him, she would be a very different person, living a very different life. Once she had had dreams of becoming a doctor. Once she had even wanted to be an astronaut. And all of that had been lost to her fear. Fear of him. Fear of the things she had done while trying to escape him. Fear of what other people would think of her.

He had given her a legacy of fear, and there didn't seem to be any way to get rid of it.

You have to face your past or you'll never have a future. Hugh's words came back to her, a mere whisper among all the frantic thoughts scrambling around in her brain. He was right, she realized. Absolutely right. She could live the rest of her life in hiding, or she could face her past and refuse to let it control her ever again.

So easy to say. So hard to do. She'd made a practice of hiding for so long that she honestly didn't know if she could find the courage to do what Hugh had suggested and what Lorna needed.

And if she did, would she really be free if her entire life was destroyed and she needed to start over again?

There didn't seem to be any answers, and Monday loomed all too close.

Chapter 13

"Hugh is still coming for Thanksgiving dinner, isn't he?" Lorna asked.

It was Wednesday morning, just five days before the judge expected Anna's answer, just two days since Lorna had run away. Two of the longest days of Anna's life. In the past she'd always believed herself to be decisive, but all of a sudden she had turned into a dithering idiot. Should she or shouldn't she?

Just this morning she had finally decided what to do, and now Thanksgiving was staring her in the face. She had a sudden urge to scream wildly.

"I don't know," she finally managed to say, hoping she sounded more pleasant than she felt. The lack of sleep the past two nights was taking a serious toll.

"He doesn't come over anymore," Lorna remarked. "Doesn't he like us?"

"I'm sure he likes us just fine," Anna said. Right now she would like to have a close, personal conversation with the person who had invented Thanksgiving. How in the world was she going to manage to make a festive day for Lorna when she felt as if the whole world were coming apart at the seams? "He's just been very busy."

"Then he'll be coming tomorrow for dinner?"

"I'll call him and ask," Anna said, wanting an end to this conversation *now*. In fact, given the mood she was in, she would like to serve Hugh Gallagher the worst Thanksgiving feast he'd ever eaten. She couldn't believe the way he had used her and then vanished from her life. No, she admitted miserably, she *could* understand it perfectly well. It was what everyone else was going to do when they learned the *real* story of Anna Fleming. Yup, she was going to come out of this with nothing at all except another miserable memory.

"Well, I hope he comes," Lorna said as she picked up her schoolbooks. "He said he would."

Which probably meant that he would, Anna thought gloomily. Whatever else he might be, he was a man who did what he promised. Except that he had promised not to hurt her, hadn't he? Yet he had hurt her worse than she had been hurt in a long, long time.

"Remember," Lorna said, "I get off early today."

"At one, right?"

"Right."

"Why don't you just come to the office, then? Dan said he'll let me off early, too, and we can go shopping for a turkey."

"Great!"

Anna watched as Lorna left on her way up to the corner to meet a friend to walk to school with. Then she turned her attention to finishing her own preparations. Thanksgiving was so late this year that she was already panicking about Christmas. So much to do at the church and with the youth group, and so little time. And the shopping. This year she had to shop for Lorna, and she was already beginning to wonder what she would be able to manage financially.

Lorna, on the other hand, seemed to have stopped worrying about everything. Apparently she was convinced she was going to live with Anna. Anna wished she was half so convinced herself.

The only thing she knew for sure was that this morning she had decided to take the risk. She would face the demons and apply to become Lorna's foster mother. But to get to that point, she had to screw up her courage and talk to the only people she knew who could give her a reference, and tell them the entire story. Now she was dithering about when and how to bring up the subject.

But first she decided to call Hugh and get that out of the way. Besides, if she waited to call him, he would be off on some job, and she wouldn't know what size turkey to buy for tomorrow.

How had she gotten herself into this mess?

Hugh answered his phone on the first ring. Apparently he was up and about and ready to start the day. Anna wished she felt as cheerful as he sounded.

"Hi," she said, feeling as if she were going to choke. "It's Anna. Lorna and I are wondering if you're still coming for Thanksgiving dinner tomorrow?"

She knew she wasn't imagining his hesitation, but finally he said, "Sure. Absolutely. What time?"

"Say two?"

"I'll be there with bells on. Thanks, Anna."

When she hung up, she was shaking. How could it be so difficult to make a simple phone call? She looked down at her hands and marveled at the way they were trembling. The same way they trembled when she called her stepfather.

She closed her eyes, drawing a deep breath to calm herself. She was just overtired, she decided. Overtired and overworried. Naturally she was shaking. All she needed was a good nap.

The phone rang, and she reached for it, half hoping it was Hugh calling back with an excuse. What she heard made her scalp prickle.

"Anna?"

It was a woman's voice, and even after sixteen years Anna still recognized it. Her throat locked, and her hand froze on the receiver. She couldn't have moved a muscle to save her life.

"Anna, it's your mother." Rose's voice sounded taut, stretched almost to breaking. Even over the hundreds of miles, Anna could hear her rapid breathing.

"How did you find me?" Her own voice sounded attenuated, strained by the effort of passing through her constricted throat.

"Someone…someone called me. Anna—"

"Who called you?" Anna squeezed her eyes shut, wanting more than anything in the world to slam the phone down, but utterly unable to.

"A private investigator."

Her heart slammed so hard it hurt. Her lips felt wooden, and her mouth was suddenly as parched as the desert. "What did he want?"

"He wanted to know about…what happened with Van."

Van was her stepfather. The man who had inhabited her nightmares for so long. And suddenly Anna was angry. She had no doubt who was behind the investigator. "So what did you tell him? That I was a lying little slut?"

"Anna! Oh, Anna, no…" Her mother's voice broke on a sob. "Anna, baby…oh, God! I told him it was none of his damn business, and if he wanted to know, he ought to ask you. But I managed to get out of him where you live, and I...Anna, I *needed* to talk to you!''

Anna's fingers were aching from the way she was gripping the phone, and she was pressing it so hard to her ear that it hurt. She ought to hang up right now, she told herself, but somehow she couldn't. ''So talk,'' she heard herself say woodenly.

''I called because...because... Anna, I was wrong. I was never more wrong in my life. I should have believed you when you first tried to tell me what was going on. I'm so sorry...so sorry.... I was your mother. I should have protected you....'' Her voice broke into sobs.

Anna listened to the woman cry, feeling so detached that she knew it was unnatural. This ought to be hurting, or making her angry, or something. Anything except leaving her so far removed that she felt less involvement than she would have felt listening to a stranger on the street.

''When did you reach this startling conclusion?'' she finally asked.

Rose's sobs had lessened, and she managed to answer brokenly. ''About five years after you...ran away, I found the photographs.''

The photographs. Anna felt her heart sink to her toes. Detachment was deserting her, being replaced by stark fear. The photographs. For all these years she had tried not to think of the pictures Van had taken of her. Of them. Pictures that were somewhere out there like a ticking time bomb, waiting to fall into the wrong hands and ruin the rest of her life. ''What did you do with them?'' Nothing, probably. Her mother had always been good at doing nothing.

''I...used them to make Van give me a quick, clean divorce. And then I burned them. All of them. Anna, I'm so sorry I didn't believe you...."

More sobs. This time Anna heard them differently. Much as she didn't want it to, her mother's grief was reaching her, however dimly.

"I've been trying to find you ever since," Rose went on, her voice shaking. "I've looked everywhere.... I didn't know you'd changed your name."

"So what do you want from me?"

"Nothing! Nothing. Really. I just...I just wanted you to know that I know. And I was really worried about this private investigator calling. Anna, somebody must want to hurt you."

So Al Lacey was trying to carry out his threat. Anna almost wanted to laugh, because she had already made up her mind to tell the truth to the only people she really cared about. There was nothing Lacey could do to her now that she wasn't going to do to herself. "It doesn't matter," she told her mother, then wondered why she even cared enough to put the woman's mind at rest. "Nobody can hurt me anymore."

A bald lie, but she said it anyway, hoping that saying it could make it true. And she wondered why she kept clinging to the phone, why she didn't just say goodbye and hang up. Surely she didn't want contact with this woman who had turned a blind eye to what was going on all those years ago?

"I realize," Rose said after a moment, her voice still unsteady, "that you've probably convinced yourself of that. I hope it's true. But I've lived long enough to know that there are always ways somebody can hurt someone. Always..." Her voice trailed off.

Anna didn't know what to say. After all these years, this

woman was a stranger to her, a stranger whose memory was shrouded in bitterness.

"Well," said Rose finally, "let me give you my phone number. Just in case anyone tries to say you lied about what happened. You can count on me to stand beside you."

Anna wrote the number down, sure she would never use it, then said goodbye to the woman who had been her mother. After all these years, she couldn't even feel vindicated. It was too late for that. Her mother hadn't believed her when it had really mattered. What difference did it make now?

But even as she thought that, her throat began to ache and tears began to prickle in her eyes. She was just feeling raw, she told herself as she wiped her eyes with the back of her hand. Too much had been going on lately. Her emotions were too near the surface, and her defenses were down.

The best way to deal with this would be to go to work and do what she had to do. Keeping busy had always been her salvation.

The church office was surprisingly quiet that morning, given that it was the day before a holiday. The preparations for the church's Thanksgiving dinner were going on in the church basement, but apparently no one felt the need for any help from either the minister or his secretary.

There was no time like the present, Anna told herself. Taking advantage of the lull, she mustered her courage and asked Dan if he could spare a few minutes to talk with her.

He put his work aside with a smile and invited her to sit. "What's on your mind?"

"Lorna has asked me to become her permanent foster mother."

"I think that's a splendid idea! The child is obviously

very happy living with you. The turnaround has been apparent to everyone.''

''Most of that probably has to do with being away from her father.''

''To be sure. But it wouldn't be as marked if she weren't happy living with *you,* Anna.'' He paused, studying her thoughtfully. ''I take it there's a problem of some kind. Don't you want to take her?''

''I do. I want to very much. But you're right, there's a problem.''

''And that is?''

Anna clenched her hands into tight fists and wondered if she was going to be able to force the words out. There were things she hated to even think about, and talking about them was so much more difficult. She couldn't even bring herself to look at Dan.

''It's all right,'' she heard him say gently. ''I've been a minister for twenty years, Anna. I don't think there's much I haven't heard.''

She didn't find that reassuring. Somehow she didn't think women around here ever confessed to prostitution. Her heart was galloping, and her throat felt tight with unshed tears. It was going to be even more difficult than she had imagined. But finally, keeping her gaze fixed on the rug, she managed to start speaking.

''When I was twelve, my stepfather raped me.''

''I gathered something like that from things you've said.''

She nodded, but she still couldn't look at him. ''My mother didn't believe me when I tried to tell her. All in all, it went on for nearly two years before I got up the nerve to run away.''

''I'm so sorry,'' he said softly. ''So very, very sorry,

Anna. I can't begin to imagine what that must have been like for you.''

"Well, it gets worse," she said, grabbing the arms of her chair and hanging on for dear life. She had to force herself to take several deep breaths so she could continue. How could she expect anybody to understand that she wasn't an innocent victim, that she had done terrible things in the name of survival and had only herself to blame? Nobody could excuse that, could they?

"How much worse?" he asked finally.

"I was fourteen. I couldn't find work. At least, not honest work.''

"Ah." His tone held comprehension.

"I stole. I got away with it, too. I stole food and clothes, but I couldn't get enough. I couldn't afford a place to live, and it was getting cold, so I…so I…" She trailed off, nearly panting from the force of the emotions that gripped her.

Then, as if from a distance, she heard Dan say gently, "So you prostituted yourself."

Stunned, she looked at him at last and found nothing but kindness on his face.

"It's an old story, Anna. And not at all uncommon for girls in your position. Why shouldn't you sell what had been taken from you by force so many times? The way your stepfather treated you taught you that such things weren't precious or special. He taught you to devalue yourself. By selling what he had taken, you even managed to regain a modicum of control over your body. It's all very complicated, of course, and I'm sure I'm making a hash out of it, but believe me, you aren't unique. What makes you special is that you didn't make prostitution a way of life."

At that a bitter little laugh escaped her. "That was pure luck."

"How so?"

"The third man I propositioned was an undercover police officer. He arrested me, and I was placed in juvenile detention. Eventually they charged my stepfather and put me in foster care. I don't know what would have happened otherwise."

"Nor is it even worth thinking about. *This* is what happened to you, and if you don't mind, I'm going to say a little prayer of thanks for that police officer."

Anna shook her head, fighting back more tears. "I don't mind. I'm grateful, too. I've been grateful it happened that way. Except that..." She looked away again. "Except that I have a police record. It's sealed, of course, but it's still there. It'll probably disqualify me from being a foster parent."

"I can't say for certain, but I'd be very surprised if it did. After all, you're living an exemplary life now, and have been for some time. The whole reason juvenile records are sealed is because we, as a society, understand that children make mistakes that shouldn't shadow their entire lives."

"Maybe." She managed a wan smile. "Regardless, I'm going to try. I'd like to use you as one of my references, but I wanted you to know about this so you wouldn't be acting blindly, and so you wouldn't be embarrassed if it all comes out."

Dan smiled gently. "Anna, I would never be embarrassed by my association with you. Never. And I'll be proud and delighted to be a reference for you. Nor should you worry that this will all come out publicly. I believe these investigations are private."

Warmth and relief started to flood Anna, but before she permitted them to take hold, she had to deal with the rest of it. "It may still come out. Al Lacey made some threats.

And this morning I had a call from my...mother.'' She almost choked on the word. ''She found me because a private investigator has been digging into my background. He called her to ask about what happened between me and my stepfather.''

For the first time Dan looked shocked. ''No,'' he said in a tone of disbelief.

Anna nodded. ''It's true.''

''I don't disbelieve you, Anna. I'm just appalled that Al would be doing something like this. Good heavens, hasn't the man already done enough damage?''

''Apparently not.'' Her hands were shaking now, as much with reaction as anything.

''But what could he possibly hope to gain?'' Dan shook his head and frowned thoughtfully. ''Unless he hopes to discredit you so he can argue that you exerted undue influence on Lorna, maybe even put her up to fabricating the story.''

''But he's already agreed to a plea bargain.''

''Has he? Then I guess he couldn't find anything useful to use against you.'' He gave her a half smile. ''Foiled.''

She wanted to smile back, but her mouth was trembling too hard. Reaction was setting in, and she feared she was going to embarrass herself by crying.

''It's all right, Anna, really,'' Dan said. ''I'll be glad to be a reference for you. And don't worry about Al. If he tries anything, I'll deal with him. As for being a foster parent...go for it. I'll be behind you a hundred percent.''

''Thank you. I was thinking about asking Sheriff Tate to be a reference, too. Do you think he'd mind?''

''I'm sure he'll feel the same way about it that I do. But why don't you let me talk to him? I can explain everything you've told me and save you the difficulty of having to repeat it. Would that help?''

Anna was more grateful to him than she could even say. When she returned to her desk, she sat for a long time trying to calm herself and get past the shakiness all the tension and fear had left her with.

Just as she was beginning to calm down and relax, Nate Tate entered the building and hung his Stetson on the coat tree. He gave her a warm smile and said that Dan wanted to see him.

And all at once Anna was nervous all over again. She managed to smile and tell him to go on in, but when the door closed behind him, it was all she could do not to scream from the tension. Oh, God, now she had to wait to see how this came out. She didn't think she could stand it.

Trying to look calm, trying to ignore her racing heart, she turned on her computer and began to type the church bulletin for Sunday. She had to keep busy, and at least doing the bulletin would occupy her mind, because, except for a few notes, Dan pretty much left it up to her to decide on layout and content. It was a task that usually gave her pleasure.

Today she could barely concentrate on it, much as she wanted to. From Dan's office she could hear the faint sounds of the men's voices as they discussed her, and she wished she knew what they were saying. It seemed to take forever, but in reality it was no more than fifteen minutes before Nate emerged.

When he did, he came over to Anna's desk and sat in the chair facing hers. ''I will,'' he said, ''be proud to be a reference for you. What's more, I have no doubt Marge would be glad to do the same, if you want her to.''

Anna felt tears welling in her eyes again. ''Thank you.''

Nate smiled and shook his head. "Nothing to thank me for. I know the woman you are now. I've seen the work you do with children. What's past is past. Besides, I don't see that you did anything so terribly wrong in the circumstances."

Anna shook her head. "I still feel awful about it. It *was* wrong."

"In one sense. But people will do far worse things to survive, sweet pea. I've seen it. In my opinion, you don't have a damn thing to be ashamed of or to apologize for. Both Dan and I are agreed on one thing—we can't imagine anyone who would be better suited to helping Lorna through the days and months ahead."

"Thank you." She wished she could say more, could find better words to express her gratitude and relief, but there didn't seem to be any. Nate's expression, however, suggested that he knew exactly how she was feeling.

"Now," he continued, "as for Al Lacey...I think I may have a private word with him. I've got a real strong distaste for people who try to obscure their own problems by messing up other people's lives. Not that it really surprises me— that tends to be the way most criminals think. What amazes me is that in all these years I never guessed what a creep this guy is." He shook his head. "And here I thought I had a good nose for people."

"It would be nice if bad people looked like bad people," Anna remarked.

Nate flashed a sudden grin. "It'd sure make my life a whole lot easier, but it ain't gonna happen, sweet pea. Well, you go ahead and use me and Marge for references. Wouldn't surprise me if half the church or more was willing to stand up for you. Folks around here like you, Anna. They like you and respect you, and I can't imagine there are too many who would ever allow an unkind word to be spoken about you.''

He rose, grabbing his Stetson and heading for the door. "Say, are you going to be helping Hugh Gallagher with his youth ranch? I know he was hoping you would.''

Anna hardly knew how to respond to that. Hugh had hardly spoken a word to her since the night he'd brought Lorna home. "I don't think he's interested anymore,'' she said finally. "I've got too many problems in my background.''

He leaned toward her, looking down at her with eyes that saw too much. "Hugh doesn't strike me as a man to make too much out of somebody's past. What's more, sweet pea, your past is only as big an obstacle as you make it.''

Then he was gone, leaving behind a gust of cold air and a silent office.

Hugh Gallagher joined Billy Joe Yuma that morning to take Thanksgiving dinner up to the vets in the mountains. Billy Joe's wife, Wendy—who was also Nate Tate's daughter—had gotten her mother and her sisters and a couple of friends to bake Thanksgiving turkeys early. Everything was being carried on ice in coolers and would have to be heated up once it was delivered, but Hugh figured those guys in the hills were going to be delighted with turkeys, stuffing, cranberry sauce, vegetables...the kind of a meal they couldn't make over a campfire. Or wouldn't bother to.

"Wendy's talking about doing hams for Christmas,'' Billy Joe remarked.

"Sounds like a good idea.'' Hugh stared out at the wintry countryside as they drove higher up the pine-forested slopes of the mountains. "You know, I've been thinking. Maybe I ought to kill the idea of the youth ranch. I could just run a halfway house for guys like those in the mountains.''

"You could.'' Billy Joe glanced at him. "I thought the youth ranch was a really great idea, though. Nate's sure been looking forward to it as a way to deal with troubled kids around here.''

"I know, but…well, I don't have the best background for dealing with kids. Not after…you know.''

"I know. I don't have the best background for flying an emergency medical helicopter, but here I am. When Nate hired me, he was taking a hell of a chance that I wouldn't just suddenly go on Saigon time again.''

"Yeah…'' Hugh didn't know quite how to express his disquiet. All the time he'd been thinking about this ranch idea, he'd known his past was going to be an issue and that somehow he was going to surmount it. But now, since his rupture with Anna, he didn't feel positive about anything anymore. Everything looked insurmountable.

"What's wrong, Cowboy?'' Yuma asked.

"Nothing, really. Just a general sort of feeling.'' Which wasn't exactly true. Anna Fleming had been the first real obstacle he'd encountered in his plan, and here he was getting all down about it, as if everything was hopeless. Damn, he wasn't going to get anywhere with anything if that was all it took to knock him off his pins.

"Life is getting you down, huh?'' Yuma said. The car slipped a little, then regained traction, as they came around a snowy curve on the seldom-used road.

"I reckon.'' He shook his head, trying to get rid of the morose thoughts that were plaguing him. "It's the holiday season, I guess.''

"Yeah. It's hard when you don't have a family.''

The remark was a shrewd one, and it made Hugh uncomfortable. "I'm having Thanksgiving dinner with Anna Fleming and Lorna tomorrow."

Yuma glanced at him. "Is that a problem?"

"No. Why would it be?"

"You tell me. You don't sound real happy about it."

"I'm looking forward to it, actually," Hugh lied. The truth was, he couldn't imagine anything more uncomfortable than facing a silent Anna across a Thanksgiving turkey. He couldn't imagine why she'd renewed the invitation, and he couldn't understand why he'd felt compelled to accept it.

"Wendy like to have driven me crazy a couple of times when we were courting," Yuma remarked.

"I'm not courting Anna."

"Oh." Yuma glanced his way. "Sorry. It was something about the way you said her name. Guess I misread it. Anyway, Wendy was a handful. That woman chased me until I damn near panicked, then she went away and came back acting like she didn't care a fig for me. I thought I was relieved."

"You weren't?"

Yuma hesitated. "You know, I really can't say. I just know that it wasn't long before I was tied up in knots all over again. I'll tell you one thing, though, Cowboy. With a woman, it never pays to be *too* damn honorable."

Hugh stared at him. "There's no such thing."

"The hell there isn't. Wasn't it you who put your mind to making me so damn jealous that I clean forgot I was trying to avoid Wendy for her own damn good? Seems to me you had a few words of your own to say on that score. Something about getting my head out of my nether regions, if I remember correctly."

Hugh had to laugh in spite of himself. He clearly remembered hanging around Wendy Tate like a fly around honey

for the few days it took to make Yuma jealous enough to
cut the crap and ask the woman to marry him. But it had
been as obvious as the nose on his face that Wendy and
Billy Joe were deeply in love.

This thing with Anna wasn't obvious at all. Right now he
just wished it would go away, because it was making a mess
of all his good intentions.

"The point I'm trying to make here," Yuma went on, "is
that a woman appreciates an honorable man as long as his
scruples don't get in the way of loving her. That's one time
she'll be just as happy to see him forget all those noble
ideas. Trust me."

"Well, I'm not in love with her."

Yuma didn't reply, which was almost as good as saying
he didn't believe it.

Hugh returned his attention to the countryside, noting that
they were within ten minutes of their destination. It would
be good to get out and hike through the snowy woods. It
would clear his head and ease the sense of doom that seemed
to be pervading his days.

No, he told himself, he wasn't in love with Anna. He was
attracted to her, but that was all. As far as he could tell, she
had too many problems to deal with, and until she dealt with
them, a man would be wiser to keep clear.

Here there be dragons, the old maps had said. A wise
man didn't venture into dragon-infested waters.

And right now he damn well didn't want to think about
Columbus.

Chapter 14

It was embarrassing, but Anna had to admit to Lorna that she didn't have the foggiest idea how to cook a turkey.

On Thanksgiving morning they'd both risen early to stuff the bird and put it into the oven. Anna had dealt with one problem by buying prepackaged stuffing, but for the rest of it, she was winging it.

"I never had to cook one before," she told Lorna. "I've always been alone, or eating at the church. My job was to bring pies." She had pies, two of them that she'd made yesterday evening. The bird was altogether a different matter.

"I never cooked one, either," Lorna admitted. "Do you have a cookbook?"

She did have one, an all-purpose cookbook that she hardly ever used because she rarely felt like cooking anything fancy just for herself. The directions for cooking and stuffing the turkey were explicit, so they set to work, opening the bag the turkey came in, only to discover that there were directions in there, too. That caused them both to laugh and set the tone for the rest of the morning.

By the time Hugh arrived, everything was just about ready. Lorna had set the table with a snowy white paper tablecloth they had bought at the store yesterday, and paper napkins. Anna didn't have any fancy dishes, but her plain blue ironstone ones didn't look bad. A bowl of jellied cranberry sauce made a sparkling ruby centerpiece. Beside it sat a freshly tossed salad. The mashed potatoes were keeping warm on the stove, and the turkey was sitting on the counter, waiting the required thirty minutes before carving.

Anna and Lorna were feeling pretty proud of themselves, and the look on Hugh's face when he stepped into the kitchen was purely appreciative.

"Boy," he said, "everything smells so good!"

"I hope you're hungry," Lorna said. "I talked Anna into buying a really big turkey."

Hugh waggled his eyebrows at her. "I didn't eat at all today so I could save room for this feast."

Anna, who'd been expecting to feel awkward, found herself relaxing. Apparently whatever was troubling Hugh was something he'd left behind so it wouldn't disturb the day. That was fine with her—at least for now—so she pasted on a smile and made up her mind to enjoy herself.

Anna asked Hugh to carve the turkey. He seemed glad to have something useful to do and joked with Lorna as she stood holding the platter for him to place slices of breast meat on.

"Hey," he asked, "does anybody like the dark meat?"

"Not me," Lorna and Anna piped in unison.

"Good, that means more for me." He promptly cut a thigh for himself.

They said grace, then sat together at the table to eat. Anna found herself thinking how nice this was. It had been years since she'd last had a Thanksgiving meal in a family setting, and she guessed the same was true for Hugh.

It would, she thought, be so easy to get used to this, to sitting around a table with Hugh and Lorna, to watching them laugh and tease one another. Even as she thought it, her heart ached with yearning. Someday, somehow, she wanted to have a family again. A real family.

But that could never be. Stifling a sigh, she made an effort to join the lighthearted conversation between Hugh and Lorna. The two of them, she thought, had somehow reached an amazing level of comfort together, a kind of comfort she wished she could share.

But there was no way she could be comfortable today, anyway. Not with the court appearance looming over her head. Not with the prospect of having her life turned inside out in public over Lorna.

But maybe none of that would happen, she told herself. Maybe the investigation would go smoothly; maybe she would even get guardianship of Lorna. Dear God, how she hoped so, because even after this short time, she knew that losing Lorna would leave a gaping hole in her life and her heart.

Hugh insisted on doing the dishes himself, since they had done all the cooking. Afterward they played cards and then a game of Monopoly that ran on until Lorna's bedtime.

The realization of the time hit Anna hard. Suddenly she couldn't avoid thinking about the court appearance Monday. The feeling wasn't a whole lot different from the stage fright she had experienced as a youngster before a school play. Butterflies settled in her stomach, and the court appearance loomed threateningly.

Which was ridiculous, she thought. Her mind was already made up. All she had to do Monday was tell the judge she was going to apply to become Lorna's permanent guardian. The approval process would drag on for months, probably, during which time she would still have Lorna. There was nothing to be nervous about right now.

Except Al Lacey and what he intended to do with whatever his private detective had managed to find out. Telling herself it didn't matter, especially now that she'd talked to Dan and Nate, wasn't the same as believing it.

"Is something wrong?" Hugh asked. He had made no move to leave after Lorna had said good-night and gone to bed. Anna wondered why he was lingering, after avoiding her for so long.

"Nothing," she answered. "Really. For some stupid reason I'm nervous about the hearing Monday. That's all."

He nodded and twisted on his chair so he could reach the coffeepot. He refilled both their mugs, then put the pot back. "So, are you going to apply to keep Lorna?"

Anna nodded, wondering how much he knew or guessed about all this. It was possible she was already the subject of widespread gossip and just didn't know it.

"Well, I can sympathize," he said presently. "Yesterday I was saying to Billy Joe Yuma that maybe I ought to just give up this whole idea of a youth ranch."

"But why?"

He gave her a rueful smile. "Because I all but get cold sweats when I imagine how people are going to react to the idea of putting troubled children in the hands of a guy who was a homeless, insane drifter for a couple of years. That doesn't look real good on a résumé."

"But it's such a wonderful idea! And you won't be doing it alone. I mean, with all the people you'll need to hire, it's not as if they'd be placing these kids in the hands of one person. Besides, whatever happened before, it's not true of you now.''

He looked straight at her. ''The same could be said of you, Anna.''

She felt punched. He *did* know, she thought wildly. And that *was* why he had stopped asking her to help with his ranch. Why he had stopped coming by to see her. Why all his friendship had so completely dried up.

''You don't know,'' she heard herself say woodenly, believing that he really did.

''So tell me,'' he suggested.

Tell him? She stared at him in astonishment. ''Tell you what?'' she heard herself ask. ''You already know!''

Now it was his turn to look surprised. ''Are we crossing wires here? You told me I didn't know. You're right, I don't know what it is you're so worried about, except that you apparently have some kind of juvenile record. So what's the big deal, Anna? Our whole relationship has been like dealing with quicksand. I never know where it's safe to put my foot, and you won't tell me. I know something has got you seriously worried, but I sure as hell don't know what it is. So don't sit here and tell me I don't know and then get in high dudgeon when I ask you to tell me, because I'm supposed to already know!''

''How can I believe that, when you've been avoiding me like the plague?''

His mouth opened as if he wanted to say something, then closed. He shook his head. ''Whoa. Can we backtrack here?''

Anna, who hadn't had enough sleep in several nights now and was looking forward to another sleepless night, was in the mood for a fight. She recognized it and considered apologizing and backing off. But then it occurred to her that among the reasons she wasn't sleeping was this man and the way he had been treating her for the past several weeks. Why not get it all out in the open so she knew where she stood? Why not clear the air?

"Sure," she said, feeling her chin thrust forward. "Backtrack."

"All right." He leaned forward, resting his elbows on the table.

He was wearing a nice shirt today, but he had rolled up the cuffs. Almost as if her eyes were magnetized, Anna found herself looking at his forearms and admiring their strength. Looking at his shoulders and admiring their breadth. He was a powerful man, but his strength had never hurt her physically. That somehow seemed very important to her.

"Backtracking," he said, "I *have* been avoiding you."

"I knew it."

He sighed. "Anna, please, just let me finish before you try to start a fight, okay? I *have* been avoiding you. But not for whatever reasons you're apparently imagining. After we…made love, and you ran out of the shower and locked the bedroom door on me…well, I decided I'd made a mistake. I'd obviously done something that had upset you— although I still don't know what. And that's the problem here. How can I avoid hurting you or upsetting you if I don't know where the mines are buried?"

She started to open her mouth, but he held up his hand. "Please. Let me finish. Then you can have your say. So I knew I'd hurt you, and I got the distinct feeling that you didn't want me around anymore." He gave a humorless half smile. "When a woman you've just made love to locks you out of the bedroom and won't talk to you, you kind of figure you've made a really big hash of things. So I left.

"And after I left, I figured I'd do best to stay away for a while. Whatever was bothering you, you needed time to calm down. I figured that later we could maybe be friends again. And I figured that trying to make us lovers was something I'd be wisest to avoid from here on out, since it apparently upset you so much."

Anna wasn't ready to buy it. It sounded awfully thin to her. "I'm supposed to believe you want us to be friends after the way you've been avoiding me?"

"Look," he said, "I'm not perfect. I'm going to admit I was weighing this whole youth ranch thing into the matter, too. I figured that I'd offended you somehow, and if I kept offending you, you sure as hell weren't going to want to help with the ranch. I thought we'd get back on a business footing a whole lot sooner if I just stayed clear so you realized I wasn't going to pounce on you every time you turned around. Now, I'll be the first to admit that sounds pretty ridiculous, but at the time I was thinking it, it actually made sense."

"So you just want us to have a business relationship?" Anna couldn't express why that disappointed her so much, when the last thing on earth she wanted was a personal relationship with a man. But she expected him to dismiss even that possibility now, anyway, since he clearly didn't want any kind of relationship with her. Why else would he have avoided her? She couldn't believe it was because he honestly thought that would help get things back on a business footing between them.

"Given what was going on, Anna, that seemed like the wisest course. I mean, you made it pretty apparent you didn't want anything else. Hell, you ran away from me and wouldn't even talk to me."

Anna suddenly felt uncomfortable, as she admitted her

own fault in all of this. What she had steadfastly refused to admit over the past weeks was that she had shut Hugh out in a way that would probably make anybody reluctant to talk to her again. Except wouldn't most people have demanded an explanation, rather than just telling her that she needed to deal with her past? She kept getting hung up on that.

"Anna," Hugh said finally, drawing her out of her thoughts, "I don't know what it is you're so afraid of, or what I did to offend you, and I'm worried about doing it all over again, because I don't know what I'm dealing with here. And that, I guess, is the real reason I've been staying away. Never mind what I've been telling myself. The truth is, I'm scared to death I'm going to step on a land mine. That doesn't make it very easy to relax and trust somebody."

The first trickle of belief began to run through her. He wasn't lying, she thought. He really didn't know the whole story.

"Talk to me, Anna. Tell me what it is. That way I'll know where the mines are, and maybe we can get back to being friends."

Why not? she found herself thinking. Why not. She'd already told Nate and Dan and survived. Why not tell Hugh what he was so eager to know? He talked as if there was some little obstacle they could just ignore once she explained it, but she knew better. Once he knew the truth, there would be no further possibility of "friendship."

"You know my stepfather molested me," she said finally. "Oh, why not be blunt about it. He *raped* me. Repeatedly. With force. With threat of force. With threats of harm against my mother and my friends if I didn't do exactly what he told me to do and if I didn't keep my mouth shut. I used to pretend to be asleep when he came into my room at night, hoping he'd go away. But he'd just go ahead and do what he wanted anyway. It didn't matter. The only thing that mattered was that I didn't fight him too hard or make too much noise, because then he'd hit me and threaten to do something really awful, like telling my friends about me, to shut me up."

She couldn't look at Hugh, but she could feel him looking at her. It was like laying her soul bare, and her stomach roiled uneasily. But now that they'd started, the words just kept coming, as if the spillway had opened on a dam, and nothing was going to stop the flow now.

"I tried to tell my mother, but she didn't believe me. She accused me of lying because I hated my stepfather. When she didn't believe me, I didn't think anyone would."

"I can understand that."

Anna nodded, fixing her gaze on her clasped hands. What she needed to do was get through this without breaking down or throwing up. She wondered with a strange detachment if she was going to be able to do it. She hadn't told anyone about it with this kind of detail since she'd received counseling after the police picked her up.

"It went on for nearly two years," she said tonelessly. "At one point I took a hammer and put it under my bed, figuring I'd pull it out and threaten him the next time he came. Or maybe I'd beat him over the head with it when he was all limp and weak afterward." Something in her voice betrayed bitterness and disgust now, but she didn't try to rein it in. She was lost in her memories, seeing them almost as if they had happened to someone else.

She fell silent then, remembering how she had waited night after night, looking for the right moment…a moment that never seemed to come. "I would have killed him," she told Hugh. "I really think I would have killed him. But I never got the chance. He found the hammer, and he told me if I ever tried anything like that again he was going to use it on me."

Hugh swore softly.

"Finally...finally I got to where I didn't feel much about it one way or the other anymore. It was like it was someone else he was touching and using. I'd go away in my head, you know? I'd make up stories, or imagine I was in some beautiful place all by myself. I got really good at it."

Her eyes were starting to burn, but she ignored them, the way she ignored her tightening throat.

"I'm not sure exactly when I decided I wasn't going to take it anymore. I'm not even sure why I suddenly decided to run away. I mean...it just happened. Like it had been building without me being aware of it until...boom! There it was. I was going to run away.

"I didn't have any money to speak of, but I stole some from my mother, packed a couple of things in my schoolbag and left for school one morning. Only I never went to school. I got on a bus and went to New York."

"Why New York?"

Startled, for she had almost forgotten he was there, she looked at him. "Because it seemed far enough away and big enough that he could never find me there."

Hugh nodded. He started to reach out, as if he wanted to touch her hand, but he drew back at the last moment. "That was a brave thing to do."

"It was a stupid thing to do," she said flatly. "In retrospect, I had a lot of better options. I just didn't think anybody would believe me. I was sure everyone would think just what my mother had, that I made it up because I hated my stepfather. So I ran away, figuring I could pretend to be older and get a job or something.''

''I'll bet it wasn't that easy.''

''Of course it wasn't. Back then, kids didn't have to have social security numbers for the IRS, so I didn't have a social security card or any way to get one. Not that anybody would have believed I was sixteen. I was fourteen, and I looked twelve. Nobody ever bought my story about being older. Not once.''

She looked down at her hands again. ''Sometimes a business owner would feel sorry for me and give me a few bucks. It wasn't long before it was obvious I was a runaway. I mean, I didn't have any place to stay where I could clean up, not on a regular basis. Sometimes I'd meet older kids who would let me crash with them for a few nights, but I couldn't stay permanently, because I couldn't help with the expenses. So I started stealing food and clothes when I could, and washing up in public rest rooms. But then it started to get cold.'' Her voice grew unsteady.

Once again Hugh reached out toward her, but she pulled her hand away. She couldn't bear anyone to touch her right now. Not anyone.

''I decided there was one job I could do where nobody would ask me for a social security card. One job where my age was an advantage. Besides, Van had taken it any time he wanted. Why shouldn't I get money for it?''

''Oh, Anna,'' Hugh said quietly, sadly.

''It felt worse, though,'' Anna said. There was a pressure growing in her chest, making it difficult to breathe and talk, but she forced the words out anyway. She didn't know if she was doing it because she wanted to punish him for asking, or because she finally, at last, just needed to tell someone about what all this had done to her.

"It was worse," she said again, "because this time I was choosing to do it. They didn't rape me or force me. They paid me. And I hated myself for it. I really did. I felt even worse than Van had made me feel. I figured I didn't deserve to live at all anymore, and one of these guys was going to kill me. I told myself it was going to be a good thing, that I deserved to die."

She drew a deep breath. "It was the worst thing I've ever done. Worse even than stealing. It seems stupid, but that's how I feel about it. Anyway, I was lucky. The third guy I propositioned was an undercover cop. He arrested me."

"And that's what you're worried about? A juvenile record for prostitution?"

She nodded and reluctantly dragged her gaze to his face. He didn't look disgusted or even very surprised. "I'm applying to become Lorna's guardian, but I don't think I'll be approved. And with a background like mine, I wouldn't be an asset for your youth ranch, either. I know you were thinking I could balance out your problem, but I just have a bigger one, Hugh. A much bigger one. Nobody will want a former prostitute looking after kids."

"And what about what happened between us?" he asked. "Why did you run from me like that?"

"Because..." It was suddenly almost impossible to speak. All her clinical detachment evaporated in an instant, and pain pierced her. "Because I felt...cheap. Like I was...doing it all over again."

He nodded slowly. "What we did wasn't cheap, Anna. It was beautiful. The most wonderfully intimate and affirming thing two people can do together if they care about one another. I wasn't using you. Believe me, I wasn't."

She was breathing rapidly now, trying to hold back tears once again. "Really?"

His expression grew sad. "Really, Anna. Really." He rose and came around the table. Taking her hands, he drew her to her feet. "I swear I wasn't using you. I wanted you, yes, but I thought you wanted me, too. I wanted us to be together and share that wonderful experience. And if it seems that I cast you aside afterward, because I've been avoiding you, I'm really, really sorry. I wasn't casting you aside, I was trying to do the only thing I could think of to avoid making the situation worse. I guess I made some stupid choices."

Before she could decide how to respond, he continued. "Thanks for telling me what the problem was. I appreciate it. Don't worry about it anymore, Anna. From here on out, you can set the limits between us. I'd like to spend more time with you, but I'm not going to push you. And if you want me to go away, I'll go. All you have to do is say so."

"Don't go." She could hardly believe she was saying it, but she was. She was actually asking a man to stay. Her heart hammered wildly, and she felt as if she were climbing out of some long, dark tunnel.

He searched her face, then wrapped his arms around her, hugging her close with a tenderness that made her throat ache anew. "It's okay," he said. "It's okay. You'll see. To hell with the rest of the world, sweetie. It doesn't matter a damn what any of them think of you. All that matters is what you think of yourself. And as far as I can see, you've got a whole hell of a lot to be proud of."

She turned her face up to him, filled with a sudden fierceness. "And so have you, Cowboy. So have you."

He smiled then. "So okay. We'll face 'em all down." He squeezed her gently, then brushed the lightest of kisses on her lips. "Meantime, I'm going to skedaddle. You look exhausted. In fact, you've looked exhausted all day."

"I haven't been sleeping well."

"I can tell. You go to bed now. I'll come over tomorrow evening, if that's okay, and we can talk more then."

Her heart gave a strange little leap when she realized that Lorna was planning to spend tomorrow night with Mary Jo again. But she was also too tired and feeling too emotionally wrung out right now to think about what that might mean. She walked Hugh to the door, accepted another light kiss and said good-night.

Then she stood at the living-room window and watched him walk to his truck and climb in. For the first time in what seemed like forever, she actually felt that things were starting to get better.

And that night, for the first time in days, she slept soundly and well.

It wasn't until the next morning that it struck her that once he'd heard her story, he'd been in an awfully big hurry to leave.

Chapter 15

Monday morning, while Anna was getting dressed for court, the phone rang in the living room. She heard Lorna call out, "I'll get it, Anna!"

Her first thought was that it must be Hugh, and her heart leapt with an eagerness that was almost frightening. This time, instead of telling herself that Hugh had left early the last few nights because he was disgusted, she was trying to believe that he had left for the very reasons he had cited. She had a tendency, she was beginning to realize, to interpret people's actions in the worst possible ways—a tendency to assume that they were acting out of disgust for her. It was becoming increasingly clear that that just wasn't the case. Just look at Nate and Dan. There was no reason to assume Hugh couldn't be just as generous.

So she found herself hoping it was him, but when Lorna didn't come back to get her, it became apparent it must have been one of her friends. She felt deflated, then scolded herself with a reminder that he had said he would be coming by tonight.

She chose her prettiest dress to wear that morning, a navy blue A-line with a white collar and long sleeves. Looking at herself in the mirror, she wondered if it wasn't high time she bought a few things that were less conservative. The church-secretary image was fine for work, but surely she could be a little brighter on her own time?

When she came out of her bedroom, Lorna was sitting on the couch in the living room, wearing a violet dress and white stockings. Her long blond hair was caught in a butterfly clip on the back of her head.

"Don't you look lovely," Anna said approvingly.

"Thank you."

Lorna sounded subdued, and Anna felt a spark of worry. "What's wrong, honey?"

Lorna shook her head.

"Are you nervous about today?"

"I guess."

Anna stared at her in perplexity. Lorna hadn't been nervous about going to court before. "Are you worried about making a decision about the plea bargain?"

"No." The girl shook her head. "I'm fine, Anna. I'm just tired this morning."

It was possible, Anna thought. "Who was on the phone?"

"Wrong number."

She couldn't have said why, but in that instant Anna knew that Lorna was lying. But why? She considered pressing the issue, then decided to wait and see what might develop. She all too clearly remembered herself at that age, and how stubborn and angry she could get when an adult pried into private things.

The meeting this morning was being held in the judge's chambers rather than the courtroom. Anna expected to get there and find just the judge and a court reporter present.

Instead, to her dismay, Al and Bridget Lacey and his attorney were waiting in the anteroom.

"No, don't go in there," the bailiff said. "You two ladies are to go directly in to the judge." He guided them through the door across the hall into the conference room where they had met Judge Williams to take Lorna's statement weeks ago.

But as fast as the bailiff moved, it wasn't too quickly for Anna to see the significant look that Lacey sent his daughter. Lorna seemed to shrivel.

"That was inexcusable," Anna told the bailiff as soon as the door closed behind them. "Do you know what that man has done to this child? He's not supposed to be anywhere near her!"

"I'm sorry, ma'am," the bailiff said. "He wasn't supposed to be here this early. His hearing isn't until nine-thirty."

Anna was furious and wanted to shake somebody, but she couldn't do any more. Lorna sat at the long table, looking frightened and shrunken, as if she wanted to curl up on herself. Anna would have blamed it entirely on the encounter with her father, except that it had started before they'd left home. What in the world was wrong?

The judge entered the room, along with the court reporter, and greeted them warmly. "This should only take a few minutes," she said. They waited while the stenographer typed in the information about the hearing and its purpose, then Judge Williams turned to Anna and Lorna.

"Miss Fleming, have you decided whether to apply for permanent guardianship of Miss Lacey?"

"Yes, Your Honor, I have. I'm going to apply."

"Excellent. I want you to know that both Reverend Fromberg and Sheriff Tate have spoken to me personally about your application. I'm aware that there may be...some difficulties, although I doubt it. So I want you to know that I'm going to keep a personal eye on your application to ensure that it's handled properly and processed as quickly as possible. In the opinion of people I respect—and in my own opinion, for that matter—there is no guardian better suited to this case. In the interim, your guardianship is re-affirmed indefinitely.''

''Thank you, Your Honor.'' Anna felt her heart swell with the first stirrings of hope. Maybe it all *would* work out so that she could keep Lorna.

''Now, Miss Lacey. I explained to you on Monday that a plea bargain has been offered in the case against your father for sexually abusing you. The terms are that he has to move away, that he can't have contact with you again, and that he'll be on probation for the next five years. Neither can he have contact with any minor child, including your sister. I've decided to increase that probation to ten years. I'm also going to require him to attend a program for sexual offenders. How do you feel about this? Should the court accept or refuse this bargain, keeping in mind that if it is refused, the case will have to go to trial?''

Lorna didn't answer. The judge waited a few moments, then said, ''Miss Lacey?''

''I...don't know.''

Judge Williams sat back in her chair and looked kindly at Lorna. ''I understand this must be difficult for you. Are there any questions I can answer that might help you make a decision?''

''W-what will happen if...I say I lied?''

Anna felt her heart slam. No! There was no way this child had lied about this. No way! She opened her mouth, but the judge waved her to silence.

Francine Williams's voice was gentle. "Did you lie, Miss Lacey?"

Lorna's head was bowed, and her hands were twisting on her lap. "What if I say I did?"

"It's a crime to lie to the court, Miss Lacey. But the important thing right now is that you tell me the truth, whatever it is."

Lorna nodded.

"Did you lie, Miss Lacey?"

Lorna lifted her face, and her cheeks were streaked with tears. "My mom called me this morning. She said...she said if I tell you I lied, I can come back to live with them, and I can have a horse of my very own. She said my daddy would never touch me again, that he promised. But if I don't tell you I lied, she said I'll never see my sister again. Not ever."

The room fell silent as Judge Williams pondered. Anna's hands formed fists, and it was all she could do not to say anything. Every cell in her body wanted to shriek with shock, anger and disbelief that anyone, most especially a mother, would put a child in this position.

"Miss Lacey," the judge said finally, "it appears you have a difficult decision to make here. From what you just told me, it's apparent that you did *not* lie on your deposition when you made your statement to me under oath. I can't prevent you from recanting your earlier statement, if that's what you decide to do. But I want you to think very carefully about what it means if you do. Not only will your father not be punished for a very serious crime, but you will be branded a liar in front of the whole world. You might be charged with perjury.

"Now, regardless of what you decide to do here today, you are going to have to do it under oath. That means that you *must* tell the truth or commit the crime of perjury. Do you understand?''

Lorna nodded, fresh tears running down her cheeks. The judge administered the oath, and Lorna swore to tell the truth.

''Miss Lacey,'' Francine Williams said, ''did you lie to this court when you made your earlier sworn statement that your father sexually abused you?''

Lorna gave a great hiccuping sob. ''N-no…''

Anna felt a huge surge of relief flow through her, and she reached out to put her hand reassuringly on Lorna's arm. At that moment, she thought, she could cheerfully have killed Bridget Lacey.

''Did your mother call you this morning and try to per- suade you to say you lied when you testified that your father had sexually abused you?''

''Y-yes.''

''Do you still say that your father sexually abused you?''

''Yes.'' The girl's voice was growing steadier with each response, and her tears were easing. ''He hurt me just like I said. But I don't want to lose my sister.…''

''I can't make any promises on that score, Miss Lacey. Your sister's custody is not an issue before this court, and the court can only deal with matters in its jurisdiction. The only thing I *can* do, and something that I am going to do, is forbid your father to have any contact with any minor children during the term of his probation. Do you know what that means?''

Lorna shook her head.

''It means that for the next ten years, your father cannot see your sister. At all. What I cannot do is remove your sister from your mother's care. Her parental rights can't be terminated unless she does something to warrant termination. This winds up meaning that your father can't live with the family anymore.''

Lorna nodded.

"If your father does, for *any* reason, have contact with your sister—or any other minor child—he'll go to prison for the rest of his sentence.

"Now, I told you that social services will be investigating the family situation. If they should decide that your mother can't be trusted to keep your father away from your sister, they'll probably ask the court to remove your sister from the home. The same will apply if they feel your sister is at any risk of being abused at any time, even after your father's sentence is completed. Do you understand?''

Lorna nodded, looking miserable.

"As for you being able to see your sister—well, I'll speak to social services about it. I don't see why something can't be worked out. I'll definitely do what I can to ensure it.''

The judge asked a few more questions, then returned to the issue of the plea bargain. Lorna agreed to accept it rather than testify.

Judge Williams ended the hearing, but indicated that they should remain where they were. "I have some business I want to take care of before the two of you leave here. I'll have the bailiff bring in some hot cocoa or coffee for you, if you'll be kind enough to wait for a little while.''

Anna was in no hurry to go out into the hall again, where they might run into Al Lacey. She nodded agreement to the judge, then scooted her chair over closer to Lorna so she could hug the girl.

"You did a brave thing, Lorna.''

Lorna turned and threw her arms around Anna's neck, crying onto her shoulder. "I'm so scared, Anna,'' she said brokenly. "So scared. He hurt me, but he's still my dad!''

"I know that, honey. I know that."

"Why couldn't he be like everybody else's dad?"

"I don't know." Questions like that never had any answers, she thought wearily. All she could do was hold Lorna and ache for her, and ache for all the other little children who were betrayed by the people they should have been most able to trust.

"Do you think I'll ever see my sister again?"

"If there's any way possible, we'll find it. I promise."

Lorna nodded and straightened, wiping at her eyes with the back of her hand. Anna searched her purse and found some clean tissues, which she handed to the child. Lorna murmured a thank-you and dabbed at her eyes.

"I'm sorry," she said, when her sniffling had quieted. "I was just so scared. At first I thought I had to do it, because she's my mother. But I was scared about going back there to live, because I don't think my dad would keep his promise. And I was scared about not seeing my sister again if I didn't.... I was so confused."

Anna hesitated, then went ahead and said, "Your mother was wrong to ask you to lie."

Lorna nodded. "I know she was. I mean, she always taught me not to lie, not even about little things. I couldn't believe she wanted me to lie now."

"She's trying to make this all go away, Lorna. It was wrong of her to ask that, but that's why she did it. She wants it all to just go away."

"So do I!" A fresh tear ran down Lorna's face. "I want it all to go away! I want it all to never have happened. But it *did* happen, and nothing anybody says or does is going to make it go away, Anna. How can it go away, when I can't forget it?"

There was no answer to that, either, and it struck Anna

as a very sad thing that a child should be asking such questions. "Time helps, Lorna. That's all I can tell you. Time makes it easier. You don't think about it as often. It will always hurt, but it will get so you don't think about it for long periods of time."

Unless something happened to reawaken it all. Anna looked past Lorna, thinking about how much time she had spent in the past month thinking about those very things, as if her childhood, once remote, was suddenly as close as yesterday. It would all fade again with time, but she supposed that every so often it was going to come back to her and start her hurting all over again. She hated to think that Lorna was probably going to endure the same process for the rest of her life, too.

The judge returned a few minutes later. "You won't have to worry about this happening again," she told Anna and Lorna. "I've taken some steps to ensure that it doesn't. You can leave now...and don't worry, no one is out there to bother you."

Lorna left at six to spend the night with Mary Jo, and Hugh arrived at seven. When Anna opened the door to let him in, she was surprised to see it was snowing again.

"We're supposed to get a couple of inches tonight," he said.

"That's not so bad."

"As long as the wind doesn't kick up and build huge drifts everywhere." He hung his jacket on the peg by the door and kicked his boots off, leaving them to dry on the braid rug in front of the door. "Is Lorna here?"

"She went to spend the night with a friend. They've been planning it for days." She didn't want him to think she had arranged it because he was planning to visit tonight.

He hesitated. "Did you hear what happened to Bridget Lacey?"

"No. What?" She was shocked to realize that she half hoped the woman had driven her car off a cliff.

"She was arrested this morning for witness tampering." He arched a brow at Anna. "You wouldn't know anything about that, would you?"

"My God." Anna sat abruptly on the couch. "I had no idea the judge did that."

"What happened?"

"She called Lorna this morning just before we went to court and tried to induce her to say she'd been lying about her father molesting her."

Hugh shook his head in disgust. "You really have to wonder what's wrong with some people's brains, don't you? I can't believe anyone would be so stupid—or so cruel. That woman isn't fit to be a mother."

"No, I don't think she is." Anna shook her head. "I'm certainly not going to make any more excuses for her. And Lorna's worried sick about her little sister."

"Of course she is! I can't believe they'll let that little girl stay with that family. Neither parent is fit."

"But what will they do with her if they take her away? Lorna will be heartbroken if she can't see her sister again."

"Maybe *you* ought to think about taking the little one, too."

Anna barely let herself consider the possibility, even though it appealed to her. "I'd love to, but I can't. Hugh, I have to *work*. And I can't afford day care."

"I didn't think of that. Are you going to call Lorna and tell her about her mother?"

"Absolutely not! If I call her now, it'll ruin her time with Mary Jo. She'll feel responsible and worry about it. No, tomorrow's soon enough to tell her about this.'' Soon enough, but no time would be good enough. Poor Lorna, this was going to upset her even more.

Hugh leaned over and touched her shoulder gently. ''How about a change of subject?''

Anna summoned a smile, trying to put her concerns aside for now. ''Sure. To what?''

''Oh, something like, what happened to all that leftover turkey?''

She had to laugh. They went into the kitchen and pulled the turkey from the fridge.

''Now, you let *me* make the sandwiches,'' Hugh said. ''My culinary skills may be limited, but when it comes to making a sandwich, I have no equal.''

He proceeded to construct sandwiches that would have done any deli proud. ''I take it you and Lorna had a rough morning?''

''Just a bit.''

''I'm real sorry about that. In my so humble opinion, I think the two of you have been through quite enough.''

''I couldn't agree more. Where do I lodge a complaint?''

''Beats me. If you find out, let me know, will you?''

He carried the sandwiches to the table and sat next to her. She pulled napkins from the caddy, handing one to him and spreading hers in her lap. It was nice, she thought, to be having an impromptu meal with him. It was all too easy to imagine a future where the two of them did this regularly, sitting together at the end of a long day.

The yearning made her uneasy, because it reflected a major shift in her attitude. For so long she had believed that solitude was safety, that her life was far better for living it alone. Over the past few weeks, however, she had found herself wishing for things she knew she would never have, and every one of those wishes seemed to revolve around Hugh Gallagher.

As usual, part of her mind tried to warn her that that way lay grief, but this time, for the first time, she argued back. She was entitled to want such things. She was entitled to wish for a normal life, with a husband and children. She had done nothing so wrong that she should have to spend the rest of her life paying for it with loneliness. Even if life never granted her these simple but important blessings, she had a right to wish for them.

With that small but important argument, with that small but important shift in her belief about herself, she felt a sense of freedom begin to blossom. There was, she realized, nothing intrinsically wrong with her. She had done some bad things, and some bad things had been done to her, but they didn't make her a bad person.

"Anna?" Hugh was looking at her, concern creasing his brow. "Is something wrong?"

She shook her head. "No, I'm fine. Really, I'm *fine*." She said it with a smile.

He smiled back. "What brought that on?"

"I just realized I'm not a bad person."

"Of course you're not!" He put his sandwich down and reached for her hand, clasping it gently. "I've never known anyone who was further from a bad person than you."

"But the things I did—"

"You did from necessity," he interrupted her. "I've seen people do a lot worse. The point, Anna, is that you didn't do anything to hurt someone else. The only person you hurt was yourself. Most of us can't say that."

"But I stole."

"To survive. It may be against the law, but I don't see it as a moral crime. Not when it's a matter of survival."

"That's debatable," she said, but a soft smile curved her lips. She liked having him champion her this way. She liked knowing that he didn't think she was a shamefully bad person.

"Don't try to debate it with me," he said. "You'll lose. You aren't a bad person, and you never were. Period."

"Neither are you."

"No, I'm not. I've done some bad things, but I probably saved a lot of lives by doing them. I'll never know, and I'm tired of beating myself up over it. All any of us can do is the best we can at the time. That's what you did. That's what I did. And trust me, a bad person wouldn't still be beating herself up over things she did when she was fourteen."

She nodded, feeling his words fill her heart with a soothing balm.

He picked up his sandwich again. "There, now that we've settled that…"

She laughed again, loving the easy way he lightened the moments when they became too intense. Loving the way he looked at her over the top of his sandwich, a smile glinting in his eyes. An impulse to touch him swept over her, and before she could prevent it, she had reached out and laid her hand on his arm.

He put his sandwich down again. "Aw, Anna, I'm going to have to kiss you."

"I wish you would."

The smile in his eyes was suddenly something much hotter. Her breath stuck in her throat, and she couldn't tear her gaze from his.

"Be sure, Anna," he said quietly. "Be very, very sure, because I am gonna be one mad dude if you regret this."

Even now, he made her want to smile. "I'm sure," she

managed to say, and was absolutely positive that she had never been surer of anything in her life.

He rose from the table and reached for her, drawing her up against his hard chest, cradling her as close as he could possibly get her. His kiss tasted like turkey sandwich at first, but before long she could taste the heady flavor of him.

"Anna," he whispered raggedly. "Oh, Anna...you've been driving me nuts for weeks. I dream about you every night. I wake up every morning wishing I could see you. You haunt me...."

His words reached to her soul, plucking new feelings forth, feelings of warmth and softness and trust, feelings of beauty. Oh, how beautiful he made her feel, and never, not once in her life, had she felt beautiful.

He plucked her glasses from her nose and set them on the table, then swept her up in his arms, carrying her toward the bedroom.

"Stop me now, Anna. If you're going to want to stop me, stop me now."

She didn't want to stop him. She wanted him never to stop. She could feel his muscles trembling with eagerness, and his eagerness fueled her own. "Don't stop," she said throatily. "Please don't stop...."

He set her on her feet beside the bed and gripped her shoulders, looking down into her eyes. "This can't be a mistake. I swore I was never going to do this again. Don't let this be a mistake."

If she had ever felt fear, she couldn't remember it now. If she had ever been reluctant, she was incapable of it now. She needed his hands on her flesh, his mouth on her skin, his body against hers and inside her. It seemed to have come out of nowhere, this sweeping, undeniable fire of need, but she knew it had been building since the very first time she had set eyes on him.

Always, always, she had been drawn to Hugh Gallagher, even in the months before they first spoke in the church basement. From the moment she had first spied him on the street, she had felt drawn. Only now did she realize that she had been waiting for him her whole life long.

Never had anything been so right.

He pulled her sweater over her head, then paused, admiring her small, firm breasts in their lacy cups.

"So pretty," he whispered, and ran his finger along the edge of the lace. Shivers trickled through her, and her breath began to come in small, soft gasps.

He reached behind her and released the clasp of her bra, freeing her breasts. She looked down as he drew the material away and set her free. And this time she *felt* free. She *was* free. This was Hugh, and that made everything special.

Lifting her head, she looked up at him and laughed with delight. He smiled back at her and reached for the snap of her jeans. "You don't need these, darlin'," he said. "Trust me, I'll keep you warm."

She *did* trust him. That was what was so wonderful. She trusted him so much that she was able to shed all the inhibitions and fears that had kept her away from him. He gave her a safe place to be herself. A safe place to just *be*.

When he lifted her and laid her down on the bed, she felt as light as a feather falling.

Hugh stood over her, stripping away his clothes, devouring her with his eyes. "I'm scared," he said suddenly. "I'm scared you're going to run from me...."

Anna shook her head and reached out to clasp his hand and draw him down to her. "Not this time," she said. She felt as powerful as the earth mother, and as old and wise as time. She *knew*.

His hot flesh covered hers, shielding her from everything else in the world, closing her into the haven described by his arms. Inch by inch, he trailed molten fire over her skin with the touch of his lips and hands. She thought she had awakened the first time they had made love, but it had been nothing like this. This time she felt as if she were a pure, burning flame of passion, free of all constraints. Free of all her past.

Her own hands roamed him, learning contours she had been almost too shy to touch before and discovering what a sheer delight it was to touch him. Never had she imagined how good the sensation of warm, dry sky beneath her palm could feel. Or how very sexy a man's angles and planes could be.

He seemed to enjoy her touches, making sounds that reminded her of a large, purring cat. Encouraged, she grew more daring even as his touches swept her higher on the roaring flames of passion.

His mouth found her breasts, bringing them to aching life until she arched, begging for harder touches. She felt as if her whole body were blossoming, reaching for her lover's touch in the same way a flower reached for the sun.

A deep, hard ache built in her, driving her onward, causing her to arch up against him with her hips, seeking more of him, and more.

Then, in an instant, he was sheathed inside her, filling her and completing her. A momentary satisfaction caused her to gasp; she had never felt anything so perfect, so right, so satisfying…and then hunger goaded her again, causing her to lift against him time and again, taking him deeper and deeper with each thrust. More…more…more…

He caught her hips with his hands, bringing her even closer, and that simple movement catapulted her over the cliff edge into completion.

Only dimly, as she drifted slowly back to earth, was she aware that he followed her.

"That sandwich is stale," Anna said.

They stood together in the kitchen, she in her flannel nightgown, he in his jeans.

"I hate to waste it."

"By now it's probably growing a million little salmonella bacteria."

He grimaced at her, a laugh in his eyes. "Okay, okay. Damn, you sure know how to spoil a man's appetite."

"I'll make you a fresh sandwich."

He caught her around the waist as she started to pass him on the way to the refrigerator. "No," he said. "I don't want you to wait on me."

"Don't be silly." But her breath caught as she looked up into his eyes and saw the banked fires there.

"I'm not being silly," he said. "I want our relationship to get off on the right foot. I'm a grown man, Anna. If I get hungry, I can make myself something. You don't have to take care of me."

"Oh, a liberated male." She knew she must be grinning like an idiot, but she didn't care. She was as close to delirious as she had ever been. "Fine. I don't have any problem with that. But what if I *want* to do it?"

A smile crinkled the corners of his eyes. "Oh, well, that's different."

"I had a feeling it might be."

But he helped anyway. They made fresh turkey sandwiches, laughing and talking all the while. After they ate, they went to sit in the living room, curling up together on the couch and talking in the aimless but intent fashion of people who are just learning to know one another.

"Have you ever been married?" Anna asked him.

"No. I never met anybody I felt I could spend the rest of my life with." He shifted a little, tucking her closer under his arm and running a finger along her forearm. "I kept waiting for the magic."

"Magic?"

"Yeah. You know. That feeling that *this is the one*. I came close a couple of times, years ago, but...I don't know. Something always made me back off. I can't see getting married unless I feel with my whole heart and soul that this is the right person."

"I never even came close before."

"It's kinda hard to do unless you date."

She gave a little laugh. "Just a little."

"So will you date me?"

"Date you?"

"We'll go places and do things together and see where it all goes." He looked down at her, a smile deep in his eyes. "I'm feeling lucky. How about you?"

She *was,* she realized. She was feeling very lucky. "I don't think I could be any luckier than I feel right now."

"Trust me. You could be a whole lot luckier." He started to bend his head to kiss her, but just before their lips met, the phone rang.

"I'd better get that," Anna said. "It might be Lorna."

It wasn't Lorna. It was an all-too-familiar male voice saying, "I'm going to make you sorry you got involved in all of this."

Something inside Anna snapped. She heard it in the back

of her head like a breaking twig. Fear was the furthest thing from her mind as anger surged in her.

"Listen, you disgusting, slimy toad, you don't frighten me! What are you going to do? Tell everyone in town that I was raped by my stepfather? Well, go ahead! I don't care if the whole damn world knows about it! Now go crawl back under your rock and don't ever let me see you or hear from you again. Get out of my life, and get out of your daughter's life before one of us decides to give you what you really deserve!"

She slammed the phone down so hard she thought she might have broken it, but she didn't care. Tremors of rage ran through her, making her shake violently.

"I'm going to kill him," she said. "I'm going to find a way to kill that bastard!"

Hugh came over to her and wrapped his arms around her, holding her tightly, as if he could protect her. "Want me to go knock his block off?"

"No!" Anna lifted her head and looked at him. "*I* want to knock his block off."

Hugh shook his head. "Sorry, sweetheart, but I don't think you're quite big enough to succeed. You're a tiny little woman, and he's kind of a big guy. But you sure told him off good."

"I could throttle him and his wife both. I could wring their disgusting necks!"

"I can sure see why you want to."

"Do you know what else he did?"

"No. What?"

"My mother called me a couple of days ago. My *mother*. I haven't spoken to her since I ran away from home! But she got my phone number from a private detective who was looking into my background. There's no doubt in my mind that Al Lacey hired him.''

"Probably." Concern was evident in his face as he looked sadly down at her. "I'm so sorry, Anna. What did your mother tell him?''

"Nothing, apparently. She called to warn me about it, and to tell me she was sorry for not believing me when I told her Van was raping me.''

"She did? When did she reach that conclusion?''

"About five years after I left.'' Anna shuddered and wished she could burrow right into him and hide from everything.

"What changed her mind?''

Much as she hated to even remember those pictures, she found she didn't mind telling Hugh. Telling Hugh things was surprisingly easy. "She found the photographs he took.''

"He took *photographs?*'' He was plainly appalled. "My God! What happened to them?''

"She burned them. After she used them to get a divorce.''

He nodded. "Well, thank God for that. You don't need to be worrying if those pictures might turn up sometime. Damn it, I can't believe what a jackass that man must have been. A disgusting creep, yeah. I already knew that. His kind don't deserve to live. But how stupid do you have to be to take pictures of your crime?''

Anna had never quite seen it that way before, and somehow, surprisingly, it made her feel good. She *liked* the idea that her stepfather was a stupid jerk, stupid enough to collect evidence against himself. "He *was* stupid,'' she agreed.

"An IQ of two.'' He shook his head. "Damn, it's hard to believe. But what about your mother? How do you feel about that? About her?''

Anna leaned against him, listening to the steady sound of his heartbeat, loving the way it felt to be able to lean against him this way. Loving the freedom she had found in his arms. "I don't know, Hugh. I've been angry at her for a long, long time. And I haven't seen her in over sixteen years. I don't know that I really feel anything one way or another anymore."

"But she's your mother."

"Yes. I don't know. I don't feel ready to make any kind of decision about whether to ever talk to her again or just forget she even called."

"It'll take time."

"Yes, it will."

He tipped her face up and kissed her gently on the mouth. "We have plenty of time, sweetheart. Plenty of time for getting to know each other. Plenty of time to decide things. But I'm going to leave right now."

"Why?"

"Because you're about to come under scrutiny as a potential foster parent. I don't think it would look too good if your neighbors report that you've had a man as an overnight guest."

She couldn't argue the justice of it, but she was starting to feel wounded again. Was this all he had wanted? Just to get laid?

But he was already turning away, heading for the bedroom and his clothes. Anna looked at the clock and was astounded to see it was only ten-thirty. She felt as if her entire life had changed, and it was only ten-thirty.

But nothing had changed, she told herself. Nothing at all. Hugh had gotten what he wanted, and now he was leaving again.

Before he left, he came to give her a tight hug and a

lingering kiss. "I'll call in the morning," he said. "Just to see how you're doing."

"Sure." She didn't think he would. She had told him about the pictures, and he was hightailing it out of here as quickly as he could go. It must be that he didn't think the pictures had been destroyed. Yes, that was probably it. He was afraid they might turn up sometime and adversely impact his ranch.

This time she didn't stand at the window to watch him leave. And she never expected to hear from him again.

Chapter 16

When he left Anna's house, Hugh went hunting. It was late on a Monday evening, and except for the roadhouses and bars, Conard County was pretty well settled in for a long winter's nap. Snow continued to fall steadily, but not heavily, and the roads wouldn't become impassible for hours yet, so he didn't even hesitate about driving out to Al Lacey's house.

He supposed he could get in trouble with the law for what he was about to do, but he was damned if he cared. That creep was going to stop tormenting Anna, and that was all there was to it. Besides, he wasn't going to beat the man, merely have a cautionary word with him.

But he had to do something about it. It had been bothering him all along, but he hadn't felt as if he had a right to do anything about it. It was Anna's business, after all, and unless she asked someone to intervene, nobody really should. But things were different now. He and Anna had a relationship, and he was feeling entirely too possessive to let this continue.

It struck him, when he was halfway out to Lacey's place, that he'd probably been too abrupt in his departure from Anna's. Hell, from the minute he'd realized who that call was from, he could think of only one thing: confronting Al Lacey. Now Anna was probably wondering if something she had told him had sent him into flight.

That woman's self-esteem was way too low, and if he spent the rest of his life doing it, he was going to find some way to give her back the confidence she was entitled to. She was a lovely, sweet, intelligent young woman, who shouldn't spend the rest of her life feeling so damn undeserving.

Of course, from his perspective, it could be difficult to deal with her defensiveness and her readiness to assume the worst, but she was worth it. Hell, she was worth a whole lot more than a little trouble like that.

But he sure wished he'd thought to make a more reasonable departure. Well, he would have to mend that fence in the morning, because right now, he was going to fix a wagon.

It was a quarter after eleven when he reached the Lacey house, but there were enough lights on downstairs to indicate that Al wasn't tucked into bed yet. Not that it would have mattered. As angry as he was right now, Hugh would have rousted the jerk from sleep and not turned a hair.

Al Lacey opened the door to Hugh's knock. He looked haggard and angry.

"I want you to stop making threatening phone calls to Anna," Hugh said without preamble.

"I'm not making any phone calls to anybody!"

Hugh took a step forward and jabbed his index finger into Lacey's chest. "It's like this, Lacey. I know you're making those calls. And if she gets another one, ever, I'm going to hunt you down and make you sorry you were ever born. And if I hear one whisper of gossip about that little lady, I'm going to hold you personally responsible. If you think you've got troubles now, just try me. Are we clear?''

The two men glared at one another for several seconds, but then Lacey's gaze flickered. ''What the hell do I care? I'm leaving town, anyway.''

''The sooner the better,'' Hugh said.

He heard the door slam behind him as he walked to his car. His knuckles were itching for the feeling of landing a solid punch, and just a few weeks ago, he might have done it. But not now. Now he didn't want to do anything that might upset Anna, or take her from him.

He drove home through the falling snow, trying to figure out what to tell her in the morning to smooth her feathers, because he didn't for an instant doubt he'd messed up again.

He had to learn to take his leave better, he thought. He had to learn to start explaining to her. He couldn't keep on carrying on as if he was the only person in the world, because now Anna was a part of his world, too. And next time he got a burr to do something, he promised himself, he was going to explain it to her before he went charging off.

He just hoped that by morning she hadn't decided she hated him.

Anna was roused from a sound sleep by the ringing of the phone. The sun still hadn't come up, and she could hear the wind howling outside her window. She grabbed her robe from the foot of the bed and jammed her feet into slippers, then hurried out to the kitchen to answer the phone.

It was Lorna. ''Anna? My dad called a little while ago. He told Mrs. Weeks that my mom is in jail and it's all my fault.''

"Lorna..." Anna hardly knew what to say, except that she would like to kill Al Lacey.

"It's okay, Anna," Lorna said. "Mrs. Weeks told me it's not my fault, because I didn't make my mom do things that were wrong, just like I didn't make my dad do things. She said none of it is my fault."

"Honey, it isn't. Trust me on this. It's no more your fault than it would be your fault if one of them decided to rob a bank."

Lorna gave a little laugh. "That's exactly what Mrs. Weeks said. Anyway, I'm calling because...well, we're snowed in."

"Oh, no!"

Lorna laughed again. "Yup. Mr. Weeks said he doesn't think he'll be able to get me home before late this afternoon, and I didn't want you to worry."

"Thank you. But about your mom—"

"It's okay, Anna. Really. It's like Mrs. Weeks said. I'm the kid and they're the parents. They're supposed to know better, and if they do things that are wrong, it's not my job to protect *them*. They're supposed to protect *me*."

"That's absolutely right."

"So I'm okay with it. Really. I'm just worried about my sister, but you said we'd find a way to work that out, so all I'm going to do is pray really hard that God takes care of her. He will, won't He, Anna?"

Anna's own opinion was that God didn't much bother with individual worries—if He did, would parents molest their children?—but she didn't have the heart to disillusion Lorna. "Pray hard, honey," she said. "Pray really hard. God will find a way."

Lorna sighed. "I'll be grown up before long, so maybe I can do something about Mindy myself."

"That's possible, too. We're certainly going to look into ways to make sure you can still see her."

"Okay. Well, I gotta go eat breakfast now. I'm sorry I woke you up, but I didn't want you to start worrying or anything. And I was wondering..."

Anna waited, wondering why Lorna was hesitating. Finally she prompted her. "Wondering what, Lorna?"

"I was wondering...can I call you Mom?"

Anna felt as if she were walking on air. She hardly cared that the blizzard of the decade was blowing around her house and drifting snow into banks ten feet tall that were going to challenge even the snowplows. Lorna wanted to call her Mom! She hugged the joy close and ran the conversation through her mind over and over again.

She was pacing the kitchen, drinking her second cup of coffee and thinking that life just couldn't get any better, when she heard a knock on her front door. She couldn't imagine who would be out on a morning like this and decided it must be a stranded motorist who wanted to use the phone.

Humming under her breath, she went to answer the door and was astonished to see Hugh standing there, bundled against the bitter day.

"How in the world did you get through this storm?" she asked, stepping back to let him in. All her upset of last night was forgotten in her joy this morning. She was simply glad to see Hugh and wanted to share her good news.

"I walked," he said.

She closed the door, feeling a gust of wind and icy snow blow up under her nightgown as she did so. "Why in the world did you do that? You could have just called."

"Calling wouldn't work," he said simply. "I had to see you."

She stepped back away from the flying snow as he pulled off his hat, his scarf, his jacket and his boots. His jeans were caked with snow and ice, and he looked down at them.

"Is Lorna here?"

"She's snowed in at the Weeks's house until this afternoon, probably. I just talked to her."

"Well, to hell with it, then," he said, and stripped off his frozen jeans. "Where can I hang these?"

"How about throwing them in the dryer?"

"You have a dryer?"

"The church set me up really nicely. All the amenities, and my rent is sinfully low."

"Can't complain about that."

She showed him where the dryer was and watched him throw his wet clothes into it. He was, she thought, really quite cute standing there in his flannel shirt, briefs and socks. His legs were gorgeous, and she could get quite used to the sight of him running around this way.

When he finished starting the dryer, he turned to her and asked, "Are you mad at me?"

"I'm not mad at anybody in the whole world this morning."

He raised an eyebrow. "What happened? You sound ready to burst with good news."

"I am." She savored his attention for a moment, while she poured him a cup of coffee and handed it to him.

He accepted it gratefully. "So, are you going to tell me, or do I need to beg?"

She laughed then. "I had the nicest conversation with Lorna this morning. She asked if she could call me Mom."

For an instant she feared he wouldn't understand, but then

his whole face softened, and he smiled. "Oh, Anna, that's wonderful. That's truly wonderful. I'm so happy for you."

"I'm dancing on air. I don't think anything in the whole world could make me any happier."

"Really? So you're not mad at me about the way I left last night?"

She sat at the table and reached for her own coffee cup. "Well, I was a little upset last night. It seemed like you couldn't get out of here fast enough."

"I couldn't." He pulled a chair out, turned it around and straddled it. "But it wasn't because of you, sweetheart. I realized after I left that you probably thought so, but it wasn't because of you."

"Then what was it?"

"I hightailed it out of here because I couldn't wait to have a couple of very pointed words with Al Lacey."

Her mouth formed an *O* of surprise, and her eyes widened. "Did you? Did you really?"

"Let's just say that I left him with the impression that if he doesn't leave you alone, or if he ever spreads any gossip about you, I'm probably going to rend him limb from limb."

Were it possible, her eyes grew even bigger. For an instant he wondered if he'd made a serious mistake. It wasn't beyond the bounds of possibility that she might resent him for interfering, or that she might object to him making threats of violence. He had known women who would feel that way.

Just as he thought his stomach was going to sink all the way to his boots, Anna laughed. She clapped her hands in delight and laughed, a lovely cascade of sound that made him grin in response.

"Thank you," she said. "Oh, Hugh, thank you! You can't know how good it feels to have somebody stand up for me like that! I've been all alone for so long. This is just wonderful.''

"Well..." He hesitated and cleared his throat, and finally decided there would never be a better time. "Well...if you like...I'd be happy to stand up for you for the rest of our lives.''

As his words penetrated, her smile began to fade. He nearly panicked, thinking he'd gone and said it exactly the wrong way. Or maybe he was mistaken, and she didn't care two figs about him. Maybe...

"Hugh?'' She said his name in a husky whisper. "Hugh?''

"I realize,'' he said hastily, "that there are a hundred reasons why no woman wants a guy like me. You don't have to tell me. But I've kinda...well...'' He swore and drew a deep breath before continuing. "It's the magic, Anna. I've been feeling it with you almost since the first words we spoke to each other. I've been telling myself that I was imagining it. I've been telling myself that it would wear off. But I'm not imagining it, and it's not wearing off.''

She blinked and continued to look at him as if he were speaking a foreign language. It occurred to him that he wasn't using the right words.

"It's getting stronger, Anna. I'm crazy head over heels in love with you—which is probably why I've been acting like a jerk these last couple of weeks. Damn, I'm scared! All I know is that when I'm with you, I feel like I've come home for the first time in my life. Like I've come home for good. Will you at least give me a chance?''

Her face was softening, but he still couldn't tell what she was thinking. Never had he imagined it could be so difficult to tell a woman he loved her. This was worse than going solo into enemy territory. It was easier to face a firefight.

She spoke. "A chance for what?"

"A chance to prove I can be a good husband. A chance to...well...convince you to fall in love with me."

A tear sparkled on her eyelash, and he really panicked. She hated him. She never wanted to see him again. She was just trying to find a kind way to tell him to get lost.

But then she spoke. "I love you, too, Hugh."

For an instant her words didn't penetrate. When they did, he couldn't believe them. "You do?"

"I do. I love you so much I'm terrified by it. And when I'm with you I feel...safe. Safe for the first time in my life. Safe to be me, exactly as I am. I love you, too."

"So..." He stood up, nearly knocking the chair over in his eagerness. He came around the table, and when she rose, he wrapped her snugly in his arms. "So you'll marry me?"

"But what about your ranch? What if my background keeps you from having the youth ranch?"

"Sweetheart, the way I figure it, neither you nor I has anything to apologize for, and neither one of us is going to creep around any longer as if we do. To hell with the rest of the world. If I can't have a youth ranch, I'll find something else to do. But we're not hiding any longer. Will you marry me?"

"Yes. Yes! Oh, yes!"

He kissed her long and hard, and stopped only when they both needed breath. In two minutes, tops, he was going to have her in bed with him again, but first he had to deal with something very important. "What about Lorna? I guess I should ask her, too. If she doesn't want me as part of the family, maybe we'd better hold off until I can convince her."

Anna pointed to the telephone. "Call her right now—555-1545."

His mouth felt dry, and he realized he was really concerned about this. With a slightly unsteady finger he punched in the number, identified himself and asked to speak to Lorna. Moments later he heard her cheerful voice.

"Uh, Lorna? I just wanted to know how you feel about…well, I just asked Anna to marry me. Are you okay with that?"

A moment later he turned and handed the phone to Anna. "She wants to talk to you."

"Me? What did she say?"

He shrugged, feeling that sinking sensation come back. "All she said was she wants to talk to you."

Anna took the phone. A moment later she hung it up.

"Well?" Hugh demanded impatiently.

Anna smiled. "She said, 'Go for it.' She wants to call you Dad."

Epilogue

"Mommy! Mommy, Daddy's coming home!" Seven-year-old Mindy danced into the room, her blond pigtails flying. "I saw him on the hill!"

Anna put aside the skirt she was hemming for Lorna and went to the window to look out. From her second-story aerie she could see the distant hill and the unmistakable mounted figures of Hugh and the six boys he had taken out with him for an overnight camping trip. "He sure is, sweetie. Where's Lorna?"

"Helping Miss Mildred with the birthday cake for Daddy."

Miss Mildred was the cook they had hired to help out with the meal preparations when Anna had become too pregnant to keep up her old pace. She looked down now at her rounded belly and smiled. Could life be any more perfect? she wondered.

Three years ago, shortly after she had been cleared as Lorna's permanent foster parent, the girls' mother had decided to give up Mindy, too. Apparently the constant visits of the child welfare authorities had been more than Bridget wanted to put up with. Mindy had been promptly placed in Hugh and Anna's care with her sister.

A little over two years ago they had received their first batch of troubled boys at the ranch. That program had gone so well that they were now receiving youths on a regular basis, and next Saturday they would be receiving their first group of girls. Along with the program's success had come a group of new employees to help with the care and supervision of all the children.

These days Anna wasn't able to contribute as much as she had in the past, but she was still keeping her fingers in the pie as much as possible. And she still loved living in the second-floor apartment, although when the baby arrived, they might start feeling a little crowded. Hugh was talking about building an addition.

But right now she had to go down to greet the returning group, the way a mother should. Because that was how she looked at all these children. They weren't temporary guests or transients in her life, but children she loved dearly. Hugh seemed to feel the same way, and when the kids eventually left, they kept in touch. Some of them even came back for holidays.

She passed the kitchen and called out a greeting to Mildred and Lorna, who looked as if they were having a wonderful time. She and Mindy reached the stable yard just about the same time the group of riders did.

"Hi, guys!" Anna called out. "Did you have a good trip?"

A chorus of happy yeses answered her, and soon she was awash in tales of wolves on Thunder Mountain, and coyotes, and how good the fish they had caught this morning had tasted for breakfast.

Hugh waited until all the boys had finished talking and had taken their mounts into the stable. Then he scooped up Mindy with one arm and hugged his wife with the other. "How are my favorite ladies doing?"

"Fine," Mindy answered for both of them. "We're making a surprise for you."

"Mindy, hush," Anna said gently. "You don't want to give it away."

Hugh grinned down at her. "It couldn't have anything to do with the date, could it?"

"Don't be difficult," Anna said. "Pretend you didn't guess. It's a surprise."

Lorna came out onto the porch and called a greeting to Hugh. "Mindy, come in here for a second, will you? I need you to do something for me."

Hugh set the little girl down and watched her tear across the yard and disappear into the house. And suddenly he and Anna were all alone, surrounded by the Wyoming summer afternoon.

"How's my sweetheart?" he asked softly.

"Just wonderful. How are you, darling?"

"Never been better. And never been happier to come home."

"It does feel good, doesn't it?" she asked, smiling up at him.

"Sweetheart, there's no better feeling in the world than when a cowboy comes home."

He bent to kiss her, and she lifted her arms to wrap them around his neck and hold him close. Inside her, a gentle, warm peace settled.

When Cowboy came home, she came home, too.

* * * * *

A QUESTION OF JUSTICE

To my sister Pat, for giving me courage
when I most needed it, and for some of the
best advice I ever had. And to Cris, always.

ACKNOWLEDGMENTS

My deepest gratitude to Nathaniel Brown for hours
of research into Wyoming statutes regarding rape,
and for all the advice on procedure. Most
especially, thanks for all the insight into the
personal conflict criminal defense attorneys face
daily. Without your perceptions,
this book would have been a hollow bell.
And, of course, any errors are mine.

Chapter 1

"Counselor, do you have any questions for the witness?"

"Yes, Your Honor, I do." Rising from the defense table, Sandy Keller picked up her pad and tried not to look into the sullen face of her young client. Les Walker, she felt, was going to lose on the basis of his scowl alone, never mind a damning accumulation of circumstantial evidence. In the meantime, all she could do was give him the best defense she could make out of this lousy case.

Conard County Deputy Sheriff Micah Parish sat in the witness box. He wore his inky black hair to his shoulders and bore the stamp of his Cherokee ancestors proudly on his face. She'd cross-examined him in other trials and had no illusion that it was going to be easy to undermine his testimony.

"Deputy Parish, you lifted a fingerprint from the checkout counter at Freitag's Mercantile the night of the robbery, which was later determined to be my client's."

"That's correct."

"How many other fingerprints did you lift from Freitag's Mercantile that evening?"

Micah tilted his head slightly, but met her gaze steadily. "I don't recall the exact number."

Good answer, she thought, but she wasn't going to let him get away with that. It was her responsibility to make it perfectly clear to the jury that a fingerprint, in and of itself, proved very little. "Let's see if we can narrow it down a little. You lifted more than one set of prints, is that correct?"

"Yes."

"More than...oh, a half dozen different prints?"

Micah nodded slowly. "I'm sure there were more than a half-dozen different prints, yes."

"More than a half-dozen." She glanced at the jury as she drove the point home and was glad to see they were following intently. "More than a dozen?"

"I'm not sure. I'd need my notes."

"Well, for now we'll go with 'more than a half-dozen.' Tell me, Deputy, do fingerprints come with time and date stamps?"

She was looking past Micah at the jury, but from the corner of her eye she saw him stiffen. The jury, too, seemed to grow more intent as they realized that something interesting was happening. Slowly she turned her head and looked at Micah. "Deputy?"

There was a kind of wariness around his dark eyes now, something only someone who saw him often would be able to detect. "I don't understand the question, Counselor."

"I thought it was quite clear. Do fingerprints come with a time and date stamp, like a videotape?"

"No."

"Then you can't say precisely when those fingerprints were left on the counter?"

"No."

"Which means you can't say for certain that my client

didn't leave that print there much earlier in the eve-ning...during normal business hours, perhaps?''

He shifted ever so slightly in his chair, and she saw the glimmer of admiration appear around his mouth, a not-quite smile. "No, Counselor, I can't say that.for certain.''

"In fact, Deputy, all you can say is that my client was in Freitag's Mercantile at some time recently. Is that correct?''

"Yes.''

"And just how many people pass through Freitag's on a given day?''

"Objection!'' Sam Haversham, the prosecutor, was out of his seat like a shot. "Counsel is asking the witness to speculate.''

Sandy turned toward Judge Williams. She could have ar-gued, but her point had been made, and the jury knew the answer already. "I withdraw the question, Your Honor.'' She faced Parish once again. "Deputy, were you able to identify all the fingerprints you found at Freitag's?''

"No, ma'am.''

"So...someone else also touched the counter beside the cash register?''

"Yes.''

"Someone you can't identify?''

"Yes.''

"Like the real robber?''

"Objection!'' Haversham was on his feet again.

"I'll rephrase, Your Honor.'' Now she looked directly into Parish's dark eyes. "Deputy, could one of those un-identified prints belong to the real robber?''

That thin, almost-smile again. "Yes, that's possible, but...''

"No further questions, Your Honor.''

Turning sharply away, satisfied that she had done the best

possible job she could in demolishing the importance of that
fingerprint, she returned to the defense table. It wasn't that
she wanted to get a guilty person off—she hoped she never
did that—but it was her job to make sure the jury evaluated
the evidence correctly. To make sure that they didn't put
more weight on a fingerprint than was justifiable. After all,
among the other fingerprints on the counter at Freitag's
might well be one of theirs.

Glancing toward the rear of the courtroom, she nearly
stumbled as she recognized the craggy face of a man who
was seated in the very back row. Garrett Hancock? No, it
couldn't possibly be. What reason could a Texas Ranger
have for sitting in a Wyoming courtroom, listening to a burglary case? None. Absolutely none.

She slipped into her chair and tried to pay attention as
Sam questioned Parish again, trying to undo the damage she
had done.

She couldn't afford to get distracted. This case was a dog;
she didn't stand a chance in hell of getting this young mis-
creant off, but she still had to give him the best defense
possible. That was her job, her duty and her moral responsibility.

But awareness of Garrett Hancock burned at the base of
her skull like a maddening itch, and she had to force herself
to focus on the trial. A trial that she had advised Les Walker
would be a waste of time and probably get him a longer
sentence. It wasn't as if she had any defense to offer other
than that Les's mother was willing to testify that her son
had been in his bedroom at the time the robbery was committed. Considering that the sheriff had found Les in possession of all the stolen goods, considering that he'd purchased a used motorcycle for almost exactly the sum of
money that was missing from Freitag's… Well, Mrs. Walker

was probably going to be ignored by the jury as a biased witness.

Sam Haversham finished questioning Micah, and Sandy declined the opportunity to do a re-cross. She had, after all, said all that needed saying with regard to the fingerprint. The jury would keep it in perspective now, and that was all she could ask...or wanted to.

"You may step down now, Deputy Parish," Judge Williams told him. "Mr. Haversham?"

"Prosecution rests, Your Honor."

"In that case, seeing as how it's nearly three, this court will adjourn until ten tomorrow morning." She brought her gavel down sharply.

"All rise."

Standing, Sandy watched the judge depart the courtroom. A moment later her client was leaving, too, in the company of two deputies.

"That was some hatchet job you did on Micah," growled a low voice in her ear.

Sandy whirled around and found herself face-to-face with the Texas Ranger. A torrent of conflicting feelings flooded her, ranging from pleased surprise that he evidently remembered her from their brief meeting nearly two years ago, to dismay that he was evidently annoyed at her.

And then anger drove everything else away, clearing her head and putting her on her mettle. "It wasn't a hatchet job, Ranger. You know as well as I do that a fingerprint can tie a defendant to the scene of the crime, but it doesn't prove a damn thing."

"It proves plenty. Besides, Micah says the kid has a record a mile long."

"Do you eat eggs for breakfast, Mr. Hancock?" He was

good, she thought, surprised that her abrupt change of subject didn't throw him. He didn't so much as blink.

"Yeah, as a matter of fact, I do," he said.

"Well, there's a plate in my sink right now with egg yolk
on it. I can therefore infer you must be the person who ate
eggs at my house this morning?"

"No, but—"

"Just because a person has committed six rapes doesn't
mean he committed a seventh. Or, in this case, a prior record
for petty theft doesn't mean my client committed *this* burglary."

It took a moment, but slowly one corner of his mouth
hitched up just the tiniest bit. "Point taken. But with all the
other evidence—"

"It is my job to make sure that my client is tried on the
basis of evidence, Mr. Hancock, not inference or supposition. That fingerprint does not prove my client robbed the
Mercantile. All it proves was that he was there at some time.
Just that simple. And I have to make sure the jury doesn't
give it more importance than it honestly deserves."

"You defense lawyers are always getting crooks off on
technicalities."

He was scowling at her now, and she scowled right back.
She'd stopped letting men intimidate her many years ago.
"Considerably less often than you law officers like to think.
Ninety percent of the people who are convicted are actually
guilty of the crime. What frightens me is that the other ten
percent aren't. All I'm trying to do is make sure the jury is
convinced beyond a reasonable doubt and maybe keep some
of those ten percent who are innocent out of jail. That's all."

Turning, she scooped papers into her open briefcase and
wondered why she had ever thought, even fleetingly, that it
might be nice to see this man again. Two years ago she had

been impressed by the sensitivity he had shown toward Faith Parish who, until she had fled to Conard County and met Micah Parish, had been the abused wife of a San Antonio, Texas, police officer. Garrett Hancock had come up here to extradite Faith's former husband, and Sandy had been assigned the unenviable task of representing the abusive cop as defense counsel.

She'd been impressed with Garrett then, but now she wasn't so sure. She had no use for cops who didn't understand the importance of defense attorneys.

"You ready to go, Garrett?" asked the deep voice of Micah Parish.

"Sure. Just renewing my acquaintance with Ms. Keller, here."

"That's right, she was Frank Williams's attorney." Micah gave Sandy one of his almost invisible smiles. "You'll have to come up and have dinner with Faith and me while Garrett is visiting."

She managed a smile and a noncommittal response, and then watched as Micah and Garrett left the courtroom. So the ranger was visiting the Parishes. Well, that explained what a Texas Ranger was doing in a Wyoming courtroom. After a moment, ignoring a sense of disappointment, she returned to packing up her papers. By lunchtime tomorrow, Les Walker was probably going to be convicted. She seriously doubted the jury would be out any longer than it would take to poll the members. For all Garrett claimed that criminals were always getting off on technicalities, in reality it didn't happen very often.

Well, he'd thoroughly soured her mood, she thought as she tramped across the courthouse square toward her office in a small white clapboard house just off Front Street. The house had been left to her many years ago by an uncle and had proved to be a perfect office location.

Nina, her secretary, was busily typing a brief on the computer when Sandy stepped in the side door. A glance over Nina's head told Sandy that no one was in the waiting room, which meant she could kick off her shoes and enjoy a cup of coffee before plunging into anything more.

"Hi, Nina. Anything up?"

"Yes'm." The young woman glanced up with a wry smile. "Sheriff's office called. They've got another client for you."

"It can't be my turn again already!" The county legal society volunteered its members for duty as public defenders on a rotating basis. There weren't very many attorneys in Conard County but there also weren't very many crimes. Sandy hadn't been expecting to get called to serve again so soon.

"This one isn't *pro bono,*" Nina said. "Sheriff Tate asked if you could come over ASAP. They've made an arrest, and the suspect is asking for you."

A defendant with money? That was a rarity! "Just as soon as I have a cup of coffee," Sandy told her.

"How'd it go in court?"

"About the way I expected."

Settled behind her desk, she kicked off her pumps and wiggled her toes gratefully. There was no discomfort quite like having to wear high heels all day, and it seemed to get tougher with each passing year. Maybe, at forty-seven, she ought to admit it was time to come down from three-inch to two-inch heels.

Placed in the middle of her green blotter was a stack of mail, all neatly opened and unfolded by Nina, envelopes clipped to the back of the enclosures. Ordinarily the mail was the very first thing she dealt with when she returned from court, but today she decided to let it go.

She enjoyed criminal defense work more than any other facet of the law, but it was also mildly depressing to expend so much effort knowing it was unlikely she would win. By nature she was a winner, not a loser, and every loss galled her, even a loss like the Walker case, where she hadn't stood a chance in hell.

There were two contests in every court case. The first was the plaintiff against the defendant, in this case the State of Wyoming versus Les Walker. That one mattered professionally.

But there was a second contest that was purely personal, and every trial lawyer knew it. It was Sandy Keller versus Sam Haversham, one-on-one. Who was the best? It was ridiculous to look at it that way, and she knew it, but inevitably, at a gut level, she took defeat as a personal judgment, even though it was nothing of the sort. Juries decided on the basis of evidence, not on the basis of which lawyer they liked best. Still, it would take her a day or two to shake the feeling. It always did.

Which made this a perfect time to go see her new client. Maybe she would get revved up enough to carry herself through the inevitable loss tomorrow. Of course, maybe she wouldn't want to touch this one with a ten-foot pole, either. That was the nice thing about a paying client—she could always turn him down.

But first the cup of coffee. On stocking feet, she padded back out to Nina's office and poured herself a mugful from the pot on the warming plate. Both she and Nina were inveterate coffee drinkers. Around here, the pot was never allowed to go dry.

"Did the sheriff say what the guy was arrested for?"

Nina's fingers paused over the keyboard, and she looked up. "Nope. I got the feeling they're trying to keep it quiet."

"Oh, goody." She spoke sarcastically, but the truth was, her interest was immediately piqued. If the sheriff was trying to keep a lid on it, it must be something big. Maintaining an appearance of indifference, she padded back to her office.

But her stomach fluttered with uneasy anticipation. She'd deferred major cases before, but it had been a while, and there was always a mixture of excitement and fear—excitement at the prospect of a meaty case, and fear that she might not be adequate for the task.

It wasn't as if major criminal cases crossed her desk every day of the week…or even every year. Nor did she want them to. Part of the reason she had returned to Conard County after working for several years in the larger world was because life here was more tranquil. Living on a perpetual adrenaline high didn't appeal to her.

But once in a while it felt good. Like now. She stuffed her feet into her shoes and reached for her briefcase. The desire to dawdle over her coffee had completely vanished, replaced by awakening curiosity. No point spending time in speculation. All she had to do was trot over to the jail and find out what was up.

The tension at the sheriff's office was high, noticeable the instant she stepped through the door. It wasn't so much that people were scurrying around and talking as it was that there were more people than usual and that they were unusually quiet. Something big had happened, but nobody was talking about it. That alone was enough to set off her alarm bells.

Velma Jansen, the dispatcher, didn't even bother to rustle up a smile. "Nate's expecting you, Sandy. Just head on back."

The sheriff's office was halfway down a narrow hallway with a window at the far end. The window looked as if it hadn't been scrubbed since the building was erected, and years of grime and smoke had virtually frosted it. The office door was open, and the sheriff, Nathan Tate, rose the instant he saw her on the threshold.

"Afternoon, Sandy. Micah tells me you did a good job of demolishing the fingerprints on the Les Walker case." One corner of his mouth hitched up in a faint smile that said he was trying to be pleasant. Everything else about him said he was finding it difficult.

Nate and Sandy had grown up together and gone to school together, and ever since had been tussling about the law from different sides of the criminal courtroom. Ordinarily their disagreements were good-natured and minor. Last winter Sandy had been his divorce attorney, very briefly, until he and Marge had sorted things out. Now they were back to their usual "law" and "lawyer" positions.

Sandy smiled. "Micah knows I was right. There's a limit to what a fingerprint proves."

"Good try, but it won't get the kid off."

She shrugged. "My job is to make sure he gets a fair trial. I think I went through this just a little while ago with that Texas Ranger, Garrett Hancock. Is he up here on business?"

"No, just came up to visit Faith and Micah. Maybe you remember, he was the one who investigated Faith's former husband?"

"I remember he came up here to take Frank Williams back to Texas with him. I didn't know he was close to Faith, though."

"They got to be pretty good friends after Garrett stopped Frank from stabbing her to death."

Sandy shook her head. "I never did hear that whole story."

"Get him to tell you. It's no big secret. Right now, I got other things on my mind, so why don't you just pull up a chair? Can I get you coffee?"

"No, thanks, I just had some. Nina says you have a paying client for me."

"Apparently so." Nate settled behind his desk and leaned back, a powerful man with a sun- and wind-reddened face and dark, gray-flecked hair. "Before I start talking as the sheriff, I want to say something as a friend. You want to think real hard before you take this case, Sandy. Oh, I know all the stuff about how even Ted Bundy was entitled to a fair and legal defense, the best defense possible, but you need to consider very carefully, anyway, because this is a case that's going to take a toll on you. It'll be a personal toll for sure, but it will probably also be a professional toll. You might never be able to practice law in Conard County again."

Sandy felt the skin across the back of her neck tighten. "What's he accused of?"

"It appears he raped a five-year-old girl."

Sandy didn't immediately go upstairs to meet her potential client. Nate got called away for a few minutes to handle something out front, so she sat where she was, staring at the wall behind his desk. A topographical map of the county had been enhanced with little pins and flags, but she hardly even saw them.

Accused of raping a five-year-old girl. She could well understand why Nate wanted her to think about it before taking the case. When word of this got out, indignation was going to run high, and the anger would unquestionably spill over on the defense attorney. She would be a fool to dismiss the potential fallout without weighing it and determining whether she was prepared to deal with it.

Rising, she walked to the window and stared out at the gray spring day. It looked as if it might snow again tonight, she thought absently. It was high time the weather started warming, but it appeared that it was going to be a tardy spring.

If the accused went to trial, the public attention would be incredible. Nothing like this had happened in Conard County in her memory, and the rape of a child was always guaranteed to rouse people's anger. Folks here might never forgive her for defending this guy. They would certainly never forgive her if she managed to get him off, and in a case like this…well, there was so much potential for legal missteps that even if the guy was convicted there was a good possibility he could get off on appeal. A child wasn't the best witness, and if there had been any mismanagement of evidence…

She shuddered inwardly. Defense attorney for an accused rapist. Again she shuddered, trying to slam the lid down on a coffin that she'd buried many, many years ago. Could she be certain that she would give an accused rapist the best defense? After all, she knew what it meant to be a victim. All that had happened a very long time ago, and she considered herself well past it, but…what if her feelings prevented her from providing the best defense she could?

That was the other side of this decision. Could she be sure that old ghosts wouldn't prevent her from doing the best job for him? Because that was essential. If she took this case, she had to do the best job she was capable of and set her personal feelings aside.

No easy task, sometimes.

"Sorry to keep you waiting so long."

Nate's voice drew her out of her reverie, and she turned around, managing a small smile. "That's all right. I needed the thinking time."

"You're going to need more of it when you hear the whole story," he said, resuming his seat behind the desk and motioning her back to hers. "It's not pretty. I'll give you the background first, and then we'll get to the reasons we arrested your client."

"Not my client yet."

"Sorry. It's been a long night and an even longer day. The suspect. I'll tell you about him when I get there in the story, okay?"

She nodded.

"You heard that little Lisa Dunbar was missing?"

"I heard about it this morning before court. Someone said she hadn't come home from school last night."

"That's the gist of it. Her mom works, and the eldest daughter baby-sits after school. Only last night, the older girl, Debbie, decided to go to a friend's house instead of coming home from school on the bus with Lisa. The bus driver said Lisa got off the bus alone at four. I don't know if you're familiar with the Dunbar place?"

Sandy shook her head. "Not really. It's been a while since I've been out in that part of the county."

"Well, the bus lets the kids off at the ranch gate, but it's more than a mile walk up the road to the house. Lisa evidently got snatched somewhere along there. There was absolutely no sign that she had gotten home. Mom came home about six-thirty, found both girls missing and no sign they'd come home, and she called us. The eldest girl turned up about twenty minutes later, dropped off by the friend's mother. All she knew was that Lisa had gotten on the school bus to come home.''

Nate shook his head. ''Kids. It was a kid thing for her to do, to let her sister come home alone, but now she's a mess, too, because she's old enough to feel responsible for what happened to Lisa. Old enough to realize it might never have happened if she had come home with her.''

''She can't know that,'' Sandy said. ''There's no way she can know that, Nate! Both girls might have been assaulted.''

Nate nodded. ''I don't think this was done on the spur of the moment, either. Somebody knew those girls came home at that time and had to walk up to the house from the road. Lisa wasn't a target of opportunity. No way.''

Sandy turned her head and looked out the window at the chilly, gray day. The trees in the courthouse square had only just begun to bud. It would be a damn shame if a frost killed them.

No, chilling as the thought was, she didn't believe Lisa Dunbar had been a target of opportunity, either. It wasn't as if she'd been abducted from somewhere full of kids, such as a playground or a mall. Nate was right. Someone had wanted that girl. Maybe both girls. ''How old is the sister? Debbie, isn't it?''

Nate nodded. ''Thirteen.''

''Old enough to watch her sister, young enough to get sidetracked by a friend.'' Sandy shook her head and stood up, pacing to the window and rubbing her upper arms with her hands. ''It's getting colder out there.''

''Yeah. We're supposed to get a frost tonight. It'll kill the trees.''

''Maybe. Okay, the mom called you, and the search began?''

''That's it. We verified that she'd gotten on the bus, that

she'd gotten off at her stop and that she hadn't been seen by anyone since. It was already getting dark by then, but we started a search of the ranch, thinking maybe she'd wandered off the road chasing a jackrabbit or a deer or something. It wouldn't be the first time.''

"No." There had been a case not too long ago where a child that age had wandered off from a campsite following an animal. Search parties had located him some six hours later, unharmed but scared.

"It was cold last night. Nobody wanted to halt the search for fear she might die of exposure. We started getting really uneasy, though, after a few hours, because Lisa knows the ranch. She may be only five, but there aren't too many places she could wander to within a short space of time and not find her way back. You know how ranch kids are.''

"Born with a sense of direction." She'd been one herself. By the age of five she'd wandered freely over quite a large area and had known her way home. Her brother's grandchildren were now doing the same thing at similar ages.

"She'd been missing more than two hours by the time her mom phoned us, and by the time it had been dark for a few hours...well, everyone was pretty much certain she'd been hurt somehow, and nobody was quitting. Then, in the early hours this morning, her book bag was found on Willis Road.''

Sandy drew a deep breath and turned around to look at Nate. "Quite a way from home.''

"Exactly. No more speculation after that. We knew she'd been kidnapped, and we knew she'd probably been hurt. We moved the search over to that area...and found her.''

He passed his hand over his face and shook his head. "Actually, *I* found her, on the creek bank south of Willis

Road. She was naked, nearly unconscious from hypothermia, and it was obvious she'd been raped."

"Obvious?"

"She'd been bleeding, Counselor. No five-year-old girl bleeds that way from any other cause."

She drew a long, shaky breath and wrapped her arms more tightly around herself. "Did she identify her attacker?"

"He was dark, had black hair, long in the back.... Something like that. I took it down, and it's being typed up for the report now. I'll see you get a copy."

"What was her state of mind?"

"Disoriented, crying...."

It might well classify as an excited utterance, then, she thought, which meant Nate's memory of what the little girl had said could be admitted into evidence, rather than being dismissed as hearsay. She would have to make a motion on that, try to prevent it....

And that was when she realized she had almost made up her mind to take the case. She was already planning her moves. Good Lord, did she really want to defend a child molester?

"Where is she now?"

"At the hospital."

"Nobody's questioning her, I hope."

Nate shook his head. "I'm the only one who has. Sam Haversham and her family are looking into getting a good psychologist to talk to her. In the meantime, everyone's leaving her alone and just letting her talk if she feels like it. I hear she doesn't much feel like it."

"She's got to be in a terrible state of shock."

"I'd think so."

Sandy expelled a long breath. "I take it you arrested the

suspect on the basis of her description? It isn't a very good description, Nate."

"Give me some credit, Sandy." He spoke mildly enough, but his eyes held a haunted look that she didn't like. "One of the searchers found signs of recent digging on the property across the road from where we found Lisa. We dug up her clothes. That's when I made the arrest. The guy fit her description, and her clothes were hastily buried on his property."

"What does *he* say?"

"Not a word. From the moment we read him his rights, he hasn't said anything except that he wants you for his attorney."

"Who is it?"

"Craig Nighthawk."

She shook her head. "I don't think I know.... Wait. Isn't he that truck driver who bought Hattie Maguire's acreage a few years back?"

"That's him. Always quiet, kept to himself.... Hell! Up until today I never much thought about him one way or the other." He rapped his fingers impatiently on his desk and then sprang to his feet. "Look, I know you're probably going to take this case. You were always a scrapper, and maybe you think you like a quiet life, but I know better. I'm trying to keep a lid on this mess, trying to keep folks from knowing what happened...."

"Hell, Sandy, the kid's only five. There's no reason the whole damn county has to know she was raped. If word gets out that some kid was raped, everyone will connect it with Lisa Dunbar being missing overnight. I'm hoping if we can keep it quiet for a while we can at least protect the kid's identity."

"I'm with you." She managed a thin smile. "She's suffered enough damage. But do you *really* think you can keep it quiet? You've arrested somebody. There must be dozens of people who know that.''

''I was the one who found the little girl. I called for a couple of my deputies, but none of the other searchers saw her or know that she was raped. Just me, Micah, Les and the doctors and her family know what really happened. And I'd like to keep it that way as long as possible.''

''You've got my word I won't spill the beans. As far as I'm concerned, she's a Jane Doe. So…any other evidence?''

''We're doing tissue samples—she may have scratched her attacker—checking her clothes for hairs…anything that might carry a genetic imprint. I don't know if they've found sperm samples or anything like that. I know the doctors were going to swab for samples. If anything turns up, Sam will let you know. Assuming you take the case.''

Sandy sighed and looked over her shoulder at the darkening day. Should she or shouldn't she?

''I'll talk to him,'' she said finally. ''I'll talk to him before I decide.''

''It won't be pretty. People could get really angry at you if you defend him.''

She faced Nate straight on. ''I won't let that decide me, Nate. Sure it'll be uncomfortable, but everyone is entitled to a fair trial, and the last I heard, everyone is presumed innocent until convicted. That's the point of a trial, isn't it?''

''But principles can be cold comfort sometimes.''

''Yeah.'' She wondered if she was going to be able to live up to hers.

The Conard County jail was above the sheriff's office in an armored room on the second floor. It was a small jail, having only six cells and a conference room where attorneys could consult with clients, and where the sheriff could question suspects.

By the time Nate took Sandy upstairs, Craig Nighthawk was already there and waiting, guarded by a deputy. When Sandy stepped into the room, the deputy nodded and left. She heard the bolt being shoved home with a solid thunk, and then she was locked in with a man who might well be a child molester.

Craig Nighthawk didn't say anything to Sandy, but his dark eyes never left her as she pulled out a chair on the far side of the table and sat facing him. Well, they were even, she thought, not saying a word as she opened up her briefcase and pulled out a legal pad and pen.

"I'm Sandy Keller, Mr. Nighthawk," she said finally. "I understand you've asked for me to be your attorney, but I haven't decided yet whether I'll take your case. If I decide not to, anything you tell me will not be covered by attorney-client privilege...which means I could conceivably be subpoenaed to testify. Do you understand what that means?"

He nodded, his eyes never wavering. Sandy decided he did indeed understand her, so she continued.

"Don't tell me anything you wouldn't want me to have to tell someone else. Now, I don't know why you asked for me, but maybe you can give me a reason why I should take your case."

He never moved so much as a muscle, but she had the distinct impression that he leaned across the table toward her. His intensity was palpable. "I can give you a reason," he said. "It's simple. I didn't do it."

Chapter 2

"He didn't do it."

Nate scowled at her. "Come on, Sandy! You weren't born yesterday! How many times have you heard someone say that when you knew damn well they were guiltier than sin!"

"Plenty. And I never believed them...until now. I'm telling you, Nate, this guy didn't do it. Now you can ignore me, or you can get busy finding out who *did* do it."

He settled his hands on his hips and blew out a frustrated breath. "Sandy, be reasonable. If we come up with some evidence that indicates he didn't do it, I'll get to work on it, but right now the evidence points to him, and he's got plenty of reason to lie about it."

"Nate..."

"Look. We'll collect all the evidence there is. We're waiting for the results from the lab, and we're searching the area out along Willis Road for any additional data we can find. I promise you, if anything turns up that might exonerate Craig Nighthawk, you'll hear about it. We're not in the business of burying information. And we're not in the business of sending innocent people to prison, either."

"Then—"

He shook his head. "Let me finish. We're also not in the business of proving guilt or innocence. That's the job of the lawyers. We collect the evidence, period. We'll let Nighthawk go if we find reason to. In the meantime, if that isn't good enough for you—if you want somebody to *prove* Nighthawk's innocence—maybe you'd better hire a private investigator."

A short while later, standing out on the sidewalk in front of the sheriff's office, she felt the frigid wind cut through the wool of her blue suit. This morning it hadn't been cold enough for her to need more than the suit jacket. Now she wished she had her ski parka on.

She also wished she wasn't wearing three-inch heels on feet that were aching, and that she'd had her hair cut and restyled into something more sophisticated than the bob she'd been wearing for so many years, and that she'd colored it so the gray wouldn't be so obvious...and that she weren't foolhardy enough to believe in the innocence of a man who had no more defense than his own words: "I didn't do it."

She was going out on a limb, she realized. Just because she had looked into a man's eyes while he claimed innocence—and believed him—she was preparing to take an immense risk. Every instinct told her that Craig Nighthawk was telling the truth. *He* believed he hadn't done it. *He* believed in his own innocence, and because he believed it, so did she.

But it had been one hell of a long time since she'd been young enough and passionate enough about anything to *want* to go out on a limb. Awareness of the risks gave her a queasy feeling even as it heightened her senses. But what else could she do? If she believed the man was innocent, she could hardly turn down the case. It wasn't as if defense lawyers grew on trees around here.

The air tasted of snow, she thought, and turned toward her car. Snow. Again. Much as she loved living in Conard County, after six months of winter with only the prospect of a cold spring, she was beginning to think Florida sounded good. Any place far enough south that it wouldn't snow in April and May. Easy to visualize a white beach, blue water and warm sunshine. So easy to imagine stretching out on that beach and listening to the lapping of waves on the shore.

Instead she'd been foolhardy enough to agree to defend an accused rapist for no better reason than that he said he hadn't done it. Good grief, she needed to be committed!

"Ms. Keller."

For just a fleeting instant she experienced a wild urge to ignore Garrett Hancock. She still felt bristly from their encounter after adjournment and wasn't sure she wanted to get freshly irritated. What made her turn, however, were even more fleeting urges and images, furtive feminine feelings she hadn't allowed herself to indulge for so many years.

She was attracted to the man. She'd recognized that the very first time they met. At the time it hadn't seemed like a problem, simply because he was only in town for a couple of days. She'd thought of him once or twice since, with the kind of vague disappointment that accompanied a missed opportunity.

When she'd recognized him in the courtroom earlier, all those vague feelings had rushed to the foreground, reminding her that it was indeed possible for Sandra Keller to be attracted to a man, despite all her resolutions to the contrary. One lousy marriage ought to be enough to warn anybody

off, she'd always believed. Still believed. So why did her
heart skip a beat at the sound of this man's voice?

The smart thing, she told herself, would be to tell him to
get lost. He clearly didn't have much admiration for defense
attorneys, and she was past the stage in her life where she
had any desire to defend herself to anyone. Why defend
herself to a man who would be heading back to Texas in a
few days anyway? Even if she ignored her own good sense
and tangled herself up with him, it would come to nothing.

But despite all her resolutions, despite knowing better, she
turned around with a cautious smile. "Ranger."

Garrett's face was sharply etched, strongly masculine.
Textured by wind and sun, it was ageless. He was lean and
fit, about six feet in height, and his cowboy boots added
another two inches. A good-looking man overall, but his
most remarkable feature was a pair of electric blue eyes.
They seemed to stand out in his dark face, to glow with an
internal light of their own. They probably could look as
glacial and forbidding as Arctic ice, but right now they
looked…as wary as she was feeling. He was uneasy about
speaking to her, she realized, and felt herself relax. Neither
one of them was comfortable, and for some reason that made
her feel better.

"I was on my way to Maude's to get dinner when I saw
you," he said. "Would you join me?"

A moment of common sense nearly caused her to decline,
but before she could frame a polite refusal, she heard her
own voice saying, "Thanks, I'd like that."

Maude's was only a block off the main street, facing
Good Shepherd Church. The menu hadn't changed in forty
years, and the food was still the best-tasting down-home
cooking to be found anywhere. The hour was early enough
that they had the place mostly to themselves, and Garrett

settled them in the booth against the front window so that they could look out at Good Shepherd and the slowly darkening afternoon.

"Snow again tonight," he remarked. "Don't you folks ever get tired of it?"

The question was friendly, as was the faint smile around his startling blue eyes, so she smiled back and admitted, "Often, but that doesn't stop the snow."

He chuckled and passed her one of the menus that was tucked between the ketchup and mustard bottles. "Back home in San Antonio right now, most folks are already using air-conditioning."

"Right now that sounds pretty good." She knew Maude's menu by heart, and after a quick scan of the day's special, she put it aside. "Will you be visiting the Parishes long?"

"I'll be around for a week or so, I guess. I may stay longer. I'm on convalescent leave, so my time's pretty much my own. I'm not sure whether I'll hang around here or head down to Colorado and look up some old friends."

"Convalescent leave? What happened?"

He gave her a wry smile that brought a twinkle to his eyes. "I'd like to tell you some exciting story about a shoot-out, but the simple truth is I was in an auto accident. A drunk driver ran a red light."

"How awful! Are you going to be okay?"

"Oh, I'll be a hundred percent again before long. I just need some time for all the repair work to settle in enough that it doesn't twinge all the time."

"Were you hospitalized for long?"

"A couple of weeks."

Which meant he'd been terribly hurt in the accident, Sandy thought. She wanted to commiserate, to ask exactly how badly he'd been injured, but she didn't feel she knew him well enough. Her silence was just beginning to grow awkward when Maude interrupted it with a demand for their orders.

After Maude stalked off, Garrett spoke with a kind of gruff embarrassment. "I'm sorry I gave you a hard time over your cross-examination of Micah about the fingerprint. I get frustrated sometimes with the way the law works."

She was willing to accept the olive branch—cautiously. "I think we all get frustrated about it sometimes."

"That crack about people getting off on technicalities was a cop's gripe, but one I know isn't fair. We grouse about it a lot, but basically all those technicalities just make us do our jobs better."

"That's the idea." Smiling at Maude when the older woman set mugs of coffee in front of them, she received a glare back. It didn't faze her; that was Maude's usual demeanor. "The standard of proof in a criminal case—'guilty beyond and to the *exclusion* of every reasonable doubt'— demands it. The alternative is 'guilty until proven innocent.' I don't think any of us wants to see that."

One corner of his mouth lifted. "Better that one guilty man should go free than that one innocent man should go to jail, eh?"

"That's the general idea. But it's more than that. If we make each criminal case a battleground for doing it right— for doing it *constitutionally*—then we protect the rights of everyone. Or, to put it another way, if the state can't convince a jury with *legally* collected evidence that a person is guilty beyond any reasonable doubt, then the person is not guilty. Unfortunately, sometimes that means a criminal will go free. Most of the time it doesn't, because the police and prosecutors do their jobs legally." She wanted to sound cool and objective, but instead sounded earnest and intense, something she thought more suited to a young woman than one of her years. At her age she ought to be adopting some of the armor of cynicism, but she somehow never seemed quite able to do that. Get her on the subject of the constitution and the law, particularly civil liberties, and she became as impassioned as any idealist.

Because she *was* an idealist at heart. She truly believed every criminal court case was a constitutional battleground, and that regardless of the guilt or innocence of the defendant, the constitutional right to a fair trial was the real issue each and every time. That was how she could fight as fiercely for a guilty defendant as for one she truly believed innocent...as she believed Craig Nighthawk was innocent.

She wished there was some way she could discuss the case with Garrett. Wished, actually, that she could tell Garrett Hancock that she was defending Nighthawk, and that she believed he was innocent. But she wasn't free to discuss the case, in part because of attorney-client confidentiality and in part because she wanted to help protect Lisa Dunbar's identity. Best just to stay away from the entire subject.

"It's been good to see Faith Parish again," Garrett remarked, saving her the problem of changing the subject. "I don't know how familiar you were with what happened there—"

"Well, I was supposed to represent Frank Williams at his extradition hearing, but then he escaped and tried to kill Faith, and Micah killed him...." She shrugged. "I heard he was abusive and had tried to kill her once before."

"That's right. I'd been investigating him for drug running, and he was indicted on a bunch of counts. After he got out on bail, I got this itchy feeling that something was up, so I started following him again. He made a beeline for

Faith, intending to kill her. By the time I broke into her apartment, he'd inflicted multiple stab wounds.''

''My God!'' She hadn't known and couldn't imagine why anyone would want to treat tiny Faith Parish that way. Thinking of Garrett breaking in just in the nick of time, thinking of how badly Faith must have been wounded and how close to death she must have been, made her stomach feel queasy. It was one thing to read about it happening to a stranger and quite another to hear about it happening to someone you knew and liked.

''Sorry. You don't need the gory details. The point is, I got to know Faith pretty well after that. She felt grateful, and I felt protective. My sister was in a situation like that for a couple of years, and I know just what hell it is. And, of course, Frank was intent on killing her, and I was afraid he might get another chance.''

''They didn't let him out again on bail after that, surely!''

''No.'' Garrett shook his head. ''Maybe you don't recall. He escaped from custody. That's how he got up here after her. I came up once because we got a request for Frank's rap sheet from the Conard County Sheriff, and I thought he'd been picked up for something up here...which wouldn't have surprised me, because I knew Faith had come up here. Turned out Micah was just checking up. A few days later, I was back up here because Frank *had* turned up and been arrested.''

''And then he escaped from the jail and tried to kill Faith again. I'm not normally a bloodthirsty person, but I think the world is better off without Frank Williams.''

Garrett gave her a crooked smile. ''Careful, Counselor. You'll start sounding like a cop rather than a lawyer.''

She smiled back, thinking that maybe he was okay after all. Despite her impression earlier in the courtroom, it appeared Garrett Hancock didn't take himself too seriously. She liked that in anyone, man or woman. "You said your sister had been in an abusive relationship. Is she okay now?"

"Yeah." He patted his breast pocket absently, the automatic gesture of a man looking for his cigarettes. When he didn't find them, he became aware of what he was doing and suddenly grinned. "Bad habit. I quit smoking a couple of years ago, but when I get tense I still find myself looking for my cigarettes. Yeah, my sister's okay. She dumped the guy years ago. The really scary part of it was that her husband had her convinced that she was to blame."

"That's common enough, I hear."

"Apparently so." He shrugged one shoulder. "I'm afraid this is a major concern of mine, so stop me if I get on my soapbox about it."

"That's okay. I don't mind soapboxes. I have a few of my own."

The faint smile returned to his lips. "I guess you do, Counselor."

Maude interrupted their conversation to serve them, muttering something about how the fries might not be just right because the kitchen boy had turned off the deep fryer earlier, and that grease was never quite ready when the thermostat first said it was.

"They look great, Maude," Sandy hastened to assure her. "Just the right golden brown."

"Well, you let me know if they're soggy. I've never served a soggy fry in forty-nine years, and I don't aim to start now!"

When Maude had disappeared back into the kitchen, Garrett's eyes crinkled in the corners. "She's quite a character, isn't she?"

"Always has been. She was just like this when I was a little kid. I don't think she's changed by so much as a hair."

A knock on the window drew their attention, and they turned to see one of the deputies smile and wave before he moved on down the street.

"I like it here," Garrett said abruptly. "If I live long enough to retire, I could easily see coming up here."

"No way, Ranger. You'll be like everyone else at that age—looking for a warm, sunny climate to make life easy and slow."

"I live in one of those climates right now."

"Well, I guarantee that when you're sixty-five the idea of shoveling snow won't appeal to you."

He laughed. "It doesn't appeal to me right now. But the folks here do. Guess that's why I keep coming back."

"It's why I stay. I practiced for a while in a large firm in Cheyenne, but I got tired of the pace, tired of the office politics and infighting. It was such a relief to come back here and live a civilized life."

"*Civilized.* That's a good word for it. Folks here seem to have time to be courteous. You don't find that much in cities anymore. San Antonio's a friendly town, and so's Austin, but not as relaxed as Conard City."

"When there're only five thousand people in an area the size of this county, you get to feeling like family pretty easily. It's great. Really great." She looked down at her plate and wondered why she hadn't just ordered a salad. She didn't really feel hungry. So that Garrett wouldn't feel awkward, though, she had to eat at least some of it.

"I take it you grew up here?"

She looked at him. "I sure did. Conard County born and bred. My older brother inherited the family ranch north of town and still makes a living on cattle."

"But you wanted bigger things?"

"Not bigger so much as just different. I've always enjoyed a good challenge, a good problem to solve. There are plenty of problems to solve in ranching, but not my kind. I was reading casebooks in high school. The law is endlessly fascinating." She paused to eat a fry. They *were* soggy, which gave her an excuse not to eat very many of them. "What about you?" she asked Garrett. "Native Texan?"

"Born and raised. My father was a ranger, too, so I guess you could say it runs in the family." His eyes crinkled at the corners as he smiled at her. "One Riot, One Ranger was a motto I was raised with. Made me into a self-reliant cuss, I guess. My sister will tell you I'm the most frustrating man on earth to talk to or to get information out of." He shrugged. "Can't help that I'd rather listen than talk. I learn more that way."

Sandy was surprised into a laugh. "I'm sure you do. It also keeps other people from learning very much about you."

His smile broadened a shade. "Silence is often mistaken for wisdom. My mama used to tell me that. If you don't tell people every thought in your head, she'd say, they'll think you're smart." He chuckled, and Sandy joined him. "I guess I was a chatterbox when I was little."

"Did you feel pressured to become a ranger?"

"By my dad, you mean? Nah. He used to say he didn't much care what his kids did, as long as they were law-abiding and productive citizens. I didn't exactly set out to be a ranger, either. I joined the FBI initially, because I wanted to work in counterintelligence. Spent about ten years in the Washington area, then decided I really wanted to be living down home in Texas."

He gave a slight shrug of one shoulder. "Anyhow, there

were a variety of reasons why I wasn't very content with
the bureau, so I took a position with DPS, the Texas Department of Public Safety. State police. That was okay, but
for some reason, when the test for ranger came up, I couldn't
resist taking it." He grinned. "Got selected, too. Dad was
proud enough to bust, and I kind of felt I'd finally gotten to
where I wanted to be. Still feel that way. Looking back, I
figure I wanted to be a ranger all along."

"That's how I feel about law—it was the only thing I
wanted to do. It wasn't exactly an approved career for a
woman at the time, but nobody had told me I couldn't do
it. I *did* get a little frustrated when I went to work for that
firm in Cheyenne and they wouldn't let me do any trial
work. They tried to keep me concentrating on family law. I
raised a fuss and finally got my own way, but I seriously
doubt I'd ever have made partner." She shrugged indiffer-
ently. "In the end, it didn't matter, because I was unhappy
there."

"Micah said you have a son."

"Yes, I do. He's graduating from college this year. Then
he's planning to go on to medical school." She couldn't
prevent the smile that rose to her lips. "I'm terribly proud
of him."

"I imagine you are. I was never lucky enough to have
kids. Or get married, for that matter."

"Do you regret it?"

"Not having kids? Not really. It's one of those things I
just never thought about. Mainly because I never married, I
guess. And I never married because I never found a woman
I loved who could put up with my lifestyle. When I get
involved in a case, I lose track of time, even the day of the
week."

"I do that, too. Some things just can't wait." Like the

rape case she had just taken on. She glanced out the window at the dark evening and saw that the first snowflakes were beginning to fall. She had so many things to deal with that she would probably go back to the office' this evening and start thinking about which pretrial motions she could file to buy time and control what evidence would be admitted. And she would need to get hold of Sam Haversham and find out just what he knew and was planning.

"You're taking the rape case, aren't you?"

Garrett's question jerked her sharply back to the present, and she looked at him. "What do you know about that?"

"More than most folks, I guess. I was part of the search party, and I wasn't far behind when Nate found the little girl. I heard they made an arrest this afternoon. I figured that's what you were doing at the jail. Am I right?"

She nodded slowly. "Nate wants to keep this under wraps for a few days, at least, so that the little girl's identity doesn't come out."

"I know. Believe me, I wouldn't discuss it with anyone except you or one of the other deputies. Are you sure you want to get mixed up in this, Sandy? It could get really messy."

"That's a chance I have to take." She hesitated only a moment before adding, "I honestly don't think they've got the right man."

He whistled softly. "Now, that *will* get messy. Do you have any evidence for that?"

She shook her head. "Gut feeling."

"Sandy..."

She shook her head. "You look into that man's eyes when he tells you he didn't do it, and then you tell me he's lying."

He leaned back in his chair and regarded her steadily for long, silent moments. "Okay," he finally said. "Okay. You believe him. How are you gonna prove it? From what I'm hearing, the deck is heavily stacked against him."

"I'm going to need to find an investigator, I guess. But first I want to see what the physical evidence turns up, particularly the analysis of body fluids. The whole thing may become moot."

"Always that chance. But where around here can you find a private investigator?"

"God knows. I'll probably have to bring in someone from elsewhere."

There was another noticeable pause before he cleared his throat and said, "You could ask me. I wouldn't mind taking a little busman's holiday. I'm going out of my gourd with next to nothing to do." One corner of his mouth curved up. "I guess I'd better develop some hobbies before retirement hits me between the eyes, but for right now...right now I'd like to be busy doing what I do best. So if you decide you need someone..."

"I might take you up on it, Ranger." There wasn't a doubt in her mind that he would be the best investigator she could hope to find. He might be difficult to deal with at times, and he might get under her skin, but he was definitely the best man for the job...assuming he could keep an open mind.

"This would be different from your usual investigative work," she reminded him. "You're used to looking for evidence to prove someone's guilty, not trying to find proof that someone didn't do it."

"Comes down to the same thing in the end, Counselor. I've almost never worked on what you could call a cut-and-dried investigation. A lot of the time I start out with a handful of clues that don't point to any particular person. I use that evidence to give me some idea of who might have done it. Sometimes I come up with several suspects, and then have to get together enough information to nail one of them. This really wouldn't be any different. I'd look for something that didn't fit with the theory that this guy did it, and from there I'd start looking for who might have done it. You don't just look for proof of innocence—you look for evidence of who *really* did it.''

"I don't need proof of innocence to get him off. I just need enough to raise a reasonable doubt in the minds of the jury."

"I know. But look at it from *his* perspective, Counselor. What good is it going to do to get him off if he can't live in this county because everyone still believes he's guilty? Nope, you'll have to find out who really did it if he's ever going to have a normal life again." He looked down and then raised his startling eyes to hers once again. "Assuming, of course, that he really *is* innocent. I could conceivably find more evidence that he's guilty."

"I'm aware that possibility exists." Of course it did. While she was inclined to believe Craig Nighthawk's protestation of innocence, she was experienced enough to know that he might be a world-class liar. As much as instinct told her that he was innocent, some little corner of her mind remained warily apart, alert for any indication that she was being used or misled.

"It always exists." He picked up his cup and took a swallow of coffee. "Most of the time the cops arrest the right guy, Counselor."

"But not all the time, Ranger. Ten percent of the time they arrest the wrong guy."

He nodded. "This may be one of those times. I'll have to see the evidence before I can say. I *do* have a great deal of respect for Nate Tate's police work."

"So do I. But there are a couple of things we have to get clear here, Garrett...in case I *do* take you on as an investigator. The first thing is, you're not the judge or jury. You don't decide anything from the evidence. If you make up your mind about this man's guilt or innocence from the evidence that's already been collected, you won't be any good to me. The other thing is attorney-client privilege. If you work for me, you'll be working for the accused and privilege will cover all your communications with him and all my communications with you about anything he tells me. You won't be able to repeat any of it anywhere."

"Even if he says he did it."

"Even if. So you'd better figure out if you can live with that."

He didn't answer immediately. In fact, he didn't answer at all. When he walked her back to her car, he said only, "I'll think about it, Counselor."

He wouldn't be able to live with it, she thought as she started her car and watched him walk down the street toward his own. He was a lawman, accustomed to a suspect's every admission to build a case against him. He wouldn't like the idea of privilege extending to an admission of guilt. But then, few people found that notion palatable. It was something an attorney learned to live with, but something only a lawyer or a priest could understand.

Feeling thoughtful and just a little blue, she backed out of the parking slot and turned her Volvo toward her office. She had a lot of thinking to do, and she would do it best among her law books.

Nina had cleaned the coffeepot and set everything out neatly for the morning. Sandy took advantage of it and started a fresh pot of coffee. It was going to be a long evening, she thought. The arraignment and bail hearing had to take place within seventy-two hours of Nighthawk's arrest, and she would need an argument to get a reasonable bail for him. She figured Sam Haversham wasn't going to want the man released at all and would argue for extraordinary circumstances.

Judge Williams would be inclined to give Haversham what he wanted, too, given that even by Nighthawk's own admission, his only tie to Conard County was the property he'd bought out on Willis Road. It would have been helpful if he'd paid the mortgage off, but as it stood, he had twenty-eight years left on a thirty-year mortgage. Hardly an unbreakable tie for a man accused of first-degree sexual assault. He didn't have any family in the area, didn't belong to any local church, didn't have friends who could vouch for his reliability. He was an enigma, and even after talking to him, Sandy didn't feel she knew a darn thing about him.

He was at least part Indian, to judge by his appearance and his name, and by the fact that when she had asked about a church affiliation he had said he belonged to the Native American Church. Which wouldn't help his case at all if word got out, because peyote was one of their sacramental practices, and to most white folks that would mean he was a drug abuser. Thank goodness his religious affiliation wouldn't be legally admissible in court...not that that would necessarily keep people from finding out.

Nothing was going to help him, she found herself thinking sourly. Nothing. Judge Williams would probably deny bail because of the seriousness of the charges and the fact that there was no way to guarantee that Craig Nighthawk would hang around for the trial.

And that might truthfully be best. She didn't think his hide would be worth a plugged nickel once folks around

here found out he'd been charged with raping a five-year-
old. If Lisa Dunbar's dad didn't go after him, some other
hothead would. Frontier justice hadn't been gone so long in
these parts that it was forgotten. And too many folks just
naturally assumed that only the guilty were arrested—which
was far from the truth, but not something that could be argued with a lynch mob. No, Nighthawk was probably considerably safer where he was.

He wasn't going to like it, but she decided she would
suggest to him that he should refuse bail even if it were
granted. It wasn't as if he would be able to work if he were
out of that cell. He was an interstate trucker, and there was
no way on earth he could haul loads cross-country when he
was forbidden to leave the county, which he would be while
out on bail. No advantages and plenty of disadvantages to
freedom, then.

Sighing, she reached for one of her casebooks and looked
up the Ironshell case. That was a rape case involving a minor, too, and there had been an interesting decision by the
Federal Appeals Court having to do with excited utterances.
And that was an issue she needed to address before the trial,
to see if she could find a way to get the judge to bar Nate
Tate's recollection of Lisa's statements.

She wasn't holding her breath on this one, though. And
if Nate were allowed to repeat Lisa's description of her attacker, Craig Nighthawk wasn't going to stand a chance in
hell...unless they could find out who really had committed
the crime.

Thumbing through the casebook, she hardly saw the
words on the pages before her. In her mind's eye she was
seeing Garrett Hancock as he had looked sitting across the
table from her in Maude's. Hard to believe that the man
she'd had dinner with was the same man who had accosted

her in court earlier and practically accused her of using technicalities to get the guilty off.

Hard to believe he had volunteered to help her investigate this case. She would have taken him for the type to believe that the sheriff must have arrested the right man. And maybe he was. Maybe he was just offering to help because it would be interesting, not because he believed he would turn up anything that would exonerate Nighthawk.

Did it make any difference what he believed? Texas Rangers were sort of the FBI of Texas, renowned as investigators, called in to handle the most difficult major cases. She couldn't ask for a better investigator. And she felt that Garrett had enough integrity to do the job right, regardless of what he believed.

Well, she told herself, this all might become moot if the physical evidence proved that Nighthawk couldn't have done it. A sperm sample might settle the entire case.

Maybe.

In the meantime, she had to ready every weapon in her arsenal, and the first thing she had to do was see how she could get the judge to suppress Nate's testimony about what Lisa had said. And then, if she and Garrett were going to investigate this case on their own, they were going to need time, which meant finding a way to postpone the trial date for as long as possible.

Forcing her attention back to her law books, ordinarily one of her favorite occupations, proved surprisingly difficult. Garrett Hancock's face seemed to float before her on every page, a handsome man who couldn't possibly be interested in her, and who had to be too young for her, anyway.

"Lord, Sandy," she muttered under her breath. "Getting the hots for a good-looking guy at *your* age. Don't you know better?"

Apparently she didn't.

Chapter 3

In the morning, just as she had anticipated, the jury listened with stony faces to what little defense her client and his mother could provide. Twenty minutes after withdrawing to the jury room, they were filing back into the courtroom with their verdict of guilty. Les Walker returned to the county jail to await sentencing.

Back at her office, she found that the Nighthawk case was moving forward. That morning at the ex parte hearing, the judge had approved the prosecutor's complaint against Craig Nighthawk, which essentially meant that Sam Haversham had established, to the court's satisfaction, probable cause for Nighthawk's arrest. Another message told her that the bail hearing would be held that afternoon at three-thirty. A copy of the complaint filed by the D.A. would be delivered to her that morning.

And Nina, having learned from Sam Haversham's secretary what the case was about, was frowning disapprovingly.

"You shouldn't touch this case," Nina scolded, following Sandy into her office. "You have to *live* in this county. If you get that man off, nobody will ever forgive you!"

Sandy dropped her briefcase on her desk and wondered if there might be some legitimate reason to try to get in touch with Garrett Hancock today. The sad fact was that she'd fallen asleep thinking about him last night and awakened this morning with his face before her eyes. She had it bad, and somewhere between her first cup of coffee and getting to court this morning, she had managed to convince herself that the best cure would be an overdose of the man. The reasoning sounded weak, even to her.

"Look, Nina," she said, facing her secretary of twenty years, "if he gets off, I won't be the only one involved. There'll be a judge, and probably a jury."

"Do you think anyone will care about that? Nope. They'll be sure you pulled some fancy legal trick."

"Of course," Sandy said dryly, "there couldn't be any possibility that the man is innocent."

"Of course not—" Nina broke off abruptly and stared at her boss with widening brown eyes. "Are you saying this guy didn't do it?"

"That's what he says."

Nina shook her head sharply. "No! Damn it, boss, that's what they *all* say!"

"Not all of them. Very few, in fact. But it doesn't matter, anyway, Nina. I don't believe all of them. I *do* believe this guy."

"So what's the deal? He has three unimpeachable witnesses who can place him halfway across the continent at the time of the rape?"

Sandy ignored Nina's sarcastic tone and replied levelly, "No."

"Then you don't have a case. Sandy, Nathan Tate is a good policeman. If he says the evidence shows this guy did it—"

"Nate could be wrong," Sandy interrupted ruthlessly. "He may be good, but he's not infallible. Nor do they have a whole lot of evidence at this point. From the verbal information I've been given, I'm almost surprised the judge approved the complaint."

"Well, that doesn't mean a whole lot, either," Nina said tartly. "What *is* going to mean a whole lot is what folks around here will think!"

Sandy blew out an exasperated breath and flopped into the chair behind her desk. "I'll tell you what's important, Nina! What's important is that the Supreme Court of these United States has said that under the Sixth Amendment, the accused has a right to counsel. The right to an attorney. Craig Nighthawk, whether he's guilty or innocent, is entitled to the best defense an attorney can provide for him."

"You don't have to be the attorney!"

"That's not the point! The point is that he's entitled to one. He asked for me. But even more importantly, the point is that guilt or innocence is not decided by me, nor is it decided by *you*. Neither of us is judge or jury, and the mere fact that Nate Tate arrested this man is the poorest excuse I can think of for a conviction! Innocent people *do* get arrested, and without a fair trial there's no way to be certain beyond a reasonable doubt that *any* person is guilty! Nina, you've worked with me for nearly twenty years. I'm sure you understand that by now."

Nina shook her head and sighed exasperatedly. "Forget I said that. The point *I'm* trying to make is that you might have to leave this county if you win this case! Let some other lawyer do this."

Sandy felt herself softening as she always did when someone expressed concern for her; she'd certainly had little enough of that in her life. But now was not the time to be swayed. Her principles were at stake here. "Nina, I appreciate your concern, but I'm going to defend this man. Someone has to do it. If that means I have to leave Conard County—well, that would be a shame. I prefer to think my neighbors are wiser than that, though."

"Oh, they're wise enough," Nina muttered. "Wise enough. In a year or two they might get over it. But what about you in the meantime?"

"That's a risk I have to take."

"Well, I just hope you know what you're getting into."

"I do. Believe me, I do." Sure she did. She was putting everything she had striven for on the line. Conceivably she could lose everything she had worked for. Oh, not because the anger of her neighbors would make life too uncomfortable. No, because they could simply go elsewhere for their legal services. Boycott her. And this county was small enough that a boycott would probably succeed.

But this was ridiculous, she told herself, flipping open her briefcase. She was borrowing trouble. None of those things had occurred yet, and they might well never occur, especially if she could come up with sufficient evidence to get Nighthawk acquitted.

The phone on her desk rang once, a signal that Nina was putting a call through directly, without asking first if Sandy wanted to take it. Which meant the caller was either the Sheriff's Department, Sam Haversham or her son, Gerard. She was hoping it was Gerard. Instead it was Nate Tate.

"I thought I'd give you your druthers," he told her. "We're serving a search warrant on Nighthawk to examine his house and land. Since he's incarcerated, we're going to serve *you*. Do you want us to just drop it by your office, or—"

"I want to be present at the search."

Nate sighed. "I somehow figured you would. What's the point? You know I'm not going to plant anything."

"I want to see what you find, if anything. I want to see where you find it. And I want to know where you haven't looked."

"We're pretty much going to look *everywhere*, and it's going to take a few hours at the very least. The Dunbar girl's panties haven't turned up, among other things."

"Well, I have to be in court for the bail hearing at three-thirty, and before then I need to talk to my client."

"That sure as hell puts us on a tight time schedule." She could hear him drum his fingers on his desk, a rapid tattoo. "Okay. Come on over to see Nighthawk, and I'll serve you the warrant. Then we'll head out to his place. Come three o'clock, I'll bring you back in for the hearing...and I'll give my deputies a coffee break."

He didn't have to do any of this; as far as the law was concerned, Craig Nighthawk's house could be searched on that warrant with no one present except the deputies. Nate was certainly bending over backward for her, and she said so.

"No big deal," he said gruffly. "Believe me, I want this crud convicted for what he did to that little girl, and I want him sent up for a good long time. But I *don't* want his conviction to get overturned on appeal because I did some stupid little thing wrong."

Fifteen minutes later she was in the conference room of the Conard County Jail, waiting for Craig Nighthawk to be brought to her. Sam Haversham had left an envelope for her with the dispatcher, knowing that Sandy would be over sometime today to see her client before the first hearing. While she waited, she reviewed the formal complaint as it had been filed, with the attached copy of Nate's report. Her scalp prickled uneasily as she read.

"Do you know who hurt you, Lisa?"

"Bad man."

"Do you know his name?"

"No name. No name." Child became hysterical, crying and sobbing, needed to be calmed down. Questioning resumed some five minutes later in mother's presence.

"Can you tell me what he looked like?"

"Yes."

"Tell me, Lisa. What did the person who hurt you look like?"

"Big and mean."

"What color was his hair?"

"Black."

"Was it long or short?"

"I don't know."

"Did his hair come down this far? (Chin) Or this far? (Shoulders indicated)."

Child nodded that hair was shoulder-length.

A nod. On the basis of a nod, Craig Nighthawk was in jail. He certainly wasn't the only man in Conard County who had shoulder-length black hair. Sandy shook her head and read further.

It seemed that Lisa had indicated the man's face was "mashed," which the sheriff took to mean he was wearing some kind of mask. His face was dark, she said, but not black. The mask or the assailant's skin...they couldn't be sure, could they? Just because Craig Nighthawk had deep brown skin... She shook her head again.

The judge considered the evidence, meager as it was, to

be sufficient to justify the arrest of Craig Nighthawk. But probable cause for an arrest was a far cry from winning a case in court. If the D.A. couldn't come up with any more than this, Craig Nighthawk would likely be freed at the pre-liminary hearing in a few weeks.

And then he would probably have to leave the county for a long, long time. Garrett had been correct, she thought. Nothing less than complete vindication was going to give Nighthawk his life back.

The door swung open to admit Craig Nighthawk, escorted by a deputy.

"Ring the bell when you're through," the deputy told Sandy, then left the room. The sound of the heavy bolt being driven home was loud in the silence of the conference room.

"How are you managing?" Sandy asked Nighthawk.

"Okay." He shook his head. "Not okay. I'm so mad I could bust a gut!" He jumped up from the table and started pacing. "I didn't do it. I didn't *do* it! What am I doing stuck in a stinking jail cell?"

It was sure going to be fun to try to convince this man to refuse bail if it was offered—which she doubted it would be. Watching him pace, she felt a great deal of sympathy for his plight and could understand the anger he must feel. But that wasn't going to get them anywhere.

"We need to talk, Mr. Nighthawk. We need to discuss matters calmly if we're ever going to get you out of this mess."

He paused, his back to her; then, with a stiff nod, he resumed his seat. "Sorry. I'm just real angry, and there's nobody but you to let off steam with."

"I can understand. I *do* understand. But we have more pressing things to deal with right now. Your anger may have to wait a while."

He gave her another nod, and a sigh escaped him. "Okay. What do we have to deal with?"

"A couple of things. First off, when I go downstairs the sheriff is going to serve me with a warrant to search your house and property for some specific items, among them the victim's underclothes. I told him I expect to be present during the search, so I'll be spending most of the day out there."

"All right. Damn it, maybe they'll believe me when they don't find anything! That kid was never in my house! Never on my property! At least, not with *my* knowledge."

"Well, it'll help if they don't find any more evidence that can implicate you even remotely. But by being there I can know exactly what they find as soon as they find it...assuming they find anything. That's especially important because I want to hire a private investigator, and he'll want to know what was searched and what wasn't, among other things."

"A private investigator."

Sandy waited a moment, letting him assimilate the idea. "It'll be expensive."

"Yeah. What isn't? You think it's necessary?"

"Let's just say I'd feel a whole lot better with someone out there trying to find proof of your innocence, rather than just trying to confirm what they already believe."

He looked away from her, as if restraining himself, then nodded. "It's a hell of a choice, Ms. Keller. Run the risk of spending most of the rest of my life in jail, or spend every penny I've ever saved trying to stay free. Either way, it's going to cost me damn near everything."

There wasn't much she could say to that, so she just waited for him to deal with his feelings. When he finally looked at her again, he appeared calmer. "Okay. Whatever it takes. Where are you going to find a private eye?"

"There's a Texas Ranger vacationing up here. He says he'll do it." Beneath the table she crossed her fingers, hoping Garrett hadn't changed his mind. "They're highly trained investigators."

"I didn't know there were any Texas Rangers left."

"Ninety-six of them, I hear."

"Well, okay. Hire him. What else?"

"You'd better brace yourself, because you're not going to like this at all."

"I haven't liked a whole hell of a lot since Sheriff Tate knocked on my door and told me I was under arrest for the rape of a little girl. What could be worse?"

"Not accepting bail."

The silence in the room was suddenly profound. Seconds dragged interminably while Nighthawk didn't twitch so much as a muscle. Sandy had expected almost any kind of reaction but this. She'd been ready to deal with rage and shouting, but not complete, stony silence.

When Nighthawk spoke, his voice was completely level. Expressionless. "Why would I refuse bail?"

"In all honesty, I don't expect you'll get it, but if you do, I want you to refuse it. Quite frankly, Mr. Nighthawk, you're safer in jail. Word of the charges against you is going to spread across this county like wildfire after the hearing this afternoon."

"And my life won't be worth a plugged nickel."

"It's an unfortunate possibility that someone might try to take matters into their own hands, yes."

He nodded. "Yeah. Yeah, it's a possibility." His mouth drew into a tight line, and he shook his head, as if the injustice were beyond words. "Just how long do I have to sit in this cell? Damn it, I didn't do anything wrong!"

His frustration was palpable. Sandy felt a great deal of sympathy for him, but there wasn't anything that could be done. "I'm sorry, Mr. Nighthawk. Truly. But the judge approved the complaint against you this morning, and at present there is absolutely *nothing* we can do except try to find evidence to prove you didn't do this. Until then, the safest place for you is in the Conard County Jail, sorry as that is. I wish it weren't that way, but if wishes were horses..." She shook her head and left the old aphorism incomplete.

"I know. I have to face reality." His jaw worked tensely for several moments before he spoke again. "Indians learn that early."

"I don't think your arrest has anything to do with your race, Mr. Nighthawk."

He fixed his dark eyes on her. "No, I don't think it does. That isn't what I meant. Surprisingly enough, I don't think my race motivated the sheriff. That's about the only positive thing I have to say about any of this mess, though."

Sandy nodded. "Okay, then. I'll accept the warrant, check it out and accompany the sheriff out to your place for the search. If I can get the investigator to go with me, will that be all right by you?"

He shrugged. "At this point I don't seem to have any privacy left. Why not? Anybody you want can go through my stuff. The sheriff's going to do it anyway. What's another person or two?"

She didn't need him to spell out the feeling of violation this had left him with. The tragedy was that he didn't deserve any of this. At least, she hoped he didn't.

Ten minutes later she went downstairs to get the warrant and was glad to find Garrett Hancock down there talking to Nate. Too good-looking for his own good, she told herself as she felt her heart give a little leap. A striking man, not conventionally handsome, but certainly enough to catch *her* eye. Yeah, she really needed this right now.

"What did you decide?" she asked him point-blank.

"I'm still volunteering."

"Then you're hired."

Nate interrupted the rapid exchange. "Hired for what?"

"Garrett's working for the defense as a private investigator on the Nighthawk case."

Nate turned and looked fully at the Texas lawman. "Why?"

"It'll keep me out of trouble while I'm here."

It was evident to Sandy that Nate didn't like the answer, but there wasn't much he could say about it. "Just remember you're a private citizen up here."

"I won't forget, Nate."

Nate turned to Sandy. "And don't you forget he's not a licensed P.I. Call him a research assistant or something, will you?"

"No problem. And I presume you don't have a problem with him coming along when you perform the search?"

Nate shook his head. "Fine by me. Just keep out of the way, both of you."

Willis Road was about twelve miles out of town and a long way from Lisa Dunbar's home. Garrett owned a four-wheel-drive Explorer, better for the rural roads after last night's snowfall, so they agreed to take his vehicle rather than her Volvo. With a smile he handed her the keys.

"You know a heck of a lot more about driving on snowy roads than I do."

His willingness to admit that warmed her. In her experience, admittedly not the broadest in the world, men were reluctant to admit a woman might know more about or have more skill at anything except cooking and cleaning. Her ex-husband, an attorney at the Cheyenne firm where she had worked, had been like that. He had considered her utterly inept, little more than a glorified legal secretary. It wasn't until they'd been married several years that she had finally realized his attitude toward her had been based on her sex, not on her knowledge or her ability.

Since then she had seen many examples that proved her husband was far from atypical. Some men seemed to be determined to deprive a woman of every vestige of self-confidence, as if only her total dependency on them could satisfy them. Sometimes it was just a subtle but corrosive condescension that slowly ate away at her belief in herself; other times it was open scorn. Coming as it did from someone the woman loved, it was eventually crippling. It had taken her years to reconstruct her self-esteem and self-confidence in her legal abilities alone. In other areas she had never recovered.

Not every man seemed threatened by a woman's knowledge or skills, of course. Nate Tate certainly wasn't, nor was Sam Haversham. And Garrett Hancock's remark about her ability to drive on snow seemed to indicate he was not that kind of man, either. It was nice to think he was confident enough of himself not to be threatened by other people's abilities.

Not that it mattered, she reminded herself sternly. He was heading back to Texas in a couple of weeks, and it was absolutely certain that he intended to head back alone. There was no point in allowing herself to even think otherwise.

Besides, even if he weren't heading back to Texas, he still wouldn't want her. She was a plain woman in her late forties who knew from long experience that men didn't find her attractive. And this one, who must be a decade younger than she was, couldn't possibly be interested in her at all. He was just being nice because he regretted his outburst after the adjournment yesterday.

That settled in her own mind, she forced her attraction to Garrett into the back of her mind. For the umpteenth time. Her attraction to him had a damnable way of resurrecting itself.

There was little enough in the scenery to hold Garrett's attention as he and Sandy drove out to Craig Nighthawk's place. He wasn't sure why he'd been crazy enough to volunteer for this job, but he had a pretty good idea that it involved one slightly bristly lady lawyer—the one sitting beside him, to be precise.

Oh, he was three kinds of fool for even thinking about it. He knew damn well that she wouldn't be interested in going to Texas, and he wouldn't be interested in giving up the rangers, so there was no point to it. He'd never been one for brief affairs.

But if the the only problem in a relationship with Sandy were whether she would move to Texas, he would have been willing to take it on. A compromise satisfactory to both of them might have been difficult, but not impossible.

No, it was experience that made him reluctant to pursue his attraction. He'd had two serious relationships in his life, both of them with women he'd been ready to marry. One of them had lasted right up until a week before the wedding, when he'd been involved in a shoot-out that had convinced Janine she couldn't live with a man who put his life on the line, even if it only happened once in a blue moon.

The other relationship had been just as damaging. Maybe

more so, because it had struck at the kind of person he was. Being a cop was not something he did for forty hours a week. It was his life. He ate, slept and breathed it when he was on a case that required it; anything else and he would never have been a ranger. Shortly after he'd gotten engaged to Wanda, he'd become involved in a big drug case that had demanded his every waking hour and some of his sleeping ones, as well, for a couple of months. Then, no sooner had they closed that investigation than he'd been assigned to a major police corruption case that had kept him on the streets till all hours of the morning. Within six months, Wanda had returned his ring, leaving him devastated.

Since then he'd considered himself a confirmed bachelor, steadfastly refusing to give any woman access to his heart. The simple fact was, when he fell, he fell hard, and being rejected left him feeling gutted. He was a two-time loser who was bound and determined never to give another woman a good shot at him. The thought brought a wry smile to his lips and drew his attention back to the woman beside him. He should be feeling safe, he thought. She wouldn't give up her career to come to Texas, and from what he'd heard, she hadn't even dated much in the twenty years since her divorce. She probably didn't want to put her neck in that wringer again any more than he did. That being true, she posed no threat.

He couldn't quite put his finger on whatever it was about her that attracted him. He'd been pondering the matter, because he didn't like to act without a clear-cut reason and didn't like to feel things he couldn't explain. Part of an investigator's mind-set, he sometimes thought—there had to be a reason for everything.

She was a little older than he was, maybe five years. Didn't bother him at all, nor did it surprise him that the age difference didn't bother him. Such things had ceased to matter to him a long time ago. What he did notice was the sparkle in her fine hazel eyes, eyes that had the clear-sighted gaze of the honest and honorable. He liked those funny little half eyeglasses she perched on the tip of her nose whenever she had to read, and wondered if she'd picked them to make herself look more sober and serious, especially in court. He'd gotten his own first pair of reading glasses just a couple of months ago and understood the dilemma involved in choosing something that changed your face so radically. Yeah, she'd probably picked hers to enhance her image in court. They were kinda cute, he thought.

He liked the way she hadn't colored her gray-streaked hair. It took guts for a woman to admit her age, but Sandy Keller made no bones about it that he could see. The gray in her hair was pretty, as pretty as the smile lines around her eyes and framing her mouth. He never could understand why Madison Avenue forced the smooth face of youth onto the world. Character and living were what built a face and told a story. You could look at Sandy Keller and see that she was a warm, generous person who liked to smile. And who frowned when she concentrated, to judge by the little line between her brows.

So he liked what he saw. He even liked the way her waist had thickened a little since back when he'd met her the first time. Made her look more womanly. It was a waist a man could enjoy squeezing. And when all was said and done, the woman had a hell of a calf and looked sexy as all get-out in those narrow little skirts she liked to wear to court.

It had tickled him to death the other day when he'd caught her slipping her shoes off under the defense table and rubbing the arch of one foot with the instep of the other. Poor little lady probably needed a foot rub like mad by the end of a day on those heels of hers.

And then there was her intelligence. He'd never liked a woman with a block of wood for a head. Or a man, for that matter. A little native intelligence was always helpful. In this woman's case there was considerably more than mere native intelligence. He wondered if she had any idea just how bright she really was. Probably not. She didn't seem to be at all full of herself, which was another thing he liked a whole lot about her.

She probably didn't know it, but her eyes would settle on him sometimes and then leap quickly away, as if she were afraid of being caught looking—and that told him as clearly as anything that she wanted him, too. Otherwise she wouldn't have been afraid of being caught looking at him. And that realization pleased him more than he felt really comfortable with.

Simple fact was, nothing could come of this, and he damn sure didn't want to get involved, anyway.

But that didn't stop a man from noticing and didn't stop him from wishing. Nor did it stop a woman, he thought with an inward smile as he returned his attention to the snow-covered countryside. He wondered if Sandy might be interested in a little innocent fun over the next couple of weeks. He didn't think she was the type to go to bed with a man she didn't feel committed to, but then, he wasn't that type, either. So maybe they could just date casually and make this cold gray spring a little warmer. Make the evenings a little more pleasurable. A harmless flirtation.

Sounded good to him.

Craig Nighthawk's house was set well back from the road, not visible to passing traffic. Nor was any activity along the road visible from the house and barn. Garrett commented on that as they turned off Willis Road and into the untouched driveway, identifiable only by the open gate at the roadside and the parallel rows of snowdrifts left by a winter's worth of plowing. Sandy followed the three sheriff's vehicles, feeling as if they were bucking from one rut to the next. Nighthawk needed to grade his driveway.

"What difference does that make?" she asked Garrett, her voice breaking as they struck yet another rut.

"Just that someone could have come off that road and buried something on Nighthawk's property, and chances are he'd never see 'em."

"And?"

"And it's just bugging me that the little girl's clothes were found on his property. Ask yourself, Counselor, if you'd bury the evidence on your own property."

Sandy shook her head. "*I* wouldn't, but don't forget the guy who gave the bank teller a holdup note written on his own deposit slip."

"Or the one who used a taxi for his getaway car and gave the driver his home address." Garrett chuckled and shook his head. "I know. I've met plenty of them. Does Nighthawk strike you as stupid?"

"Actually, no."

"Me neither."

"When did you meet him?"

"During the search for the little girl. We let him know we were searching his property for a missing kid. Came right out to help. Of course, a guilty man would have done the same. That doesn't mean anything at all. But I had a chance to talk with him for a few minutes here and there, and he didn't strike me as a fool. Or as a nervous man, come to that."

"And you've been thinking about that."

"Yep. Since we talked about it yesterday, I've been thinking over how he acted the night of the search, and it just doesn't strike me as the behavior of a guilty man. I've been wrong before, though."

"I'd like to find the truth. Honestly, Garrett, I'd really like to find the truth. That's something a defense attorney rarely knows and isn't supposed to care about. Defending someone rarely involves seeking the truth about what happened. My job is to make sure the defendant gets a fair trial under the law, and the decision made by the jury is one of guilt or innocence. I imagine most of the time we get a pretty clear picture of what actually happened, but that's a far cry from trying to discover the *truth.* And my job, or the prosecutor's job, is certainly not to *prove* the truth." She shook her head slightly. "Just once I'd like to know what the truth is, and in this case more than ever. If that man is innocent, this is one time when *innocence* will have to be proven beyond and to the exclusion of any reasonable doubt. Like you said last night, he'll never have any chance at a normal life here otherwise."

"So we do our damnedest to find the real culprit?"

"That's the idea." She glanced at him. "Did you think I wanted you to do something else?"

He shifted a little on the seat. "I just wasn't sure what I was supposed to do if something comes up that looks bad for your client."

"*Our* client, Ranger. Our client. What you do is tell me about it. I don't believe he did it, Garrett, but if he did, well…I want to know that, too. This time I definitely want to know that."

"That could make things uncomfortable for you."

"I'm not worried about that. But attorney-client privilege

only covers what my client tells me. It doesn't cover physical evidence. I can't obstruct justice any more than the next person."

"That considerably relieves my mind."

She glanced at him and smiled. "I kinda thought it might. No, we're no more in the business of suppressing evidence than anyone else. Just remember, anything Nighthawk tells us *is* privileged, and we can't repeat it."

"I can live with that."

Craig Nighthawk owned his own rig, a big black Kenworth to which was attached a fifty-foot trailer bearing the logo of a national transportation company. It was parked in the barn, which had been converted into a garage cum workshop. From all appearances, he also did all his own work on the truck.

"This seems a mighty strange place for an independent trucker," Garrett remarked. "How many big loads go out of this town?"

"He's got a regular hauling job with a big trucking firm. They hire owner-operators all the time."

He gave her a sheepish grin. "I'd forgotten that. But it still seems like a mighty strange place to call home. He must drive a long way to pick up a load."

She turned to look fully at him. "You can question him about that if it seems significant."

"Maybe I will, Counselor. Let's see what else turns up first."

The sheriff searched the truck first but found nothing of significance there. "Looks like he cleaned it up getting ready for another haul," Nate remarked. "Hell, the rug in the cab has even been vacuumed."

The compartments in the cab yielded nothing of interest, either.

The house, a single-story ranch, had the sterile look of a hotel room.

"Man doesn't spend a whole lot of time here," Garrett remarked quietly to her.

The only things that gave evidence of occupancy in the main part of the house were a rinsed-out coffee mug and spoon in the kitchen sink, some cereal and coffee in the cupboard, and cold cuts in the fridge. Not much. There were no family photos in the living room, no sign of personality or habitation. The back of Sandy's neck began to prickle uneasily, and more than once she glanced at Garrett to find him looking doubtfully at her.

"He's not here much," she whispered to him as deputies checked beneath the sofa cushions and chairs, and behind the curtains.

"Yeah." Still looking doubtful, he kept his attention on the searching deputies.

Sandy found she had wrapped her arms around herself, a sure sign of uneasiness. This didn't look good, she thought. A home shouldn't be sterile, not even when it was only occupied for a couple of days a month. Had she been a complete fool? Was the man simply an accomplished liar?

"I don't like this," Nate said finally, looking Sandy right in the eye. She didn't reply.

They moved down the hall, finding two bedrooms that didn't contain any furnishings. Even the closets were empty. The next room appeared to be his bedroom, with a neatly made iron bedstead that looked old enough to be a relic from the last century, complete with nicks and dings. The dresser was small, four drawers on wooden legs. A deputy searched it minutely while Nate and Sandy watched. Little there but clean underwear and neatly folded T-shirts.

In the very bottom drawer, however, they came across a

photo album, one of the old-fashioned kind with black pages and little black corner-holders that had to be glued in place. Black-and-white photos covered every page, and many were tucked in between pages.

"Family photos," Nate said, as they flipped through the album.

For an instant Sandy considered objecting, because it was highly unlikely that they were going to find a little girl's underwear tucked into the pages of a family photo album. Strictly speaking, there was no need for the deputies to even look. But she held her tongue, because they could legitimately argue that a tiny pair of underpants could be tucked almost anywhere, and a photo album would be a likely hiding place. Chances were a judge would uphold the deputies on that one.

At least they tucked the album back safely before they continued their search. In fact, the entire search was respectful of Nighthawk's property. Everything that was disturbed was returned to its original condition.

Next came what appeared to be a combination of hobby room and office. A huge sand table dominated the room. It had been carefully contoured into hills and valleys, and miniature trees dotted it. What really caught Sandy's attention, though, were the exquisitely crafted and painted tin soldiers that had been positioned on it.

"He's a war-gamer," Garrett remarked. "A really serious one, to judge by this. Almost nobody bothers with sand tables anymore."

"Looks like Austerlitz," Deputy Beauregard remarked. "Those are French and Austrian uniforms from the early part of the nineteenth century."

Nate cocked an eye at him. "You a war-gamer, too?"

Beau shrugged. "I read a lot of military history."

"Boss!"

They all turned in response to the excited exclamation from Ed Dewhurst, who had just opened a rolltop desk.

"Boss, come look!"

Sandy was right beside Nate as they hurried across the room. Her only thought was, *Please don't let it be Lisa Dunbar's missing panties.*

It wasn't. But it was almost as bad. Lying on the desk in plain sight was a color photo of a little girl, maybe two or three years old. She stood in a big metal washtub, and she was completely nude.

Chapter 4

Garrett and Sandy were nearly silent on the drive back to town. Nate had taken the photo of the little girl as evidence, and while it didn't prove a thing, it was damning nonetheless. Sandy's stomach felt queasy even as she tried to put an innocent explanation on it. She could hardly bring herself to look at Garrett, who must have been wondering what he had gotten himself into. She was afraid he was going to tell her that he couldn't continue helping her.

That thought upset her far more than it should have. After all, she could find another private investigator somewhere. But she wanted to work with Garrett, not with some stranger from Cheyenne or Laramie or wherever. The strength of her desire warned her that more than professional considerations were involved. She wanted the excuse to be near him, to see him, to talk with him. It was a purely selfish desire, the likes of which she couldn't remember having since high school.

Oh, it was ridiculous, she scolded herself. Absolutely ridiculous. She had more important things to occupy her time than her attraction to a man who would be leaving the county in a few weeks. But she couldn't help stealing surreptitious looks at him and wishing he weren't leaving. Wishing he would turn those intensely blue eyes on her with something more than friendliness.

But she had wished that before, and nothing had come of it. All the lessons life had taught her still hadn't squashed the girlish hope that somewhere there was a Prince Charming for her, a man who could make each day a joy. A man who could make her feel that she was important and needed. A man who could make her feel loved and cherished. A man who could grant all those foolish, girlish dreams that her marriage had demolished with such careless precision.

Unwittingly she sighed, then realized it when Garrett glanced her way. He was frowning, she saw, and she could almost imagine him forming the words to tell her that he'd changed his mind about working on this case. Instead, astonishing her, he said, "I think you'd better ask Nighthawk about that photo. It doesn't look good."

"No, it doesn't." In fact, sitting there and thinking about Prince Charming had been a great way to avoid thinking about that very thing. She wasn't ordinarily the kind of person who refused to look facts in the eye, but this fact was more than a little unpalatable. The thought that she might have been completely mistaken in her judgment of Nighthawk undermined what little self-confidence she'd been able to amass in the years since her divorce. If she could be this wrong about Nighthawk, then she couldn't trust her judgment about anyone.

Scary thought indeed.

"It could be purely innocent," she said finally.

"Given the reason he's been arrested, that's a little hard to believe just now."

"I know." She hated to admit it, but she was too honest to do otherwise. As an attorney she could see all too clearly the difficulties such a photo would raise if presented to a jury, and how hard it would be to overcome the doubts it would plant. If that picture was innocent, they had to prove it in such a way that it would never come before a jury as evidence.

Sam Haversham would undoubtedly try to get it admitted under Rule 402, claiming relevance because it showed a tendency toward pedophilia on the part of Nighthawk. Unless Nighthawk had a good story to explain the picture, she would have to argue from Rule 403 that the photo would excite prejudice in the jury. Somehow she didn't think she would win that one.

She sighed again and looked at Garrett, wondering what he was thinking. Here they were, confined by the cold day to this small space in the cab of his Explorer, and yet she felt utterly isolated. Which was stupid. She hardly knew this man, after all, but he seemed so far away right now....

He turned suddenly and glanced at her. "You have to be in court this afternoon, right?"

She nodded. "For Nighthawk's arraignment and bail hearing."

"Word of this is going to get out, Sandy. Nate's not going to be able to keep the lid on it much longer."

"I figure it'll get out this afternoon. Somebody at the courthouse will undoubtedly spill the beans, probably right into Kent Reed's lap."

"Kent Reed?"

"Publisher and editor of the *Conard County Sentinel.*"

"Ah, the media."

Sandy was surprised to feel a smile tug her lips. "Yes, the media. Only I don't think Kent sees himself that way.

He's not a caped crusader, merely somebody who likes to tell a story. Before Gutenberg, he would have been a troubadour, I think.''

"I'm surprised he can afford to keep a paper going in a community this size.''

"I don't imagine it's easy. He used to publish three times a week, but now he's down to once.''

"So how long does that give us before the story is the talk of every household in the county?''

Us. His choice of word left her feeling weak with relief. *Us.* "So you're not quitting?''

"Quitting?'' He glanced at her again and smiled slightly. "No. I figure he's guilty as sin, but the evidence will show that. All I'll be doing is looking for evidence. If it proves him innocent, well...'' He shrugged one shoulder. "Wouldn't be the first time I've been wrong.''

"Nor I.'' With an effort, she suppressed another sigh and looked out the window at the passing snowy countryside. "Well, if Kent publishes the story based on information he gets today, I would imagine it'll be on the front page tomorrow.''

"That doesn't give us very long.''

The muscle in his cheek was working, as if he were clenching and unclenching his jaw. "It's been nagging at me that whenever the news gets out, Nighthawk won't be the only person who could become a target.''

She felt the skin on the back of her neck crawl. "I don't think...'' The sentence trailed off as she realized that she *did* think it was possible that some person might actually choose her as a target if they couldn't get to Nighthawk because he was in jail. It sure wouldn't be the first time an attorney was threatened for defending an unpopular client.

"I didn't think that had occurred to you,'' Garrett said.

"I've been in law enforcement a long time, Sandy, and I've seen plenty of lawyers threatened by people who hold them responsible. Take a case I saw just recently, where a prosecutor was sent a bomb because he didn't get some guy convicted in a rape case. Then there was the defense attorney who got shot at for getting an accused murderer off. Funny thing was, in that case the guy *was* innocent. We found the real perpetrator just three days after the acquittal. Problem is, too many people think that just because someone is charged, he's necessarily guilty."

"I've been saying that!"

"And I've been hearing you. You're right. Innocent people *do* get charged and tried. But guilt and innocence isn't the issue so much as what people perceive to be the failure of the criminal justice system. Your neighbors are probably going to see you as some slick lawyer who's going to try to get a crud off on some technicality or other."

"They know better than that! I've lived here almost my whole life!"

"And now you're defending a man who's accused of raping a child. Sandy, they're going to believe Nighthawk is guilty, and they're going to believe that you're somehow standing in the way of justice. Oh, most of them will realize that isn't the case, but all you need is one nut. Just *one*."

She averted her face, looking blindly out at the snowy countryside. She didn't want to think any of the people she knew were capable of such things, but she couldn't deny the possibility.

Garrett was right—faith in the criminal justice system had never been lower. People were inclined to believe that anyone who was arrested was guilty. What they failed to remember was that, in many cases of acquittal, a jury—made up of people just like themselves—hadn't been convinced of the guilt of the accused. And when a defendant got off on a so-called technicality, it was because the error was so serious that it had prevented an impartial trial. Those "technicalities" were the very things that prevented innocent citizens from being beaten into confessing crimes they hadn't committed, that protected ordinary people from being tried and convicted on the basis of lies or past behavior. In reality, those "technicalities" protected the innocent more often than they protected the criminal.

Most criminals didn't get off, despite popular opinion after several highly publicized cases, such as one where the defendants had actually been videotaped in action. Most criminals who were caught were convicted.

But that was neither here nor there. The people of this county had a great deal of faith in Nathan Tate, and if he had arrested Nighthawk, then a good eighty or ninety percent of the people were going to believe that Nighthawk was guilty. Which came right back to the necessity of finding the real culprit. In this case, a verdict of not guilty wouldn't be sufficient. Not when people believed that where there was smoke there was fire. Not when public outrage would demand that someone pay for this heinous crime.

And if people believed that Sandy might keep Nighthawk from paying, then they could well make her the scapegoat.

Garrett sat in the back of the courtroom, waiting for Judge Williams to make her appearance. Sandy was at the defense table, sitting with crossed legs and talking to Sam Haversham, who was resting one hip on the table and idly swinging his foot. It was apparent that however much those two might go toe-to-toe in the courtroom, there was a great deal of liking and mutual respect between them. That spoke well of them both, Garrett thought.

The courtroom was busier than usual this afternoon. Across the hall, the municipal court was, as always, busy with traffic court and small claims actions. Here, matters tended to proceed at a slower and quieter pace, as he'd noticed during his few weeks in the county. Crimes tended to be rather minor as a rule, most cases being more like Les Walker's burglary trial. Rarely was there more than a small handful of people present, most of them older folks.

But today it was different. Word had gotten out somehow; there wasn't a doubt in Garrett's mind. There were too many people for an ordinary arraignment and bail hearing. These folks had heard that something big was happening. So much for Nate's desire to keep things quiet for a little while.

The side door opened, and two deputies escorted a handcuffed and leg-shackled Craig Nighthawk to the defense table. The man's eyes burned, Garrett noted. Those dark eyes swept the courtroom with a kind of angry disdain. It was the look of a man who'd had his worst suspicions confirmed.

Garrett watched him with a policeman's eyes, wondering if the man was really guilty. Before he'd seen the photograph of the little girl, he would have said Nighthawk was probably innocent. The man had been too calm the night of the search; nothing about him had struck Garrett as being the behavior of a guilty man. And most guilty people telegraphed their nervousness and lying somehow. But not all. Not all. And that left the question of whether Craig Nighthawk was simply an incredibly good liar and a nerveless criminal. Though they were rare, they existed.

"All rise."

Judge Williams took her seat at the bench, and the hearing proceeded. The charges were read; Nighthawk was questioned as to whether he understood them. Sam Haversham argued against bail, pointing out that Nighthawk's ties to the community were very slender. It was Sandy who broke the ritual and sent an audible ripple of shock racing through the courtroom.

"The defendant waives bail, Your Honor."

The judge waited a few moments for the murmuring to die down before she spoke, this time directly to Nighthawk.

"Mr. Nighthawk, do you understand that waiving bail means you will remain in jail during the pretrial and trial periods?"

Nighthawk didn't even glance at Sandy. "Yes, Your Honor. I do."

"Is there a reason you prefer to waive bail?"

"It appears that I will be safer in jail than at home until this is settled."

Judge Williams looked down at the bench for a few moments, then returned her attention to Nighthawk. "Unfortunately, Mr. Nighthawk, I'm inclined to agree with you. This court accepts your waiver of bail. Defendant will remain in custody until such time as the charges against him are decided."

The courtroom emptied almost immediately, substantiating Garrett's suspicion that the people had come only because they had heard about the case. Another arraignment was scheduled to follow, but as it wasn't Sandy's case, she was free to leave. Garrett joined her, walking with her out into the cold, clear late afternoon.

"People know," he said.

"So it seems. It was bound to get out."

"Yeah." His breath created clouds of ice crystals, which sparkled in the slanting, almost golden, sunlight. "Sandy, I'm probably being overly protective, but I don't think you ought to go anywhere alone until this is settled."

She stopped walking and turned to face him. Most of the

crowd from the courthouse had dispersed, and they were the only ones walking down Front Street. The homes lining either side of the street presented opaque windows and closed doors, creating a sense of privacy. Even the snow added to a sudden sense of isolation as it muffled all sound.

"I can't hide, Garrett," she said. "I can't allow myself to become a prisoner of fear. I learned that a long time ago."

He looked down at her, admiring her fine eyes, wide and clear and straightforward, and wanted to ask her how she had learned that lesson. Instinct warned him that it was not something she would be willing to discuss with a near stranger. "I'm not suggesting you become a prisoner of fear. Just asking that you be cautious. Instead of walking between the courthouse and your office this way, maybe you ought to take your car. Don't go out alone after dark. Just that simple kind of stuff."

For an instant she hesitated visibly. Then she shrugged and resumed walking. "For a woman, danger doesn't exist only on the streets, Garrett. It just as often exists in the home and among friends."

He stared at her back for a moment before he took a couple of quick steps and caught up with her. "What's that supposed to mean? I'm aware of domestic violence, but that's not the issue here. I'm worried about what one of your neighbors might take a notion to do if he starts to think you might get Nighthawk off."

"And I'm telling you that I refuse to live my life in fear. If I did that, I'd have to hide in a windowless, doorless room and never talk to anyone again!"

Her words struck him. Something about the words she'd chosen told him that she had faced fear, real fear, and conquered it. That she had measured in very real terms exactly what the cost would be of letting it control her.

His entire perception of her shifted sharply. For whatever reason, it had never occurred to him that she might have known serious hardship and fear. It gave him a better idea of just how much courage she really had and raised his estimation of her even higher.

It also made him even more concerned for her. Such courage was founded in innate strength, but it could also be very fragile precisely because it had once been so severely tested. There was simply no way to know in advance.

"I'm probably worrying too much," he admitted. "It's part of being a cop, to expect the worst of people."

They turned onto the sidewalk leading up to her office and climbed the steps onto the porch. "That's okay." She glanced up at him with a faint smile. "It's nice that you care. I just don't think folks around here are like that. They may get angry at me during the course of this case, but I honestly don't think anyone would attempt violence."

Violence, he thought as he escorted her inside, was not always necessary to create terror. Terror could be as intimidating as any actual threat of violence, and it could be just as psychologically damaging. It wouldn't take much for someone around here to scare Sandy half to death.

But he kept that thought to himself.

"Someone needs to open a Chinese restaurant here," Sandy told the empty room. The lack of Cantonese and Szechuan fare was about her only complaint about Conard County. Tonight, sitting on her living room floor surrounded by copies of all the prosecutor's files on the Nighthawk case, she was faced with a choice of canned chow mein or frozen pizza. Neither one tempted her.

She loved to cook, but cooking for one was a pain in the neck, and shopping for one was just about as bad. As near as she could tell, frozen foods were designed for one, but everything else was designed for three or more. It became tiresome to have to buy enough food for three and then repackage it…and then go to all the trouble to prepare a single stuffed pork chop. If she got the urge for lasagna, she made the smallest one she could manage, froze the leftovers in individual portions…and wound up eating lasagna for the next eight weeks.

Hence, frozen dinners, canned chow mein and French-bread pizza. Faced with that selection, she once again postponed dinner, even though her stomach was growling. The only other alternative was to go to Maude's, and she hated to dine out alone—even though she'd had plenty of practice at it. Besides, the night had turned blustery, and even in her cozy living room, with the curtains drawn, she could hear the rattle of snow blowing against the windowpanes.

The physician's report on Lisa Dunbar was uncomfortably graphic, even though it was couched in medical terminology: vaginal lacerations and contusions; bruises around her neck as if her assailant had choked her; assorted other cuts and bruises indicating that she had struggled and been struck; a mild concussion consistent with shaking.… Sandy felt her gorge rise, and along with it fury at a man who could do such things to a small child.

There was no doubt Lisa had been brutally raped, but whether physical evidence—vaginal swabs and nail scrapings—would yield any conclusive evidence about the identity of her attacker remained to be seen.

Which left a lot of circumstantial evidence. The girl's clothes had been found hastily buried on Nighthawk's property, the girl herself had been found along a stream bank just across the road from Nighthawk's property, and a photograph of a nude toddler had been found in Nighthawk's house. Other than that, there was a vague description of a man with a dark, "mashed" face and long black hair.

And not one other thing. What they had right now shouldn't be enough to convict. If genetic testing wasn't conclusive, then the jury shouldn't return a verdict of guilty. But the jury probably would, anyway. Sandy felt it in her gut, and knew that if she were on the jury and was presented with this crime and this evidence, it would be damn hard to maintain a reasonable doubt. An act of this nature cried out for retribution and punishment. She would need a lot more than Craig Nighthawk's protestations and a lack of definitive evidence to get him acquitted.

And now, in the privacy of her own mind, she could admit that, after finding the photo, *she* needed more than that, too. She didn't want to spend the rest of her life wondering if she had gotten a guilty man off merely for lack of evidence.

She wasn't sure she could live with that. The man who had hurt Lisa Dunbar deserved to go to prison for what he had done. But more than that, he had to go to prison to protect other little girls. It was a sad fact that people who committed crimes of this type rarely committed them only once. The man who had raped Lisa was a threat to every little girl he would ever meet. That couldn't be allowed.

So this time, lawyer or not, she needed more than a reasonable doubt. This time she needed proof. She needed to be sure that the real criminal was found and convicted. Her intuition told her that Nighthawk was telling the truth, and for that reason she would take the case. But beyond that, she couldn't allow intuition to guide her. This time she had to *know*.

After having lived for many years in the belief that it was not innocence that needed proving, but guilt, she found it strange to be taking the opposite position on this case. It was uncomfortable to realize that the principles she had always espoused were not enough this time. That she, like most of the rest of the world, needed definitive proof of innocence.

If Nighthawk wasn't guilty, then they had to find out who was. Discovering the real rapist was essential for so many reasons.

And if anyone could discover who'd really done it, she suspected Garrett Hancock could.

With a mental shake, she tried to drag her thoughts back to the file folder in her lap, but her stomach growled, and her mind wanted to wander down byways that involved Garrett. The man was taking up too much of her time, invading her thoughts at the most unexpected moments and making her want to moon over him the way she hadn't mooned over any man since her marriage.

Shaking her head again, she forced herself to start reading the paper in front of her. It was the physician's record of his interview with Lisa Dunbar, reporting the questions he had asked about her injuries and her responses.

"Was it a man who did this to you, Lisa?"
Child nods.
"A grown-up?"
Nod in response.
"Did he put something inside you here?"
"Hurt me!"
"Yes, I can see you're hurt, Lisa. It must have hurt very badly."

Just then the doorbell rang. Sandy hesitated, thinking that whoever it was could just go away. It had to be a salesman, because any of her friends would have called first. On the other hand...

Sighing, she put the folder aside and struggled to her feet, wincing as her legs protested a little from being folded up under her for so long. "Use a chair next time, Keller," she muttered to herself as she headed for the stairs. "That's what they invented desks for!"

For convenience's sake, her office and home were in the same house, with her office downstairs and her living quarters upstairs. Moving the kitchen upstairs had been the most expensive part of the transition, but it had given her a truly cozy apartment.

But it also meant that she had to descend the stairs into the darkened office to answer the doorbell, and even though she flipped on the stair light, she found herself strangely uneasy. All Garrett's talk about people getting angry at her, she thought, it must be working on her subconsciously, although she quite seriously believed she had nothing to fear from her neighbors, other than a few harsh words.

Rationalizing her uneasiness didn't keep her from peeking around the edge of the curtain that covered the window beside the door. A relieved breath escaped her when she recognized Garrett. What was he doing here?

It took her only a moment to throw the dead bolt and fling the door open. "Garrett! What's wrong?"

"Not a damn thing," he said with a wry half smile. "I went to Maude's for dinner and realized I didn't feel like eating alone. So..." He held up a big brown bag. "I talked her into making us some roast beef sandwiches and a salad. Please tell me you didn't already eat dinner?"

A laugh escaped her as the wind swept icy snow up from the yard and tossed it against her face. "Come inside before we both freeze!"

Garrett followed her upstairs. "So, you haven't eaten, have you?"

"No, I haven't. I was just trying to figure out which canned or frozen concoction I could stomach tonight. I'm famished!"

"Well, there aren't a whole lot of fast-food places around here to add to your options. I considered the drive-in for hamburgers, but then I decided Maude could do better than that. Wait till you see these sandwiches."

The sandwiches were as great as he'd said; Maude had spared nothing in their construction. Garrett's presence made her cozy apartment seem even cozier, and she began to enjoy the icy rattle of snow at the windows and the whistle of the wind around the corners of the house. It was a great night to be indoors.

"So what's that all over the living-room floor?" Garrett asked while they ate.

"All the information the prosecutor has on the Nighthawk case."

"Can I look at it?"

"Sure." She felt a pang of disappointment that he was going to get absorbed in the files. It would have been nice to spend an evening just chatting and getting to know him. As soon as she had the thought, she warned herself to cut it out. There was no room in her life for a footloose Texas Ranger. Besides, he would want sex, and she was no good at sex. Not since she'd been raped, for sure. She always got panicky and...

"What do you think of the case?" he was asking her. "Strong? Weak?"

"Weak. Very weak. Everything is so circumstantial without a positive ID. If Lisa pointed her finger, or if the physical evidence points to Nighthawk, then we've got serious trouble. But as it stands..." She shook her head. "It really shouldn't be enough to convict him."

"But you're afraid he might get convicted, anyway."

"Yes. I am. Juries are an unpredictable element in any trial. That's why the jury system is probably the best method ever devised for deciding guilt, because their decisions can be tempered with mercy. Unfortunately, they can also swing the other way, so I'm going to recommend that Nighthawk waive a trial by jury. I really think a bench trial would be a better choice for him, given the type of case and the weakness of the current evidence. However, I think Sam is going to insist on a jury."

"Can he?"

She blinked, surprised by the question, and then remembered that not everyone had her acquaintance with the inner workings of these things. A policeman probably wouldn't know about such maneuverings, since his part in them would be limited to being told when to appear to provide his testimony. "Yes, he can. The constitution guarantees a trial by jury only to the accused, but the Supreme Court has upheld the prosecution's right to insist on a jury trial. Given the emotions that are bound to surround this case and the weakness of the evidence as it stands now, Sam's best hope for a conviction is a jury. A judge would dismiss the whole thing at this point."

"Well, I'm sure they're going to come up with a lot more evidence before matters get that far."

"Probably. But I'm sure hoping *we'll* come up with some to exonerate him."

He had been just about to take another bite of his sandwich, but he paused and looked at her. "This is getting to you, isn't it?"

Reluctantly she nodded. "You've heard me spout off about the defense attorney's role in guaranteeing a fair trial under the constitution and the law, and how it's not my job to determine guilt or innocence, but only to make sure the verdict is reached based on legally admissible and legally sufficient evidence.''

One corner of his mouth edged upward. ''I've heard you.''

''Well, I believe that. I really do. I kind of hang on to that like a floating log in the middle of a river, because most of the people I defend are as guilty as sin and I know it. But I have a job to do, a responsibility to uphold, and I can't afford to have nightmares about getting a guilty person off. But this time...damn it, this time I'm scared to death of the consequences if we don't get the guilty person behind bars. I have to *know* the truth!''

He nodded slowly and put his sandwich down. ''Are you beginning to think Nighthawk might be guilty?''

Her head jerked a little, as if the question in some way astonished her. ''No. Actually no, I still feel in my gut that he didn't do it. But that doesn't solve my quandary. My gut could be wrong, and I know it. That's the first problem. The other is, what if we don't catch the right guy? What if this happens to some other little girl because we tried to nail the wrong man...or because we *do* nail the wrong man?''

''Yeah. I've been kind of worrying that around myself. I know Nate Tate thinks he has the right man. But...well, I might have thought so, too, except that you're so sure he didn't do it, and there wasn't anything at his house except that one photo, so I'm wondering, too. By the way, did you ask him about that picture?''

''Of the little girl? Not yet. I only got to see him for that little bit of time in the courtroom, because they had an appointment to collect some tissue samples from him. I'll see him in the morning, and that's soon enough, I guess.''

"I'd like to come with you, if you don't mind. I need a chance to talk with him."

"Sure. I don't think he'll object. I told him I was hiring you. Is there something specific you need to ask him?"

Garrett shook his head. "I just want a chance to watch his face and listen to his voice when he responds about the photo."

"A lie detector test?"

He smiled broadly at that. "Sort of. I'm sure you know just how much can be revealed by the subtle way a person reacts to things that make him feel uncomfortable."

She knew; that kind of perception was indispensable in the courtroom. Both the jury and witnesses had to be continuously monitored for those subtle shifts of eyes and posture that could betray everything from boredom to disbelief, emotional distress to lying. "Well, I'll have to ask him, of course, but I honestly don't think he'll mind talking to you."

Later they sat together on the living-room floor and pored over the files. The doctor's report on Lisa was every bit as distressing to read as Sandy had anticipated, but she forced herself to wade through it even though her mind rebelled. And despite her distress, one thing was tragically clear: nothing Lisa had said in any way definitively identified her assailant. At this rate, whoever had committed the crime might very well walk free.

"It's not a whole hell of a lot," Garrett said as he set the last of the files aside.

"Enough to uphold the charge, but not enough to convict."

"A jury might convict, anyway."

"They might. It would probably get overturned on appeal, though. But we're far from through gathering evidence. I'm hoping against hope that the genetic testing proves unequivocally that Nighthawk didn't do it. That would settle it fast. But..." She chewed her lip and looked away.

"But you want the bad guy caught and put behind bars. Yeah. Me, too."

"I keep getting afraid that maybe people will stop looking for the truth because they think they have the right man in custody. That the real rapist will hurt another little girl. And that an innocent man will rot in jail."

"That's a concern in every serious case," Garrett replied, speaking slowly. "Most of the time the obvious suspect *is* the right one, but there are always cases where the immediately obvious isn't the correct choice. It's an investigator's nightmare. I don't think the Sheriff's Department will limit the scope of its investigation simply because they've made an arrest."

"That's the ideal, of course. The reality is that we see what we expect to see and are blind to anything that doesn't fit our preconceptions."

The crow's feet at the corners of Garrett's eyes deepened as he smiled. "Are you concerned that I might be blind?"

Her cheeks burned faintly for the first time in more years than she wanted to remember. Good grief, the man could make her blush! "I could be blind myself, Garrett. I keep wondering if I'm refusing to see something that's right under my nose, and it's driving me crazy."

"I don't think you're refusing to see anything. The evidence as it stands now isn't conclusive. As an investigator, I'd feel I'd hardly begun, and I imagine Nate feels pretty much the same. But it *is* enough evidence for an arrest and a charge. If the case doesn't get any stronger, then I imagine the charge will be dropped."

"I'm not so sure about that," she admitted glumly. "Public pressure to convict somebody may force the issue. It wouldn't be the first time.''

"Now, that's borrowing trouble!'' But he spoke gently, not scornfully, and edged closer to her.

Their shoulders brushed, and in a heartbeat Sandy found herself acutely aware of him as a man. He didn't wear cologne, so she was able to smell the soap in his clothes and on his skin, and underlying that, a delicious masculine aroma. In the most absurd way, she wished she could just close her eyes and inhale him.

But her eyes had to remain open, and because they did, they wandered over the parts of him she could see without being obvious. His legs, clad in starchy-looking jeans, stretched out before him on the floor, long, hard and lean. Cowboy boots, something he was apparently never without, disappeared under the jeans, so she couldn't judge the shape of his calves. But she *could* judge his thighs, and what she saw made her mouth go dry.

Garrett Hancock might be an urban cop, but he rode horses and rode them often. She recognized a cowboy's legs when she saw them; she'd grown up among cowboys, after all. Powerful legs, accustomed to tightening around a horse or standing in the stirrups.

Gads, when had she developed a thing for men's legs? When she'd looked in the past, she'd discovered a weakness for male posteriors. This was a new one.

A tremulous little sigh escaped her, and she forced herself to look away. No point thinking about it. She'd put the rape long behind her, but its aftermath—a husband who held her somehow responsible for the attack and a tendency to freeze up during sex—had convinced her that she was better off avoiding sexual entanglements. And for all these years she *had* kept clear of involvement. It wasn't that she never yearned for the warmth and strength of a man; it was that she didn't know if she could withstand another rejection in such a vulnerable state. Far better to keep her guard up. Far better not to sigh over powerful legs encased in sexy denim.

And denim *was* sexy, she thought with an inward smile. She wasn't sure what about it struck her that way, but it beat gray flannel hands down any day of the week. Her fingers were just about itching to reach out and run over Garrett's thigh. The thought almost made her blush again.

That was when she became aware that Garrett was watching her, and something in his expression told her that his thoughts were wandering in the same direction.

The realization nearly stole her breath. When was the last time anyone had desired her? She couldn't even remember. But suddenly a pair of blue eyes were trained on her with an intensity that left her almost light-headed. They wandered over her face slowly, leaving her feeling almost as if he were touching her gently. Her lips parted helplessly, just a little, in unconscious invitation. At once his eyes wandered to her mouth, resting there almost softly before moving on.

Please, Garrett. Please. She couldn't have spoken the words out loud—she couldn't have spoken just then to save her life—but when he drew a quick, sharp breath, she knew the plea was written on her face. For an instant she hung suspended in breathless anticipation, sure that he would kiss her.

But then his eyes drifted downward, slipping lazily across her sweater in a way that seemed to paint fire on her breasts. The caress of his gaze was almost as exciting as a physical touch, and when his eyelids began to droop and *his* lips parted, she felt a clenching thrill of arousal unlike any she had ever before known. This man unmistakably found her attractive.

But though his eyes wandered over her in an incredibly seductive manner, leaving her breathless and weak, he never touched her. She would not have believed it possible to be seduced by the way a man looked at her, but Garrett had done it effortlessly.

And when, slowly, so slowly, his eyes lifted once again to hers, she could tell by his faint smile that he was aware of it. But he didn't give her a chance to resent his knowledge. Instead he spoke in a husky voice that sent warm shivers running along her spine. "You're a beautiful woman, Sandra Keller. Beautiful."

She could have arched like a cat being petted. His words made her *feel* beautiful, and his smile seemed to reach deep within her to pluck a golden chord.

But much to her disappointment, he didn't kiss her. Didn't even touch her in the smallest of ways. Instead he sat up a little straighter and reached for one of the manila folders strewn about the floor.

"I guess we need to start thinking up a plan of operation," he said. "This investigation has to start somewhere."

For a moment so fleeting she felt it only as a pang, she nearly wept. And then she straightened her own shoulders and focused on the task at hand.

No man had ever really wanted her. No reason to think a miracle would happen at this late date.

Chapter 5

He squeezed the tennis ball until the cords in his arm stood out. The effort didn't help his mood any.

Sitting in his room at the Lazy Rest Motel, Garrett watched green neon blink outside his window as he did the exercises a sport physician had prescribed for him. Unbeknownst to anyone but himself, Garrett was fighting for his future. The accident had left him with nerve damage in his right arm, damage that kept his grip weak and his arm unsteady when he raised it. Fact was, he wouldn't dare fire a gun the way his arm was now, and if he couldn't fire a gun, he couldn't remain in law enforcement. They would give him a medical retirement the instant they heard about it.

So he had to be sure they didn't hear about it until he had no alternatives left. Holding the tennis ball in his right hand, he squeezed it again and again, working toward greater strength. The sport doctor he had seen felt there was a slim chance that he could encourage nerve regeneration by working out. It certainly couldn't harm him. So, slim though the chance was, Garrett exercised his arm religiously.

It seemed to be getting stronger, he thought as he watched his fingers tighten around the green tennis ball, then relax. It looked as if they were compressing the ball more than they had a couple of weeks ago. In his suitcase was a small device for measuring grip strength. He could take an objective accurate measurement right this very moment.

But he didn't. At the end of his convalescent leave, there would be an inevitable reckoning when he tried to go back to work. He would have to pass a rigorous physical before his return to duty, and that would be soon enough to know if his efforts amounted to anything. Right now he didn't want to risk discouragement, because it might make him feel that he was wasting his time. These exercises were the only thing he could do to help himself, so he was going to do them and leave the results in the hands of the Almighty.

At least the physicians who had cared for him in the hospital hadn't told his bosses that he would never be fit for duty again. They'd told Garrett it wasn't likely that he would ever recover full use of his arm, but they'd been vague with his bosses, saying that only time would tell.

But he didn't have a whole lot of time. In just a very few weeks, he might be taking his last shot at the job that was his whole life.

But he didn't want to think about that right now. Right now, about all he could think about was one sexy-as-sin attorney and the mess she was dragging him into. Just the way she had reacted when he looked at her had been enough to arouse him, and it had been extremely difficult to resist the offer implied by her gently parted lips.

But he knew himself far too well. When he fell, he fell hard and held nothing of himself in reserve. And when he was jilted, the pain was almost more than he could endure. It wasn't a risk he was prepared to take again, not after two bad experiences. Time had taught him not to open himself up and give himself so quickly, but whether he fell fast or slow, the cost of rejection would be devastating.

So he refused to fall. And he suspected that Sandy was no more in the market for a serious relationship than he was. She had evidently managed to remain unattached for quite some time now, according to what Micah had been able to tell him. Sandy had divorced nearly twenty years ago and avoided entanglements ever since.

And that was another good reason for him to keep a safe distance. The woman plainly wasn't interested in involvement with *anyone*. Hell, she probably had as many good reasons as he did, and if he had half a brain he wouldn't be thinking about her. Nothing but pain lay along that path.

He squeezed the ball again and watched his hand tremble. An oath sprang to his lips, but he swallowed it. Swearing wasn't going to help matters, nor was getting frustrated and angry...although he was sorely tempted. Life had handed him the short end of the stick yet again, and while he ordinarily found self-pity disgusting, tonight he was tempted to indulge in just a little of it.

But he wouldn't. Self-pity was a waste of time and energy and never made anything any better. Instead he forced himself to think about the Nighthawk case.

After he had a chance to talk to Nighthawk tomorrow, he would be in a better position to know whether the man was an accomplished liar or an innocent victim. It wasn't that Garrett didn't trust Sandy's judgment, but he had a lot more experience with skillful liars than she could possibly have. It wasn't as if she dealt with criminals on a daily basis; he had. Most people were lousy liars, saying too much, being too quick with explanations...in general betraying themselves by revealing that they were aware they had something to explain or conceal.

But every so often a skillful liar came along, one who never volunteered anything, who never betrayed prior knowledge. A liar who could look you straight in the eye and feign both shock and innocence in exactly the right way. He'd questioned more than a few of them and had learned to detect them more often then not. Which was not to say he was never wrong, because of course he was, sometimes. But he would feel a whole lot better if tomorrow he reached the same conclusion as Sandy about Nighthawk's innocence.

Thinking about Sandy again. He exhaled a quiet breath of amused frustration and wished he still smoked. Wished he could reach for a cigarette and forget the warm heaviness that pooled in his groin when he thought of that woman.

And what a woman! Tonight he'd been frank in his perusal of her, letting his eyes fill themselves as they chose, and he had realized that every time he looked at her he wanted her even more. Insanity. Sheer insanity. It could be nothing but a mistake for both of them.

But she did have lovely curves, and that silk blouse she had been wearing had kind of slid over them in the slinkiest damn fashion every time she moved. He wouldn't be the least surprised, he realized, to discover that beneath that silk she had been wearing equally enticing lingerie. She looked like a satin-and-silk woman, despite the no-nonsense wool suits she wore. Heck, those high heels of hers gave her away. She was a woman who liked to feel feminine. If not, she would have worn flats of some kind. He would have staked his last dime on it.

But she wore those nice three-inch heels with her suits, a startling contrast to the half eyeglasses she peered at the jury over. He would be willing to bet that somewhere in her closet there was a pair of red heels. And maybe a red suit for special occasions. She sure would look nice in it.

And this was getting him nowhere. Damn it, why couldn't life be easy? Why couldn't he simply suggest they explore the attraction and then say adios once the fires had cooled?

Because he wasn't that kind of bastard. Because she wasn't that kind of woman. Because somebody would get hurt.

So he squeezed the tennis ball until the veins on his arm stood out and tried to think of all the questions he would ask Nighthawk tomorrow, if he had the chance.

If he had the chance. There were few enough of those in life. And Sandra Keller was a chance he wasn't going to take.

There was nothing like a man for ruining your sleep, Sandy thought irritably as she drove to the sheriff's office for her appointment with Nighthawk. Garrett was supposed to meet her there at eight, and she hoped he looked as exhausted as she felt. It would be nice to know his sleep had been as disturbed as hers.

Oh, this was ridiculous! At her age, to have been kept awake by yearnings she had buried a long time ago. To have lain in bed like a college girl, hugging her pillow and remembering every look, every word, every nuance. Remembering the way he had looked at her. The way his eyes had touched her with such intimacy.

With such approval.

Another errant thrill ran straight to her womb, causing her to clench deep inside. Approval. When you came right down to it, the approval Garrett's face had reflected was as sexy as anything she had ever seen. As a woman, she needed to know that she appealed to a man, to know that it was *her* he wanted and not just a convenient body. And it had been so very long since anyone had looked at her that way, as if they liked every line of her.

At her age!

Another thrill, softer this time, trickled through her. She couldn't afford this. She didn't have time for this, and she'd never been the type for a brief fling...although the notion was certainly appealing right now. If she could be sure she wouldn't get emotionally wounded, she might have a terrible time talking herself out of this attraction. But she knew better. Nothing but pain could come of a few weeks with Garrett Hancock.

Besides, she would actually have to test herself as a lover, and that was something she had steadfastly refused to do for a *long* time. After all these years, the pain of failure had faded, and it would be easy to forget what she already knew—just how deeply wounding it was to have a man look at her with pity. Or disgust. Or any of the other things a man thought when he found out that a woman was a lousy, inhibited and possibly frigid lover.

But even if Garrett didn't let her see those things, she would know she had failed when he didn't want her again. And she *would* fail. She had *always* failed.

And this was definitely not the time to be thinking of these things. Actually, there was no good time to think about her failure as a woman, a deep-rooted pain she had lived with for a long, long time. Better just not to think about it at all.

The sheriff's office was already bustling when she stepped in the front door. Shifts had changed, and the men who had been on graveyard were busy filling out reports. Nate Tate's voice drifted from his office at the back and was answered by Micah Parish's. Velma Jansen, the dispatcher, nodded from behind her console.

"Hancock's waiting for you upstairs, Sandy," she said.

"Thanks, Velma." So he was already here. The notion unsettled her for some reason. Silly to have hoped she would have a few more minutes to herself, a couple of minutes to prepare inwardly. Well, he was up there waiting, and there wasn't a darn thing she could do about it.

Upstairs, she found Garrett in conversation with the jailer. He looked over at her with the kind of smile one stranger gives another, and a brief nod. Irritation scorched her cheeks, ridiculous though it was. After the way he had looked at her last night, how dare he look at her now as if he'd never seen her before.

But, of course, he regretted the moments of intimacy they had shared, brief and fleeting though those moments had been. For just a few moments they'd both lowered their guards, and now they were both uncomfortable with what they had revealed. It was a silly way for two adults to act, and she knew it even as she gave him a distant smile and turned to follow the guard to the conference room.

"I have to make sure that Nighthawk is willing to talk to you," she reminded Garrett as she turned away.

"I know. I'll be right here."

Snow melting from the roof had formed an incredible fringe of icicles right outside the window of the conference room. One of them reached from the top of the four-foot barred window nearly to the sill and was so clear that the slanting morning sunlight made it glisten like a diamond. Beyond the window, the courthouse square was still quiet, buried beneath its blanket of snow. Only a flock of sparrows were to be seen, hopping around the base of the feeder the high school shop class had built and still maintained.

Behind her, the heavy steel door opened. She turned and summoned a smile for Craig Nighthawk. He looked like hell, she thought. He apparently hadn't slept, either.

"Good morning, Mr. Nighthawk."

He nodded briefly and waited for her to settle at the table before he sat facing her.

"Do you need anything?" she asked him. "Cigarettes... books...?"

He started to give a sharp, impatient negative shake of his head, then caught himself. "Sorry. I'm kind of irritable this morning."

"Trouble sleeping?"

"Yeah. Cages don't fit me. But that's not your problem. A book would be nice. Science fiction, maybe."

"Great. I'll get you A. L. Tierney's newest. She's almost your neighbor, but I guess you know that."

"No."

"Oh. Well, she's Amanda Laird. She and her husband run a sheep ranch not too far from you."

He nodded slowly, his eyes never wavering. "I met them once."

"Are you close to anybody at all around here?"

"Not really. I'm on the road most of the time. Just nodding acquaintances around here."

She wanted to sigh, but that wouldn't do any good, so she suppressed it. "Garrett Hancock is outside. He's the investigator I hired. Do you mind if he sits in with us? Anything you say in his presence will still be protected by privilege."

"I don't have a damn thing to hide, Ms. Keller." Impatience edged his voice. "Bring him in."

Nighthawk stood when Garrett entered the room. The men shook hands, and there was no mistaking the measuring way they looked at one another. Garrett stood in the corner, leaning his shoulder casually against the wall and folding his arms as he listened attentively.

"Why did you decide to move to Conard County, Mr. Nighthawk?"

"Because it reminds me of home, but it's prettier. Because the price was right on the ranch."

Sandy cocked her head attentively and waited. As she expected, after a moment, he continued.

"I was raised on the rez—reservation—in North Dakota. Once I managed to get away, I sure as hell didn't want to go back. But this is my part of the country. I like the wide-open spaces. The solitude. I heard about this place at a truck stop east of Des Moines, if you can believe it. This other guy and I got to talking about how we'd like to retire someday, and when I mentioned I wanted a ranch in the Dakotas or Wyoming, he sent me out this way to talk to a shipper who was trying to unload his parents' spread. Simple as that."

"Unusual choice for a bachelor," Garrett remarked.

Nighthawk looked up at him. "I was married once. Been there, done that, as they say. No desire to be a fool a second time, Hancock. I figured that once I could afford some cattle, I could get my sister's family down here to run the place while I'm away. I'd like her kids to have a better chance than I ever did."

Sandy felt an uneasy prickling at the base of her skull. He wanted to bring his sister's family here. Kids. Surely... She wouldn't even let herself complete the thought. It was too terrible. "There was a photo on your desk, Mr. Nighthawk. A photo of a little girl in a washtub."

He nodded. "My niece."

"The sheriff has taken it as evidence."

"Evidence?" He sat up straight. "Evidence! What the hell for?"

"She's...not wearing any clothes."

"Oh, for God—" He broke off, jumping up from the table so quickly that the chair slid across the slick tile floor and hit the wall. "Damn it!" He strode to the window and stood there holding the bars as he stared out at the brilliant day. "Damn it. Filthy minds!"

"Tell me about it," Sandy said gently after a moment.

"That's my sister Paula's daughter. Paula sent the photo in a letter I got the day before I was arrested."

"Where is the letter?"

He gave a quick jerk of his head, as if he were trying to shake off an annoying mosquito. "I tossed it."

"Why?"

His tone grew impatient. "I don't keep stuff like that. Why would I?"

Sandy considered that, never taking her eyes from his back. "It's a summertime photo." She was careful not to be accusatory, but it was a point that had to be made.

Nighthawk whirled around. "Actually, it was taken just a couple of weeks ago. They don't have indoor plumbing! Paula has to bathe the kids in a washtub, usually inside in front of the stove, but the weather was nice that day, so she decided to keep the mess outside. A friend took the picture, and she thought it was so cute she sent it to me. And if you don't believe me, ask *her!*"

"I have to ask these questions, Mr. Nighthawk. If I don't, someone else will, most likely in court. Okay, it's your niece, and your sister sent the photo. If you'll give me her number, I'll call and verify it, and maybe we can get the photo excluded from evidence as being irrelevant. Needless to say, if a jury gets a look at that, it will probably prejudice them.''

He swore harshly. "Do you realize what a sick society this has become? A picture of a two-year-old splashing in a washtub is going to *prejudice* a jury? My God, it's unbelievable! It's a damn witch hunt! There was a time when people thought pictures like that one of my niece were *innocent!* What the hell has happened?''

"What has happened," Sandy said quietly, "is that little girls like Lisa Dunbar are being sexually assaulted. A five-year-old girl, Mr. Nighthawk. When that happens, people get very upset. And a picture like the one of your niece can appear very suspicious. So give me your sister's phone number. Once I verify this, I'm sure the photo will be removed from evidence.''

He looked away. "My sister doesn't have a phone. You'll have to send her a letter and ask her to call you. Or get somebody to go out on the rez and question her.''

Sandy nodded. "Okay. Give me her address, or some kind of information on how to find her, and I'll see what I can do. If I write, do you think she can get to a phone easily? She can call collect, so it won't cost her anything.''

He shrugged. "It might be a week or more before she picks up her mail. She only goes to the post office every couple of weeks, because I'm the only one who writes to her.''

Sandy glanced at Garrett. This didn't sound good. They didn't have all the time in the world to collect information and get ready for trial. "Then I'll see about getting somebody to hunt her up and get her to a phone. Any suggestions?''

"Tribal police would be your best bet, I guess. They'd probably get to her quickest.''

"That's what we'll do, then." Sandy shoved the pen and pad across the table. "Give me her full name and address, please."

"Do I have to get her involved? I don't even want her to know this is happening!"

"I'm sorry, Mr. Nighthawk. Truly I am. But consider what's at stake here. You can't afford to leave any stone unturned, because if you get convicted, you're going to spend a long time in prison. And then, for the rest of your life, you'll have a record as a sex offender. Weigh that against getting your sister involved just this little bit."

He resisted a little longer, but finally nodded. Seated once again at the table, he wrote down the information Sandy had requested. "Can you...ask them to break it to her as gently as possible?"

"I'll do what I can. I promise."

He shoved the pad and pen back across the table to her and shook his head. "God! I can't believe all this is happening because of an innocent photo of my niece."

That question led Sandy directly to another topic she needed to discuss with him. "That's not all they have, Mr. Nighthawk. They arrested you because the girl's clothes were buried on your property and because you appear to fit the girl's description."

His head jerked as if he'd been struck. "I didn't—I never— Damn! It must be a frame!"

Garrett spoke. "Who would have a reason to want to frame you?"

Again an almost helpless look from dark, anguished eyes. "I don't know. I don't know! All I know is that I didn't do it!"

Sandy waited a moment before continuing. "Appearances right now aren't so good. From the description I had from the prosecutor, the clothes were found on your property, approximately one hundred and fifty yards behind your house.''

''*Behind* it? But that's farther from the road!''

''Exactly. Somebody had to go right by your house to get there.''

''I would have heard a car.'' Nighthawk's eyes moved from her to Garrett and then back again. ''If anyone had driven up, I would have heard them. It's not the kind of sound I could ignore, not out there.''

''So,'' Garrett said slowly, ''you're suggesting a scenario in which somebody walks up your driveway and past your house in the dead of a dark cold night to bury clothes a hundred and fifty yards behind your house. Somebody who's just dumped a little girl on a creek bank across the road from your place. On a creek some two hundred yards from the road. So this person leaves the child, hikes back up to the road, then up your driveway and past your house. Do you know how *unlikely* that sounds?''

''Unlikely or not, that has to be what happened, because I damn well know *I* didn't do it!''

''Then maybe you'd better start trying to figure out who might want to go to so much trouble to make you look guilty.''

''Is that it?'' Nighthawk demanded. ''Unless I can figure out who's done it, I'm going to get screwed?''

''There's still the physical evidence,'' Sandy said quickly. ''Genetic tests may show beyond a doubt that it wasn't you.''

''Of course they—'' He broke off sharply as her choice of words struck him. ''Are you saying there's a chance they might not prove I'm innocent?''

''They can be inconclusive, yes.''

"How can that be? No two people are exactly alike."

"That's true, and a complete genetic code for a single individual is unique to that individual. Even more unique than a fingerprint, I hear. I've been reading up on it, as you can probably tell." She gave Nighthawk a small smile. "However, the lab can't test for a one-to-one comparison, because there are just so many genes, so the method is to pick a half-dozen alleles... Well, suffice it to say they make a comparison of a number of points on the chromosome. The test is highly accurate, although in your case I could probably demolish the importance of a match in court—"

"You won't have to demolish it," he interrupted tautly. "It won't be my DNA."

"I don't expect it will be." She shook her head slightly and smothered a sigh. "What I'm trying to do is prepare you for the possibility that genetic testing may not prove anything at all, least of all that you're innocent. In the first place, the tests won't work if the sample is contaminated or damaged in some way. Then, of course, there's the possibility that they might not have found any DNA samples at all other than the victim's because the rapist wore a condom...or that if they did, there might not be a sufficient quantity to permit both the initial test and the confirmatory test. FBI procedures require that the test be duplicated before they'll call it a match. That protects *you,* of course, although it may not feel like it if they say the sample is insufficient."

He absorbed the information stoically, staring steadily at her from dark eyes. When he spoke, his voice was strained. "I was counting on genetic tests to clear me."

"They may well do that. I'm certainly hoping they will. But while we wait for the results, we need to keep working on the case. Trial is set for nine weeks from now, and there isn't a whole lot of time to waste. And maybe, if we're lucky and turn up something really definitive, we can settle this without going to trial."

But what, she wondered later, could they possibly turn up that would accomplish that? The real rapist? If that were going to be easy, the sheriff would already have done it.

Garrett followed her back to her office and took a seat facing her across her desk. He gave Nina an absent smile when she asked if he wanted coffee, then looked at Sandy.

"Well?" she asked.

"It's a picture of his niece but his sister is hard to get a hold of? He just happened to have thrown the letter away?" Garrett shook his head. "Too slick. Bet they can't find the sister at all."

"You think he was *lying?*" Sandy couldn't believe it. Everything about Nighthawk's demeanor and responses had seemed honest and open to her. "Garrett, not everyone in this country has a telephone, and life on the reservation is hard. So many of the Indian population are dirt-poor! If someone doesn't have indoor plumbing, they're hardly likely to have a phone!"

"I realize that. I'm not saying it's impossible. It's just too damn convenient, that's all."

"It's convenient only if he's guilty and that photo is some kind of kiddie porn."

"Exactly."

"You think he's guilty, then?" Her head almost felt as if it were spinning, because her belief in Nighthawk's innocence had been reinforced by this morning's conference. How could Garrett have received such a different impression?

"I'm reserving judgment," he answered. "I'm *not* convinced he's innocent. But then, I'm not exactly convinced he's guilty, either. Just keep in mind that this sister story is a little too convenient. Don't be surprised if the tribal police say they can't find her.''

Rising, Garrett thrust his hands into the pockets of his jeans and began pacing to and fro before her desk. "The entire thing is difficult to believe. First off, I honestly can't imagine the perp risking discovery by burying the clothes so far from where he left the little girl and on somebody else's property...unless the property is his own. Otherwise he risks being seen and identified by the occupants of the house.''

"In the middle of the night? Come on, Garrett!''

"Well, tell me that it makes any sense to bury the stuff there instead of somewhere far away where it would never be found!''

"Exactly! Nighthawk doesn't strike me as the kind of fool who'd bury the evidence in his own backyard.''

"You'd be surprised what fools criminals can be. Take the guy who told the cops he hadn't meant to rob the store, that he had really meant to rob the place next door. My point is that it's far more likely, in my experience, that the criminal would bury the clothes someplace on his own property, thinking it was far enough away from where he left the girl, than that he'd go creeping through strange country in the dead of night and risk discovery by an irate householder, just so he could bury them on somebody else's place. And if he's going to go creeping around the countryside in the dead of night, it would make a hell of a lot more sense for him to drive ten, twenty, even thirty miles away before burying the stuff.''

Much as she didn't like to admit it, Sandy was beginning to see the logic in his argument, and it didn't look good for Nighthawk. "Somebody *could* be trying to frame him.''

"It's possible. But considering that he claims not to know anyone around here, I wouldn't bet my hat on it."

Neither would she, when she considered that Lisa Dunbar had probably not been a simple target of opportunity, given the isolated place where she had been snatched. No, someone had been stalking her, and if someone had been stalking her, it had to be someone from around here. Someone would have noticed a stranger.

The phone rang sharply, and she looked at Garrett. "Excuse me."

"Go ahead." He crossed to the window and stood staring out at the snowy street.

She picked up the receiver and heard Sam Haversham on the other end. "Sandy, word of Lisa Dunbar's rape is getting around."

Sandy sighed, but before she could reply, Sam continued.

"Anyway, somebody heard about it and showed up at the sheriff's this morning. It seems he saw Craig Nighthawk talking to Lisa Dunbar outside Soop's Supermarket last month."

Sandy's stomach sank with a sickening thud as her hand tightened around the receiver.

"We need to take his deposition," Sam said. "The sooner the better. Can you get over here sometime this morning?"

Stunned, feeling as if she had to force herself to move, Sandy drew her calendar across the desk and looked at it. "Uh...yeah." She'd been planning to spend this morning drawing up the wills for Mel and Doris Dahl, but that could wait. "I'm free until three." When she had a consult on a deed dispute.

"How soon can you come over?"

"Right now."

"I'll have Nate shuttle the guy over here, then. See you in about twenty?"

"That'll do."

After she hung up, she turned her head slowly to look at Garrett. He had turned to face her.

"What's up?" he asked.

"It seems Nighthawk knew Lisa Dunbar after all. He was seen with her about a month ago."

He stiffened, and she realized that the news had shocked him as much as it had her. He didn't want to think he was working for a rapist who was an accomplished liar any more than she did. Her stomach lurched again, a sickening feeling.

"Sam's going to depose him," she said, forcing herself to speak through a dry mouth. "I need to go over there right now."

"I'll ride shotgun."

She hardly heard him. Once before she had been this mistaken in a man. Then it had been her husband. This time it was a client. Damn, how could she be such a fool?

Dudley Willis was one of the community's more respected members. Sam Haversham couldn't have asked for a more credible nail to drive into Nighthawk's coffin. The Willis family had been in the county almost as long as the Conard family and had been one of the great powers until financial reverses had cost them most of their cattle empire just after the Second World War.

The empire might be gone, but Dudley Willis continued the tradition of community service. He was an active scoutmaster, a pillar of his church and he ran several of the biggest charitable fund-raisers in the county. Everyone knew Dudley Willis, and no one would question his word.

When she saw him, she suddenly experienced the uncharacteristic wish that she could just crawl into a pair of powerful arms and hide. Preferably Garrett's arms. Not that it would do any good. Nighthawk was hung, she found herself thinking. Whether or not he had raped the Dunbar girl, he was hung, because two and two made four even when the answer was really five...and Dudley was the second "two."

"I couldn't believe it this morning when I heard from Kent Reed that the little Dunbar girl had been raped, and that Craig Nighthawk had done it."

Sandy felt again the unpleasant lurching in her stomach. It was difficult for her to believe Kent Reed had revealed the little girl's name to anyone. She had always thought him far more responsible than that. Since it wasn't the point of this interrogation, however, she remained silent on the subject.

"The first thing that flashed into my mind when I heard about it was Nighthawk showing the little girl the cab of his truck."

"You saw him do that?" Haversham asked him.

Willis nodded. "Right in front of Sooper's. Ben Dunbar and I got to talking in the checkout line about that robbery over at the Watering Hole the night before. Anyhow, we came outside, and there's little Lisa sitting up in the cab of the truck. It was parked right out front of the store. Only place to park it, I guess."

Sandy scribbled on her notepad: *? Lisa outside w/o supervision?*

Sam asked another question. "What was your initial impression when you saw her sitting in the truck's cab?"

Willis didn't even hesitate. "I felt kind of uneasy. Well, it's these times we live in. You see kids with adults who aren't their parents, and you start wondering what's going on."

"So you know the Dunbars pretty well?"

Willis nodded. "Pretty well. From church and school activities. My daughter is in Debbie Dunbar's class."

"Johnna is your thirteen-year-old, correct?"

"That's right."

"So it was your daughter Debbie was with when she didn't come home on the bus Monday evening with Lisa?"

Sandy thought Willis stiffened a little, as if sensing an accusation, then relaxed. "I don't know," he said. "My ex-wife is remarried and lives in town. The kids live with her. I guess Debbie could have been there. Do you want me to find out?"

Sam shook his head. "Never mind. I'm just trying to get events clear in my mind. Okay, you and Ben Dunbar came out of Sooper's and found Lisa sitting in the cab of Craig Nighthawk's truck. Was Nighthawk in the cab with her?"

"No."

"Where was he?"

"Standing on the truck step."

"So he was off the ground, standing on the step. And what was he doing?"

Willis shrugged. "Talking to her, I guess. I don't know."

"What was his demeanor?"

"How do you mean?"

"Did anything about him seem…unusual?"

Willis thought about it a moment. "No, not really. He was just standing there."

"What about Lisa? How did she strike you?"

"I'm not sure." He sighed. "I was alarmed to see her in the cab of his truck. Whether that was because of the way she was behaving or just instinctive…well, I can't say for certain.''

Sam looked at Sandy. ''Do you have any questions?''

''Yes, I do. Okay, Mr. Willis, you felt alarmed when you saw Lisa Dunbar in Craig Nighthawk's truck. Do you know Craig Nighthawk?''

''No, I don't.''

''So your alarm didn't come from anything you know about him?''

''No.''

''If you don't know him, how could you be sure it was him standing beside the truck?''

''I've seen him around.'' He shook his head quickly. ''He lives right up the road from me, Ms. Keller. When he first bought his place, I stopped in to invite him to the church. Other than that, I just see him around sometimes.''

''Didn't he buy his property from your aunt, Hattie Maguire?''

''Yeah.'' Willis made a disgusted sound. ''I asked her to hang on to it a little longer, until I could buy it, but she needed the money. Ah, well. I offered to buy it from Nighthawk last year, but he isn't interested in selling.''

''So you *do* know him?''

''To nod to. What's this got to do with anything?''

''I'm just trying to determine how you could be so sure it was Mr. Nighthawk you saw with Lisa.''

''Well, ask Ben, then. He recognized Nighthawk right off, too.''

''How did *he* react?''

''He was upset. He shouted out, 'Lisa, you come down from there right this minute!' Nighthawk reached right up and lifted the girl down to the ground.''

''Did you see him touch her at any other time?''

Willis hesitated briefly. "No. Just when he lifted her down."

"The little girl didn't seem disturbed in any way?"

"Well, I can't say exactly. I mean, it happened fast, and she was sure upset once her father shouted at her. Maybe she was upset before he shouted. I couldn't tell you."

Little by little Sandy pinned him down to exact descriptions of what people were wearing, and how long he and Dunbar had chatted at the register, so that by inference they could judge how long Lisa had been unattended. With each detail that was added, she was in a better position to determine his truthfulness. More importantly, by drawing out details, she could prevent him from speaking in sweeping generalities when he testified. Generalities tended to leave juries able to draw sweeping conclusions that were not necessarily accurate.

By the time she finished questioning Willis, she was convinced the episode was innocent...and utterly damning, given that the little girl had been raped. And even though the episode had been innocent, could the same be said about the motive behind it?

God, this case was an attorney's nightmare! At this rate, whatever the outcome, she was probably always going to wonder if justice had been done.

What if Nighthawk went to prison and he was innocent? And far, far worse, what if Nighthawk were guilty and acquitted, and went free to rape again?

Chapter 6

"Well, you're in for it now, Sandy," Nina said the instant Sandy stepped into her office.

For an instant, just a fleeting instant, Sandy had an overwhelming urge to throw something. She had never once in her life thrown a thing—other than a snowball or a softball—but right now she wanted to pitch something and hear the satisfying sound of shattering glass. It never rains but it pours, she reminded herself, quoting her mother's favorite adage. She'd taken on this damn case, and now she was just going to have to endure the doubts and concerns that went with it...and still handle all of life's usual complications. That was, well, life.

The thought leavened her mood just a little and made it possible for her to turn attentively to Nina. "What's up?" she asked. Being "in for it now" could mean almost anything, from a new case to trouble with the central heating system.

"The hate calls have started."

Sandy stared at her blankly for a moment, almost as if her secretary had spoken Greek. "Hate calls?"

"I don't know what else to call them. I've had three calls this morning from people—men, actually—who want to know if you've lost your mind to be defending a child molester. Only they weren't quite so polite about it. And, frankly, I don't want to answer any more of those calls!"

"You mean they used foul language?"

"I mean they were foul, vile and threatening! And whether you like it or not, I called Nate Tate and told him I'd had three threatening calls—"

"Nina, you didn't!"

"I did!" Nina folded her arms beneath her breasts and scowled at her. "And Garrett said—"

"You didn't tell Garrett!" She couldn't say why that upset her so much, but it did. It was almost as if something dirty had touched her, and she didn't want anyone to see it. "Nina, don't get so upset about it! Anonymous callers—good grief, they haven't got the guts to do anything or they'd say it to my face."

"Right. And cows fly. Don't be stupid, Sandy. People are mad enough that you're defending Nighthawk to pick up the phone and make threats. Someone could get mad enough to actually try to do something about it. You can't afford to take the risk!"

"And I suppose Nate told you there wasn't a damn thing he could do about it."

"Actually, he suggested we call the phone company and have them put a tap on the line so they can trace the calls and give those folks hell."

"Calls like this go with the territory, Nina. Have you forgotten some of the nasty calls we got when I defended the toxic waste dumpers?"

"These were different." Nina shook her head sharply. "Very different, Sandy. These calls scared me."

Much as she wanted to, Sandy couldn't ignore her secretary's assertion. Nina *had* laughed off the calls during the toxic waste trial, and some of them had been pretty vulgar. That these calls had been different enough to frighten her...

Absently she crossed the front office to look out on the quiet street that fronted her house. The leafless tree limbs reached to the gray sky. The snow was melting away, leaving patches of brown grass and dark earth visible. Winter was always so pretty when it first arrived and always so ugly as it slipped away. The ground had already started to thaw before this last snowfall, and now, stepping off the pavement, one was apt to sink into several inches of mud.

She was trying not to think the unthinkable. Her neighbors, she had always believed, were essentially good and law-abiding people. She couldn't imagine any one of them failing to understand the legal system to the extent that they somehow transferred the blame from the perpetrator to the attorney.

Yet she knew a lot of people did that. The justice system was often blamed, as if it were somehow responsible for the crimes people committed. It was as if the mere fact that justice were being meted out fairly, impartially and legally somehow rubbed the taint of the crime onto the system that dealt with it.

Not fair, certainly, nor even logical, but certainly it was human. It was also something she could understand. Recent highly publicized trials had created a public impression that guilty people always walked on technicalities, and that juries were capricious and out of touch with reality. Nothing could be further from the truth.

But that perception often made lawyers appear to be the enemy, as much as any criminal. And that perception had led to a number of violent attacks on members of the legal profession.

Yes, it could happen. The question was, did she think it could happen here in Conard County?

She shivered, feeling suddenly cold despite the warmth of the office. She knew what men were capable of. It was not mere speculation for her, because a long time ago a man with no motive other than his own need to inflict pain and fear had leapt out of the darkness of a winter night and raped her in the snow not a hundred yards from her office.

She had long since put the trauma behind her. It flickered into her mind only rarely now, when some event or circumstance made her suddenly uneasy. What she had never been able to forget was that a total stranger had come out of the night to hurt her.

Eventually she had overcome her lingering fears, had put the assault behind her and learned to live without the constant companionship of fear.

Until this very instant, she had believed that she had put it all behind her. Until right now, when she quite suddenly realized that she didn't feel safe. Other people lived in the blind belief that such things couldn't happen to them. Sandy Keller knew better, because it *had* happened.

She couldn't ignore the possibility, much as she longed to. One of her neighbors had raped a five-year-old girl. Could she really delude herself into believing that others couldn't possibly be capable of violence against her because they felt so morally outraged by her defense of the accused rapist?

She turned and looked at Nina, who was still watching her. "All right. Call the phone company and get a tap put on the line."

Nina expelled a relieved breath. "Good! Nate says we

both need to be more careful for a while, too. Not go any-where alone, especially after dark. Make sure windows and doors are locked—that kind of thing.''

Sandy chewed her lower lip briefly, a characteristic ges-ture when she was unsure how to say something. ''Nina... Nina, if you're uneasy, you don't have to come to the office until this case is over. I hadn't thought... Look, I don't want you to be here alone while I'm at court and dealing with other things.''

Nina put her hands on her hips. ''And just who's going to handle the phone, the appointments and typing the briefs? Sandy, you can't function without a secretary! You couldn't possibly get ready for court without me, never mind all the other stuff on your desk!''

''Well, I'm damned if I'm going to think of you spending hours here all alone and scared because of phone calls and maybe other stuff.''

''They're not threatening *me,* Sandy.''

''If somebody's crazy enough to take the law into his own hands, can you be sure you won't be caught in the cross fire?''

''Well, you can't get along without me, so that settles it!''

''No, it doesn't. Look, you can take the laptop home with you and work there. At least you won't be all alone, because Dex will be right nearby in his shop.'' Dex was Nina's husband, an electrician who ran a shop out of his home. These days Dex stayed in his office running the show while younger men did the footwork for him.

''I don't know....''

''Look, you can come in here several times a day when I'm here. We can catch up then, and you can ferry disks back and forth as necessary. I just don't want you to be here all alone if you're frightened!''

Nina wasn't inclined to back down any more than Sandy was, and that amused Sandy just a little. They could advise each other to be careful but were loath to take the advice themselves.

"I don't want you to be alone here, either,'' Nina said finally. "You're in far more danger than I am, and you're alone a lot more.''

"That's my problem. I'll deal with it. What I don't want to do is put you in a dangerous position. I chose to take this case, after all, but you didn't. No reason you should suffer for it.''

For a moment it appeared Nina was going to argue, but finally she compressed her lips and nodded. "Okay. Have it your way.''

In her own office, Sandy settled down at her computer and logged on to a national law database system to read court decisions involving cases with issues similar to Nighthawk's.

The law was not carved in stone but was constantly growing and changing as new cases were tried, new rulings handed down. Yes, there were laws against rape, but the way a rape case was tried, what kind of evidence could be admitted, what factors could be used in jury selection... those were changing all the time.

The first case she called up was a recent one dealing with the admission of DNA analysis in a rape case. The Wyoming Supreme Court not only agreed with the admissibility of DNA matching as evidence but had decided that the statistical evaluation of the evidence was also admissible.

Ordinarily no statistical claims could be admitted in a trial, because regardless of what statistics claimed, they were not relevant to a particular case. Or to put it another way, just because a third of all women were abused by their spouses, that did not mean that a particular woman had been abused by her husband.

In this instance, though, the court felt that failure to admit statistical evidence would deny a jury the information to evaluate the relative importance of the DNA matching process.

And that gave her some ammunition, should the DNA point to Craig Nighthawk. If statistics could be admitted, then they could be used to undermine the importance of a DNA match, especially in the case of a Native American, where the likelihood of matching the wrong person was a thousand times higher than it was for a Caucasian.

Some people would call that a technicality and get mad at her for using it, but the simple fact was that DNA evidence was not infallible. There *was* a chance the wrong person could match, especially in the case of a Native American suspect, because Indians tended to marry among themselves, and the gene pool was small to begin with. That increased the likelihood that the markers used in DNA testing might match the wrong person. No chicanery was involved in making sure the jury understood that possibility, just as there was no chicanery involved in proving that a witness lied. They were the same thing, a matter of making sure the jury understood the real value of the evidence and testimony being presented.

But the DNA test would exonerate Craig Nighthawk. It had to. If there was enough genetic evidence collected, then it would prove beyond a reasonable doubt that Nighthawk was *not* a match. That much, DNA samples could do.

And despite all evidence to the contrary, she was still convinced that Nighthawk hadn't committed the crime.

But that testimony from Dudley Willis this morning was going to make it appear that he had. It was circumstantial evidence of the worst kind: the victim had been seen in the company of the accused. Sam was going to call Ben Dunbar in to give a deposition about the incident, too, but she had no reason to believe Dunbar's statement would be materially different from Willis's. Two men had seen the victim sitting in the cab of the accused perpetrator's truck a couple of weeks before the rape. Who was going to believe there wasn't a connection?

Why hadn't Lisa Dunbar's father remembered the incident right away? Why had Willis been the first person to show up in the sheriff's office with the story? Had Dunbar somehow failed to hear who had been arrested in his daughter's case? Had he just forgotten the entire thing? Could such an event have seemed so insignificant to a little girl's father that he didn't even remember it? How likely was that?

Her head was still spinning with unanswered questions when she logged off the database and realized that she had a client due in fifteen minutes.

But the client didn't show.

"I don't understand it," Nina said. "I called to confirm the appointment yesterday, and they said they'd be here."

"Maybe something came up." But she didn't think so. No, she had an edgy, fluttery feeling in the pit of her stomach that said her clients had decided not to keep the appointment because she was defending Nighthawk.

"They said they're going to find another attorney," Nina told her twenty minutes later, after calling the people to find out what was wrong. "Because you're defending a child molester."

Something inside Sandy seemed to snap. She rose swiftly from her desk, slamming a law book shut with an emphatic gesture. "Why the hell are we bothering with a trial? No-body's heard a smidgen of evidence, but they're already convinced the man is guilty! Why don't they just hang him right now?"

Garrett's voice reached her from the outer office. "Wouldn't surprise me if some folks are talking about that very thing right now." Two seconds later he filled the door of her office. "It's started, has it?"

Nina forestalled her. "You better believe it. I'm going to call the rest of the day's appointments and see how many more are planning not to show up."

"Let's not exaggerate this, Nina," Sandy said quietly.

"I'm not exaggerating anything! You have a right to know if people are going to show up or not. It's just common courtesy!"

"Let her call, Sandy," Garrett said. "If you find out you don't have any appointments this afternoon, you can come with me."

Her heart seemed to skip a beat at the thought of spending an afternoon with Garrett, but almost before it rose in her, she repressed the feeling of excitement. He wanted to discuss the case, that was all. Probably wanted to ask her about the deposition this morning.

Then, in a moment of uncomfortable clarity, she faced her initial reaction and what it meant...and the emotional danger it put her in. She couldn't afford to care one way or another whether this man wanted to spend time with her. Not only could she not afford it, she absolutely didn't *want* to care. Caring had been a cage in which she had nearly suffocated once before, and she had promised herself that she would never again let any man put her in such a posi-tion.

But some integral part of her didn't want to listen to reason. It wanted to kick up its heels and fall madly, wildly in love, and damn the consequences. Some unfulfilled part of her yearned for all the promises that had never been met, hungered for the dreams that had never come true. She knew better—life had certainly taught her that those dreams were just dreams, never to be matched by reality—but some part of her apparently couldn't quite relinquish the longing.

"Go ahead and call," she told Nina, managing a small smile. "I know when I'm outnumbered."

Turning away from Garrett, she reached for one of the books on her desk, meaning to put it back in the floor-to-ceiling bookcase that covered the wall behind her desk.

As suddenly as if someone had flipped a switch, she found herself remembering something her mother had said a couple of years ago, after reading a romance novel. "I could never write one of these," her mom had said. "I'm too old and I was married too long to even remember what it felt like to fall in love."

At the time Sandy hadn't paid much attention to the statement, primarily because she couldn't remember, either, and had no desire to. Now here she was, facing those scary, uncertain feelings again and trying to turn her back on them. Sad, she thought abruptly. It was so damn sad. Sad that her mother couldn't remember those feelings, and sad that she herself only wanted to avoid them.

"Are you okay?"

Garrett's concerned voice right behind her made her aware that she had sighed. "I'm fine, Garrett. Just disgusted, I guess."

"Hardly surprising. It never fails to amaze me how rarely most people bother to think things through. Most of the folks who'll be giving you hell about this case would agree in principle that a man's innocent until proven guilty. Most of 'em would agree that everyone is entitled to a defense attorney, and that a miscarriage of justice can't be tolerated. Funny how fast they forget all that when somebody's arrested for a terrible crime. Unfortunately, this kind of crap goes with the territory, Counselor.''

''I know that.'' She turned her head so she could glance at him over her shoulder. ''I know, but it doesn't make it any less disgusting. The whole point of the system is to make sure that innocent people don't get sent to prison, but that's what everyone seems to forget the instant someone gets arrested.''

''I think we're all guilty of that.''

Sandy expelled a soft breath, letting go of some of the tension. ''Even me, and I'm an attorney.'' A quiet, rueful laugh escaped her, and she faced Garrett. ''I imagine you want to hear about the deposition this morning.''

''What I want to hear about it are your impressions. I can read the actual statement when you get a copy. Are you going to interview the girl herself? What about members of her family?''

''Sam's going to have the father come in tomorrow to give a statement. We're both kind of curious as to why he hasn't told us about finding his daughter in Nighthawk's truck.''

''Me, too.'' He frowned faintly and rubbed his chin absently. The skin of his forefinger rasped against the darkening stubble of his beard. ''I'm also wondering why Nighthawk didn't mention the incident.''

''Believe me, I intend to question him about that.''

Garrett shook his head. ''I'm beginning to wonder about a lot of things. When you stack it all up, my feeling is that Nighthawk isn't being real helpful. Why didn't he mention that the girl had been in his truck?''

"Maybe he doesn't know that was the little girl who was raped."

"That's possible, I guess, but it makes him look even more suspicious. Who in their right mind puts strange little girls into their trucks?"

"I have to agree it wasn't the brightest move in the world, but you can't hang a man for stupidity."

"Oh yes, you can! Work in law enforcement for a little while, Counselor. You'd be amazed how many people get into serious trouble over *stupidity*." His startling blue eyes seemed almost to glare at her, but his mouth framed a slight smile.

Well, she thought, maybe he was genuinely exasperated at the way things were happening. She knew she was. Every time she turned around she seemed to be discovering something that boded no good for her client. Inevitably she was being nagged by doubts about his innocence.

And while that shouldn't matter—couldn't matter—to a defense attorney, in this instance it mattered one hell of a lot to her. She had taken this case with the blind conviction that the man was innocent. The sorry fact was, if she had believed him guilty, even all her principles couldn't have forced her to take the case.

Apparently her principles weren't as steadfast as she'd always believed, and that realization was as unsettling as an earthquake. The ground on which she had so firmly stood for so long had shifted, leaving her feeling disoriented.

"Damn," she whispered softly. "Damn."

"Sandy?" Garrett's expression had lost its unnerving intensity and now reflected concern. "What's wrong?"

She shook her head, not wanting to discuss it. "This case is just making me uneasy."

"I can sure understand that. I wish I had something positive to offer, but I'm having trouble finding anything."

"What do you mean?"

"Well, I was kind of nosing around this morning, trying
to find out if anyone around here knows Nighthawk."

"And no one does."

"Not quite." One corner of his mouth lifted just a hair.
"Dirk Bayard at Bayard's Garage knows him. Nighthawk
goes in there from time to time to order parts, and they
apparently shoot the breeze."

"Did he have anything useful to say?"

"Only that Nighthawk seems decent enough, and Bayard
would never in a million years believe Nighthawk could hurt
a kid."

It was kind of a relief not to be the only person on the
planet who thought Nighthawk couldn't have done it. Not
that that helped a darn thing. A man's opinion was a long
way from evidence. "Nothing else?"

"Afraid not. I'll keep poking around, Sandy. Nighthawk
said he didn't know anyone around here, but it turns out he
did regular business with Bayard, and Bayard knows him.
There are probably other people who know him the same
way. Maybe somebody can shed some light on things."

"But why didn't he mention Bayard when I asked who
he knew around here?" Another troubling omission.

"Maybe," Garrett said, "he's just unassuming."

"What do you mean?"

"I mean that maybe he doesn't think Dirk Bayard would
remember him, because Bayard does business with so many
people. Maybe it never entered Nighthawk's head that Bayard would consider him to be an acquaintance."

"Possible, I guess, but it seems to me that someone facing

what Nighthawk's facing would be clutching at any straw, not dismissing things that don't seem important.''

"Maybe that's how you'd handle it, but Nighthawk's a different person with a different outlook. Maybe you need to jog him a little bit and get him to thinking.''

"I'm sure going to try.''

"So are you going to get to question the little girl?''

Sandy shrugged. "As soon as the doctor says it's okay. The sooner the better, actually. As time goes on, her memory won't be as good.''

"I don't envy you.''

"Me either.'' She gave him a crooked smile. "I have this nightmare of her testifying on the stand and me having to cross-examine her. Lord, I don't want to have to do that.''

"*Can* she be allowed to testify? I thought kids weren't brought into the courtroom in these cases.''

"They can be, and the Wyoming Supreme Court has already declared that a five-year-old was a competent witness in a similar case. All that's necessary is for Judge Williams to determine that Lisa Dunbar is competent to testify.''

After a moment Garrett shook his head doubtfully. "Is there any way you can prevent that?''

"I'm sure going to try to. The simple fact is, if Lisa takes the stand, I'm going to *have* to cross-examine her. That's my constitutional duty. I *have* to verify the accuracy of anything she says. And regardless of the truth of her testimony, the jury is going to see me as a nasty old witch giving the poor little girl a hard time, and that hostility will be transferred to my client. So when all is said and done, I'd be very happy to have the judge declare Lisa incompetent.''

Nina tapped on the door and poked her head in. "Sorry, Sandy. You've got the rest of the day off. Two more cancellations, one over the Nighthawk case, the other not saying why. And the third appointment rescheduled for tomorrow. Car broke down.''

"Thanks, Nina. That's not too bad.'' She managed a smile. "I still have one client left.''

Nina sniffed. "They may change their minds by tomorrow!''

The corners of Garrett's eyes creased as he looked down at her. "Great. Now you're mine for the rest of the day.''

All her concerns about the case faded as sparklers of excitement ignited within her. "All yours? For what?''

"I want to go out to Willis Road and take a look at the crime scene. Nate gave me the go-ahead.''

The flares of excitement winked out as suddenly as they'd burst into life and left her feeling crabby. It was a disappointing plummet.

"You'd better change into jeans and boots,'' Garrett said. "It'll be pretty muddy out there.''

The afternoon sun shone brilliantly in a cloudless blue sky. The warmth of the sun's rays had melted the snow in patches, leaving bare ground and brown growth visible like islands in a shrinking sea. The air was still chilly, though, a stimulating contrast to the heat of the sun.

Because Garrett drove, Sandy was able to relax in the seat and soak up the delightful sunlight through the windows. She had forgotten how good it felt to just let the sun beat down on her and drive all the tension away.

In fact, it suddenly disconcerted her to realize how long it had been since she had simply taken the time to relax. How long it had been since her last vacation. She'd grown so accustomed to working all the time to support herself and Gerard, that she had forgotten how to do much else. And now finances weren't even an adequate excuse. Actually, she had no excuse whatsoever not to take an occasional vacation.

Except that how much fun could a vacation be all by oneself? Maybe she needed to look up that all-women's travel group one of her acquaintances had mentioned. Or maybe she ought to just poll some of her friends. There were probably a few of them who would love to take a vacation away from their families.

That thought almost made her smile. For all that she often felt a little lonely, she knew plenty of her friends envied her independent lifestyle. Funny how different positions could create such a different perspective.

They turned a corner, and her cheeks felt bereft when shadow replaced the sun. Opening her eyes, she turned and looked at Garrett. "What do you hope to find out here?"

"Nothing, really. I just want a chance to look things over and get them fixed in my mind. Sometimes you can get an inkling of what the perp was thinking by following his footsteps."

He pulled over suddenly and braked, leaving the engine running. "Aspen Meadows Ranch," he announced, pointing at the open gate and cattle guard. "The Dunbar girl was dropped off right here by the school bus. I called ahead, and they said it's okay to drive up the road to the house and check things out."

He put the Explorer in gear and turned onto the rutted private ranch road. "She had to be snatched somewhere along here. It seems to me that if the car had been waiting within sight of the gate, the bus driver would have mentioned seeing it. Hell, he probably would have asked the girl if she knew who was in the car."

"Probably. You can be sure I'll ask him about it, though."

"I figure he drove far enough up the road that he couldn't be seen from the bus when it pulled up, and certainly far enough up so that nobody could see him snatch the kid. We need to find out if he was wearing a mask when he kidnapped her, or if she ever saw his face."

"There's a lot we need to find out as soon as she can talk to us," Sandy agreed. "She may well remember a lot of little details, particularly from earlier, before he started hurting her, that could help clarify things considerably."

"We can hope." He glanced in the rearview mirror. "Okay, from here you can barely see the top of the gate. Let's see how much farther before you can see the ranch house, and that'll give us a pretty good idea of where he must have snatched her."

"Why would he care if anyone could see from the house? If it was a planned kidnapping, he'd know that no one would be there."

"Would he? How could he be absolutely certain? How would Nighthawk, for instance, know the schedule June Dunbar follows that gets her home after six? Or that Ben Dunbar would be working in town that day? I hear his job is part-time and intermittent, according to when the feed store wants him to help with deliveries."

"I didn't know that." She turned a little in the seat so she could see him better and was surprised when he flashed her a smile.

"That's why you hired a detective. Okay, Ben Dunbar ranches, but they're not exactly making ends meet out here, so June works year-round as a dental hygienist, and during the winter months Ben takes whatever work the feed store offers. There was no way for somebody to be *sure* he wouldn't be home that day…except maybe a good friend or someone at the feed store."

"Neither of which fits Craig Nighthawk."

"Exactly."

They hadn't driven too much farther up the road before Garrett braked again. "There's the roof of the house. If I were planning to snatch a kid, I wouldn't want to be this close to the house when I did it." After turning the vehicle, he set the hand brake and looked at Sandy. "I'm going to walk back toward the highway and see if I can spot anything along the side of the driveway here that might tell us something. "You follow behind me in the car."

He walked down the middle of the narrow track, scanning from side to side. The snow hadn't helped a whole lot, but now that it was melting back from the edges of the drive, there was a slim chance he might discover something, though he wasn't holding his breath.

Bringing Sandy along had been a spur-of-the-moment idea when he had realized her clients were deserting ship. Better to keep her distracted than let her spend the afternoon brooding about what those canceled appointments meant. She had faced the possibility of this happening when she decided to take the case, but this was one of those life events that tended to feel a whole lot different when it actually happened than she'd expected it to.

She was bound to feel hurt by what was happening. No way to escape it. These folks weren't strangers to her, the way they might well be in a big city. Nope, these folks were her neighbors. She probably knew damn near every one of them, and this had to hurt like hell.

And it was going to hurt a whole lot worse. He kinda figured those canceled appointments were like the sweeping arc of stratus clouds on the leading edge of a hurricane. Once this case became a topic of local discussion, she was probably going to hear a lot of not-so-nice stuff to her face.

The thought made him clench his fists. One of his biggest failings was the way he felt protective of folks he considered to be his friends. The way he felt protective of women, in particular. Lots of women didn't much appreciate that anymore, and he'd been told more than once that they could take care of themselves. On the other hand, there had been some who'd tried to take advantage of that weakness of his by inventing troubles and asking for his help. Good thing he'd learned to harden his heart long ago, or it would have been busted a whole passel of times instead of only twice.

But he felt extremely protective of Sandy Keller. So protective that he'd had to battle an urge to ask Nina for the names of the fools who'd canceled their appointments so he could go have a talk with them about the constitution of these United States and all the civil liberties people held so dear...until they applied to someone else.

But he'd stomped down on the urge. Instinct told him that Sandy wouldn't have appreciated it at all, and he had the sense to see he would only have made her look like some kind of a fool by his interference. No, she had to handle this herself so she wouldn't look weak.

Well, she had to give the *appearance* of handling it herself. Sure enough, if he could find unobtrusive ways to help her through this, he would.

Of course, it would probably be better if he just stayed clear. He knew better than to get involved, but Sandy Keller would have been one easy woman for him to get involved with. Something about her had him thinking about slippers before the fire and other nonsense to do with long, lazy evenings and the company of a loving woman.

Dreams he'd given up on years and years ago.

Funny how a woman could resurrect wants and needs that

were buried and ought to be dead. Real funny. So damn funny that he didn't feel at all like laughing.

From time to time he heard her rev the engine, slip into gear and catch up with him. He was as aware of her eyes on him as he would have been if someone had been stalking him. And maybe it wasn't so different, considering that he'd seen his own wanting reflected in her eyes last night when he'd looked at her from head to foot.

He'd known how bold his look had been, but he hadn't been able to stop himself. There was a peculiar kind of hunger in him for her, and it worried him considerably. It wasn't the simple sexual hunger a man often felt for an attractive woman—a hunger he'd felt countless times over the years. Nope. This was a hunger for scarier things, and alarm bells were going off inside both his head and his heart.

Just then he noticed a tire track off to one side, a scar in the muddy ground. It could have been almost anything, one ranch vehicle pulling aside to let another one pass, the mailman, or someone stopped because they'd taken a wrong turn. He moved in for a closer look anyway and saw small footprints right next to the track. Footprints that might have been made by a five-year-old girl coming home from school in her boots.

He straightened and motioned Sandy to pull up alongside.

"I may have found a tire track belonging to the kidnapper. Hand me the cellular phone, will you? It's under the console cover between the seats."

The connection was pretty good—not surprising, since there was a repeater just outside of town. Nate Tate promised to send a deputy immediately to make a cast and asked if Garrett would please wait there to protect the track until the deputy arrived.

"Not that anything's likely to happen to it," Nate said, "but why take a chance?"

"No problem," Garrett assured him.

When Sandy had hung up the phone and closed the console, he motioned her to slide over so he could get in behind the wheel.

"Chilly out there," he remarked, rubbing his hands together briskly.

"How come you never married, Garrett?"

The question came at him sideways, utterly unexpected from Sandy Keller. Astonished, he turned his head so he could look straight at her and found her blushing violently.

"I'm sorry," she said quickly. "I don't know where that question came from. Just an attorney's insatiable curiosity about people, I guess."

But he knew where the question had come from. Women started wondering about things like that when they were interested in a man. His heart took an unwelcome leap of delight even as his stomach sank with a dread he knew all too well.

Damn it, he couldn't afford to get involved! It always wound up hurting too damn much. And from the horrified expression on her face, he would guess that Sandy Keller was no more eager to get involved than he was. Nothing but pain could come out of this if they weren't careful. Nothing but god-awful pain.

"I got jilted twice," he heard himself say. And that was when he knew he was in serious trouble.

Chapter 7

"Jilted? Twice?"

He had her attention now, he realized, and there was no way he could refuse to answer, not when he'd brought it up himself. Nope, he was just going to have to bite the bullet on this one and tell the gruesome tale.

The strange thing, though, was how difficult he suddenly found it to discuss something he'd honestly believed he'd come to terms with. It was as if the hurt he'd felt so long ago had never really gone away. Or maybe it just wasn't easy to admit to someone else that he didn't measure up. That he'd been rejected.

Stupid, he told himself. How could it hurt to admit that a couple of women had left him because of his job? It wasn't as if they'd rejected *him.*

"Back when I was twenty-seven, I was engaged to a wonderful woman named Janine. She was what I thought I wanted back then. You know, the Donna Reed kind of thing. She wanted to stay home and raise kids and bake cookies. About a week before the wedding, I was involved in a shoot-out with some drug dealers. Didn't get a scratch on me, and it's not very often most cops even get into a shooting match. Hell, I've known plenty of cops who've gone their entire careers and never had to fire their guns except on the range.''

"I suppose you told her that." Sandy could easily hear him making that argument to Janine.

"Of course I did." He felt almost embarrassed now to realize the degree of passion that had entered his voice, embarrassed to realize that he still felt it necessary to defend his career as he once had to Janine. It was apparent even to himself that this scar wasn't as faded as he'd been telling himself. In fact, it sounded suspiciously fresh, to judge by the degree of emotion in his voice. He cleared his throat and tried to sound detached.

"It happens, of course. I couldn't promise her that I'd never get shot at again, or that I'd never get killed. The fact is, though, that I don't do the kinds of work that are most dangerous to the average cop—traffic stops and domestic disturbances. And I'm not involved in any undercover work, so my job is probably safer than some." But not so safe that he didn't need to carry a gun. Not so safe that he could promise he would always come home in one piece. Not so safe that the tremor in his hand was of no concern. No, he had to be able to use that gun.

"Then there was Wanda," he continued. "I was a little older and a hell of a lot more cautious then. I'd given up on the Donna Reed idea. I wanted a woman who could stand on her own two feet and not be scared to death that I might not come home. Scared that she might be left with kids to clothe and feed by herself. Wanda didn't especially want kids, but what attracted me to her was that she had a good career in a telecommunications firm.'' He shook his head a little ruefully, remembering.

''What happened?''

''Well, Wanda believed that you put in your forty hours and a couple extra if you really needed to, and then you came home and forgot about it until the next business day. Unfortunately, I'm not like that.''

''Me either.''

He flashed her a smile. ''You probably understand what I mean when I say I'm a Texas Ranger twenty-four hours a day. When the job needs it, I don't quit except to sleep. Now, I reckon that's not necessarily something to brag about. Some folks would call it obsessive, I guess, but that's the way I am. I don't blame Wanda for getting fed up with it, though. A little while after I met her, I got assigned to a really tough case and…well, it started to take all my time. I lost count of the dates I had to break, or the weekends I worked. She finally had enough.'' He shrugged. ''I guess any woman would.''

''Was that unusual for you, or typical?''

''Unusual. Oh, the occasional case comes along that just devours every minute of every day, but most of 'em work out a little better than that. I work a lot of evenings and weekends, but not *all* of them. She saw the worst of it, wham, bang. Can't really blame her for backing out.''

''Well, you saw what I was doing when you dropped by last night. Up to my ears in work. Gerry—my ex—used to be annoyed by that, but I always felt he was being unfair, because he used to bring work home from the office, too. We were employed by the same legal firm, and I don't understand why he could never comprehend that I had just as much work to do as he did.''

Garrett tilted his head. ''Simple to explain. Your work

wasn't as important because you're a woman," he said
wryly.

Sandy's eyes widened a little. She'd figured that out herself a long time ago, but she had never expected a man to
understand it. Everything in her ex-husband's attitude had
devalued her simply because she was a woman. He would
praise her cooking but never her legal briefs. He bragged
about the clean house she kept but never about her trial
work. The effect had been subtle but ultimately devastating:
she had lost confidence in her abilities as a lawyer. His refusal to even acknowledge that her work was as important
as his had been undermining in a very indirect way. Just his
insistence that her work could wait while she cooked a meal
or ironed his shirt had evinced a priority that demeaned her
efforts.

Except for his comments about her sexuality, his attitude
had been one of simple male superiority and so much a part
of the times that it had taken her years to realize what was
happening to her. To this day she didn't blame Gerry. Lord,
no! The man's attitudes had been bred in him since birth,
part and parcel of his society. And she had accepted them
because she had been raised with the same attitudes. Only
when she came to realize that he was wounding her did she
develop the anger necessary to fight for her personhood.

The anger had resulted in the death of her marriage and
her own resurrection as a competent, capable, *independent*
woman. A woman who didn't *need* a man. But a woman
who wanted one, anyway.

She glanced at Garrett, but he was looking out over the
sun-drenched, snow-dappled countryside. Apparently he
didn't expect an answer to his remark, which was just as
well, because she really couldn't think of any casual response. The issue was too emotionally loaded for her.

"Right about here," he remarked lazily, "I could think I'm in West Texas. As long as I don't turn a little and see the mountains."

She gave a quiet laugh. "Getting homesick, Ranger?"

He turned to smile at her. "Reckon I am, a little. I think you'd like San Antonio, Sandy. One of these days you'll have to come visit and let me show you around."

"I'd like that." And she would, she realized. She would like it a whole lot. If she could ever make herself take a vacation.

Garrett straightened a little and peered through the windshield. "Somebody's coming. Hope it's a deputy. I'd like to get on out to Willis Road."

Nate had sent two deputies, and after chatting a few minutes with Garrett, they sent him and Sandy on their way.

Since they had left town, clouds had begun to appear over the western mountains. As they drove toward Willis Road, the sun sank low enough in the west that the heavy gray clouds swallowed it.

"More snow?" Garrett asked as gloom seemed to suffuse the world.

"Looks that way."

"Isn't that unusual?"

"To have this much snow at this time of year? Unusual, but not unheard of."

"I wish the light were better. Well, we might as well check things out anyway. If it snows again, there's no telling how long before it'll melt enough."

He parked the Explorer on the shoulder of Willis Road. Looking out across the range toward the creek where Lisa Dunbar had been found by Nate Tate, Sandy was glad she'd worn her winter boots. It looked muddy and unwelcoming.

With the disappearance of the sun behind the clouds, the

omnipresent wind had strengthened and taken on an icy edge. Sandy snapped her parka all the way to her chin and tugged on a stocking cap and gloves. Garrett wore a shearling jacket and leather gloves, but only a cowboy hat. She guessed his ears were going to get really cold.

"All right," he said. "I'm going to assume the guy assaulted her somewhere else and brought her here to dump her. As I remember, it was pretty damn cold that night. Cold enough that he probably took her somewhere that was heated. Then he needed to get rid of her. Common sense says he takes her somewhere away from his place."

"Not right across the road, you mean?"

Garrett looked down at her. "You'd think so, but not necessarily. Was there any reason to think that the searchers would look for her out here? We're seven or eight miles from where she was snatched. He probably figured that before anyone looked here she would have died of exposure."

Sandy repressed a shudder. If she lived to be as old as Methuselah, some of the things of which people were capable would never cease to horrify her. "Except for her book bag, you mean."

"That's right. That's what moved the search in this direction. How did the sheriff find out about that?"

"Someone called the office and reported that a little girl's book bag, full of schoolbooks, had been seen alongside the road here."

"Where?"

"I'm not sure, exactly. The report didn't say. You'd need to ask Nate to point out the place to you."

"So somebody called and said they'd *seen* it? Not that they'd found it?"

Sandy shook her head. "Weird, isn't it? No, somebody called, said they'd seen a kid's book bag alongside the road, that they hadn't touched it because they'd heard about the Dunbar girl being missing, and then before Velma—she's the dispatcher—could get their name or anything, they hung up.''

"Pretty much everybody knew the kid had turned up missing, huh?''

"You bet. The Dunbars have been here a long time, and lots of folks know them. When the sheriff formed search parties, it was inevitable that word would spread like wildfire. I figure nearly everyone must have heard about it by midnight. Certainly by the next morning, when they got to work.''

"So that part of it isn't suspicious.''

"Not in *this* county.''

"What time did that call come in to the sheriff?''

Sandy racked her brain. "Mmm, maybe around eight in the morning. I can check the report for the exact time. It's in my briefcase in the car.''

"Don't bother. We can check the time later. The call is suspicious, though.''

Sandy tilted her head back a little so that she could look directly at him. "Why?''

"Well…it sounds to me like it might have been the perp calling.''

She put her hands on her hips. "Why in the world would he do that?''

"Couple of reasons, maybe. It's not unheard of for the perp to suddenly get a conscience. Could be he put her out there but didn't want her to die. Could be he started to get really uneasy about it and changed his mind about letting her die. Could be he figured she was already dead, and he wanted her to be found before the search extended too far and turned up something he didn't want to turn up. Or maybe he was thumbing his nose at the sheriff. Or...maybe he was trying to point the finger at somebody else.''

''You mean Nighthawk?''

''Could well be.''

''Good grief.'' She turned and looked over the wintry countryside, shivering a little as the wind snaked into the collar of her jacket.

''The book bag keeps bothering me,'' he continued. ''It's unlikely that little Lisa was in a condition to think of shoving it out of the car like Hansel and Gretel leaving bread crumbs behind. Not at that point, right before he dumped her. I also don't think it's likely it just fell out of his vehicle when he pulled her out. You said it contained schoolbooks. No way he wouldn't have heard it fall out, even in the dark.''

''You think he left it by the road deliberately?''

''You might say the thought keeps crossing my mind.'' He turned a slow circle, taking in the gentle rolling of the land here. There were a lot of dips and gullies to hide things. ''Without that book bag, they might not have found that girl's remains for years.''

Sandy nodded, unable to find words to describe how it was making her feel to listen to him list possibilities that could only be coldly calculating. The thought that anyone could have considered such matters—could have treated such a little girl's survival in such terms—utterly horrified her.

''Come on. Let's walk down to the creek.''

She grabbed a notebook and pen, and stuffed them into a deep pocket. Experience had long since taught her to be prepared to take notes at any time.

The remaining snow wasn't very deep, and before long they started trying to walk in it in preference to the soggy and often slippery ground where the snow had melted away. The ground had become a web work of shallow gullies carved by spring runoff. None was much more than a foot or so deep, but they made the walk treacherous.

"Why would he have carried her all this way?" Sandy demanded breathlessly at one point. "I seriously doubt she walked."

"She couldn't be all that heavy, a little five-year-old. He probably wrapped her in a blanket and slung her over his shoulder. It's only about five hundred yards, and you have to remember, he wanted to conceal her. If he put her too close to the road, there was always a chance she might make enough noise to be heard. Or might wander back to the road. We need to ask her if she *did* wander around after he left her. She might not even have been abandoned on the creek bank."

The creek itself was swollen and muddy with early spring runoff. The water was icy and raced swiftly between its banks.

"In a few more weeks this'll be a real torrent," Sandy remarked. "I imagine all the gullies will be full of running water."

"Most likely." Garrett squatted and pointed downstream a little way. "That must be the cottonwood copse where Nate found her."

Sandy nodded. The only other visible trees were quite a distance upstream. "That's what he described in the report."

"And it's right across from Nighthawk's place, like he said. Come on, let's hike down that way along the bank. I figure he had to have dumped her just before dawn."

"Why?"

"Well, it couldn't have been too long before that or she probably would have frozen to death."

"She came damn near it, from what the doctor said."

"I imagine so. Anyway, he would have wanted to dump her and get out before it got light, so nobody would see him. The easiest way to navigate would be to follow one of the gullies to the stream, then follow the stream to the trees."

"Why would he even think it necessary to take her to the trees?"

"Because that way she wouldn't be spotted from overhead by an air search."

Sandy shivered again, not from cold. Garrett was thinking like the perpetrator, and the efficiency with which he did it was chilling. She was, she realized, getting a glimpse into the criminal mind. There was no doubt that thinking this way helped him to be a better investigator, but it unsettled her nonetheless to have this look into what must be a sick mind. "God," she whispered softly.

"Horrible, isn't it?" he agreed levelly. "Our perp is no idiot. He did an awful lot of thinking about this."

"Which means?"

"Not a whole hell of a lot. Yet. Okay. He kept the kid all night. And that means nobody would wonder about his whereabouts if he didn't show up for a while."

"That means someone who's single." Like Nighthawk.

"Not necessarily." He took a few more cautious steps along the slippery bank and gave her a hand to steady her. "From what the kid said about his face being 'mashed,' I figure he was wearing some kind of mask."

"That's what Nate figures."

"There aren't many masks he would have found comfortable to wear for twelve hours, which is approximately how long he had her. That means he must have had a place to stash her so he could get out of the mask for a while. He might not have done anything at all until hours after the kidnapping.''

"So he could have been home until the wife and kiddies fell asleep, and then left to rape Lisa? Good God!''

"Awful, isn't it? But yeah. It could have happened that way. All he'd need is some place to keep the kid until he was ready.''

The thought that the rapist might have calmly gone home to a wife and children left Sandy feeling ill in a way that was impossible to describe. Bad enough to think the perpetrator might have been some slug living alone in a solitary world, but far, far worse to think of him raising his own children. She shivered, slipping a little on the muddy creek bank.

Ordinarily she found the rushing sound of water soothing, but all of a sudden it seemed to be an isolating cocoon, cutting out the sounds of the larger world, making her feel as if she were moving through a separate world. She found herself wondering what it must have been like for a little girl in the icy predawn air after a night of terror. Dropped out here to die. Only saved, perhaps, by a belated twinge of conscience. Or by a simple, inexplicable accident that had left her book bag by the roadside.

"You know," Garrett said suddenly, "the best proof of Nighthawk's innocence is that damn book bag.''

"Why?''

"Because if he buried her belongings out behind his house, wouldn't he have buried the book bag, too? The more I think about it, the more convinced I become that somebody left that bag out there on purpose.''

To point a finger at Nighthawk. He left the implication unspoken, but it hung in the air like the leaden clouds above. The wind blew a little harder, seeming to push her forward as it swept between the creek banks. Like a giant hand on her back.

Why would someone want to frame Nighthawk? Had a little girl been raped because someone bore a grudge against him? No, no one could be capable of such a thing. The girl would have been abducted regardless. Framing Nighthawk was simply a way for the rapist to protect himself.

And all of this had been planned. The earmarks were unmistakable. Someone had, like a repulsive spider spinning a web, plotted and planned every move in this heinous crime. She couldn't have said why, but she would have found it all a lot less revolting if it had been an act committed on the spur of the moment.

"All this premeditation," she said to Garrett as they worked their way toward the copse of leafless cottonwoods, "doesn't fit with the idea that he had an attack of conscience after he dumped her."

"Sure it does." He stopped walking and turned to face her. "The truth of it is, the perp gets high on the adrenaline. He gets higher and higher through all the planning and through the commission of the act. Sexual excitement propels him, too, as often as not. And what happens in the aftermath, Sandy? Surely you remember what happens when the sexual compulsion is satisfied."

"Afraid not." She didn't know why she let those words pass her lips. She had guarded her secret for years and years, and now, standing beside an icy stream on a cold, wintry day in the middle nowhere, she let the truth come out.

Garrett grew suddenly still in a way that told her he had not missed the significance of the words. His brilliant blue eyes bored into hers, seeking answers. But he didn't ask. Thank God, he didn't ask. He left her secrets alone.

"Sexual compulsion is a powerful motivator. It's pretty

good at silencing conscience and fear, actually, which is why so many kids get into trouble. Our perp has a thing for kids that's probably been goading him for years. Given that no other child molestation appears to have happened around here, I'd say he's either very new to the area or he's been controlling the urge for a long time.

"Let's go with the latter, since I don't think Nighthawk did it. So this guy has been repressing some very, very powerful urges for a long time. And suddenly they start to get the better of him, propelling him to satisfy them. Probably when he started planning this, he told himself he'd never carry it out. Told himself he was just fantasizing, but that he'd never do this thing.

"Only as he got more and more into it, it began to seem more and more possible. More and more likely he could pull it off and never be detected. And as he thought more and more about it, the compulsion to do it kept growing. Until finally it was controlling him rather than the other way around. It seemed so easy to do it, and it was just about impossible to stop.

"So he does it. Satisfies the compulsion. It loses its driving grip on him, and his brain begins to kick in again, just a little. Fear sets in. He ditches the girl and leaves a trail pointing to someone else, the way he'd planned it. Then he gets home…and the adrenaline quits. Without the high, he's scared, alone, facing reality, possibly for the first time in weeks. And then he thinks about that little girl lying out there on an icy creek bank and his conscience starts to work on him. No one'll ever find him, he tells himself. He pointed the finger at somebody else. But does the little girl have to die?"

Sandy drew a shaky breath. "So he picks up the phone, calls the sheriff's office, and tells them about the book bag."

"That's about it."

Something in the way his gaze slid away from hers told her that he was withholding something. "What's the rest of it, Garrett? What aren't you saying?"

He turned a little, so that she was looking at his profile, and kicked a loose stone into the rushing water. "Just that what this guy did goes beyond pedophilia. It's not a mere sexual quirk but something more. That's apparent by the fact that he abducted her, kept her for approximately twelve hours and left her to die. I've investigated more than one case of this nature, unfortunately. Usually the perp goes through a strong period of remorse and shame, but then the compulsion starts to take root again. As a rule, they do it again. And the next time is worse. He needs more to get the same high."

He looked over his shoulder at her. "This guy will move again, Sandy. I can't say when. There's no way to predict his schedule based on one incident. But the chances are good he'll work himself up to it again fairly soon. It just gets easier and easier for him each time. He's done it once, and now he'll do it again."

She nodded. "That possibility has been scaring me to death. We've got to get the right man behind bars."

A small boulder, left there long ago by a rushing torrent or a glacier, rested half in and half out of the water. It looked dry, and Sandy sat on it, electrically aware when Garrett settled beside her. She stared back up the stream coursing so hurriedly between its high banks, a swiftly moving muddy torrent from the clean white snow on the mountains.

This case had moved far beyond a matter of providing a defense as required by the constitution. It had become a matter of saving an innocent man and finding a vicious serial rapist before another child could be hurt. Sandy had never met Lisa Dunbar, but that didn't matter. She was a mother, and she'd had a five-year-old, and the thought of *any* child experiencing any part of what Lisa Dunbar had...

She shook her head, wiping the horrible thought away. It made her want to kill, when she really thought about it. A person who could do such things to a child was unfit to live.

The sheriff thought he had the right man. So until she and Garrett could prove otherwise, they would be the only people on earth trying to find the real perpetrator. The real rapist. The man who had to be stopped before he did it again.

And she knew Garrett was right. She hadn't made a study of it, but over the years she'd read here and there enough to know that people who committed this sort of crime never committed only one. Instead they would do it again and again in an ever-escalating spiral of violence, each act coming sooner after the last. If the rapist in this case had indeed just committed his first crime, then they might have weeks or even months before the next attempt. But if this wasn't his first...

She shivered again. The rock felt cold beneath her, almost icy even through her jeans. She shouldn't sit here long, she thought absently. She would quickly lose body heat through contact with the rock.

But she didn't move. It might be cold as all get-out, but she could feel Garrett's arm just brushing against hers, and she didn't want to lose that contact, even with the layers of clothing between them.

Some deeply buried place in her seemed to be opening, reminding her of things so long forgotten. How long had it been, for example, since a man had placed his arms around her shoulders? Oh, so long! She ached now for just that simple contact. That feeling that someone on this planet truly wanted to be close to her. How badly she needed to be hugged.

Before she could deny the yearning, Garrett seemed to read her mind. What was more, he didn't even try to be casual about it. He turned, looking fully at her, waiting until she turned tentatively to look back at him. When he had her full attention, he draped his arm over her shoulders and tucked her up against his side.

Her breath locked in her throat as she tilted her head back farther and looked up into his amazing blue eyes. Such a wonderful blue, she thought hazily, as her whole world seemed to narrow to this man, this moment.

He was going to kiss her. A flare of panic erupted within her, then faded, as a warm, needy feeling filled her. It had been so long, and Garrett was such a unique man, that this risk didn't seem too terrifying. A kiss. Just a kiss. How much harm could come from a simple kiss?

She let her eyelids flutter closed as his head bowed toward hers. This much trust she could give him. This much she had in her. It was, she told herself again, just a kiss. Nothing to fear.

That was her last coherent thought. Garrett's lips touched hers with warmth and tenderness, a gentle questing that demanded nothing and offered so much. Soft little kisses, sprinkled against her mouth with hardly more pressure than a warm raindrop, that made her soften internally, driving everything else from her mind before a tide of yearning.

The darkening afternoon spun away; the cold was forgotten. Nothing existed except Garrett and the blossoming hunger within her. Her head fell back, inviting a deeper invasion, and Garrett's tongue joined his lips in caressing her. Soft, sweeping strokes that made her mouth tingle, a tingling that seemed to spread through her in the wake of the softening warmth and arouse forgotten needs.

What could be the harm in a simple kiss? Now she knew. If he had wanted to sweep her beneath him and take her on that cold boulder, she would have let him. Awareness of her danger struck her like a bolt of lightning. In an instant she stiffened and pulled back, arousal and warmth lost in the frigid awareness of her inadequacy.

As soon as she stiffened, Garrett released her. She feared he would question her, would demand to know what was wrong. Instead he dropped a quick kiss on her forehead and slid off the boulder.

Turning, he offered her a smile and a hand. ''We'd better hustle, or night is going to catch us before we're done.''

Her legs felt like rubber as she followed him along the bank toward the cottonwood grove. Looking up, she saw that the clouds were scudding swiftly and seemed to be almost low enough to touch. If they didn't have snow, they were sure going to have some rain.

It was easier to think about the weather, about the case, than it was to think about what had just happened, so she pondered the cold spring, the slippery bank and the mind of a man who could abandon an injured child out here on a cold, dark night.

The distraction would work for a while. It always did. But later, when she was trying to fall asleep, she was going to have to deal with that kiss somehow. Deal with her reaction to it. She felt as if everything inside her had somehow been shaken free and was now drifting, rearranging itself, taking on a new and different configuration.

But she couldn't deal with that right now. That would have to wait. She didn't dare confront her confused feelings until she was safely private.

*   *   *

It was extremely unlikely that they would discover any new evidence among the trees where Lisa Dunbar had been found. Even in the slowly failing light, they could tell that the ground had been pretty well trampled.

"Crime-scene unit went over this with a fine tooth comb," Garrett remarked. Yellow streamers of plastic tape strung from tree to tree, still demarcated the area. Garrett didn't even bother to cross the line, just circled the area, looking at it from all angles. Leafless tree branches above nearly obscured the sky, they were so thick.

"A hell of a place to dump the kid," he said. "He sure didn't want her to be found. Let's walk up to the road now."

From here the terrain wasn't too difficult. Not impossible to cross at night, though it would require some care, Sandy thought. The hay had been mowed before winter set in, and the brown stalks were just thick enough to have concealed the passage of someone on foot. He had picked his ground well.

Garrett spoke. "So he made his way down to the stream with the kid. Probably had her wrapped in a blanket. Came back this way with the blanket, went to his vehicle, which could have been anywhere along this road at that time of night. I doubt anybody would drive along here before dawn, but even if they did, they probably wouldn't pay any attention to a vehicle pulled to one side unless there was something unusual about it. If he parked right at the end of Nighthawk's drive, nobody would notice at all."

"Probably not."

"So he gets back to the road, gets the girl's clothes from his trunk or wherever and then hikes up Nighthawk's driveway and buries the stuff behind the house."

By the time they had walked up the driveway and then the hundred and fifty yards to where more yellow tape was strung from stakes around a hole in the ground, Sandy was convinced of one thing: every step had been deliberate. Nighthawk would have buried the clothes near Lisa, not on his own property. Not behind his house.

"Somebody is framing him," she said.

Garrett nodded slowly. "I reckon," he said.

"But who? And why?"

"Well, darlin', at this point I'd kind of guess somebody has an ax to grind. And I think we need to ask Nighthawk again about anyone who might have a grudge. Although, often enough, people really *don't* know someone is mad at them."

Darlin'. The absent endearment stuck with her as they drove back to town. He hadn't meant anything by it, she told herself. It had just slipped out and he didn't even realize he'd said it. Some people called *everyone* darling or honey.

Except that Garrett didn't seem to. At least, she'd never heard him do it before. But then, how well did she really know him?

Twilight had descended just about the time they reached the pit in Nighthawk's backyard, but it didn't linger long as the clouds swallowed the last of the light. The wind strengthened, each gust of its cold breath causing the Explorer to shudder, forcing Garrett to constantly correct for it.

It was not snow that began to fall, finally, but heavy drops of windswept rain that rattled against the windows of the car.

"It's damned inhospitable tonight," Garrett remarked as he slowed down and leaned forward a little to better see the wet road.

It even *sounded* cold, Sandy thought. Turning in her seat,

she looked at Garrett and spoke before she could change her mind. "Why don't you stay and have dinner with me?"

He shot her a sharp glance, then nodded. "I'd like that. Thanks."

Only as they neared her house did she realize how that invitation might have sounded to him, coming as it did after their kiss earlier.

A blizzard of panic instantly filled her with ice. What if he took her invitation to dinner as an invitation to make love? Oh, God, what had she done?

Her stomach began to flutter nervously, and her brain scurried around frantically, trying to find an excuse to change her mind that wouldn't sound rude but also wouldn't reveal her panic. She didn't want him to know how scared she was of making love. She didn't want *anyone* to ever know that.

Nor did she want to face her fear. It wasn't fear because she had been raped, though that had been a brutal experience that had left an aftermath of problems for her to deal with. What scared her was not that Garrett might hurt her, but that he might humiliate her, as Gerry had done so many times.

That Garrett would discover she was frigid and would come away dissatisfied and scornful. That, even if he said nothing to humiliate her at all, her failure as a woman would still lie exposed to the glaring light of someone else's knowledge.

Her inability to respond to her husband after the rape had scared her as no mere rape could have. What if she tried to make love with Garrett and the old ghosts reared their heads, and she froze? What if, as had happened so often with Gerry in the immediate aftermath of the rape, she closed her eyes, felt a man's hands on her body and panicked? What if revulsion filled her and caused her to twist away as if Garrett were the attacker?

But that had only happened for a brief time after the attack. What had happened thereafter had been the direct result of Gerry's response to her panic and revulsion. She quite simply froze up inside. Withdrew to someplace safe in her own mind and refused to let any of it touch her, so that when he began to say those vile things about her frigidity, they wouldn't be able to touch her where it hurt.

And the root of the problem was that deep inside she believed Gerry had been justified. Throughout their marriage she had been sexually inhibited, but after the rape...well, what had been a perfectly normal reaction to the assault had been turned by Gerry's condemnation into something considerably worse.

It had, however, resulted in her facing what a farce her marriage had become. His lack of support for her after the attack had forced her to look hard and long at all the other ways he had failed to support her. All the ways he had undermined her.

And leaving Gerry had unquestionably been one of the smartest moves she had ever made. Little by little she had pieced herself back together, had nurtured her own confidence and strength...and had unquestionably raised a better son as a result. She had never, and would never, regret the divorce.

But there was a part of her that had never healed. A part that she had chosen to bury, rather than deal with all the painful scar tissue. A part of her that she was being forced to look straight in the eye as Garrett helped her down from the Explorer, as they entered her house and climbed the stairs to her apartment above the office.

Like a frightened horse, she had a wild urge to bolt. If

she just turned and ran out into the rain-lashed night, Garrett would take the hint and never trouble her again.

But was that what she really wanted?

At the head of the stairs, on the landing, he took the key from her trembling hand and slipped it into the lock that kept her apartment inviolate during the day when the lower part of the house was open for business. She heard the thump as the dead bolt slid back, the creak of hinges as the door swung open. Garrett reached across her and felt for the light switch.

Oh, God, she thought, her heart hammering wildly, what now?

Light flooded the landing, and Garrett looked down at her. There was barely a breath of air between them, making her certain he must be able to hear her heart hammer.

He smiled, the corners of his blue eyes crinkling attractively. "Can I see your file on the case after dinner?"

It was as if he had pulled a plug; all the tension seeped out of her, leaving her almost weak. "Sure," she said. "After dinner."

Dinner and work. That was all. Relief should have made her giddy. Instead, all it did was disappoint her.

Chapter 8

For dinner she made a stir-fry and had the unique experience of being assisted in the kitchen by a man who actually knew how to slice vegetables.

"Now, that's a female chauvinist attitude," he teased her when she commented. "I've been living alone a long time, darlin'. It was either learn to cook or spend my whole paycheck in restaurants."

"I take it you don't like that old staple, the fast-food hamburger?"

"If I'm going to eat a burger, it has to be all beef, thick, cooked rare and smothered in onions and Swiss cheese."

"Picky, picky."

After dinner they sprawled on the floor with the file again, just as they had last night. Tonight, though, Garrett was particularly looking for the record of the phone call to the sheriff about the little girl's book bag being seen along Willis Road.

"Here it is," he said. "'Male caller at 8:33 a.m. Said he'd seen what looked like a kid's book bag while driving to work. Said he hadn't touched it, but wondered if it might belong to that little girl who was missing. Disconnected abruptly without identifying himself and didn't call back.'"

Garrett, who was sitting on the floor, closed the file and leaned back against the couch. "I don't like the sound of it. Something fishy as hell about that call. How many people live out along Willis Road?"

"I'm not sure. I could find out."

"In the morning. We'll check it out in the morning." He tilted his head back and turned it so he could look at her. She was curled up with her feet tucked under her, leaning against the couch at the opposite end. Avoidance, he thought. Something had made her as skittish as a doe about the time she'd asked him to have dinner with her.

At first her distancing had struck him as strange, but now, as he thought it over and put it together with her abrupt pulling away when he had kissed her, he had to conclude that she was afraid of the sexual attraction between them.

Well, he couldn't blame her for that. If he had a grain of the common sense he'd always prided himself on, he would get up right now and get out of here before he followed through on a growing desire to wrap his arms around her and hold her close. Because once he got her close—if she let him—he might not be able to keep it casual.

He might not be able to let go.

Looking away, he pretended fascination with the toes of his socks. Problem was, or so he tried to tell himself, that as he got older, he got a whole lot more discriminating about women. In practical terms that meant it had been many months since he'd held a woman, and one hell of lot longer since he'd made love to one. That was the price of pickiness. And that meant that when he met a woman like Sandy Keller, a woman who appealed to his head and heart as much as his body, he was damn near a pushover.

Time to get out of here, before he did something they would both regret. Refusing himself an opportunity to change his mind, he rose to his feet in a single swift movement. Sandy looked startled, then quickly unfolded herself and stood. "Leaving?" she asked.

But he couldn't make himself. Silly as it was, he couldn't make himself reach for his boots and get the hell out of there. Instead he reached for Sandy. His arms stretched out toward her, open, his palms turned upward a little, beseeching. If she had stiffened, if she had run, if she had made the least movement or sound of rejection, he would have turned and left.

But she didn't. She licked her lips nervously, looking from his arms to his face, probably never realizing how much he read in her expression. Like a mistreated child, she both yearned for the offered affection and was terrified of it.

If he had any doubts of the wisdom of escaping, that should have settled it. Whatever had happened to this lady, he was hardly likely to be able to fix it. Maybe he couldn't even deal with it. How could he possibly know? And if he *mis*handled it, he might make her problems worse. He didn't dare risk it.

Which was precisely why he stepped toward her and, ignoring her fear and uncertainty, swept her into a bear hug that hauled her flush to his body. Ah, hell, he thought dismally, and squeezed her even closer. She felt so damn good. A bundle of feminine softness, complete with the faint, enticing fragrance of woman.

"It's okay," he heard himself say huskily, though he hadn't the vaguest idea what needed to be okay. Nor did he have the dimmest idea of what he might be promising. "It's okay," he said again.

He felt a shudder rip through her. If her hands had tried to push him away, he would have let go instantly. Instead they clutched at him, crushing the front of his shirt in a death grip. She was scared to death, but the lady didn't want to be somewhere else.

In which case… Taking a huge chance, he tilted her head upward with the gentle pressure of one finger. Her eyes were closed tightly—too tightly—but she didn't try to pull her head away.

So he kissed her. Kissed her and hoped to hell he wasn't making a huge mistake. He would hate it if Sandy got angry with him or wouldn't have anything more to do with him. For an instant she grew really stiff against him, but then nothing else seemed to matter, for her lips parted beneath his, and there was no mistaking the way her head fell back in timeless surrender.

The woman softened for him. There was no greater aphrodisiac in the world than realizing that a woman wanted him, and this one did. She was scared, maybe even terrified, but she wanted this kiss as much as he did. Taking care not to scare her, he touched her lips gently with his tongue, then slipped it inside tentatively, alert for any sign of fright or rejection.

None came. A little more boldly, his tongue foraged in her warm silky depths, and he found himself wishing his whole aching body could slip into her just like his tongue. In this woman's depths he would be able to forget everything else, would be able to put aside all his problems and worries for a little.

Even as he had the thought, he felt guilty. She wasn't an anodyne to his problems, and he had absolutely no right to even think of using her in such a fashion. She was a woman with feelings and needs every bit as important as his own, and she deserved to be treated as such.

But even the fleeting attack of guilt couldn't make him let go. Couldn't make him stop kissing her. His need for her warmth and closeness was almost desperate.

But not desperate enough to make him forget that she was frightened. Her breasts, belly and thighs were pressed snugly to him, but before they could make him forget his good sense, he lifted his head and tucked her against his shoulder.

"You're a beautiful, sexy woman, Sandra Keller. I'd better get out of here before I get carried away." He didn't mind admitting what she made him feel. What he hoped was that she might confide in him about her fears.

But she didn't. A soft, regretful sigh escaped her, and slowly she pulled away. Reluctantly he let her.

Two minutes later he was standing outside next to his Explorer, with icy rain slapping his cheeks. It was a dark, cold night, and he didn't think he'd ever felt so alone.

"Ninety-nine...one hundred." He let the tennis ball go and watched it bounce across the dingy motel carpet. No question but that he was about ready to chew the furniture. The wind howled noisily around the corner of his room, the rain rattling loudly against the window, beginning to sound very much like heavy sleet. Everyone in Conard County except him had probably gone to sleep hours ago.

He resisted the urge to get out his pistol and see if he could hold it steadily yet. No point in even attempting it. He might heal. It was entirely possible that he would regain full use of his arm. But there was no way he could gauge improvement, and no way that simple improvement would be enough to get him back on duty. That arm had to work flawlessly, and he still had plenty of time before he had to face that. In the meantime, there was absolutely no point in riding a roller coaster of emotion from day to day as he tried to tell if he was improving.

But it was close to driving him crazy, this wondering. With a disgusted sigh, he flopped back onto the bed and tried not to think about his hazy future. Tried, too, not to think about a certain lady lawyer who was preoccupying far too much of his thoughts lately.

Only a damn fool would get involved under these circumstances. She was as skittish as a woman could get, obviously afraid, probably a mess from her marriage. He was leaving shortly, and anyway, he might not even have a job at this rate. How could he even consider getting involved?

And involved was what he was going to get if he spent too much time with Sandy Keller. Something about her kept tugging at him in the most uncomfortable way, despite the fact that she seemed to be as determined as he to remain uninvolved.

Ready to growl, he looked at his watch and decided that *this* time his sister was going to have to put up with being awakened, the way she'd roused him so many times when Bobby had gotten drunk and abusive.

Damn! His hand paused over the phone, hovering, as he remembered his sister's seemingly endless marriage. How many times had he begged her to leave, offered her a safe haven, promised to protect her from that crud? But like so many victims, Ginny had been sure Bobby meant it when he wept and swore he wouldn't do it again. Believed it when he blamed her for his rages, saying he wouldn't have hit her if only she hadn't done some little thing like make the mashed potatoes too creamy. Believed that if only she were a better wife he wouldn't hit her at all.

"Hell!" The word escaped him, briefly filling the silence and emptiness of the motel room. It was always hard from the outside looking in to understand why anybody put up with that crap. Hard to fathom why anybody would take that treatment for so long. Some took it for a lifetime. His sister hadn't, largely because she'd had alternatives.

He'd been rousted out of bed in the middle of the night a lot of times in his life. For one thing, it went with his job. Then there had been Ginny. How many times had he picked up the phone and heard her frightened, weepy voice begging him to come and get her and the kids because Bobby had been drinking again? How many times had he begged her to file charges and then listened to her insist that she'd banged her face on a door or fallen down? Or worse, had insisted that Bobby hadn't meant to hit her, and no, she wasn't going to send him to jail over a few little bruises. Besides, it had been *her* fault because…because…because. The stony silence when he had persisted.

Finally one night Bobby had beaten her so badly that Garrett had to take her to the hospital. That night Garrett had returned to the house with a city police officer, who arrested Bobby for assault with intent to kill. Because that time Garrett had arrived in time to see some of it with his own two eyes.

The years since had been good, watching Ginny put herself back together with the aid of counselors, watching the fear gradually fade from her eyes and the eyes of the children.

And, of course, there was the memory of the fear in Bobby's eyes when Garrett had told him in no uncertain terms that if he ever came near Ginny or the kids again, Garrett would shoot him.

It really wouldn't be very nice to disturb Ginny's sleep

with a phone call. What would he say to her, anyway? Hi, I'm fine, and I'm trying like mad not to get involved with a lady who wouldn't want me, anyway? Ginny would immediately want to know all about Sandy, then would badger him to go for it and remind him that he would spend the rest of his life alone if he didn't at least make an attempt.

He found himself grinning at the ceiling, realizing that he didn't even need to call Ginny, because he'd already had the entire conversation. But he lifted the receiver and dialed her number, anyway. It had been a week or more, and he got to worrying about his little sister.

"Garrett!" She sounded sleepy but pleased, and brushed away his apology for calling so late. "I woke you up more times than I can count. Are you okay?"

"I'm fine, Ginny. Fine. Just got to hankerin' for the sound of your voice. How are you and the rug rats doing?"

"We're doing just fine."

But there was a very faint hesitation when she answered, just enough to alert him that she was worrying about something. He would let it ride a bit, see if she brought it up herself. If she didn't, he would pin her down. It wouldn't be the first time.

"Bobby Jr. is collecting bugs for a school project. Did I tell you about that? Well, I opened the microwave last night to put the broccoli in, and there was a jar full of bugs. Garrett, I swear! He doesn't want to kill them the way the teacher told him to, because it takes too long and he doesn't like hurting them. So he microwaved them!"

Garrett couldn't have stopped the laughter that rolled out of him. "Makes sense to me."

"Well, not to me! It makes my skin crawl to think of him putting those filthy things in there, where I cook food! Even if they were in a jar." A quiet chuckle escaped her. "Actually, it reminded me of you, and I can't for the life of me say why."

"A jar of bugs reminded you of me?" He tried to sound offended but didn't quite succeed.

"No, silly, not the bugs. No, it was the way Bobby Jr. handled the situation. Creative problem solving, to say the least."

She went on to tell him a few amusing tales about her two younger children, but he didn't hear a thing that could have caused her any concern at all. Finally he asked her point-blank what was worrying her.

For a few moments silence hummed between them on the line. Finally she spoke in a subdued voice. "The parole board sent me a letter."

"And?"

"It seems Bobby's going to get out of prison next month. It's mandatory, they said."

Garrett swore, knowing how that news had to make her feel. "Listen, Ginny. I promise I'll be home before then. You won't have to deal with this alone."

"Isn't there some way they can make him stay in jail?"

"I'm afraid not. If they said it's mandatory, then he's got enough time served and enough good time to get out, and there's nothing anyone can do about it. It's the law."

"Well." She managed a shaky laugh. "He's stupid, but not stupid enough to try to come after me."

"No, I don't think he is. He knows I'll kill him if anything happens to you, so I expect he'll stay far away. But it doesn't matter, anyway, because I'll be there. I promise."

Right, Hancock. As if you can keep another person absolutely safe twenty-four hours a day. Besides, the last time he had looked, there hadn't been a big yellow *S* on his chest.

"I'll get back there soon, and we'll deal with it, Ginny. I swear. He's not gonna hurt you or the kids ever again."

Thanks to that little piece of news, they never got around to discussing him, which was just fine, because sure as shootin' he would have mentioned Sandy. Then it would have been the third degree for sure.

Later, wishing for a cigarette, he worked the tennis ball over some more and listened to the cold rattle of sleet against the windowpanes. The problem, he told himself, was that you couldn't always tell who was going to be a repeat offender. Spouse abusers and child abusers tended to keep right on doing it, no matter how many times you put them away. Problem was, they were prosecuted under the same assault laws that applied to knocking somebody down on the street because they drove into the side of your car. Consequently, the "good time" calendar and mandatory parole were applied evenly across the board, regardless of whether a person was liable to commit the same crime again.

It was an unhappy fact that, no matter what he'd told her, his sister was in considerable danger from her ex-husband. If Bobby Taylor felt Ginny was responsible for his incarceration, he might well take a mind to teach her a lesson. Or to get even. And there was no real way to know if he was that kind of person. The only thing anyone could know for sure was that, all too often, when somebody like Bobby Taylor got out of jail, he went after the person he perceived to be at the root of all his troubles: his ex-wife.

Well, he would worry about that when he got home and could actually do something about it. Until Bobby was released, there was no threat and absolutely no point in wondering if he would be what his sister needed when the time came.

He had enough demons on his plate right now, mainly

wondering what he was going to do if he couldn't go back to work. He talked about it as if it didn't matter, but the fact was, early retirement was about as appealing as a case of cancer to him. Either one would gut him and kill him. But no point thinking about that right now, either. Some things could only be dealt with when you looked them right in the eye.

What he needed to be thinking about was the Nighthawk case. After tramping around out there earlier, he was convinced that Nighthawk was being framed. Simple as that. Oh, he could be wrong—that was always a possibility—but the way things looked now, he would bet the ranch on Nighthawk's innocence.

Which meant that the best way to exonerate Nighthawk was to figure out who was trying to frame him. Nighthawk didn't seem to think he had any enemies around here who would want to do that, but it wouldn't necessarily be someone who was mad at him. The little girl's father, for example, might be the perp. In fact, in far too many of these cases a relative was to blame. So just for argument's sake, say it *was* Dunbar who'd hurt the little girl. Why would he choose to frame Nighthawk, of all people?

Because Nighthawk had been seen with Lisa last month. Because someone else had seen the little girl in Nighthawk's truck and would remember it. Easy to frame the Indian. And that would explain why the initial report of the incident had come from what's his name—Willis—instead of Dunbar. If Dunbar were guilty, he wouldn't want to make himself obvious by bringing up the information first. But he might well have reminded Willis about it, jogging the man's memory, so to speak.

Perhaps the most frightening thing about the thoughts running through his head at the moment was their plausibility.

Ben Dunbar the bad guy? Yeah. It made all too damn much sense.

And it made his stomach churn. There was nothing more horrible than a parent doing something like that to his own little kid.

In an instant, the night became a time of terror for Sandy. She'd been snuggled into her bed with quilts drawn to her chin, sleeping deeply, when something had startled her into wakefulness with a pounding heart.

The sense of threat was unmistakable. Ordinarily, when a sound woke her during the night, her mind registered it with a ready explanation that allowed her to turn over and go back to sleep. A tree limb brushing against the side of the house. The wind moaning around the corner. A car backfiring....

But this time she awoke with a definite sense of threat. She had heard something that was not a normal night sound, and her hammering heart demanded more air than she was getting.

Eyes wide open, she stared into the dark and listened so intently that her ears felt strained. Even when the night remained as silent as only the night could be at around four in the morning, she couldn't escape the sense that she had heard some*one* rather than some*thing*.

But there was no other sound, and after endless minutes of nerve-stretching fright and alertness, she began to relax. It had just been an odd sound from outside. Maybe some kid driving by in a car had shouted something and she'd mistaken it for a threat of some kind. Perhaps a cat had howled and her mind had registered it as a scream. Maybe she'd just been having a bad dream that had somehow commingled with a night sound to make something perfectly ordinary seem threatening.

Finally, facing the fact that she wasn't going to fall back to sleep soon, she sat up, tucked her feet into slippers and padded out to the kitchen to make tea.

The sky had cleared since bedtime, and moonlight fell through the uncurtained kitchen window, reflecting off icicles on the leafless tree just outside. The wind had died, leaving the night utterly calm.

Without turning on a light, she lit the burner beneath the teakettle and took a tea bag from the canister beside the stove. Moonlight, she thought, was so coldly beautiful.

Then she heard it again. Something was inside the house. Downstairs. She had heard it move.

She stopped breathing and reached over to turn the flame off beneath the kettle, wanting absolute silence from which to listen.

A mouse, she told herself. Some poor little field mouse must have come in from the cold and was—

Again. A sound so soft it was almost impossible to hear. As if… As if someone were climbing the stairs to her apartment.

For several heartbeats she was paralyzed, unable to move at all as her ears strained to listen but she could hear nothing except her own galloping heart. There was a dead bolt on the door between her apartment and the stairs, and it was a solid core wood door. It would take a little time for the intruder to break in.

That awareness released her from paralysis. Heedless of whether she made any sound, she scurried across the kitchen and grabbed for the wall phone. The sheriff was the first number on the autodialer, and she punched the button, listening to the familiar series of tones impatiently. Not even a machine could dial fast enough for her.

A sleepy-sounding Virgil Beauregard answered the phone.

"Beau, this is Sandy Keller. There's someone in my office downstairs, and it sounds like he's coming up here—"

"We're on our way, Sandy," Beau said abruptly, no longer sounding sleepy. "Keep the phone off the hook. I'm going to keep the line open, okay? Now, make sure the door is locked, then go hide in a closet."

But she couldn't bring herself to go hide in the closet. If the intruder managed to get through the door before the sheriff arrived, she didn't want to be trapped in a confined place with no escape route. After a moment's hesitation, she went to the cabinet beside the stove and pulled out a heavy cast-iron skillet. If anyone came through that door, she was going to be waiting right behind it.

But there was no further sound from the stairway—at least nothing that reached her through the closed door. From far away she could hear a siren and wondered if that could be the sheriff heading for her house.

But no, they would approach without sirens and probably without lights, so they wouldn't alert the prowler and cause him to run. Reaching behind her, she felt for the cord of the wall phone. The receiver was dangling almost to the floor, and she had to bend to find it. At last she tucked it to her ear.

"Beau?" she whispered.

"Aren't you hiding yet?" he growled. "There's a car pulling up two doors east of you. The officer is going to approach the house on foot. Now you go hide."

"No. I'm staying right here. If he tries to get through the door, I'm going to hit him over the head."

"Damn it, Sandy, this is no time to play hero!"

"I don't have the right build to be a hero," she managed to whisper shakily. Her mouth was so dry that her lips were sticking to her teeth, and her hand ached from holding the handle of the skillet. From below, she heard no sound at all.

"This is no time for humor, either," Beau grumbled. "Okay, the officer is approaching the house right now. This is the dangerous part, Sandy. No matter what you hear, keep that door locked until I tell you it's safe to come out. Hear?"

"I hear." God, if minutes could move any slower, they would encompass aeons. But even as she wished the officer outside would hurry, she felt concerned for him. It would have to be awful to walk into a dark building with no idea whether someone was in there, or if the intruder was armed. Closing her eyes, she said a little prayer that no one got hurt. "Who's the officer, Beau?"

"Ed Dewhurst."

Ed. She knew Ed pretty well, had dated him a couple of times after his first wife died and before he remarried. Now he had four kids, the eldest of whom was thirteen. Oh, Lord, don't let anything happen to him.

"He's at the front door, Sandy," Beau told her. "Someone definitely broke in. The glass has been knocked out so he could reach the doorknob."

"Tell Ed to be careful."

"Backup's on the way," Beau reassured her. "Should be there any second. He won't be alone."

There was still no sound from downstairs, but that could have been because she was hanging on to Beau's voice in her ear like a lifeline, so it was hard to listen for faint sounds from below.

But maybe the intruder had already left. The floors tended to creak up here when she walked, and it was audible downstairs. Or perhaps he had heard her call the police. She hadn't exactly been quiet about it.

Oh, how she wished she weren't alone right now! Thoughts of Garrett suddenly filled her with something that was almost despair. If she hadn't stiffened when he kissed her, maybe he would still be here. Maybe she wouldn't be alone.

She was so *tired* of being alone, locked in a prison of self-doubt about her womanhood. She didn't see how she could possibly escape it, though. Not when the only way out was for some man to make her feel sexually adequate, and that was unlikely to happen when she panicked every time anyone kissed her.

Nor was that entire subject something she wanted to be thinking about when something terrible could happen at any moment. At this point she didn't know which she wanted more—to hear something from downstairs or to hear nothing at all.

"They've finished checking around outside, Sandy," Beau said in her ear. "Ed's coming in now."

Probably the same way the thief had gotten in, she thought, through the door with the broken-out glass. But even though she strained to hear, there was still no sound from below. Ed must be as silent as a cat.

More minutes stretched tautly, and now Beau couldn't even give her a blow-by-blow, because Ed was busy checking out the house and was probably being silent. Sandy let the skillet dangle by her side and wondered if her fingers would ever uncramp.

And then, at last, Beau said, "Sandy? Ed's coming up the stairs now. You can let him in. No one's below."

"Thanks, Beau. Thanks."

"No problem. This is what we're here for."

Moments later Ed was smiling at her from the landing. "Whoever it was is gone, Sandy. Maybe you want to come down and tell us what's missing, though. He got into some stuff."

She pulled on a velour robe over her flannel nightgown and followed Ed downstairs. Light blazed everywhere—he'd evidently turned on every light in the place when he'd finished checking things out. Another deputy, whose name she didn't know, was standing near the front door.

"Somebody broke in through that door," Ed said. "Broke out the one pane so he could reach in and get hold of the knob. He broke into your secretary's desk and into a file cabinet in your office. Looking for money, I guess."

He'd found some, too, Sandy saw. The petty-cash box had been pried open and emptied of everything except receipts.

"There was definitely cash in there," she told Ed, "but exactly how much is something Nina will have to tell you. Couldn't have been more than a couple of hundred, but judging by the receipts, it was probably a good deal less."

Her office was another matter. Someone had broken into the locked file cabinet where she kept her case files. The top drawer had been pried open, probably with a crowbar, and files had been rifled. Her files from this year. Her stomach sank with a horrible sense of violation.

"He was probably just looking for money," Ed said, trying to be soothing. "What interest could anyone possibly have in your files?"

Plenty, thought Sandy grimly. Plenty. There was probably enough blackmail material in those files to fuel a crime wave. But she was reluctant to say so to Ed, reluctant to discuss such possibilities with someone who enjoyed gossip as much as anyone else in the county.

"We'll have to dust the files for prints," Ed told her. "Sorry, Sandy. It's going to be a mess."

For an instant she wanted to stamp her foot and protest all of this like a two-year-old. Not only had she been robbed, not only had the secrets of her neighbors been pawed through, but now the guardians of law and order were proposing to mess things up even more. She couldn't have said at that moment whether she objected more to the idea of black fingerprint powder all over everything or to the idea of police officers going through her confidential files. They wouldn't read anything...would they?

"You can't dust the files," she said flatly. "Anything else, but *not* the files."

"Look, Sandy—"

"No, *you* look, Ed! I realize you want to catch this jerk, but I can't have you going through my files. Those things are protected by attorney-client privilege. I can't let anyone else look at them. I won't allow it."

"But—"

"Absolutely not! Half the people in this county are my clients! How would *you* feel if you found out some cop had been dusting *your* file for fingerprints and maybe reading parts of your will and discovering you'd— Oh, never mind! This stuff is confidential, and confidential it remains."

Uncertain how to handle it, Ed called Nate. Twenty minutes later, looking slightly rumpled and with a pillow crease still visible on his cheek, Nate showed up.

"She's right," he told Ed. "Attorney-client privilege is protected by law. What's more, I don't feel like dealing with an irate Henry Freitag or a furious Steve Stephanopoulos if you guys come within five feet of their files here. As far as the files go, only Sandy touches them." He turned to her, almost glaring. "And you go through them and see if anything is missing."

For the first time since she'd been awakened, she felt things were genuinely under control. A crooked smile tugged her lips as she nodded to Nate. "You got it."

Nate spent the next half hour checking things out, too, and finally concluded it was the Walker kid. "It has his M.O. all over it," he told Sandy and Ed. "Even got through the front door exactly the same way. Damn it, Williams gives the kid a suspended sentence, and the next day he's out doing it again!"

Sandy wasn't so sure about that, but remembering Les Walker's sullen expression, she didn't see how she could argue.

"Did that kid know you had a cash box?" Nate asked her.

She opened her mouth to say that all businesses kept a petty-cash box and everyone knew it, when she had a sudden memory of Les Walker delivering lunch from Maude's two days before he was arrested for the Mercantile break-in. And Nina taking the petty-cash box out of the bottom drawer of her desk.... "Yes, he knew."

"Well, that about settles it. Guess I need to have a long talk with that kid."

Sandy turned back to her files, still not convinced—until five minutes later when she discovered that one file was indeed missing: Les Walker's.

By the time she climbed her stairs, dawn was beginning to lighten the eastern sky. From outside she heard the slam of the sheriff's car doors as Nate and his deputies drove away. This night was a lost cause, she thought. There wasn't a chance she could go back to sleep now.

Finally, risking it, she called Garrett at the motel and asked him if he wanted to join her at Maude's for breakfast. If she didn't talk to somebody, she was going to burst a gasket, or so she felt. And there wasn't anybody else she wanted to roust out of bed to have breakfast with. Or anybody else she wanted to talk this over with. Nina or any of her other girlfriends would all probably be seriously alarmed and start demanding she move out of her apartment above the office to someplace safer. She wasn't quite sure what that safer place might be. Heck, there wasn't a safer place in the country than right here.

Although at the moment it sure didn't feel like it.

"Give me twenty minutes, Sandy" was Garrett's response to her invitation. He didn't sound sleepy at all.

She had taken only one step from the phone when it rang, a jarring sound in the early morning quiet.

"I saw the cops outside your place, lawyer," said a muffled male voice. "Getting scared? You ought to. Maybe if somebody raped you, you wouldn't be so quick to defend the guy who hurt that kid."

With a loud click, he disconnected.

Sandy stared blankly at the kitchen wall, at first too stunned to even react. Cold waves began to wash through her, and her knees threatened to buckle. Then an electric jolt of anger strengthened her, and she slammed the phone back into the cradle. How dare he? How dare *anyone?*

When she arrived, Garrett was already at Maude's, sitting in the booth by the front window, stirring a steaming mug of coffee. The way he looked at her as she slid into the seat facing him warned her that he didn't at all think this was a casual invitation.

''What happened?'' he asked as soon as Maude brought Sandy coffee and a menu.

''My office was broken into. Someone took whatever was left of the petty cash and broke into my filing cabinet. Les Walker's file is missing, and Nate thinks Walker did the break-in.''

''Why? Just because his file is missing?''

''No, he said the M.O. is exactly like Walker, too. The way the windowpane on the front door was broken out so he could reach inside and unlock it.''

''That's hardly a unique way of breaking in.'' Garrett shook his head slightly. ''I have all the respect in the world for Nate, and maybe y'all don't have a whole lot of burglars around here, but that's hardly enough to hang Walker on.'' He lifted his mug halfway to his mouth, then paused. ''Something else is bugging you. You don't think it was Walker, either.''

''No, I don't. There was no reason on earth for him to take his file. It's not like I had proof of his guilt or innocence stashed in there. But whoever it was took the money, too. And that *is* like Walker. Oh, I don't know.'' She shook her head impatiently. ''I probably shouldn't even worry about it. It probably *was* Walker, and he probably took his file to thumb his nose at me. He never liked me.''

''I gather the feeling was mutual.''

She smiled wanly. ''You could say that.''

They ordered breakfast, Garrett going for a double stack of Maude's sourdough pancakes, sausage and eggs, and Sandy preferring just an English muffin. Then Garrett leaned back and looked out the window, drumming his fingers absently on the tabletop. He wanted a cigarette, Sandy thought. She wondered how he found the willpower to keep telling himself no.

"The break-in isn't all of it, Sandy," he said, surprising her. "What aren't you telling me?"

"When did you start reading minds?"

He gave her a wry smile. "After I became a cop and realized that most people weren't telling me everything. Something in the way your eyes moved, I guess. So what else happened?"

"Just a nasty phone call."

"At the office?"

"No, in my apartment. Right after I called you." She shrugged, as if it were nothing, but she could tell he wasn't buying it.

"What did he say?"

"How do you know it was a he?"

"Because it almost always is. What did he say?"

"Nothing, really. It was—" She broke off and looked away, fixing her gaze on the snowbank between the sidewalk and the street. It would be the last part of winter to vanish from Conard City. But thinking about snow couldn't help her right now, as she realized that the call had affected her far more than she had guessed. It shouldn't have been hard to repeat what had been said, but she found it incredibly difficult.

"Sandy?"

"He asked if I was getting scared. Said I ought to be." She couldn't continue.

"And?"

"And what?"

Garrett sighed. "Damn it, Sandy, you don't expect me to believe that you're this upset about a phone call simply because someone said you ought to be getting scared."

"That's enough, isn't it?"

"No." He leaned forward, locking her gaze to his. "He threatened you in some way, didn't he?"

"Not exactly." She saw the impatience sweep over his face, and somehow it made her blurt out the last of it. "He said maybe if somebody raped me, I wouldn't be so quick to defend Nighthawk."

Garrett swore. "That was a threat, and you know it! Did he say anything else?"

"That was all. He hung up right away."

He reached across the table and covered her folded hands with one of his. "You feel like ice." He squeezed gently but didn't let go. "Why didn't you want to tell me that? Something all but locked the words in your throat."

It wasn't something she talked about. In fact, she didn't think she'd mentioned it to anyone since returning to Conard City.

But now, without warning, she heard herself say, "A long time ago, I *was* raped."

Chapter 9

Suddenly Garrett understood a lot of things about her that had vaguely puzzled him before. Her interest in him that was countered by her stiffening when he touched her. The fact that she had apparently avoided men for a long time.

"I'm sorry," he said quietly. "That must have been terrible for you."

"I think it was worse for my husband." She looked quickly away.

Uh-oh, he thought, tightening his grip on her hands to let her know he was still with her, even as the words dried up in his throat. Worse for her husband. That said a hell of a lot, none of which made him very happy.

"Why?" he asked after a few moments. "Why was it worse for him?" There were a lot of reasons why men withdrew from their wives after they were raped, everything from feeling the woman was somehow sullied or tainted by the rape to a fear that perhaps she had enjoyed it, even asked for it, to a simple concern that making love might reawaken the memory of the rape. Some men even became impotent.

And none of that was very good for the woman who had been victimized by someone else and now found herself a pariah in her own bed.

The restaurant was beginning to fill up with local business people who wanted breakfast, and when Sandy glanced around at the growing crowd, he knew she wasn't going to answer him. Nor could he blame her; anyone could eavesdrop.

"I suppose," he said, "that your office is a mess right now."

"Slightly. Fingerprint powder all over the place."

"I'll come back with you and help clean it up." When she smiled at him, he knew he'd gotten over the rough spot. Later, he promised himself. Later he was going to get her to tell him all about it.

The newspaper broke the story of the rape that morning. Lisa Dunbar's name wasn't mentioned, but Craig Nighthawk's was, and so was Sandy's. By noon the answering machine had recorded more than thirty calls from people who were angry at Sandy for being Nighthawk's attorney.

There were no calls after that, and Sandy felt it wasn't nearly as bad as it could have been...or as she had feared it might be. Of course, she didn't seem to have any clients left, but she figured that would change in a week or two when the furor died down a little. People would remember she was a neighbor, someone they had known all their lives. The reaction this morning was simply a way of expressing their revulsion at the crime.

"You're a lot calmer about it than most people would be," Garrett remarked.

"It'll get better." She had to believe that. What was the point of believing anything else? She had taken this case for valid reasons, and she wasn't going to allow herself to be intimidated into quitting. "Actually, this will give me more time to concentrate on the Nighthawk case, which will make me feel a whole lot better."

"An optimist, I see." He turned in a slow circle, looking around the office and reception area. They had cleaned up all the fingerprint powder and moved the files from the damaged cabinet into a new one. The place looked ready for business, but there was no business. The phone had stopped ringing, and the afternoon appointment book was empty.

"What say we get out of here for a while?" Garrett suggested. The last thing she needed, he felt, was to sit around here and brood about her evaporating practice and the nasty phone calls.

"Where to?" she asked. She was staring glumly at the telephone on her desk, as if waiting for it to ring with more bad news, and Garrett felt an uncomfortable tug in the vicinity of his breastbone. She would bounce back, he was sure, but he wanted to help her feel better faster.

"Well," he said slowly, "I can't ask you home to look at my etchings, because Texas is a little too far to go in a single afternoon."

"I could almost—" She broke off and looked up with a sudden smile as she realized what he'd just said.

He winked. "How's about we just get in the car and drive? The roads are pretty clear, and at the very least we can hit a restaurant in the next county for dinner. Just to add a little spice to life."

It actually added quite a bit of spice in her life, Sandy thought as they drove north toward the next county and what were supposed to be some of the best steaks in Wyoming. At least, that was what she'd heard, but she'd never wanted to make the trip by herself. Evidently someone had been telling Garrett about the place, too, because he was convinced it was worth driving more than a hundred and fifty miles.

"It's not so common these days," he told her, "but it wasn't so long ago folks in Austin didn't think anything of driving to Dallas for dinner...about three hours each way. I'd think folks in these parts are pretty much used to driving those kinds of distances, too."

"Most of us are, I guess. It's just not something I want to do alone."

"I can understand why," he said after the briefest hesitation. "It's a dangerous world for women. I talked to my sister last night."

The sudden change of topic came as a relief to Sandy, who'd been afraid he was going to question her about her rape. That would be her own fault, since she had brought it up herself, but it wasn't something she wanted to dig up. "How's she doing?"

"Pretty good. Kinda strikes me as ironic that just about the time she's getting herself back together and living a normal life, the parole board writes and tells her that her ex is getting out."

"Didn't she have a chance to protest?"

Garrett shook his head. "This is mandatory parole. No choice. So he'll be back on the street sometime next month. I've got to be back down there by then."

Disappointment filled Sandy as she faced how short a time Garrett had left here, but she forced it down. "Do you think he'd...come after her?"

Again he shook his head. "I wish I knew. There's just no way to predict something like that."

"Has he made any threats against her since he was sent up?"

"Not that I'm aware of. Oh, he said a few things to her right after the trial, but then he seemed to let it go. Impossible to tell if he was just blowing off steam or if he really meant any of it. Impossible to know if he still might feel that way."

"But some of them do."

"They sure do."

It was Sandy's turn to shake her head. "It's just terrible the way some men treat women. Just terrible."

"Terrible the way some women treat men, too," he said. "I've been called to more than one domestic disturbance where it was the woman beating up the guy."

She glanced at him with a wry smile. "Point taken. Terrible the way some people treat their spouses."

"Amen to that."

"How are you going to be able to watch over your sister, though? Does she live nearby?"

"I had her and the kids move in with me after she left Bobby. The house was sure big enough, and it was the best way to make her feel safe and help her get back on her feet. She's almost ready to graduate with a degree in math." He smiled to himself. "She was always a whiz with figures. Me, I can barely get my checkbook to balance."

"You and most of the rest of the world."

"Anyway, Ginny is supposed to graduate this December, and I want to see that she makes it. It'd be a damn shame if that idiot of an ex of hers got in the way."

"Does he know where to look for her?"

"I reckon. It sure wouldn't take him long to find out, anyway. It's not as if she tried to disappear. She still has friends near where she used to live, and I can be found in the phone book."

"Maybe you ought to move her somewhere else for a little while, to see if Bobby actually comes after her."

"I've been thinking about it," Garrett agreed. "But her friends know she's going to college, and there's no reason they'd keep that a secret."

"So he could track her to the campus."

"Yup." Garrett wanted to pound the steering wheel in frustration as he thought about all the possible complications arising from Bobby's release. If he sent Ginny up to live with his folks or their brother, she wouldn't be able to graduate in December. At this point in her education, she would lose a lot of ground if she transferred. "I'm going to have to think long and hard about this. There's got to be a way to keep her and the kids safe and not totally disrupt their lives."

"The kids? Would he hurt the *kids?*"

"He has before."

"My God." She knew about such things, of course. She didn't live in a make-believe world where everyone was nice and perfect, but child abuse struck her as the most heinous of crimes. "At least get the kids away from there for now, Garrett. You can protect your sister pretty well, I'm sure, but it'd be easier without children to worry about."

He could protect his sister pretty well? The thought almost made him laugh bitterly. Yeah, right. With his damaged arm that couldn't lift a gun. Maybe he'd better say to hell with Ginny's education for a little while, and get her and the kids safely moved to someplace where Bobby couldn't find them. At least until he could be sure that Bobby didn't want to get even.

They pulled into the restaurant parking lot around six-thirty. The place looked full already, as if folks had come from miles around. Which they probably had, thought Sandy. The place must do a good steak.

The decor was an attractive rustic Western, and the music was quiet country. The barn-size structure had been divided up into smaller rooms, creating a pleasant feeling of coziness. A waitress gave them a private corner booth.

"This is really nice," Sandy told Garrett. Not until that moment had she realized just how much she had needed to get away. The slow uncoiling of tension was making her feel as if she were melting, particularly her neck and shoulders. Her head nearly drooped with relaxation. A glass of burgundy helped.

Garrett spoke. "Have you heard anything from the reservation about Nighthawk's sister?"

Sandy shook her head. "Nina called the tribal police. They said they'd locate her, but it might take a few days to get around to it. I guess they're understaffed, and this hardly qualifies as an emergency. I just need to get that photo yanked from evidence before trial, but that's nearly two months from now."

"How can you do that? I mean, even if it is a photo of his niece, why shouldn't the prosecution be able to present it? They *did* find it in his house."

"Rules of evidence. Probative value is outweighed by its prejudicial effect. Basically, it doesn't prove anything one way or the other, but it will probably prejudice the jury. That's enough reason to keep it out. A lot of evidence gets evaluated that way. On the other hand, if it turns out not to be his niece, it'll probably be admitted, even though pedophilia is not an indicator for the kind of crime that was committed against Lisa Dunbar. Most pedophiles, in fact, don't commit violent rape.'' She shrugged. ''The court has to weigh that kind of thing all the time.''

Garrett nodded, but it was apparent to Sandy that he hadn't really been listening. Why should he? He probably knew all this already, anyway. His blue eyes had taken on a faraway look, and he'd begun to draw patterns on his folded napkin with the edge of his fork handle.

''The perp thinks he's smart,'' he said abruptly. ''And he isn't dumb. But he's not as smart as he thinks, either.''

''What do you mean?''

''He left a false trail that points the finger at Nighthawk, but he did it so obviously that if you stop to think about it for a minute, you realize it stinks to high heaven. I'll bet Nate has started to wonder, too. I mean, you'd have to have the brains of a gnat to leave a book bag out on the road and bury the victim's clothes in your backyard if you really committed the crime. Now, I'm not going to say I've never seen a criminal that dumb, because I have. But Nighthawk isn't that kind of stupid. No way. So our perp is smart, but not smart enough. He frames Nighthawk, but does it in such an obvious way that I'm sure as hell not buying it.''

Sandy nodded. Hadn't they discussed this same thing just yesterday? ''Right. I know.''

''Okay, so now we have an M.O. for the guy. When he does something, he points the finger elsewhere.''

''You can't extrapolate from just one—'' She broke off as understanding struck. She felt all the color drain from her face. ''You're saying he broke into my office last night and tried to make it look as if Les Walker did it?''

Garrett nodded slowly. ''I also figure he called you after the police left.''

''Then he was watching....'' She thought she was going to be sick. *Maybe if somebody raped you....* ''But why, Garrett? Why would he break in? Why would he want to scare me?''

"Maybe he just wanted to look at Nighthawk's file and see if you had any information that could get Nighthawk off so he could counteract it somehow.''

"But I had all the information upstairs!''

"He wouldn't know that before he looked.''

"But…'' She shook her head. "It doesn't make sense. Oh, wanting to look at Nighthawk's file, I guess I can see. But the call?''

"Simple. He's already pointing the finger away from himself. So if he breaks in again to get the file, you'll think it's a would-be rapist.''

"That's…'' She trailed off again, thinking about it. In a perverted sort of way, it made sense. "He can't possibly be hoping to scare me off the case, can he? What good would that do? Another attorney would just take it.''

"Another attorney who might not be quite as committed to getting Nighthawk off. Someone who doesn't believe Nighthawk is innocent. Someone who won't hire a private investigator to poke around looking for the real culprit.''

Suddenly she didn't feel quite so relaxed. "What do you think he might do?''

What he was thinking was not something he wanted to share with her right now. Or any time, for that matter. "I need to think some more about it,'' he said. "There's really not a whole lot to go on.'' What he was beginning to fear was what might happen if the perp began to feel that Sandy was a threat to him. It was essential that Sandy be aware there might be danger—otherwise she might not be careful—but he didn't want to scare her half to death without something more to go on than an uneasy suspicion.

The truth was, after last night, he'd begun to feel seriously concerned for her. The man who had hurt Lisa Dunbar would not be interested in Sandy Keller in the same way, because she wasn't a child. But he was perfectly capable of harming or even killing someone he perceived as a threat. Trouble was, they didn't have a whole hell of a lot to go on.

"When are you going to question Lisa's father?" he asked.

"I'm going out to the ranch to see him in the morning. It won't be a deposition—Sam has that scheduled for Monday morning—but I want to just get a feel for the situation."

Garrett nodded. "So you're thinking along those lines, too."

Sandy's mouth drew tight, and she looked down at the napkin she was absently creasing. "He's the most obvious suspect if Nighthawk didn't do it." Which was about as sorry a comment as you could make.

"Yeah." Garrett leaned back as the waitress slipped a platter of prime rib in front of him. "And what about questioning the little girl?"

"Probably Monday. Sam said the doctor figures she'll probably be up to it by then. Apparently she's had some complications with infection that set back her recovery."

"It's going to be years before she recovers, if ever."

Sandy glanced away and down, hoping he couldn't read the knowledge in her face. *If ever* was about where she fit. Some scars never completely faded.

"Want to tell me about it?"

Garrett's voice, almost gentle, came quietly to her ears. No pressure, no insistence, in his tone, just a simple question. Reluctantly she dragged her eyes up from the napkin and met his gaze. What she saw was not ordinary curiosity but a look of understanding, as if he already knew what she would say. She drew a shaky breath.

"It was a long time ago," she said finally. "A long time ago. It doesn't matter anymore."

"Sure it does," he said quietly. "It affected you, and you dealt with it. The ways you dealt with it made you the person you are now. So it matters, Sandy. Even if it doesn't hurt anymore, it matters."

Her fingers closed into the palm of her hand and formed a fist. How could you tell someone about something like this? Where could you even begin?

"Did you know the assailant?"

As if he understood her dilemma, he asked a question. It was a policeman's question, but it was a starting point, and the phrasing of it somehow allowed her to gain a measure of detachment.

"No, I didn't know him. I had no idea who he was."

"Did they ever catch him?"

She shook her head. "No."

"If it's any consolation, they probably caught him later on another incident. These guys rarely act only once."

"I was hoping maybe he'd been hit by a trailer truck before he could hurt anyone else. Or trampled to death by an angry mob."

The corners of his mouth lifted, and his eyes crinkled. "That's always a possibility."

"Not a likelihood, though. No, I figure he'd raped a number of women before me, and he probably raped a few after me, and chances are he never got caught at all. Not as long as he kept picking women who didn't know him."

"Did he hurt you badly?" He waved a hand almost before he finished speaking. "Bad way to put it. I know he hurt you badly. I meant—"

"Did he break any bones or sever any major arteries?" She smiled mirthlessly. "It's okay, Garrett. No, I didn't need to be hospitalized. A few cuts, scrapes and bruises were the only injuries. He took me at knife point, but he didn't cut me. Which kind of surprised me, actually, because all the time it was happening, I was absolutely convinced he was going to slash my throat as soon as he was done with me."

Garrett didn't say anything, which was just as well. If he'd made a sound it would have given her the excuse she needed not to continue. His expression grew grim, almost remote, but his gaze never wavered.

"Well, he didn't," she continued. "He called me some vile names, hit me a few times, then left me. Then I was raped again. Oh, not really," she amended hastily, "but back then cops were pretty hard on rape victims. I'm sure you know the attitude I'm talking about."

"Yeah. I've seen it, though not as often anymore. They treat you like *you're* the criminal, as if it was your fault it happened."

She nodded. "And as if it never would have happened if I were a decent woman. Gerry kind of felt that way, too."

"Gerry?"

"My ex-husband. Oh, he wasn't a total clod. He understood that I'd been hurt and all that, but he was of the opinion that it never would have happened if I'd stayed home in an apron instead of going out to work."

"Your fault for venturing into a man's world."

"That about sums it up." She didn't intend to continue, but somehow she did. Part of her was appalled that she was even saying these things, and part of her was relieved to have it out. To let Garrett know the truth about her. "I, um, had some sexual problems after that."

"Hardly surprising. It would have been surprising if you hadn't."

"Well, Gerry never thought I was much of a lover, anyway, but after the rape I kind of...froze." She couldn't look at him. "I'm, um, frigid."

"And I suppose your ex lost no opportunity to tell you that." He swore. "Well, darlin', don't worry about it. You may be scared, but you're not frigid."

"You can't possibly—"

He interrupted ruthlessly. "I've kissed you, remember? You're as responsive as any woman I've ever held and more responsive than most. You're scared, all right, but scared and frigid are worlds apart." He suddenly flashed a smile. "But relax. I won't demand that you prove it."

It was as if a great big balloon of tension suddenly popped and drained all the nervousness and worry from her. It was a relief to have it out in the open. Now she didn't have to worry about any misunderstandings. Now she didn't have to wonder if something would happen and she would wind up being ashamed and embarrassed.

And now that he had made it clear that he wouldn't put her in that position, all she wanted was for him to do precisely that. She wanted him to reach out and draw her into those strong arms of his. To press her head onto his solid shoulder while he held her and told her it would be okay.

Silly, she thought, even as the yearning turned into a deep ache. Silly. A pair of strong arms couldn't hold reality at bay, and a murmured reassurance couldn't make everything all right. She was not all right and never would be, and she had long since given up wishing for the kind of love and passion that fairy tales were made of. They just didn't exist.

Maybe he was right that she wasn't frigid but just afraid. Hadn't she even once read in a medical book that frigidity was most often simply a lack of knowledge on the part of the couple rather than a real inability to respond? Yes, she'd read all that, even tried to convince herself that her problems had arisen from fear and inexperience, not from a real physical problem of some kind.

She even believed it. But that didn't counter the very real fear she felt. Not just the fear that had resulted from the rape—she honestly believed that had long ago faded away—but the fear she felt that her next lovemaking experience would be exactly the horror it had been with Gerry. All the technical explanations for what had happened, all the understanding of the physical and emotional dynamics of those last few episodes couldn't soothe her fear that they would be repeated.

Nor could she tell Garrett what would need saying if a repetition were to be avoided. How could you tell a man you'd never been to bed with that your former lover had never troubled to arouse you sufficiently, that after you were raped, fear kept you from getting aroused at all, and that rather than be patient your husband had forced the issue, causing you severe pain?

She looked hastily down at her plate as she felt color stain her cheeks. How could you tell a man who had never been your lover that another man's voice spewing scorn and condemnation had drilled a hole in your brain, that you couldn't even think about making love without hearing all those horrible accusations and names?

How could you tell a man who had never been your lover that you wanted him to be as patient as a saint and make love to you despite all those hang-ups?

You couldn't, she admitted miserably. You couldn't say, "Garrett, give me all the time and patience I need, even if it takes all night, and help me to get over this." No, you could only hope that if you were foolish enough to make love with him that he wouldn't grow impatient and react in the same way your husband had. That you wouldn't hear those awful words spilling from the mouth of yet another man.

The rape hadn't scarred her nearly as much as her husband's reaction to it and its effects. How could she tell Garrett that?

So she remained silent on the subject and began to talk about other things.

Garrett let her. She would never guess how much he had seen flitting across her face, nor would he tell her. He had seen both her yearning and her fear, and felt he understood them. The question was whether he wanted to deal with them. It would be no simple task, he thought, to get around this woman's barriers. And there was no point in doing so unless he planned to stick around.

Which he absolutely did not intend to do.

The moonlight was bright, the sky so clear that the stars hardly twinkled. The roads were clear, but the grasslands and hills were still covered in snow, and the reflected moonglow turned the night coldly brilliant. Sandy had a quick, flashing memory of standing in the moonlight in her kitchen last night, trying to hear whoever was downstairs.

She shivered, wishing she didn't have to go home tonight. Wishing she wasn't going to spend the long dark hours sitting up wide-awake for fear the man who had made the phone call might come back. Wishing she could find an excuse to say, "Take me to Laramie, I want to spend the night there, where he can't find me." Wishing she didn't have to be alone.

"That was a great dinner," Garrett remarked. "Well worth the drive."

"It sure was." A three-hour trip home. It was likely to be after midnight by the time they pulled in. Could she invite him in for coffee without seeming to suggest something more? Hadn't he said he wouldn't demand that she prove she wasn't frigid? Surely that meant he had no desire to make love to her.

But if that was the case, why had he looked at her the way he had the other night? Why had he kissed her as if he didn't want to let go? She might be a mess sexually, but she had always been able to tell when a man was interested. But maybe her confession tonight had killed that. It would hardly be surprising.

Stifling a sigh, she kept her eyes fixed on the passing moon-drenched countryside. The mountains seemed to glow eerily in the cold blue light. And Thunder Mountain, the highest of them all, seemed actually to brood.

What would a mountain brood about? she wondered idly, remembering the fantasy stories she had once read with such appetite. Time would be on a completely different scale for a mountain. It couldn't possibly worry about such fleeting things as a kiss or a touch.

Or about having not been touched in so many years. It was something she never wanted to think about, because it did no good. All she could do was ache when she thought about how long it had been since someone last had held her, or hugged her with genuine affection. And when she *did* think about it, she wondered if the nerves of the skin of her back could actually hunger for the squeeze of an arm, the stroke of a loving hand. Because it sure felt like it some-times.

Like right now. It wasn't even lovemaking she wanted so

much as the loving touch of someone who cared. Someone who would hold her close and give her the blessing of human touch and caring. Such a little thing, something that most people took for granted. Something *she* had taken for granted until she had done without for so long.

If Garrett just wanted to put his arms around her and hold her for a few minutes, she would be grateful. She was that needy. She hated being so needy, hated the weakness that it signified, and yet she was honest enough to admit it was a natural need, one that every small child felt just as keenly. It wasn't a weakness, it was human.

She glanced over at Garrett. His face looked like a carved wooden mask in the pale glow of the dashboard light. What was he thinking? What did it matter? Even if he put his arms around her and held her, it would only be for just a few moments. He'd all but said in so many words that he wasn't interested in a long-term relationship, and a one-night stand would just about kill her.

Wishing for the moon, that was what she was doing. Just like a coyote on a long summer night, howling at the heavens. Or, as her grandmother had once told her, "If you're going to wish, you might as well wish for something impossible." Yup. That was exactly what she was doing, and that was why it would never come true.

Good grief, at her age she ought to know better. Prince Charming existed only in fairy tales. The reality of life could never measure up to a wish. Never.

But that couldn't keep her from yearning.

They arrived back in Conard City shortly after midnight. By that time Sandy was wishing she'd eaten more of her dinner than a nervous stomach had allowed. Well, she could rustle up something once she said good-night to Garrett.

He followed her up the stairs to the landing and waited while she unlocked her door. "I'll see you in the morning," he said. "I want to do some poking around, and I'll stop in before I head out."

"Okay." She tried to smile brightly, when in actuality she felt as if someone had just dropped a stone in her stomach. He had plans for tomorrow, and they didn't include her, apparently. Well, of course they didn't. But it disappointed her, anyway.

"Good night, then," he said, then turned and started down the stairs.

As if paralyzed, she stood where she was and watched him descend. She didn't want him to go, but the words that would have stopped him stuck in her throat.

Halfway down, he stopped. After a moment's hesitation he turned and started climbing back up to her.

"Garrett?" His name escaped her as little more than a husky whisper.

He didn't say a word, just climbed.

Instinctively, she inched backward, but something kept her from flying. Maybe it was the look of stony determination on his face or the brilliance of his blue eyes, but somehow she just couldn't run.

When he stood one step below her, he stopped. "Good night," he said, and before she could react, or even draw another breath, he hauled her into his arms and covered her mouth with his.

In that incredible instant, everything inside her turned warm and soft. Melting. She was melting like chocolate left in the warm sun, and at any moment she was sure she was going to puddle at his feet and slip slowly down the stairs.

His tongue found hers, and there was nothing playful in its touch. He meant business, and he wanted her to know it.

She was at once terrified and exhilarated. Oh, God, she thought wildly, this man wanted her! How was she going to deal with that? How could she possibly cope?

Terror started to well inside her, threatening to swamp her. But just then he lifted his head, freeing her mouth.

Then his stomach growled, loudly and emphatically. Garrett swore.

And Sandy laughed as all the tension drained from her. It was impossible to be afraid of a man whose stomach was growling, and it was exactly the unromantic, humorous touch she needed to set her free.

"I think you ought to come in for a snack," she said, and giggled.

A slow, rueful smile dawned on his rugged face. "You'd never guess I finished a big meal less than four hours ago. I'm starving."

"Well, come on in. I bet I can make us some nachos."

He closed the door behind them, taking care to throw the dead bolt, and followed her into the tiny kitchen. "There's no way on earth a Wyoming lawyer can make a decent nacho."

"You wanna bet, Ranger?"

"It wouldn't be fair to pluck your feathers, little pigeon. Lord, you can't possibly find a decent jalapeño up here, never mind a decent corn chip. It wouldn't be gentlemanly to take your money."

In the end, however, he allowed as how he might have been the pigeon. They sat together at her table, laughing and talking as they hadn't been able to do all evening. Sandy wasn't sure exactly what had happened, but something had, removing the last barrier between them and leaving them as comfortable together as old, old friends.

Which was probably why she didn't try to avoid it when

he turned from stacking the dishes on the counter and drew her into his arms. It probably explained how it was that she sank against him as he leaned back against the counter and quite naturally tipped back her head so that they could kiss.

This time it felt right to be in his arms, as if she were coming back to a familiar and cherished place. Amazing, she thought vaguely, how quickly one could become accustomed to something new.

But she wasn't interested in analyzing her reactions. All she wanted to do was revel in the experience. For the first time in years, she felt comfortable in the arms of a man. Felt safe and secure, rather than threatened and afraid. He made her feel that all she had to do was let him take care of her.

It was easy, so very easy, when he spread his legs to allow herself to be drawn between them until she was resting intimately against him. A shiver of fear passed through her and then was gone, soothed away by the gentle touch of his hands on her back.

"Ah, Sandy," he whispered as he lifted his mouth from hers and began to sprinkle soft, wet kisses all over her face. Those gentle little brushes of lips and tongue somehow relaxed her even more. It was as if some deep part of her, some place beneath conscious thought, judged that no one could touch with such tenderness if they meant any harm.

She softened even more, and Garrett drew her closer, allowing his hands to cross her back so his arms could hold her snugly. She felt so good against him. God, he wondered, had a woman ever felt so good in his arms as this one did?

He was sure, absolutely sure, that never in his life had he wanted to hold someone as much as he wanted to hold Sandy. Never had an embrace felt so satisfying to his soul as this one did.

And that should have scared him to death, because there was no hope for a long-term relationship with her. Their work and lives might as well have been at opposite sides of the country, and neither of them was likely to give up their way of life. He could only get hurt.

If she had wanted a man in her life, she probably could have had any of dozens. And even if she should suddenly change her mind, she wouldn't be able to take life with a Texas Ranger. A couple of women had already proved that beyond a shadow of a doubt.

If he would ever be a ranger again. That scared him as much as anything, that he might not heal fully enough to return to his job. And then what would he have to offer any woman? A disability check?

God!

Just then, just as he was summoning words to frame a good-night that wouldn't leave her feeling raw and used, she made a little whimper. Just the softest of sounds as she nestled even closer, reminding him of something warm settling into its safe burrow.

It was enough to deprive him of his common sense. The warning voice faded away in an upsurge of need, as if this woman had somehow unlocked everything he had kept buried for so long.

He wanted her. He would deal with the pain later. Right now he needed the warmth of her love and laughter the way a parched plant needed water. He could no more deny his need for her than he could have stopped breathing.

He widened his stance even more, half expecting a protest, but she merely snuggled even closer, like a contented kitten. Her lips were close and inviting, and he couldn't resist them. Kiss followed kiss as she grew softer and more pliant, leaning more and more into him until he couldn't stifle a groan.

The groan seemed to startle her, yanking her back from the haze of desire that had been enveloping them. The instant he felt her stiffen, he slackened his hold. It wasn't easy to let go when every cell in his body was screaming for him to hang on, but he managed to do it. The last thing on earth he wanted to do was frighten this woman.

A shaky sigh escaped her, and she started to back away. Nobility demanded that he let her go without a protest, but he didn't quite make it.

"Sandy?"

"I'm...sorry, Garrett. Sorry."

"There's nothing to be sorry for, darlin'. Nothing. Did I scare you?"

She shook her head swiftly, backing away another few inches. "I'm sorry. It's just that...just that... Oh, I don't want to disappoint you!"

He liked her forthrightness. Liked the lack of coquetry in her answer. She wasn't trying to pretend that the past few minutes hadn't been exactly what they were. She wasn't hiding from the fact that he wanted to make love to her, and that she probably wanted very much the same thing. She was simply telling the truth, difficult as it was.

"You won't disappoint me, Sandy."

"Yes, I will!"

"No. You won't. You can't disappoint me, because I have no expectations of you. None whatsoever."

Chapter 10

For an instant her heart stopped beating as she wondered if she had completely misunderstood the direction their embrace had been taking. Had she made a fool of herself, leaping to a wrong conclusion? She would die of embarrassment.

But no, she hadn't been mistaken. Relief hit her in a soft wave as Garrett reached out and cupped her cheek in his hand.

"I won't be disappointed if you send me on my way," he said gently, "because I don't have a right to expect anything else from you. I won't be disappointed if you ask me to stay, because that would be more than I ever dared hope for. I won't be disappointed, because all I want is to be allowed to make love to you."

"But I'm... I can't... Garrett, I told you!"

"And I told you that I don't expect anything at all from you. I meant that. I don't expect you to perform. I don't expect you to react in any particular way. If I touch you and you freeze into a block of ice, it won't be a disappointment, Sandy. Not for me. I understand."

She shivered visibly, a great ripping wave of movement that passed through her from head to toe. Her worried eyes lifted to his, looking at once shy and scared. And there he saw her yearning as plainly as if she'd spoken it.

Moving carefully, he reached for her again and drew her close. "Just let me," he said, as he tucked her head onto his shoulder. "You don't have to say a word. Just let me. I won't promise to make this wonderful for you, because I'm not sure I can. All I can promise—the *only* thing—is that I won't be disappointed."

She didn't pull away, but she didn't say no, either. The slightest movement of her head against his shoulder seemed to be a nod, and he took it as consent. He would dearly have loved to sweep her off her feet, but he couldn't trust his arm that far yet, and he would hate like hell to have a tremor overtake him and be forced to lower her. Instead, he took her hand and guided her toward her bedroom.

She followed his urging without any hesitation.

This would be no passionate tumble on the living-room couch or the thick pile of her pale gray carpeting. No, that kind of lovemaking, romantic though it could be, was too subject to inadvertent distraction, anything from bumping into something to falling off the couch. He couldn't risk that with Sandy. He wanted nothing to jar her from the soft, willing mood that had overtaken her, and the best way to keep that soft cocoon wrapped around her was in a soft bed beneath warm blankets.

He left the hall light on and the bedroom door open a few inches, giving them just barely enough light to see by. He didn't want her to feel shy or embarrassed about her body, but he wanted to be able to see her.

Standing beside the bed, he kissed her eyes closed and then began to undress her. She had donned a simple dress for dinner, a subdued navy blue jersey. One button fastened at her neck, and the zipper slipped easily down her back. She gave a soft gasp as he pulled it down to her hips, and he bent his head, kissing her deeply but gently, soothing her before he pulled the dress away.

His hands were shaking a little, but not from his injury. No, he was trembling with nerves and eagerness as he hadn't since he was a boy. He wanted this woman more than he had ever wanted any woman, including the two whom he had almost married. He couldn't put his finger on why, and he really didn't care. All he knew was that he thirsted for her and felt as if something in him would be wounded irretrievably if he couldn't get closer...and closer....

The jersey slipped to the floor with a soft whisper, leaving her in a navy blue slip. He let his hands wander over the smooth, creamy skin of her shoulders, along the fragile line of her lovely neck, and then lower to her breasts.

Gently he traced light circles around her breasts, taking his time, giving her a chance to get used to the familiarity. When her hands lifted and gripped his waist, he knew a moment's triumph. Frigid? No way! But he had to be careful and cautious, taking into account her bad experiences. Since most of her bad memories probably involved lying beneath a man, Garrett kept them both standing beside the bed. He wanted everything about tonight to be new for her.

Stepping back just a little, he ripped open the snaps of his shirt and tossed it aside. Her eyes fluttered open, and a slow, absolutely feline smile tugged at her mouth. He nearly grinned back with relief. She liked what she saw.

Not one to waste an advantage, he stepped closer and wrapped her in the warmth of his arms. Kiss followed kiss as he gave her time to grow used to being so close to him, time to grow familiar with the bare skin and soft hair of his chest. At first she felt stiff against him, but slowly she began to relax and rub her cheek against him, as if savoring his textures.

It was unconsciously sexual, and it nearly drove him out of his mind. He had to grit his teeth and draw a couple of deep breaths while he forced his raging hunger to subside. She had no idea, he thought. No idea just how sexy and responsive she really was. And he didn't know how to tell her without sounding as if he were making it up and just telling her what he thought she wanted to hear. She would never believe it. Not yet, anyway.

But those concerns began to drift away on a rising tide of sensations. Satiny tricot, soft warm skin, the faintest little murmurs as her pleasure began to grow and her fear to subside. Encouraged, he began to lift her slip, delighting in the way it slid over her skin with a quiet swishing sound. Everything else slipped away with it, leaving him conscious of nothing but his desire to love this woman and his concern for her fears.

When the slip fell away, her eyes fluttered open. He saw the flash of concern in them, but before it could take root, he wrapped her once again in his arms and drowned her in a rain of tender kisses. And once again she softened into him with a little sigh that told him that she wanted to be here with him, flickers of fear notwithstanding.

That touched him deep in places that had been cold and empty for so very long. He had refused to think about Sandy in more than superficial ways. They had both been looking the other way, pretending nothing was happening, that they were in control of their feelings…and now this. It was as if old barriers inside him were crumbling like a weak seawall before a storm tide. This was going to hurt. It was going to hurt like hell.

But he was damned if he could save himself.

Gentle touches drew her on, carrying her past instinctive fears and hesitations into the hazy land of love—a place she was beginning to realize she had never visited before. No one had ever touched her this way, as if the touching were a joy, as if giving were as important as receiving.

As if pleasuring her were important.

A soft shudder ran through her as she began to understand that she was being loved—not taken, but loved. Loved in a way she had always believed was the fantasy of novelists. This man actually cared about what she was feeling.

Slowly, slowly, she tilted her head back and looked up at him from passion-sleepy eyes. "Please..."

It was a breathless whisper, barely audible, but a gentle smile tugged up the corners of his mouth. "Yes, darlin'," he murmured huskily. "Yes, darlin'..."

Her bra slipped away, but all she felt was relief that another impediment was gone. When he bent and tugged her panty hose and panties down, she let her head fall back and gave herself up to feeling. It might come to nothing, but she didn't care. At the very least she needed this feeling of being loved and cared for, something she had always lacked. Passion was the least of it. Had he simply wanted to hug her and stroke her like a kitten, she would have been content. He was loving her in the way that mattered.

She felt cool, crisp sheets beneath her back, and briefly she felt the upsurge of fear, but then Garrett was beside her, warm and naked and oh, so very real.

But instead of feeling threatened by that, she felt protected. Probably because of the gentle way he drew her close and because of the touches that never stopped, touches that soothed and...

And excited. Oh, heavens, she felt the early blossoming

of excitement at her center, and she hoped against hope that it wouldn't desert her, leaving her cold and frustrated and alone. But the slow, undemanding touches that flitted over her kept the glow alive and fanned the embers.

"You feel so good," Garrett whispered as he nibbled on her earlobe. "So good..."

The husky whisper in her ear sent runnels of excitement trickling along her nerve endings and awakening her in ways she had never imagined. How was it that she had never known it could feel so good to be touched? How had she missed this all her life?

But she could ask those questions tomorrow; right now all she wanted to do was gobble up the experiences Garrett was sharing with her.

And it *was* the most incredible sense of sharing. What before had always left her feeling lonely now made her feel a closeness she had despaired of ever knowing. Turning onto her side, she snuggled into his arms and kissed him, wanting to give him as much as he was giving her.

All fears of her own unresponsiveness fled before the caress of his hands on her flesh. Each touch set off little explosions that raced along her nerves to add to the pooling heat at her core. Gently, almost unconsciously, she began to rock her hips in response. Never in her life had she grown this aroused, and it was only just beginning.

For an instant she trembled on the edge of fear again, afraid that this would all vanish in a puff if some caress should jar her. But she pushed the fear aside, needing this experience enough to take the risk.

Garrett. For days now she had been responding to him in ways that had scared her, ways she had tried hard to ignore. Now he was touching her, his hand cradling her soft breast and pinching her aroused nipple in the most delicious way.

If dreams could come true, then that was what was happening at this very instant.

Garrett's lips followed his hands, and she knew she had never felt anything as exquisite as his mouth on her breast, sucking gently, and later his teeth nipping softly.

Then his hand slipped between her legs. She arched in sheer delight, and a low moan escaped her, followed by a soft whimper that was almost a plea.

He chuckled gently and kissed her soundly on the mouth, while his fingers continued to dance maddeningly in her soft curls. Each touch was electric, filling her with fresh waves of excitement.

She ought to be doing something, ought to be reciprocating, but when she reached out blindly with her hands, he hushed her and whispered that she was just to relax and enjoy.

Higher and higher his fingers teased her, until she was seeing flares of colored light behind her eyelids and arching helplessly, her entire body reaching for more and yet more. What was happening to her was no longer a matter of conscious will but a helpless response that could not be denied. She was caught on the arc of a welder's torch, burning... burning...burning....

"Let me," Garrett whispered. "Let me...." Gently he urged her legs apart and then completely deprived her of breath by slipping his finger into her.

She was his. As easily and simply as that, her last inhibition and uncertainty slipped away. It hardly mattered whether she climaxed or continued to feel aroused. What she needed and what he was giving her was this shattering, compelling intimacy. It nurtured some hungry place in her soul, and her heart cried out for more. *Come closer, Garrett. Closer.*

When he moved between her legs and entered her, there was no flashback to the rape, no memory of her misguided, unintentionally abusive husband. There was only now and the bell-like clarity of feelings never before experienced. There was only Garrett and the closeness of two human beings who cherished one another.

Because that was how he made her feel. And if she never again knew a moment like this, she was never going to forget what it felt like to be truly cherished.

"Fly with me, darlin'," he urged huskily. "Fly with me."

Amazingly, fantastically, she did just that.

He didn't say it. Sandy would have forgiven Garrett if he'd remarked that she wasn't frigid after all. If he had shown any justifiable signs of pride over what had just happened. But he didn't. Not even by the merest hint did he beat his breast in triumph.

Instead, all he did was cuddle her close and murmur, "Darlin', you're incredible."

The incredible thing was that she *felt* incredible. Absolutely, amazingly incredible. Fairy tales, fantasies and dreams *did* come true. She could have laughed with sheer joy.

The window at the head of the bed rattled as the wind kicked up. Unmistakably came the clatter of large rain drops against the glass. It sounded cold and miserable out there, and the sounds made it easier for her to slip her arms around Garrett's strong neck and murmur, "Please stay."

A rumble of laughter rose from deep in his chest and spilled into the darkened room. "You'd have to kick me out, Sandy. This bed is warm, you're warmer, and I'm not moving until I've made love to you again."

She liked the sound of that. She *loved* the sound of that.

494 *A Question of Justice*

Some corner of her mind kept trying to nudge her back to reality, to remind her that Garrett would be leaving in a few short weeks, that she was going to get hurt because of her incautious behavior tonight and that she would be a fool to give this man any part of her heart. But she didn't want to think about that right now. Tomorrow would be soon enough to deal with reality. Tonight she wanted to enjoy the fantasy of her Texas lawman lover as if it would be forever.

"I'm thirsty," Garrett murmured. "Can I bring you anything?"

"Just some water, please."

She envied him his lack of selfconsciousness as he slipped from beneath the sheet and padded out of the room. He left the door open a little wider, so that the hall light spilled across the bed. She was glad of the blankets that covered her to her chin, because she'd never been entirely comfortable with her body and was less so now that life had taken a bit of a toll—stretch marks, long since faded, from giving birth to her son, a waist that wasn't quite as youthfully thin as it once had been.

But even as she wished for a perfect body, she knew she was being silly. Garrett hadn't wanted a perfect body or he wouldn't have made love to her tonight. No, he'd wanted something else, and considering that there were far more likely prospects for a brief affair around here, she began to wonder what exactly he had seen in her.

There were no answers in the quiet night. No explanations for what seemed inexplicable. She had seen the desire in his eyes and had felt it in his body, and she could only believe that for some totally incomprehensible reason, he found her desirable. And that notion tickled her no end.

Garrett returned, closing the door enough so that only a

small crack of light streamed into the room. As if he understood her uncertainty, she thought. Perhaps he did.

He handed her a glass of icy water. "I love how cold the water is here," he remarked as he sat on the bed beside her. "In Texas, it's usually about room temperature from the tap, but here it's practically refrigerated."

"I hadn't even thought about that."

"I also like that it isn't as heavily chlorinated. The stuff I get at my house, you can smell the chlorine when you turn on the tap."

"You trying to talk me out of visiting?" As soon as the words passed her lips, she regretted them. He would probably think she was trying to angle for an invitation, and she didn't want to make him feel that he was being put on the spot. Embarrassed, she tried to think of a way to salvage the moment.

But what he did was bend over her and brush a sweet kiss on her damp lips. "Anytime you want to visit, you just give me a shout. I'd love it. I'll even buy bottled water."

She couldn't help it; she giggled, as much from relief as from humor.

"Utopia spring water," he promised. "Real Texas water before the treatment plant got to it."

When she finished her water, they settled back against the pillows, Sandy's head cradled on Garrett's shoulder. Once, long ago, she had discovered how delightful this intimacy was, this lying together of a man and woman after lovemaking, with no more hesitations and games between them. That had been when she was first married, and she had long since forgotten how delightful it was.

But she was rediscovering it now. There was nothing to quite compare to the sense of freedom that followed lovemaking. No longer did anyone have to conceal their desires or pretend they weren't interested. No more hiding behind propriety. She was free to reach out and touch Garrett if she wanted to and not be concerned about being misunderstood. More importantly, she was no longer afraid.

"I can't believe," she murmured. "I can't believe how... what... Oh, Garrett, I've never felt what you made me feel!"

He turned on his side and hugged her close, squeezing her as if he wanted to draw her inside himself. "That was never your fault, Sandy. Never. You're the most wonderfully responsive woman I've ever made love to. I could throttle the man who made you feel otherwise."

"He didn't..." She shook her head, not certain how to explain. "I don't think it was purposeful, Garrett. Really. He wasn't a cruel man. Just... Well, I guess maybe we were both inexperienced."

He shook his head a little and let it go, but what he thought was that it didn't take experience as much as it took caring. All you had to do was pay attention to your partner's responses and care enough to follow all those subtle little hints of sounds, sighs and movements. No genius needed. And before this night was out, he was going to prove it once again.

Just then the phone rang. Sandy looked at him, startled, and hesitated. He would have reached for it, but she wasn't sure she wanted anyone to know there was a man in her apartment this late at night. This was a very small town, after all.

She reached past him and lifted the receiver from the cradle, putting it to her ear. "Hello?"

Even in the dark, he could see the tension come into her face. Moments later she leaned over him and slammed the phone back into the cradle.

"What was that?" he asked.

"Some idiot who wanted to warn me not to get Nighthawk off."

"Was that all he said?"

"Yes." She shook her head. "It wasn't the guy from last night, if that's what you're worried about. No, this was someone else who apparently had a couple of beers too many, from the sound of it. I'm not going to worry about it."

"It'll probably get worse as matters progress and the case gets a higher profile."

"Probably," she agreed, and sighed. "Heck, I wouldn't be astonished to see a TV news crew out here from one of the bigger cities. Cases like this always make headlines."

"They draw a lot of flak, too." He hesitated a moment before saying, "I've seen some pretty serious threats leveled at attorneys during high-profile cases. Usually no one acts on them, but it's not a risk you should take, Sandy."

"What am I supposed to do? Hire a bodyguard?" She was suddenly furious. The ugliness of narrow minds had filtered into the sanctuary of her bedroom and was destroying the most beautiful night of her life.

Throwing back the covers, she scrambled out of bed and grabbed her robe from a nearby chair. The mood was completely shattered, and there was no way she could lounge around in bed. She needed to move, to do something. It didn't much matter what, but she was too upset to hold still.

For the first time in her life, she wished she smoked. Lighting a cigarette and puffing rapidly on it would have provided an outlet. Instead she went to the kitchen, flipped on the light and began to clatter around making hot chocolate. Not that she really wanted it; it was just something to occupy her hands and expend nervous energy on.

What she really wanted was to throttle someone. Maybe several someones. The problem was, she simply didn't know which someones. And the truth was, she might as well admit, that even if she *had* known who to throttle, she was too law-abiding to do more than wish.

She slammed the microwave door on two cups of milk and turned it on. Just then, gentle arms slipped around her from behind and drew her securely backward against a hard chest and into a warm embrace.

"It's okay, darlin'," Garrett said quietly. "Blow off the steam, but don't be afraid. You're not going to be alone."

"I'm not afraid!" Frustration filled her, along with anger, but not fear. And now, with Garrett's arms around her, she felt a positively debilitating desire to just curl into his strength and pretend that everything would go away. The urge, fleeting as it was, infuriated her even more. She had learned a long time ago to stand on her own two feet and not depend on anyone else. It was easy and kind for Garrett to reassure her, but when push came to shove, she would be on her own. Not because Garrett would fail her, but just because that was the way life was. You had to stand up and face things on your own.

The microwave beeped, and she pulled out the mugs. "Cocoa?" she asked Garrett.

"Thanks." He let her go as soon as she started to move away, and she felt relieved when he sat at the table. His eyes never left her, but at least he wasn't within touching distance any longer. Somehow the urge to touch him seemed to weaken her resolve...and everything else.

She spooned cocoa into the mugs and stirred vigorously, hardly conscious of the almost emphatic way she moved the spoon, clacking it against the side of the mug. Garrett was aware, though, and the faintest of smiles lifted the corners of his mouth as he watched her.

"I don't know why," she said, "people are always so sure that the person who is arrested is the guilty one. For heaven's sake, Garrett, the most recent statistics I've seen indicated that fully thirty percent of the time the DNA samples found at the crime scene *don't* match the DNA of the accused. Which means that thirty percent of the time the wrong person is arrested—and that's just in cases when DNA samples are found. I shudder to think that percentage may apply across the board and include people who are arrested when no genetic evidence is available."

"I didn't realize it was that high."

"Well, it is! And it's estimated that ten percent of the people who are convicted are actually innocent, which is equally appalling. Despite that, people are absolutely convinced that the criminal justice system is a circus where the guilty walk free because of some legal technicality. In short, everyone is guilty until proven innocent, and even then he was probably guilty, anyway, but some fast-talking lawyer just got him off."

"I've heard that more than once."

"I just wonder how those same people would feel if they were being tried for something they didn't do and they couldn't even have an attorney to defend them because everyone knew they wouldn't have been arrested if they weren't guilty!"

"High-profile cases sometimes create a different impression."

"I know that. And I can think of a number of them offhand where justice *did* miscarry. I agree it's appalling, but the bottom line is, not everyone who is arrested is guilty. And not everyone who is tried is guilty, and sometimes the jury is right to acquit despite the weight of public opinion. But whether the accused is guilty or not, he deserves legal representation, unless we want trial by kangaroo court!''

She placed the mugs of hot chocolate on the table but ignored hers, preferring to pace agitatedly. ''This perception of a revolving-door justice system really infuriates me. Good grief, we keep a higher percentage of our population imprisoned than any Western country except South Africa. That says more about our society than about our justice system. Yes, there are mistakes, but they're far outnumbered by the thousands of convicts who presently fill our prison system to bursting.''

She shook her head and wrapped her arms around herself as she came to a halt at the kitchen window, staring at her reflection in the dark glass. ''I'm sorry. I just get so angry about this kind of thing. That guy who called tonight evidently doesn't have any faith in his neighbors who'll be on the jury in the Nighthawk trial. He evidently thinks I'll somehow be able to blind them to the truth. I'm afraid I just don't think juries are that stupid. Most of the time they do a pretty damn good job of sifting through the evidence and reaching a reasoned conclusion. And it's the juries who decide, Garrett. Not the prosecutor or the defense attorney or the judge. A jury. Ordinary people, like the guy who called tonight.''

She shook her head. ''It's not my job to pull fancy tricks. It's not my job to distort anything. My job is to make sure that the jury reaches its conclusion on the basis of legally obtained evidence, not on the basis of gut emotions and misinformation. Yes, I'll defend Craig Nighthawk. But what a sorry state of affairs it would be if he could be tried without a chance to present his side of things. What a sorry state of affairs it would be if an arrest warrant were a conviction."

"Unfortunately, you're going to pay the price for those attitudes, Sandy."

She nodded. "I know. That's become obvious. Well, I can stick it out. I have enough savings to get me through the next few months, and I imagine folks will come around once this settles down."

"It would still be best for you and Nighthawk if we could find the real culprit."

"Goes without saying." She turned and leaned back against the counter, giving him a wan smile. "But there's hardly anything to go on, Garrett. Hardly anything at all."

"That's why I'm impatient for you to question the little girl. She might give us some little tidbit that could be really useful."

"Monday morning." She shook her head again. "I'm sorry, Garrett. That call got me really wound up."

"Perfectly understandable. Sandy, I've been guilty at times of the same attitude, complaining that some slick lawyer pulled fancy stuff and got some scum off. But the truth of the matter is, more often than not when that happens, it's because the cop did something wrong and collected evidence illegally. Or there just plain wasn't enough evidence to convince a jury. And for all my bellyaching about it, I wouldn't want to see people going to jail on the basis of illegal or inadequate evidence."

"Apparently the rest of the world doesn't agree with you."

He smiled then. "Come on, that's exaggeration, and you know it. A few meatheads don't agree; that's all. And a case like this gets people really upset. Hang in there, Counselor. It'll get worse yet."

"Probably."

At last she came to sit at the table and tasted her cocoa. It was just about drinking temperature now, but she no longer wanted it...if she ever had. Holding the mug just gave her something to do with her hands. What she really wanted to do was reach out to Garrett, but she didn't feel free to do that.

The fact that they had made love really didn't mean anything, she told herself. Her insides might be quaking and her entire perspective might be altered, but Garrett could very well regard this as just another pleasant episode in his life. What did she know about his personal life, after all? He might be used to having a different woman every night of the week. Wasn't he a confirmed bachelor?

All of the questions she had refused to consider because she had been so blinded by her own fear of making love now reared their heads. Questions she should have asked beforehand looked stark and scary in the aftermath.

Aftermath. Not afterglow. The afterglow had vanished with the intrusion of the caller and his threats. She was beginning to feel very mistaken in her assessment of her neighbors, and that left her wondering about her assessment of Garrett. She'd been wrong about people before. Tragically wrong.

"What's that sigh for, darlin'?"

She looked at him, wishing she could explain, terrified that he might guess her doubts, feeling the horrifying prickle of tears behind her eyelids. Oh, God, she didn't want to turn into an emotional wreck in front of this man.

"It's okay." In an instant he was around the table, reaching for her, drawing her to her feet and into a tight embrace. "Sandy, it's okay. If you want to cry, go ahead."

"I'm not like that," she argued, even as she struggled to steady her quivering jaw.

"Not like what?" His hand found its way into her hair and stroked gently. "Not human? Is that what you mean? Look, it's three o'clock in the morning, you just got a nasty drunken phone call and…well, earlier, with me, you lowered a lot of emotional barriers. I'm not surprised all your feelings are right near the surface. It would be strange if they weren't. It doesn't mean you're weak if you cry. It just means this has been an emotionally draining night."

But she stubbornly blinked back the tears, anyway. "I'll be okay."

"Of course you will. You're okay right now."

Gently but inexorably, he led her back toward the bedroom. Soon he had them both tucked in beneath the warm blankets while wind rattled the windowpanes. It sounded so cold out there, she thought. But it was so warm in here.

It felt good to snuggle against Garrett, to feel held and protected and safe. It wouldn't last, but for right now she didn't care. It had been a long, long time since she had felt so cared for…if she ever had.

"Don't worry about a thing," Garrett whispered soothingly. Softly his hands moved over her, slowly stoking fires that seemed not to have died but rather to have become embers awaiting a breath to bring them to fiery life.

And as his hands brushed flame over her sensitive hills and hollows, one realization struck her above all others: he wanted to make love to her again. He actually *wanted* her again! The understanding rose in her like a tiny bubble of joy, making her feel light and airy and wonderful.

And it gave her courage. Reaching out with her own hands, she began to shyly explore him. At first her touches were tentative, but his husky whispers of approval encouraged her to greater boldness. How smooth and warm he felt! Contrasting textures of skin and hair pleased her palms in ways no words could describe.

His body was hard and lean, and the simple act of touching him awakened deep yearnings in her. She had nearly forgotten the textures of masculinity, had nearly forgotten how exciting a man's hardness could be in contrast to her own softness. She had forgotten, indeed, that she could want anyone or anything as much as she wanted Garrett.

"You're so sweet," he whispered in her ear. "God, Sandy, your touches are driving me wild...."

Her confidence was growing by leaps and bounds. Each touch she dared to give him met with such patent approval and such obvious pleasure that her hands began to roam in ways that just a short while ago would have seemed impossible. Hard...smooth...furry...crisp curls...a banquet of sensations.

He turned suddenly, carrying her with him, and she found herself straddling his hips in the most intimate of ways. In the faint golden light that poured through the door from the hall, she saw the smile that curved his lips.

"Here, darlin'," he said quietly, and let his fingertips brush her hardening nipples.

Instinctively she moved, and when she moved her breasts brushed against his fingers. Electric sparks shot wildly through her, causing her to move yet again and brush against him yet again in the most incredibly erotic and teasing dance.

"That's the way, honey," he whispered. "That's the way."

She forgot all her inhibitions and rocked gently back and forth, feeling his arousal pressed firmly to her, feeling the brush of his hands against her breasts, and feeling incredibly feminine, incredibly sexy. All her self-doubts slipped away on the liquid heat of desire that filled her. She was his, and somehow he made her feel as if she were the only woman in the world he wanted to be with.

"Faster…"

He must have whispered the word, for she was in control. She obeyed and dimly realized that she wasn't in control after all, that he was….

"Harder…" That might have been her voice; she couldn't be sure. Did it matter?

"Lift up…."

"Yes…"

Suddenly he was within her, filling her to her very soul, making her feel complete in a way she had never before known. She threw back her head, savoring his possession and knowing real freedom for the first time in her life.

He found her sexy. He wanted her. He liked her touches and responded to them in the most exciting ways.

He found her adequate as a woman.

She might have wept then, at last, releasing the pain that had scarred her for so many years, but already he was sweeping her past thought, up and away from all of the cares that burdened her. Carrying her far beyond to a world where nothing existed except their joined bodies.

"Now, Sandy…now…"

Whether that was a command or a plea, she hardly knew or cared. It served to unlock something inside her, something tightly wound that uncoiled swiftly like a compressed spring.

When it snapped, it hurtled her over the edge into a blinding oblivion of delight. Dimly she was aware that she didn't go alone.

Chapter 11

"How will you live with yourself if you get that creep off?"

The question was flung at her as she crossed the hospital parking lot on Monday morning. By then she was beginning to get used to it. Sunday morning she had been the topic of a sermon in which Reverend Fromberg had gently chided those who were condemning her and had reminded his flock that every man was entitled to a defense, and that everyone was innocent until it had been proven otherwise. She had appreciated the gesture, but noticed that the dark looks she received did not in any way lighten.

Grocery shopping yesterday afternoon, she had been grateful as all get-out that Garrett had decided to accompany her, because otherwise she would have been scared half to death rather than just getting angry when three cowboys hurled nasty comments at her. She didn't even know who they were, or if they were capable of carrying out their implied threats, but they looked like the type she would be defending on a drunk and disorderly charge one of these days...assuming they hadn't moved on to a ranch in another county by then.

She couldn't say she hadn't expected it, she thought as she entered the hospital, aware that Garrett was only a step behind her. She'd known she would face some of this. The problem was, she hadn't really believed it. Yes, the rape of a child was one of the most heinous acts that could be committed. Yes, the rapist ought to go to jail, preferably for the rest of his days. But until someone proved to the satisfaction of a jury that the man accused was in fact the rapist, he had to be presumed innocent. He was entitled to a defense.

And she was beginning to feel like a broken record. Even her own thoughts were running in circles on the subject. The bottom line was that if it was this bad now, it was going to get worse. Maybe her sarcastic comment about getting a bodyguard hadn't been so far off the mark.

Lisa Dunbar was sitting up in bed wearing bright pink pajamas and playing with a doll. Sam Haversham stood to one side, talking with Lisa's mother. Garrett waited out in the hallway, because both Sandy and Sam feared that the presence of a strange man might inhibit the child. Lisa's mother gave Sandy a cool nod and retreated to a corner of the hospital room, where she sat and picked up a magazine.

"This is Sandy Keller, Lisa," Sam said, introducing her to the girl. "You've seen her at church."

Lisa nodded. "Lots."

"Okay, then. We just want to ask you a few questions this morning. Later on, we might bring another person to see you, too. A court recorder. Have you ever seen one on television? The lady who sits at a tiny typewriter in the court and types down everything people say?"

Lisa nodded, but it was impossible to tell whether she

was giving them the reply she thought they wanted or really knew what Sam was talking about.

"It's very important," Sam continued, "that you tell us the truth, Lisa. Do you know about telling the truth?"

These were the selfsame questions a judge would be asking Lisa later to determine if she would be a competent witness. Sandy watched the child intently.

"Mommy says to always tell the truth," Lisa told Sam and gave him the tiniest smile. "To be a good girl, so God doesn't get mad at me."

"That's right. You should always tell the truth. Do you know what a lie is?"

"When I make something up?"

"Good girl. A lie is when you tell something that didn't really happen."

Lisa nodded emphatically.

"Can you tell me a lie right now?"

Lisa tilted her head and pursed her lips. "My doggie is orange."

Both Sam and Sandy smiled. "What's the truth, Lisa?"

"My doggie's black and white. He's a damnation."

"Dalmatian," Mrs. Dunbar said hurriedly. Sandy had to choke back a laugh.

"So the truth is that your doggie is black and white, not orange at all."

Lisa nodded again. For a while Sam talked about ordinary things—school, church, what she wanted for her birthday. When Lisa seemed completely relaxed about talking with him, he began to circle in on the abduction.

"Now, Lisa, we need to talk about the bad things that happened to you. About when you were hurt. Can you talk to us about that?"

Another nod, but her eyes left Sam and became fixed on her doll.

"I know you don't want to think about it, honey, but we need to catch the bad person who hurt you, so you have to help us. Okay? Was it a man who took you away after you got off the school bus?"

Lisa nodded vigorously. "Bad man. Bad."

"Did you see what he was wearing? What kind of clothes?"

She nodded.

"Can you tell us?"

"Pants. Like mine. Jacket. Mittens."

Little by little Sam got a description of the clothes—perfectly ordinary jeans, boots, gloves. Nothing that seemed to have stuck in Lisa's mind as being interesting. As for his face, they got nothing at all.

"Did you see the man's face, Lisa?"

She nodded.

"What did he look like?"

"Mashed. Squished."

Sam and Sandy exchanged glances. Sam turned back to the little girl. "Do you know the man, Lisa?"

She stared back at him.

"Do you know who hurt you, Lisa?"

"Nighthawk."

Sandy's heart stopped dead, and the room seemed to recede as shock shook her to her very core. Nighthawk. As simply as that....

"But you said you didn't see his face, Lisa," Sam said gently. "Did you see who he was?"

Lisa shook her head. "He was wearing something funny over his face. Black."

Sandy spoke through stiff lips. "How do you know it was Nighthawk?"

"My daddy told me."

"Well, that sure as hell shoots it in the foot," Sam said a few minutes later as he and Sandy and Garrett stood in the hallway and held a low-voiced discussion. "There's no way she can testify, Sandy. No way. Her entire testimony would be suspect now! Damn it, I told those people not to discuss this with her at all."

"Maybe they didn't," Sandy said. "Maybe she overheard her dad say that to someone else."

Sam looked at her from hot eyes. "Guess who my next suspect would be if Nighthawk turned up innocent."

Sandy nodded and looked away. The father was always a prime suspect in these cases; all too often he *was* the perpetrator. "But she'd know her father. Even a mask wouldn't keep her from knowing him."

"Not necessarily," Garrett remarked. "Kids have great imaginations, and it wouldn't take much effort to convince a five-year-old that she was talking to a superhero or to a total stranger. Hell, all he'd have to do is keep his face covered and wear some funny aftershave. She sure wouldn't *want* to believe it was her dad."

"You may be right about that," Sam agreed. "But insofar as her testimony is concerned, it doesn't matter. She's a tainted witness. Useless."

Sandy agreed. "There's no way we can tell how much of what she says is accurate recollection and how much has been filled in since by overheard conversations."

"So we have to go with what she said to Nate when she was found. It doesn't help Nighthawk any."

"No, but it isn't a hell of a lot against him, either."

Sam nodded grimly. "I want a solution to this case, Sandy. Damn it, I can't stand the thought the culprit may escape."

"Me either," she agreed. "I still don't think it was Nighthawk, but I'd sure like to be able to prove who it really was."

"Before he strikes again," Garrett said.

Sam glanced over at him. "God, don't even suggest it."

"Can't you question her a little more?" Garrett asked. "I realize you can't use her as a witness, but she might know some things that would help, anyway. Like where did he take her? Does she know? When did her book bag disappear? Stuff like that. Maybe we can pick up a clue or two."

So they went back into the hospital room and began to question Lisa gently about events. Garrett stayed back by the door, but this time they left it open so he could hear.

"We went to a house," Lisa told them.

"Did you see the outside of it?"

"No."

"Do you know whose house it was? Who lived there?"

"The stinky man."

"Why do you say he's stinky?"

"Peeyew!" She held her nose.

That could mean almost anything, Sandy thought, but it sure didn't fit Nighthawk.

They questioned her further, discovering that she had seen only one room of the house, that there had been a bed and a chair and a picture of an old woman in it, and that she'd been tied up most of the time while he hurt her. That she never once saw his face, and that she had been alone in the dark for long periods of time.

And that the man knew her name.

"I guess that's all, Lisa," Sam said finally. "I don't have any more questions. What about you, Sandy?"

"I think that's it for now. Would you mind if I come back and visit you tomorrow?" she asked the little girl.

Lisa shook her head slowly. "More questions?"

"Maybe." Sandy smiled gently. "And maybe we'll just play a game. We'll see. Do you have any questions for us?"

Lisa looked straight at her with a child's wide, perplexed gaze. "Why are you trying to get the bad man out of jail?"

It was like taking a punch to the stomach. She couldn't even breathe. She was saved from trying to find a reasonable answer by the arrival of the local scoutmaster, Dudley Willis. He was wearing his uniform and smiling broadly as he stepped into the room with a large beribboned box. He nodded to Sandy and Sam, then turned to Mrs. Dunbar.

"The boys took up a collection to get a little something for Lisa. Is it okay?"

The woman beamed at him. "Sure, Dud. Lisa will love it."

In fact, Lisa was already clapping her hands in excited anticipation, and the hopefulness on her face showed all the joy and delight of a child on Christmas morning. Sandy's throat tightened painfully, and for a moment her vision blurred. Right now Lisa looked the way a child should look, with none of the terrible knowledge that had been so apparent on her face but a short time ago.

When Dud Willis handed her the box, she tore at it eagerly and squealed with delight when she pulled out a beautiful and very expensive talking doll. Evidently one of her friends had one, because she needed no instructions to make it work. While she explored it, Willis stood beaming with pleasure.

Garrett slipped into the room and stood beside Sandy. "Who's he? Apart from being a scout leader."

"Dudley Willis," she whispered back. "One of our more prominent citizens."

He gave a brief nod, never taking his eyes from the man and the little girl. Willis at last said that he needed to get on back. He went to Lisa's side and bent over her, telling her to get well quick.

As he got close, Lisa flinched and turned quickly away, crying, "No!"

Willis immediately stepped back from the bed. "I'm sorry," he said, looking horrified. "I forgot she'd probably be afraid of men...." He turned with an agonized expression and hurried out into the hall.

"It's all right," Mrs. Dunbar said quickly, going after him. "Dud, it's okay. You didn't do anything."

To Sandy's amazement, Garrett went right after them and in the rudest imaginable way stepped right between them and took Willis by a shoulder. "She'll be okay," he said to the man. "I'm sure she was just startled. I've seen cases like this before."

Willis looked up at him, and after a moment he nodded. "Yeah. I just feel bad about upsetting her."

Then, just as swiftly as he'd intruded, Garrett stepped out of the way. He turned and looked at Sandy through the open door, gave a little jerk of his head and walked away. She wanted to follow and ask what had gotten into him, but instead focused on Lisa, who was clutching her new doll as if it were a lifeline and staring warily at the people in the room.

"Are you okay, honey?" Sandy asked her.

Several long moments passed before the little head nodded.

"Did something scare you?"

This time there was no answer at all, just a stony silence. Then Lisa touched the back of her doll and it began to recite a poem.

"I'll stop by tomorrow to see how you're doing, okay?" Sandy said. That elicited another nod, but Lisa didn't look at her again.

Sandy found Garrett waiting in the main lobby for her. "What got into you?" she asked him as they walked to her car.

"Just had an idea I want to check out. I'm going into the big city tonight. Want to come along?"

She hesitated and then thought, Why not? She certainly didn't have any appointments to take care of, and she didn't have to be in court again until next week, when she was handling a routine DUI. "I'd like that."

They checked into one of the better motels and shared a dinner in the restaurant. Afterward Garrett suggested they go to the mall. Though he spoke casually, Sandy guessed that this was what he had come into the city for, and she longed to ask him what he wanted to check out. She bit back the questions, though, because she was sure he would tell her when he was ready to. It wasn't easy to suppress her natural curiosity, but she respected Garrett's judgment and figured that whatever was compelling him wasn't yet clear enough to him that he felt comfortable sharing it.

The mall was busy, filled with crowds that made her think of the Christmas rush. Easter was just behind them, and now Mother's Day was very much in evidence in the card shops and a few of the department stores. Garrett seemed in no particular hurry, and if he was heading somewhere in particular, she couldn't tell. More than once he suggested they wander through one of the stores when something in the window caught her eye.

"You'd look great in that," he told her when she paused to wistfully eye a turquoise silk blouse.

She hesitated a moment longer and then shook her head. "I need to be good. I don't know when I may ever have another client."

He looked somberly down at her. "They'll come around eventually, darlin'. You're a good attorney, and I think the vast majority of your neighbors really like you."

"You could fool me. I expected fallout from this, Garrett. Truly. I expected to lose some clients, and I expected nasty phone calls. Maybe even a veiled threat or two. But I didn't expect to have my business completely collapse."

"I'm sure that's just temporary. Really." He took her hand and squeezed it, then kept it tucked warmly within his as they continued their stroll through the crowd. "I'd bet money it's just a first shocked reaction on the part of most of your clients and an instinctive desire not to have their names associated in even a remote way with this mess. Once the initial furor dies down, things'll pretty much go back to normal."

"I hope so. I hate to think of having to move away and start all over again elsewhere."

"I'm sure that won't happen."

But his reply had been a beat too late in coming, and she felt her heart give a crazy leap. Could he possibly be wishing that she would consider pulling up stakes and coming to Texas? Lord, she didn't know if she would have the gumption to start all over again—and so far away, besides! It would be so different.... No, she couldn't possibly consider it.

But she glanced up at him, anyway, wishing he would

say something about it. Wishing against hope that somehow, magically, everything could work out so she could spend the rest of her life with this kind, understanding, wonderful man.

"When will you be done with convalescent leave?" she asked him finally, when he said nothing more.

"I...don't know." He turned abruptly, leading her into a lamp-lit restaurant. "Let's get some coffee and dessert."

Chocolate cheesecake was about as sinful as you could get, but she decided to splurge on it, anyway. Garrett ordered Dutch apple pie and asked the waitress to keep the coffee coming.

"Why don't you know when your convalescent leave will be over?" she asked him when they were alone. "Is something wrong?"

He didn't want to tell her. Saying it out loud somehow made it seem more real, which was utterly ridiculous, but superstition had been dogging him ever since his life had gotten out of his own control. He tried and tried not to think about it, the same way he tried not to think about how much he wanted Sandy Keller and how much that wanting scared him. He wasn't a coward, not by a long shot, but there were some things it just did no good to worry about, so a wise man set them aside and moved on to the things that *were* under his control. Besides, Sandy had enough on her plate with all this fallout from the Nighthawk case. She didn't need to be hearing his problems.

Yet he couldn't bring himself to equivocate or prevaricate. She'd been utterly honest with him, and she deserved no less in return. If he was washed-up as a cop, she deserved to know it.

"I've...had some residual damage," he told her. The words didn't come easily. "My right arm isn't as strong as it needs to be. I'm working on it, but there's no guarantee I'll be able to pass the physical.''

"Oh, Garrett, that would be awful for you!" All she could think of was how she would feel if she couldn't practice law anymore. It would be like having a big chunk of her heart cut out. She longed to reach out and offer comfort of some kind, but there was simply nothing she could say that would make this any better. Regardless of whether it might embarrass him, she reached across the table and squeezed his hand. "The waiting must be terrible."

He shrugged. "Can't be helped. And, of course, every day is another day I can exercise my arm."

"Is it helping?"

"I think so." He clenched his right hand into a fist. "There's no doubt it's stronger than it was. And the tremor is nowhere near what it was. The question is whether it'll improve enough…and in time."

He spoke with masculine stoicism, but she wasn't buying it. She had discovered that Garrett possessed the normal complement of human feelings, and although his expression of them was subtle, that didn't mean he wasn't feeling just as intensely as she would. He would, however, probably get embarrassed if she made too much of a fuss about it.

"Have you thought about what you'll do if you don't pass?"

He shook his head, smiling faintly. "I'm a stubborn cuss, Sandy. I refuse to even consider the possibility. Well…not much, anyway."

Even as faint as his smile was, she found it infectious. "Was that why you were making all those references to figuring out some kind of hobby before you retire?"

"I guess so. Much as I don't want to even allow there's a possibility, it's not something I can entirely ignore."

And now she understood why he had wanted to act as an investigator on this case. Better to be busy than to sit around and brood. It was perfectly understandable, but her stomach sank anyway. So he hadn't wanted to work on the case as an excuse to be near her. It was only right then that she realized how much some little corner of her heart had been hoping precisely that. That Garrett had simply wanted to be with her.

Which was ridiculous, she told herself sternly. Utterly ridiculous. Neither of them wanted to get involved. Both of them had been burned too badly. No, it was far better that he was investigating this case for reasons that had nothing to do with her. Far better.

But it hurt a little anyway.

And because it hurt, she ate the entire slice of cheesecake instead of the three or four forkfuls she'd promised herself. Ah, well. Didn't chocolate contain the same chemical that was released when you fell in love? She could sure use a little pick-me-up right now. A pick-me-up about the size of a one-pound box of chocolates, actually. It was a silly train of thought, but the silliness picked up her mood almost as much as the chocolate.

"Have you heard any more from your sister?" she asked him.

He shook his head. "I asked a buddy of mine to look into her ex-husband's parole, though. If there's anything at all I can do to keep that guy behind bars, I'll do it. It makes me so damn mad the way these abusive guys can keep coming back at women."

"Not all of them do that, though, do they?"

"Not all. But how the hell do you know? Anyway, I'm going to make sure he doesn't get a chance at Ginny. We should know pretty quick after he gets out if he's the kind who wants to get even.''

Back on the concourse, feeling as if she had eaten far too much and was going to swell into a beach ball, she was glad to be moving again. They browsed in a music store, and Sandy treated herself to a CD she'd been wanting for a long time.

And then, to her amazement, they entered a tobacco shop. ''I used to smoke a pipe,'' Garrett told the tobacconist. ''I'm thinking about taking it up again, only I can't remember the name of the tobacco I liked so much.''

The man nodded to him. ''What can you tell me about it?''

''It's not a widely smoked kind. I know that much. Very aromatic, but not at all sweet. Sort of heavy, and a little musty. Bitter.''

The man pulled a couple of glass jars down from the shelf and removed the stoppers for him. ''See if you recognize either of these aromas.''

Garrett took a sniff of the first jar while Sandy wondered why he was all of a sudden talking about smoking again. He'd seemed to be proud of the fact that he'd quit, even though he often patted his breast pocket, looking for that pack of cigarettes.

''This is the stuff,'' Garrett told the man. ''I'm sure of it.''

''Latakia. One of the better Turkish tobaccos. It's not one of the most popular, because it isn't sweet at all. Would you like some?''

Garrett bought a few ounces, along with a briar pipe and the other mysterious accoutrements that men used with pipes. When they were outside, Sandy asked him, ''Are you sure you want to start smoking again?''

He glanced down with an enigmatic half smile. "Only for a little while."

She shook her head. "I hear it's about the toughest addiction there is to kick. You might regret fooling with it."

"I might. But I quit once, and I figure if I could do it once, I can do it again."

"Ah, but does it truly constitute quitting if you start up again a while later?"

He laughed. "It's been three years. More than 'a while.'"

"I just don't want to see you get hooked again."

His expression softened. "Thanks for caring," he said gently. "Trust me. I won't."

"'Trust me' is always the last thing the hero says before everything goes to hell," she reminded him.

They were both laughing when they stepped out into the parking lot. The night had grown crisp, the stars were brilliant and unwinking in a black velvet sky. The air was still, however, and there was an almost hushed sense of expectancy to the world.

Garrett paused after he unlocked the car door for her. "Back to our room?"

There was no mistaking the message in his eyes. Sandy's heart quickened with excitement. It was still incredible to her that this man found her desirable. Still wonderfully impossible at the way all her doubts and fears fled when he touched her. In some inexplicable, almost magical way, she became new and fresh and untainted when he reached for her. Somehow he had peeled away all the years, all the scars, all the detritus that had closed her away for so long.

She was also scared to death. It was terrifying to feel so open, so exposed. All her defenses were down, and there was nothing left to protect her from hurt.

And she *was* going to get hurt. She wasn't naive enough

to believe there could be any other outcome. All her feelings had gotten tangled up with Garrett; that had probably been inevitable from the moment of their first meeting. Heavens, she hadn't been able to forget him in the two years since!

She would have missed him when he left if they had never made love. But they *had* made love. Gloriously. Wonderfully. Repeatedly. In a mere three nights, she had grown accustomed to his presence beside her in her bed. Had grown to love the reassurance of waking in the dark and seeing his shadow beside her in the night. Had grown to love the sound of his deep breathing, and even his light snoring in the early morning hours.

Her life, which had seemed complete and fulfilling only a brief time ago, was now going to seem empty when he was gone. A bed that had been hers alone would now forever seem lonely.

She had been foolish, she admitted, as they drove back to their motel. Utterly foolish. She had believed herself to be immune to these dangers after so many years. Even as she had felt herself slipping over the precipice of caring too much for Garrett, she had convinced herself that it wouldn't become more than she could handle. She had never for one moment realized that there was no safety in his inevitable departure, had never admitted that that wasn't safety at all.

Her only safety had been in never becoming involved at all. But she had slowly and steadily grown to care more and more...until finally she had cared enough to risk making love with him. And that had sealed her fate beyond redemption. He had shown her that she was a whole woman. He had desired her and cared for her and had made long-dead dreams come true.

How could she have failed to love him?

But now she *did* love him, and there was no hope. No

ending but a painful one. He had given her no indication that she was anything more than a pleasant diversion, and he'd warned her at the very outset that he wasn't marriage material.

A sigh escaped her, but Garrett failed to hear it, and she was grateful. There was no way she could have explained her mood to him. Better to try to put a happy face on it until he was gone. If nothing else, she could preserve her pride.

It was small consolation, but it was amazing how much backbone a little pride could provide.

Garrett had registered them in a single room as boldly as if they were married, and it was a kind of illicit thrill for her. She'd never done anything like this before in her life...which perhaps said something about how limited her experiences really were.

Once they were in the motel room, Garrett turned her into his arms as easily as if he'd been doing it for a lifetime and covered her mouth in a hungry, devouring kiss. "God," he said moments later, sounding as if he were on the edge of laughter, "you've been driving me crazy all evening. Damn it, Sandy, I don't think you have any idea how naturally sexy you are! You even breathe sexy."

The gleam in his brilliant blue eyes and the humor in his tone unknotted something inside her, and a bubble of laughter spilled over her own lips. The foreshadowing of pain faded into the distant recesses of her mind, leaving her feeling open and free.

The magic of the night seemed to come into the room with them. Dark velvet feelings filled her as Garrett's hands moved over her, removing unwanted clothing, painting sensation over her nerve endings. The confidence he had been instilling in her made her bold enough to reciprocate. With unabashedly eager hands, she helped him out of his shirt and tugged away his boots and jeans. When at last they tumbled naked onto the bed, they were both laughing and breathless.

And then their eyes locked and their hearts locked and laughter became sighs and soft whispers. She felt as if she fit perfectly into the curve of his body as he held her close and explored her with gentle fingers, leading her steadily deeper into the beauty of lovemaking. She had the craziest feeling that she had been made for this man, for these moments, for this brief stolen time. As if her entire life had been focused on this mating.

Crazy, she told herself. Crazy. But she was past caring. She needed his touches and kisses to the very depths of her soul, needed to be filled with him in every one of her senses. The sound of his voice, rough with passion, was as sensual as a fur coat slipping over her ultrasensitive skin. His aromas, of soap and man and just a tinge of the tobacco he had earlier sampled, filled her nose and seemed to spread like warm waves to the farthest parts of her body. And his touches...his touches claimed every inch of her, making her feel surrounded by him, protected by him, cherished by him.

She knew it was an illusion, but she felt as if she could just crawl into him and be held safely forever. The yearning to do just that was as intense as the desire to feel him fill her body. It was appalling to realize how long it had been since last she had felt cared for, and equally frightening to realize just how much she needed to feel that way. The years behind her suddenly looked so barren, and the future held no more promise, because this man would return alone to his home in Texas.

Near panic froze her for an instant, and suddenly, to her own horror, she was weeping huge, silent tears of impending loss.

"Sandy? Darlin', what's wrong?" Garrett's concerned face hovered over her in the dusky room, and his arms changed their hold, becoming less demanding and more comforting. "Sweetheart, what's wrong?"

She shook her head emphatically and squeezed her eyes shut against the tears. She would rather face demons than admit to this man that she was crying because he would be passing out of her life.

"Don't shake your head," he said gently, his voice laced with real concern. "Did I hurt you? Are you worried about something?"

"Nothing…nothing…sorry. Guess I'm just tired…." The tears were drying almost as quickly as they had begun, leaving her feeling foolish for having shed them. She wanted to turn her face away and hide, but Garrett prevented her. He kept her cradled safely to his chest, her head upon his shoulder, and kissed away the tears he could reach.

He held her for a long time, convinced that he must have done something to upset her. He knew Sandy; she wasn't the type to burst into tears easily. Something was seriously troubling her, and since nothing had happened in the past several hours, he could assume only that he had somehow upset her himself.

But no matter how many times he played the day over in his mind, particularly the last half hour or so, he couldn't find anything that should have caused her tears. The last time a woman he'd held had cried for no apparent reason, she had been getting ready to tell him that she was leaving him.

So perhaps Sandy was planning to break it off with him. His heart lurched painfully. But of course this was coming to an end, he told himself. That had been inevitable from the outset. He had known from day one that she wouldn't abandon her law practice, and he wasn't about to abandon his career as a ranger.

But instead of the calm acceptance he thought he should feel, he was nearly overcome by a terrible sense of loss. It gripped his chest like a vise and tightened his throat until it nearly hurt to breathe. But this was just transitory, he told himself. He'd learned the hard way not to give his heart away, and he wasn't the type who forgot his lessons. No, this was just a momentary feeling, and he would be over it by tomorrow.

For the first time, he and Sandy fell asleep together without making love. But throughout the night, they never entirely let go of one another.

Chapter 12

The first thing Sandy saw when she and Garrett entered her office the next afternoon was a note taped conspicuously to her desk. Nina wanted her to know that Sam was going to depose Ben Dunbar. Could she be at Sam's office at nine the next morning? She was supposed to call Sam.

The second thing she saw was the broken window in Nina's office. Someone had hurled a large rock through it. A piece of paper was tied around the rock, which lay amid scattered slivers of glass.

"Don't touch it," Garrett said sharply. "Let's get the sheriff over here."

The Conard County sheriff's deputies were always prompt to respond, and this time was no exception. Micah Parish was walking up to her door within five minutes of her phone call. Then Sandy had to endure the incredible frustration of waiting to find out what the note said while photos were taken and the rug was marked where the rock had fallen. Only then, after painstaking preparation, did Micah put on a pair of gloves and carefully untie the note.

Written on ordinary blue-lined notebook paper, it was brief and to the point. Penciled in block letters was the message: *An eye for an eye. If you get the rapist off, you will pay.*

"Oh, great!" Sandy said in frustration. "Just great! What's next? A Molotov cocktail? A burning cross? What is the matter with everyone?"

"It's not the matter with everyone," Micah said in his deep, slow voice. "Just a few nuts. You must have expected this."

She sighed and scooped her hair back from her face with impatient hands. "Yeah, I expected it. I just didn't expect to be so scared by it! Damn it, Micah, what kind of person does something like this?"

"Generally someone who's too much of a chicken to look you right in the eye and say it," Garrett told her. "It's a cheap shot. I wouldn't worry about it, darlin'."

"Me either," Micah agreed. "This isn't a serious threat."

"What *would* be serious?" she asked. She didn't at all like the feeling that the threat wasn't being taken seriously enough. If people were willing to throw rocks through her windows, who was to say they wouldn't be willing to do something even worse? Micah and Garrett were being entirely too sanguine about all of this.

After Micah had departed with the pictures, the rock and the note, Garrett helped her tape cardboard over the broken window and clean up the glass that had sprayed all over the rug.

"This really isn't something I think you need to worry about," Garrett told her seriously. "I wouldn't kid you, Sandy. This is more of a kid's prank than a real threat."

"Well, I don't like it anyway!"

"I don't blame you. But if I'm right, we should catch our

culprit pretty soon, and then this whole abominable mess will be put to rest.''

She turned and faced him directly. ''What's going on? And why do you keep putting me off when I ask?''

''Because I want you to observe something without knowing what you're observing, okay? Can we go to see the Dunbar girl sometime tomorrow?''

''Sure...I guess. Let me find out and set it up.''

He smiled. ''Thanks.''

''This better be good, Hancock. That's all I have to say. Curiosity killed the cat, and I've got more curiosity than any cat.''

He chuckled at that. ''Trust me. I just want you to see what I saw, so that when I tell you about it you won't think I'm crazy, okay?''

She hesitated, wondering if he were planning something that could put her entire future on the line. Then she shrugged inwardly. Her future was apparently already on the line, and besides, Garrett was a Texas Ranger. There was no reason to think he would do anything illegal.

In the morning, Ben Dunbar's deposition did nothing to clarify matters. He'd forgotten, he said, all about Lisa being in Nighthawk's truck that morning in front of the supermarket. It just clean went out of his head until Nighthawk was arrested.

Why hadn't he come in right away to tell them about it instead of waiting until they questioned him? Because his mind was on other things, namely his little kid being so hurt, and besides, Nighthawk had already been arrested, anyway.

Why had Lisa been alone out in front of the store? ''Well, you know how it is with kids. I didn't even know she'd gone off by herself until Dud Willis saw her out there. I thought she was right there while we was talking.''

"Fishy as hell," Sam muttered when Dunbar had left.

Sandy thought so, too. The stenographer was quietly packing up, so she refrained from saying anything about it until they were alone. What struck her most was that Sam was apparently beginning to consider the possibility that Nighthawk wasn't guilty.

"It's making me uneasy as hell," he admitted when she mentioned it. "Basically what we have is a lot of circumstantial evidence that's beginning to look *too* circumstantial. Of course, the genetic tests aren't in yet, and it's possible they might prove the case."

"But you don't really think Nighthawk did it." She couldn't have said why, but it was somehow important to her that Sam admit doubt about the case.

"No, I don't really think Nighthawk did it," Sam said heavily. "No, damn it, I don't. I've talked to him, and the impression I keep getting is of somebody who's very decent. Of course, everybody thought Ted Bundy was a decent guy, too, didn't they?'' He shook his head irritably. "I want more evidence. One way or another, I want something more to go on. It'll probably be three more weeks on the DNA matching, though."

"That long?" She'd never worked directly on a case with DNA evidence until this one and hadn't realized the analysis could take so long.

"It averages about five weeks, they tell me."

"Well, if you're so doubtful about Nighthawk's guilt, why don't you drop the charges?"

"And get myself run out of town on a rail? Be realistic, Sandy. He's the only suspect I've got, and I'm damn well going to hang on to him. The court approved the charges, and that's where we stand until something changes."

"Nothing's going to change if you don't look for anything."

He gave her a crooked smile. "You've hired a private eye, and you're not getting anywhere any faster than we are."

It was on the tip of her tongue to tell him that Garrett thought he'd solved the case, but she bit back the words. In the first place, she didn't know what Garrett suspected or what he was up to, and Sam would probably hit the roof if he thought Sandy or Garrett knew something material to the case and was concealing it. In the second place, Garrett was being secretive for a reason, and she had to respect that. For now.

So all she said to Sam was "I guess not."

"So, for lack of any evidence to the contrary," Sam continued, "Nighthawk remains accused. It's just getting to be an unpleasant feeling in my gut, that's all."

The prosecutor had an unpleasant feeling in his gut but was going to hang on to the suspect until there was something to prove the man's innocence. That seriously disturbed Sandy, but she could understand it. The *only* evidence they had pointed to Nighthawk, and it was sufficient that a judge had upheld the arrest warrant. Sam *couldn't* let Nighthawk go for no reason other than an uneasy feeling. And even if he had, from the looks of it the county would have hung him and then hung Nighthawk, so it wouldn't have done anyone a damn bit of good. Any way you looked at it, Nighthawk's incarceration was damn near protective custody.

"How'd it go?" Garrett asked her when she stepped out of Sam's office. He was waiting outside as he always was now, never leaving her alone. Like a patient watchdog. No, like a concerned lover, she amended. He was acting like a concerned lover. Too bad it was just an act.

No, that wasn't fair, either, she scolded herself. Garrett was a decent man, and his concern was genuine. It just wasn't permanent.

"Okay," she said. "I think Sam wishes he could pin this on Ben Dunbar. The man *is* behaving suspiciously."

Garrett shook his head. "No, he's acting like a not-too-bright man who's got more on his plate right now than he can handle."

"You're so sure he's innocent?"

"Sure enough to place a bet. Twenty bucks says I can prove it wasn't Dunbar *or* Nighthawk."

"I don't bet." She sniffed, but almost in spite of herself, a grin caught the corners of her mouth and tugged them upward. "Twenty bucks, huh? Doesn't sound like you're all that sure."

"Well, I'd bet a hundred without batting an eye, except that it would be like taking candy from a baby. I have *some* morals, you know."

"Not any that I've noticed," she joked, managing to purse her lips primly.

He leered. "You've been looking in the wrong places."

They were still laughing when they arrived back at her office, but the smiles faded before they finished climbing the porch steps. Spray-painted in black on the light gray wood porch floor was the warning *Justice must be served!*

"A somewhat literate vandal," Garrett remarked as he studied the mess with a dark frown. "Go get in the car, Sandy. There's probably more. I'll check things out first."

"No." Anger bubbled up from deep within her and began to boil. "Damn it, what do I have to do? Sit on my front porch with a shotgun twenty-four hours a day? Has the world gone mad?''

''No, the world hasn't gone crazy,'' Garrett said soothingly. ''Just a few cranks, is all. This really looks like kid stuff.''

Almost as quickly as it had bubbled up, Sandy's anger slipped away. ''Yeah. Kid stuff. I'm sorry, I sound like a broken record. I must have asked that same question a hundred times in the past few days.'' She shook her head. ''Now I have to have the porch painted. Maybe the whole damn house. Do you know how much that costs? I only had it done last summer....'' She turned quickly away, blinking back unwanted tears. This was not the time to fall apart.

Garrett's arm settled around her shoulders, a reassuring weight. ''I'll help you paint the damn place. We'll start the day after tomorrow.''

Even through the closed door and windows, they could hear the phone inside start to ring. It was the distinctive chirrup of her office phone.

''Let me answer it,'' Garrett said as she shoved her key in the lock. ''Let me handle it.''

The call turned out to be for him, anyway, a friend of his in the rangers. Garrett's responses were clipped, revealing almost nothing, but when he hung up, he turned to Sandy, looking for all the world like a man who wanted to smile.

''That was Blue, my ranger buddy. I told you about him.''

She nodded, remembering some middle-of-the-night conversation when he had mentioned that he'd asked a friend to check out the details of his sister's ex-husband's upcoming release. ''Good news?''

''Maybe. It seems Bobby got involved in a fight. It's pretty serious, and he's in the hospital. They're not sure he'll make it.'' He shook his head. ''Damn, it's awful to feel a man's death would be a lucky thing. Anyway, even if he does live, he's probably not going to breathe free air for a long time. They found drugs on him."

"Either way, that sounds like a reprieve for your sister."

"Yeah." He shook his head as a slow grin spread over his rugged face. "Yeah. Look the other way if I disgust you."

But she couldn't. She could understand all too well his feeling that this was news worth celebrating, and it was hardly mitigated by the fact that a man had been hurt. Your conscience could twinge, but sometimes you just felt it was justice anyway.

And speaking of justice... She looked around her office, wondering if anyone had gotten in and damaged things. The spray-painted warning out front had left her feeling...violated. Angry. Helpless. There was nothing on earth quite like a sense of helpless outrage.

"I'm going to walk around outside and see if there's any other graffiti," Garrett said. "If the phone rings, let the machine get it. I'll deal with any crap when I get done outside."

"I'm perfectly capable of answering the phone," she told him. "Actually, what I really need is a picket line out front."

Halfway to the door, he paused and looked back. "What?"

"A picket line. Put a dozen people out front with signs condemning me as the Whore of Babylon or some such nonsense because of the Nighthawk case, and I'd be as safe as a babe in a cradle."

Again that charming, lazy grin spread over his face. "You know, that's not such a bad idea. I wonder if I can arrange it."

Startled, she couldn't think of a thing to say before he

disappeared out the door. She'd only been joking. Surely he didn't mean to actually have her picketed?

But she was beginning to wonder just what Garrett was capable of.

In the morning they drove out to the Dunbar ranch again, this time to talk to Lisa Dunbar, who was now home from the hospital. Garrett carried a white plastic garbage bag in which could be seen the vague outline of a stuffed doll. He also carried a box containing another doll.

"For Lisa," he said.

"I hope this isn't a nasty trick."

He put his hand over his heart. "I'm wounded. Hey, look, I promise it's not a nasty trick."

Mrs. Dunbar invited them in pleasantly enough and offered them coffee and cake. "Lisa's out with her daddy looking at the colt that was born while she was in the hospital. Ben says it's going to be Lisa's very own." The woman shook her head and looked at them from haunted eyes. "I don't want to turn into an overprotective mother, but it's not easy. I can't even stand to have her out of my sight now. How am I ever going to go back to work?"

Sandy didn't know what to say to that. Once a sense of safety was shattered, it was nearly impossible to put it back together.

"And my older girl is feeling nearly as bad," Mrs. Dunbar continued. "She's so sure that if she'd come home on the bus like she was supposed to, none of this would have happened. It *was* wrong of her to go to Johnna Willis's house after school—"

"Johnna Willis?" Garrett repeated. "I didn't know Dud had kids."

"Oh, yes, he's got four girls. His wife up and left him

about three years back, never did say why. They moved into town, and Dud stayed out on the ranch. Anyhow, it was because he gave his daughter a movie that she and my girl had been wanting to see forever... Seems like forever to that age, anyway...." She smiled faintly. "Anyhow, that's what tempted my oldest to go to Johnna's house instead of coming home. What she should've done was take her sister with her, but—" she shook her head and looked away "—hindsight's always clearer."

Just then the little girl came dashing into the kitchen with a big smile on her face. "Oh, Mommy, he's beautiful, and Daddy says he's mine! My very own!"

The instant she saw Garrett and Sandy, however, her smile faded, and she sidled toward her mother. It was apparent that the sight of them had brought back memories of the past week.

"It's okay, honey," Mrs. Dunbar said gently. "It's okay. These folks just wanted to give you a present and see how you was doing. I'm right here, Lisa. You're safe."

Sandy's heart squeezed for the little girl, and the look she shot Garrett was a warning.

"Actually, I brought you two presents, Lisa. My niece in Texas loves these, so I thought I might as well get you two of them. She's always begging me to buy another one for her."

Lisa looked at him around her mother's shoulder. "Is she my size?"

"My niece? Yep. She's five years old, and she has long black hair and blue eyes like mine."

Lisa edged toward him. "What's her name?"

"Sylvia."

"I like that name."

"So do I. Sometimes I call her Silly for short."

Lisa giggled at that and apparently decided that Garrett was okay. She opened the box first, pulling forth a soft doll whose body was covered in pale pink satin. Her delight was palpable as she squealed and showed her mother, and asked Garrett if she could call the doll Silly-for-short.

"We-e-e-ell, I guess so," Garrett said, pretending reluctance. "Just don't ever tell Sylvia I said you could use her name."

Really eager now, Lisa reached for the bag as Garrett explained he had damaged the box. But when she opened it, she froze.

"Lisa?" Her mother looked instantly concerned. "Lisa, what's wrong?"

The little girl lifted frightened eyes to Garrett and stepped backward, dropping the bag as she did so.

"Lisa?" Mrs. Dunbar's voice sharpened. "Lisa, what's wrong?"

Sandy bent over in her chair, reaching for the bag Lisa had dropped. As she opened it and pulled out the doll, she understood just what Garrett had done with the pipe and Latakia tobacco he'd purchased. She shot him a furious look and then turned to Lisa.

"It smells funny, doesn't it?"

Lisa nodded.

"I'm sorry. It can be washed out, if your Mom will throw it in the machine."

"That's easy enough," Mrs. Dunbar said. Her arm was snug around the little girl, holding her close to her side. "You okay, baby?"

Lisa didn't answer.

Sandy wanted to shake Garrett, but she restrained herself and instead tried to give Lisa a reassuring smile. "Is it a bad smell?"

The small head nodded.

"Does it make you feel sad?"

"Scary," Lisa blurted. "The bad man smelled like that."

"Ahh…" The satisfied sound came from Garrett, even as the little girl looked at him warily, as if suspecting him of being the bad man. "I'm sorry, Lisa. The smell will wash out. You can keep the doll, and your mommy can fix it."

Lisa shook her head vehemently. "No. I don't want it!"

Mrs. Dunbar looked torn between chiding her daughter's rudeness and cuddling the child close.

"It's okay," Sandy told her. "Lisa has every right to refuse the doll. We'll get it out of here so it can't distress her anymore."

A few minutes later, as they were jolting down the rutted driveway to the road, Sandy exploded. "Garrett, how could you? How could you do that to that poor little girl! What if you've traumatized her all over again! Good God—"

"Willis is our rapist, and that little girl is a hell of a lot tougher than you're giving her credit for. It's just a smell, and I'm sure the whole thing is already forgotten, because nothing bad happened."

"There's no way you could have known that before you gave her the doll. No way you could be positive she wouldn't go catatonic or something!"

"I've worked on these cases before. Trust me, darlin', the child is all right. And now we have to nail Willis."

"Willis?" It suddenly penetrated her anger. "You think Dudley Willis did it? Garrett, do you have any idea of who that man is? Of his importance…?"

"Important people do terrible things, too. Yes, I think it was Willis. Did you see how Lisa reacted when he came close to her bed? I don't know if you remember, but when he started to leave, I made a point of stopping him. I wanted a good look at him, in case something about his appearance reminded the kid of her abductor, but when I got close, I smelled the tobacco, and that fit better than it being something about his appearance that upset her, because she only got agitated when he came close. But I had to be sure the agitation was from the tobacco smell, not just because a man got too close. Therefore the doll.''

''It was still a mean thing to do, and a tobacco odor doesn't mean a damn thing. There could be hundreds of men in this county who smoke that tobacco.''

''If we were talking about chewing tobacco, I'd agree with you, sweetheart, but we're talking about pipe tobacco. About a particular type of tobacco that's usually tossed in small quantities into blends where it offsets sweetness a little. A tobacco that's smoked pure by very few people. It's too strong, too bitter and too aromatic. Anyway, I've noticed that pipe smokers don't exactly grow on trees around here. Yes, it's possible someone else smokes Latakia around here besides Willis, but I wouldn't bet the farm on it.''

''It's still not enough to persuade me.''

''Well, why don't you add to it the fact that it was Willis who showed up hotfoot to tell us about Nighthawk showing his truck to the little girl.''

''Circumstantial. Not enough to even arrest him.'' But suspicious as hell, she admitted, as her anger began to seep away. Awfully suspicious. ''Garrett, Willis is one of the most prominent and important people in this county. If you point a finger at him, no one is going to listen.''

''Then I'll have to get more evidence. At least now I know where to look.''

She turned in her seat and stared straight at him. ''Don't do anything illegal, Garrett. You may be acting as a private individual here, but you're working for me. If you get up to something doubtful, I could wind up disbarred."

He nodded and glanced her way. "Haven't you heard? Honest lawyers are an endangered species and have to be protected."

"Damn it, Garrett, this is no time for lawyer jokes! If you do anything shady, I could wind up disbarred, you could wind up in trouble with the law, and Willis will get off scot-free—if he *is* the perp. I want you to walk the straight and narrow on this."

He gave her a quick, reassuring smile. "Relax. The very last thing I want to do is get you into any kind of trouble. I'm just going to talk this over with Nate Tate."

She had to be satisfied with that.

"Do you have any idea who Dudley Willis *is?*" Nate asked Garrett as they faced each other across Nate's desk.

"Yeah. Conard County's George Washington and Abe Lincoln all in one."

Nate shook his head, chuckling. "Sorry, old son. Nope, not quite. Oh, his great grandaddy had something to do with settling this county, and up until the depression they owned most of it, except for the parts owned by the Conards. But that's not who Dud is. Dud is involved in damn near every one of our community activities, from theater to scouting. He's active in the church—one of its biggest contributors, as a matter of fact—and he heads up at least a dozen charitable organizations. He's not George Washington, but I think there's hardly a soul in the county who doesn't think highly of him. *Very* highly."

Garrett stifled a sigh. "Important people do bad things, too."

"Yeah, and I'm not saying it's impossible. Just that

you're going to need a hell of a lot more than a suspicion
in order to hang Dud Willis, and right now you haven't even
got enough for a search warrant.''

"But—''

Nate waved him to silence. "The fact that he smokes a
brand of tobacco that has a smell that the little girl associates
with her rapist merely puts him in a class, and you know as
well as I do that you can't get a warrant because somebody
is a member of a certain class of people. That's like trying
to get a warrant because somebody watches a certain TV
program. Yeah, him and nineteen million other Americans.
You put that together with him having seen Nighthawk with
the little girl, and it's still meaningless. Completely and totally meaningless. And I'm never going to persuade Judge
Williams to issue a warrant just because the guy smokes the
wrong kind of tobacco and because he found the little girl's
clothes on Nighthawk's property. Damn it, we had over a
hundred people out searching that night. Any one of them
could have found the kid's clothes. You know as well as I
do that you have to have something that links *one* person to
the crime.''

"*He* found the girl's buried clothes? Damn it, Nate, you
can't tell me all of this put together doesn't raise your hackles just a little!''

Nate pursed his lips and blew out a long breath. He stared
hard at Garrett for several moments before rising and going
to look out his office window. "Yeah, it raises my hackles.
My skin is crawling, and the back of my neck is prickling.
Problem is, that won't convince the judge to issue a warrant,
either. Hell!'' He slapped his palm against the window
frame. "I would never in a million years have suspected
Dud Willis of something like this. Cheating on his taxes,

yeah. That I'd believe. But doing something like this? Never.''

He turned abruptly. "But we still need something more to get a warrant. I'm going to put my investigator on it. In the meantime, you stay clear, Garrett.''

"I understand. What you need is a reliable informant to say he saw some kind of evidence.'' And as long as Garrett was acting as a private individual, the Fourth Amendment didn't cover him.

Something in Garrett's eyes must have warned Nate, because he went back to his desk and leaned over it, resting his weight on his hands. "I don't want to know if you're planning anything foolish. I don't want to know a damn thing about it. Just remember—if you bring anything out of Willis's house, I can't use it.''

One corner of Garrett's mouth lifted in a half smile. "By the way, I want you to know I'm giving Sandy my resignation as her investigator this evening. I am no longer working for her.''

One of Nate's brows lifted, then he nodded. "I understand. I hear you. But remember, *don't touch a damn thing.*''

Garrett cooked dinner for himself and Sandy that evening in Sandy's kitchen. She felt awkward about letting someone else do the cooking, particularly a man. Never once in her entire life had a man cooked dinner for her. Her son, of course, didn't count. The thought brought a smile to her lips.

Garrett was up to something, she thought. She was convinced of it. He was planning something, and he wasn't going to tell her about it, because she would object. She wondered if losing her entire client base wasn't the least of the trouble she was going to get out of the Nighthawk case.

542   A Question of Justice

But Garrett had said he wouldn't do anything to get her into trouble, and silly woman that she was, she wanted to believe him. She didn't want anything to mar this evening, and she certainly wasn't going to confront him about the Willis idea. He'd told her that Nate had said he couldn't get a warrant based on what they had, and she agreed. It wasn't enough by a long shot. Garrett had seemed to accept that easily enough, and she had to presume he planned to continue investigating in the hopes of finding enough evidence to provide probable cause for a search warrant of Willis's house.

Not that she thought Dudley Willis would have been stupid enough to keep anything incriminating around. She didn't think of him as a stupid man. But then, she didn't think of him as a child rapist, either. Trouble was, her alarm bells were going off just like Garrett's. There was just too much coincidence in the girl's reaction to the tobacco odor and Willis having found her clothes buried on Nighthawk's property. Too much. It wasn't enough to act on, but it was enough to make her feel they had to look into it somehow.

But Garrett wasn't telling her what he was planning. While she could have demanded some kind of explanation or statement of intent—he was working for her, after all—she couldn't help the cowardly feeling that it was better to let sleeping dogs lie. He'd promised not to get her into any trouble, and with that she had to be content.

For now.

He served up a really outstanding chili—not a bean in sight, and hot enough to launch a rocket. It was thick with chunks of steak and served with corn chips. While they ate, he regaled her with tales of Fiesta in San Antonio, and tempted her with talk of strolling along the River Walk at the height of the holiday season. The Alamo, he assured her, would probably disappoint her, tucked as it was in the heart of the city, and smaller by far than most people anticipated. He chuckled as he told her that a painting of John Wayne playing Colonel Travis was enshrined there. He also told her that Davy Crockett hadn't died the way the tales told it but had in fact surrendered to Santa Ana and been tortured to death.

"What's the deal with the saying about one ranger, one riot?" she asked him.

"The saying is One Riot, One Ranger. But that isn't what was really said, though the gist is the same. Capt. W. J. MacDonald was sent to Dallas to prevent a prizefight, and a lot of trouble was expected. Anyhow, when MacDonald stepped off the train, the mayor asked him where were the others? And MacDonald told him, 'Hell, ain't I enough? There's only one prizefight!'"

"That's a delightful story."

"I think so. MacDonald had one hell of a great attitude. Another thing he said that was drummed into us was, 'No man in the wrong can stand up against a fellow that's in the right and keeps on a-comin'.'"

Sandy somehow suspected that Garrett had had that drummed into him from a very early age by his father, who was also a ranger. It was an attitude that, to her, epitomized Garrett.

Later she was touched when he brought out his tennis ball and let her see the amount of effort he was expending in his attempt to encourage nerve regeneration.

"Another month or so," he told her. Not much longer at all. What he didn't tell her was how much trepidation that caused him. What he wanted was six more months. Months he would use to solidify his position in Sandy's life so that she would actually consider coming to Texas with him.

Or so that he might actually consider staying here with her. But there was no work for him here, and at this rate there might be none for her, either. No, he needed her to come home with him.

And he was damn near sure she wouldn't. That made him a fool, didn't it? Yeah, it did. He knew better than to get involved with a woman. All he ever got out of it was heartbreak. Well, at least this time he would get away with his pride intact, for what that was worth. He would go cheerfully to hell before he laid himself open again by asking any woman to marry him.

When he looked at Sandy, though, it was almost impossible to remember all his resolutions. This woman was becoming as essential to him as the air he breathed.

Oh, man, he was in deep trouble.

Chapter 13

Dud Willis owned an independent insurance agency, with its office located across the courthouse square from the sheriff's office. That was the first place Garrett stopped in the morning to ask when Willis was expected in. An obliging receptionist with a megawatt smile checked the appointment calendar and informed him that Mr. Willis was expected in the office at ten, but only for an hour. He would, however, be back at about two that afternoon. Would Mr. Hancock like to make an appointment?

He made one for two o'clock, thinking only that he didn't want this woman relaying to her boss that a man had been asking about his schedule for no good reason. This would make his visit appear completely innocent.

It was anything but. If Willis was expected to be in his office at ten, then Garrett could safely be at Willis's house at ten. Nobody could be in two places at once.

He knew what he was about to do could get him into serious trouble. Breaking and entering was a crime, one that could get him a jail term and cost him his career as surely as his arm might. There were a dozen valid reasons why he ought to turn his car around right now and head back into town. At least a dozen. And there were only two good reasons to do what he was doing right now.

The bad guy had to be stopped, and the innocent guy had to be cleared. It was, quite simply, a question of justice. It wasn't often that a cop really had a chance to serve justice in such a clear and important way. He'd spent his whole damn life trying to guarantee justice one way or another, and one way or another it had never seemed quite as important as it did this time.

Maybe because the crime was so awful. But he'd worked on child molestation cases before. Maybe because the bad guy was in danger of going free. But he'd worked on plenty of cases where that happened. Maybe it was because an innocent man was accused. It happened once in a while. Maybe because he really felt that there was some good that would come out of this if the bad guy was caught.

In the first place, it would keep Willis from hurting another little child. The horrifying fact was that the perpetrators of this kind of crime tended to strike more frequently and with more violence as time went on. It became harder and harder for them to get the same high, and easier and easier to quiet their consciences. The next little girl might not be as lucky as Lisa Dunbar...and wasn't that a horrifying thing to contemplate, that little Lisa had actually been lucky?

This crime also had another victim—Craig Nighthawk. That man's life was ruined until and unless the real rapist was caught and convicted. Even if the jury let Nighthawk go free for lack of evidence, the people of this county would always believe him guilty. And if he went to trial and was convicted, the injustice would be of criminal proportions.

And that didn't even take into account the losses Sandy was suffering for her belief that every man had a right to an attorney. For her belief that Nighthawk was innocent...as he was.

He shook his head irritably and hardly noticed that Dud Willis passed him going in the opposite direction. Without giving it a thought, he nodded in response to the man's casual wave and kept on driving.

Garrett was gone when Sandy awoke in the morning. At first she didn't think much about it, other than wishing they'd had some snuggling time. He tended to be an earlier riser than she, and she'd already wakened a couple of mornings to find that he'd gone out for an early walk.

There was a pot of coffee awaiting her, and what apparently was going to be a long, empty day. Having no clients was not only a financial disaster but also an emotional one. She hated not to be busy, hated the sense of uselessness that kept trying to steal up on her. All her life she had worked, at first on her father's ranch and then at odd jobs throughout school, until finally she had achieved her lifelong ambition to be a lawyer. And since then she'd hardly ever missed a day, even for illness.

Until this. Lord, it was awful to feel useless and unwanted, and other than writing all kinds of motions to try to help Nighthawk before the trial, there wasn't a damn thing she could do except hope that Garrett or the sheriff managed to come up with something to prove who the real criminal was.

And much as she respected Garrett's judgment, she had serious trouble imagining Dudley Willis as the rapist. Of course, if she stopped and thought about it for a while, there wasn't *anyone* she could imagine doing such a terrible thing. So why not Willis?

Sitting over her coffee, she found herself wondering why Willis's wife and daughters had left him. From all she knew of the man, she would have expected him to be an exemplary father and husband. Not the kind of man a woman with children usually left.

Almost without thinking about it, she pulled out the phone book from the drawer where she kept it, and leafed through it, looking for Adeline Willis's number and address. Over on Whitcliff Lane, at the east edge of town. Making an instant decision, she reached for the phone and dialed the woman's number. Thirty seconds later, she was talking to Adeline Willis.

"Addie, it's Sandy Keller."

"Well, hi, Sandy! It's been a while. I haven't been in church much lately, I'm afraid."

"Neither have I, which I'm sorry to admit. I hate to bother you so early in the morning, but maybe you know I'm working on the case of the little girl who was raped?"

There was a perceptible hesitation from Addie, but instead of the chill Sandy expected to hear, there was only caution. "I've heard. Terrible, terrible thing that was."

"Yes, it was. Just awful. But what I understand is that the older Dunbar girl was at your house after school the day the little one was abducted."

"That's right. She came over here to watch a movie Dud gave our girl that morning. Some vampire thing they were both dying to see." She sighed and sounded indulgent. "You know how kids can be at that age. I'll never understand what can be cute about a vampire, but you should have heard those two girls squeal while they watched it."

Sandy laughed quietly. "I seem to remember being that way about a few things when I was their age."

"The Beatles," Addie said. "We were all screaming about the Beatles."

"Addie, why did you leave Dud?" There was no easy way to ask the question, so dropping it as an unexpected bomb seemed like the way to get at the truth most quickly. She hated herself for prying, but if Dud had a proclivity toward little girls, maybe his ex-wife suspected it.

Instead of being startled into blurting something, however, Addie became silent. When she finally spoke, there was no mistaking her suspicion. "Why?"

"I...just wondered."

There was another long silence, with nothing but the hum of the line stretching between them. "You don't think Dud had something to do with that little girl being hurt, do you?"

Sandy hesitated long enough that her silence was her answer.

"I see." Addie, too, fell silent.

It was then that Sandy suddenly realized that Addie wasn't behaving like someone who was outraged by her suggestion. She was being far too quiet, protesting nothing at all. "Addie, I don't know anything for sure yet, but...I think the wrong man is in jail."

"Oh, Lord, have mercy!" Addie barely whispered the words. "I've been so scared, Sandy! Ever since I heard it was the little Dunbar girl who was hurt. Dud made such a big deal about our girl being sure to invite the older Dunbar girl over to see that film.... Oh, God, I've been so worried!"

Sandy almost couldn't breathe as shock hit her forcefully. She could hardly believe her ears were hearing correctly. "You...you think Dud is capable of this?"

"Not trying to kill a little child. I never would have

thought...but... Oh, my God! I left because... Oh, I don't
know how to say this! I left him because there was something...not right in the way he touched our girls. I don't
think he ever... But I can't be sure! I wasn't there every
minute. I couldn't be! What if he hurt one of my babies?''

The cry was anguished, but there was no answer Sandy
could possibly give her.

''I never thought he'd hurt somebody. Never!''

''We can't be sure he did, Addie.'' It was thin, and both
women knew it.

A few minutes later Sandy hung up, hoping she hadn't
distressed Addie unnecessarily. She was now convinced that
Dud Willis must be the guilty party. She wanted to tell Garrett about the conversation, but he still hadn't returned. Feeling frustrated and excited all at once, she headed back to
the bedroom to get dressed and try to decide how best to
use this new information. She would go talk to Nate, she
guessed, if Garrett didn't get back soon.

That was when she noticed the plain white business envelope on top of her dresser. At once her heart started hammering uncomfortably as she wondered what Garrett had to
say that he couldn't tell her to her face. That he was going
back to Texas? Goodbye, it's been swell, but...

In the envelope she found Garrett's neatly typed letter of
resignation as her investigator. Effective immediately.

That was when she knew what he was doing.

And realized she had to stop him.

The Willis place was deserted, of course, and invisible
from the road. Garrett pulled his Explorer around behind the
house so that anyone driving up wouldn't see it. No point
in advertising his presence, even to the mailman.

His heart was thundering in his chest. He was not at all

deceived about what he was doing. He was proposing to break the law to catch a lawbreaker, and he knew if his captain ever heard about this, his goose would be royally cooked. It wasn't that he'd never bent the law a little, but never before had he consciously set out to commit a criminal act. His mouth was dry.

Getting in was no problem. He didn't even have to jimmy a lock. That made him even more uneasy. Surely if Dudley Willis had something to hide he would lock his doors. Even though no one out here ever apparently locked anything.

Inside he could hear the whoosh of the heater in the basement and the hum of the refrigerator. The kitchen was as neat as a pin, somehow surprising for a man who lived alone. There was even a crocheted tablecloth on the dinette.

The living room looked as if the furniture had been placed there around the turn of the century and never moved since. Maroon horsehair covered the couch, and the rug had a raised, multicolored floral pattern unlike anything he had seen in recent memory. The walls were papered in dark green, giving the whole room a musty, closed look.

Willis's bedroom was on the first floor, and the furniture there was just as old as the furniture in the living room. When he thought about it, Garrett was a little surprised that a man who was, by all accounts, quite prosperous had furnishings so old. Beside the bed were framed portraits he took to be of Willis's wife and daughters. A heartwarming touch.

He would look in the drawers later, he decided, if he didn't find anything elsewhere. Somehow he didn't think Willis would have left any incriminating evidence in his own bedroom. What Garrett *did* hope to find was the room in which Lisa had been held. The room with the picture of the woman on the wall.

And find it he did. Upstairs, at the back of the house, he found Lisa Dunbar's prison. The windows had been covered in thick black material. An iron cot stood in the middle of the room on thick padding—presumably to prevent any sound from the bed being transmitted to the room below. His little prisoner could toss and turn and shake the bed and never alert anyone who might happen to stop by. It made Garrett sick to think about it.

On the wall at the foot of the bed was the portrait of the woman. An old photograph that had been touched with color in the style of the twenties and thirties. Why the hell had Dudley left something so identifiable in plain sight? Or had he simply grown so used to it that he had forgotten it was there?

The closet was bare except for a cardboard box. Garrett had kept his thick leather gloves on when he came into the house so he wouldn't leave any fingerprints. Now he didn't hesitate to squat down and look into the box by the harsh light of the single overhead bulb.

Ropes. Leather slave cuffs. Material that could have been used for gags and blindfolds. God, he was going to be ill!

And also in the box, a tiny pair of cotton panties—white with little pink roses. And a black nylon stocking.

All the proof they needed.

Sandy's only thought was that Garrett had to be stopped before he ruined his entire future. Damn it, he could be sent to prison! And somehow she didn't think a Wyoming jury would feel any too sympathetic toward a Texas lawman who had broken the law. She thought about calling Nate but stopped herself even as she reached for the phone. Nate was a lawman; he would be obliged to go out there and arrest

Garrett. No, this was one time when she had to keep the law out of it.

And this was one time when she simply ignored the potential consequences to herself. If she were found on Willis's property she could be arrested as an accomplice, and she seriously doubted that any jury would believe she'd gone out there to *stop* Garrett. Heck, they would think she was crazy not to have called the cops.

Which she was. But, after a life spent serving the law and the pursuit of justice, she found herself unable to go to the law. "I'm sorry," she heard herself telling an imaginary jury. "I just love him too much...."

She turned her car out of town toward Willis Road. "God, what a fool," she told herself. What a complete fool. It wasn't even as if Garrett reciprocated her feelings. As if she could hope for any kind of a future with him. Nope, the whole damn thing was hopeless, yet here she was, racing out to Willis Road to try to keep him from committing a crime. It was probably too late, though. He'd probably already gotten into the house. She was probably wasting her efforts, and in the process, making herself appear guilty of complicity. If she had half a brain, she would turn around and go straight to the sheriff.

But she didn't have half a brain. She was a woman in love. The thought brought a sad smile to her lips.

Garrett stiffened, thinking he heard something downstairs. The creak of a hinge? But although he listened intently, he heard nothing further. Still, it was time to get out of here and radio Nate about what he'd found so that Nate could get a warrant based on "information from an informant."

He straightened and turned out the light, then stiffened again, once more thinking he might have heard something.

The trouble with being caught inside someone's house like this was that the householder could shoot you and no one would ever question his right. Least of all when the intruder was wearing a gun.

Hell! It was absolutely essential for him to get out of here without Willis knowing he had been here so that the guy wouldn't destroy the evidence.

That was when he realized he'd been a fool. Damn! Willis had passed him on his way out here, and now Garrett was hearing noises from downstairs.

Swearing under his breath, Garrett listened intently, absolutely convinced that Willis was somewhere in the house. The man would have seen Garrett's car out back and would guess that Garrett was somewhere in here. If he suspected that Garrett was on to him, he'd want to shoot Garrett as a trespasser and destroy the evidence before the cops arrived. Yep. So Garrett had to somehow get out of the house and draw Willis with him so that the evidence would be preserved. And then…well, a little rope would probably solve the issue. And get him sent up the river for unlawful imprisonment, along with the breaking-and-entering charge.

But none of that mattered next to getting an innocent man out of jail and putting a guilty one away before he could hurt some other little girl.

But to do that, he had to live. Which meant coming up on Willis before Willis came up on him.

It also meant pulling his gun from its holster, and just the thought of doing that made him pause. It had been a while since he'd tried to hold his gun, and he was extremely reluctant. What if it shook visibly in his hand, the way it had the last time, right after he'd got out of the hospital?

But he had to risk it. It might be his only defense against Willis. Slowly, with a hand that suddenly felt like lead, he unsnapped his belt holster and palmed the butt of his 9 mm. He held it barrel-up by his shoulder and absolutely refused to check if his hand was trembling.

Wishing he'd had the sense to wear jogging shoes, he began to move toward the hallway, taking care to set down his feet as gently as if they were puffs of down. Even the slightest sound suddenly seemed deafening.

There were no further sounds from downstairs, and he began to wonder if he'd simply heard the noises any old house makes, and not someone moving around downstairs at all. Yet, if he were Willis, he would wait downstairs, knowing the intruder would have to come downstairs sometime. Easy enough to play cat and mouse and wait for your intended victim to try to ease down the stairway.

That was when he noticed another sound, the distant drone of an approaching engine. It crossed his mind to wonder why he hadn't heard Willis approach. Then he wondered again if anyone else were in the house at all. Maybe he'd imagined it. Maybe if he got out of here now, Willis would never know he'd been in the house.

But no, that wasn't the drone of a truck engine, and Willis had been driving a full-size pickup. This was the sound of a smaller four-cylinder engine. Like Sandy's.

All of a sudden his heart was in his throat. Damn, he'd never imagined she would come after him. Never! He'd known she would figure out his intentions when she read his resignation, but he'd believed she would stay clear, which was what he had wanted her to do.

Now this. Moving carefully, but as quickly as he could, he went to the window and pulled the dark curtain aside, trying to see down the driveway. The angle was sharp, and he had to press his cheek flat against the window in order to see the driveway at all. But there it was, sure enough—

Sandy's car. Only by the greatest effort did he keep from swearing out loud. The question now was whether Willis was really downstairs, and if he was, whether he would send Sandy on her way, figuring she knew nothing about this, or whether he would be sure Sandy was Garrett's accomplice.

Probably the latter. His stomach clenched into a tight knot. What now? He couldn't let that bastard hurt Sandy.

When Sandy pulled up, the house appeared to be deserted. No cars were parked out front. Maybe Garrett hadn't come out here after all. But no, if he were going to break into someone's house, he would have the sense to hide his vehicle from casual view.

But still she hesitated, uncertain what to do next. She could get out and go ring the doorbell. If by some strange circumstance Willis answered, she could excuse her presence by saying she needed to ask him something more about his statement. On the other hand, if Garrett was inside, alone, no one would come to the door. That was hardly going to get him out of there.

But if he was already in there, the crime had been committed and there was nothing she could do now to stop him. In fact, all she could do was make herself an accomplice. She ought to turn around right now and get out of here.

But before she could move, she saw Dud Willis come out the front door, carrying a shotgun casually cradled in his arm. At once every one of her alarm bells went off. Her instinctive reaction was to get out of there, but even as she reached to release the hand brake, she realized it was too late. If he wanted to hurt her, he was close enough to blow her away with his shotgun. The only thing to do was brazen it out.

So she rolled down the window and leaned out with a

bright smile. "Dud! I was hoping I'd find you here. I have a couple of questions, if you wouldn't mind answering them."

"Sure." He smiled. "Come on in. I'll make us some coffee."

Obviously Garrett couldn't be around, Sandy thought, or Dud wouldn't be inviting her inside for coffee. Now she had to get through this charade as quickly as possible and get out of here. Where could Garrett have gone?

Keeping her smile firmly in place, she switched off her ignition and climbed out of the car. "Thanks. Coffee sounds great."

But as she started to walk toward the house, he moved in behind her, and she felt something hard press into the small of her back, right against her spine.

"Don't move, Sandy," he said quietly. "One shot here will make you a paraplegic if it doesn't kill you. Hold your hands up where I can see them."

She could feel icy sweat bead on her brow almost instantly. Slowly and very carefully, she lifted her hands. "Dud, what's wrong? Why are you doing this?"

"You know damn well why. That investigator of yours is inside my house. Damn fool left enough tracks for an idiot to follow. Some Texas Ranger."

"Why would he do that? Dud, this is ridiculous!"

"Nothing ridiculous about it, lady. He thinks I hurt that little girl. Is that what you came out here for? To help him?"

"I came out here to talk to you! I told you that."

"And I'm a brass-plated fool. Walk straight up to the door, and don't try any funny stuff, lady. You're trespassing, and no court'll hang me for protecting my property."

"That's not true! It's—"

He interrupted her ruthlessly. "Shut up. Just shut up and keep walking. This gun is loaded, and I'll use it."

Garrett heard the door slam and knew that Willis had indeed been in the house, and that now he was going outside to meet Sandy. And that scared the bejesus out of him. Forgetting everything else, he hurried down the stairs and out the back door, taking care not to let it slam shut. Then, exercising every talent he possessed for moving silently, he crept around the house to the front.

What he saw when he peered around the corner nearly stopped his heart dead. Sandy, hands held high, with a shotgun at her back, was walking slowly toward the front of the house.

There was no question in his mind now that Willis knew what was up. And there was no question in his mind that Willis would kill them both rather than be exposed as a child molester.

At least his eyes hadn't been affected. He could clearly see that Willis had his finger on the trigger of the shotgun. That brand of gun didn't have a hair trigger, but that was scant help. If anything startled him, Willis might well pull that trigger, and Sandy wouldn't stand a chance in hell.

Halfway between her car and the house, Willis told Sandy to stop. Then, keeping the gun firmly planted at her back, he hollered, "Come on out, Hancock. I know you're in there. I've got a gun pointing at Keller's back."

He had a clear shot. Problem was, he didn't trust his hand, and besides, if he shot Willis, the man might well squeeze that trigger. If he could just get him to turn…

Willis called out again. "Come on out, Hancock. You wouldn't want me to get mad and shoot her."

"No, I certainly wouldn't."

Garrett stepped around the corner of the house as he spoke and leveled his automatic at Willis. As he had hoped, his appearance from a different direction startled Willis into turning, and as he turned, Willis brought the barrel of the shotgun around with him. It was an instinctive movement, one he would have remedied immediately.

Except that Garrett was faster. He aimed, vaguely noticing that his hand was rock steady, and fired before Willis could fully assess the situation. An instant later, Willis crumpled to the ground, moaning.

"Run, Sandy! Around back. Call the sheriff!"

She took off, those long legs of hers eating up the distance as if she were the wind, and vanished around the other side of the house. Then Garrett cautiously approached Willis.

The shotgun was still within the man's reach, and he couldn't be sure Willis was down for the count. He might reach for the gun....

But Willis had more important things on his mind...such as survival. "Don't shoot me," he begged between moans. "Oh, God, don't shoot me again."

Garrett kicked the shotgun away and then squatted by Willis, who was holding his side. Blood oozed darkly between his fingers.

"You're going to live, you son of a bitch," Garrett told him roughly. "You're going to live so you can pay."

Chapter 14

Nate scowled at Garrett. "You know what I could charge you with."

Garrett nodded. "Plenty. Believe me, I thought about all of it."

"And Willis could make a case that he was just protecting his property, and that you had no business shooting a man who was just trying to protect his own."

"Except that I was there, Nate," Sandy said quickly. "Damn it, he asked me to get out of my car and come in for coffee, and then he put a gun to my back! With the evidence against him on the Dunbar case, nobody's going to believe Willis was just trying to drive off trespassers."

"That's not the point," Nate growled. "The point is that this fellow here ought to know better! He's a lawman, for heaven's sake! A little patience would have gone a long way!"

"Not for Nighthawk," Garrett said flatly. "An innocent man was in jail. Were we going to wait for another rape to happen, one while Nighthawk was in jail, so we could be sure he didn't commit it?"

Nate's scowl didn't lighten much. "It's messy. Damn messy. Messier than I like. Be that as it may, Sam agrees we're not going to charge you. I think he'd like to wring your neck, though. It's a damn good thing Willis decided to confess to everything, because there's some question about whether using you as a reliable informant to get a warrant would have stood up. He keeps muttering that someone could have made a good Fourth Amendment case and gotten all that stuff thrown out."

"I doubt it," Sandy said. "I seriously doubt it. Garrett wasn't acting in any official capacity. Since he was acting as a private individual, the Fourth Amendment doesn't cover him."

Nate shook his head. "I somehow suspect that would have been argued until the sky fell. Anyway, it's over and done with, and we have a signed-and-sealed confession, and all I want is for you to quit acting like the Lone Ranger in my county. Enjoy your vacation and keep your nose clean." Then he grinned. "And thanks. I just won't say for what."

Outside, the sun was high and the air as clear as crystal, so clear that the mountains looked close enough to touch.

"I'll walk you back, Sandy," Garrett said. "You can fill me in on exactly what Willis told Sam."

"Most of it I guess you figured out. He planned the abduction in advance, and he bought the movie for his daughter because he knew how much she and the Dunbar girl wanted to see it. He delivered it that morning so that his daughter couldn't watch it until after school, and he made a really big point about how she had to invite the Dunbar girl over, because he'd promised her she could see it, too. Anyway, that's how he separated the sisters. I talked with Mrs. Willis that morning before I came looking for you, and that's pretty much the way she told it, too."

He nodded. "When we get to the part about you coming after me, remind me I want to holler at you."

"Somehow I think you'll remember," she said dryly. Inside, though, she was aching with fear and anticipated loss. Now that the case was over, this man wouldn't have any reason to spend time with her. In fact, now that he knew he could shoot his gun without any trouble, he was probably chomping at the bit, wanting to get right back to Texas and pass his reinstatement physical.

"Yeah, I probably will. Okay, so the girl was separated from her older sister."

"That's right. He wore the nylon stocking you found to conceal his face and drove an old car that Lisa wouldn't have recognized, because she's always seen him in his truck. He took her to his place and kept her until just before dawn. He dumped her, buried her clothes on Nighthawk's property, then left the book bag out on the road, figuring someone would call the cops about it. In the end, he got too worried about the girl dying, so *he* called to report it."

"I was wondering if that was him." Garrett nodded, satisfied, and smiled down at her from those amazing blue eyes. "Not too bright."

"He was also the one who called me that night, as you suspected." She smiled at his nod and tried to ignore the way her throat kept wanting to tighten.

"But why did he want to frame Nighthawk?" Garrett asked. "Just because the guy had been seen talking to the girl?"

"No, that's more interesting. Nighthawk bought a parcel of land that used to be in the Willis family. I don't know if you've heard, but the Willises used to own one of the biggest spreads in the county. Anyway, the land that Nighthawk bought had belonged to Willis's aunt, who lives in Cheyenne. She had some kind of grudge against Dud and refused to sell him the parcel, though he'd tried more than once to buy it. She sold it to Nighthawk instead, and Nighthawk refused to sell it to Willis. So Willis decided that if he could frame Nighthawk for this crime, the land would eventually come onto the market as a foreclosure, and he could get it then. It was evidently some kind of an obsession with Dud, but according to Sam, the map will show you why. Nighthawk's property is evidently a big hole in Willis's spread.''

Garrett nodded slowly. "That makes a perverted kind of sense."

"And there you have it. Nighthawk probably wouldn't have been involved at all, except he had the misfortune to own a piece of land Dudley Willis wanted. Kind of chilling, isn't it?"

"To say the least."

At the office, Nina was back behind her desk, busily taking messages and calling clients, trying to fill up the appointment book once again. Sandy appreciated her efforts, but the bottom line was that this whole affair had left a very bad taste in her mouth, and she wasn't sure if she wanted those clients back. She had thought of them as her friends, but it seemed they weren't her friends at all. They had turned on her the instant they objected to another one of her clients. That was their right, of course, but it didn't leave her feeling eager to deal with them.

"Messages," Nina said, handing her a small stack of pink slips, and handing Garrett one.

"Well, hallelujah," Garrett said as he scanned his. "My ex-brother-in-law is being charged with criminal possession of a controlled substance with intent to deal. The feds are going to put him away for a good long time, if he ever gets out of the hospital. I think Ginny will be safe for a while now.''

''That's good news.'' Sandy tried to smile but couldn't quite manage it. The corners of her mouth were developing the most distressing tendency to tremble and pull downward. Surely she wouldn't cry? Not now!

She forced herself to look down at her own stack of messages, and all of a sudden, despite her proximity to tears, she couldn't prevent a laugh. ''Will you look at this? The phone company is ready to put the tap on the line. Do we still want to do it?''

Garrett and Nina both chuckled.

''Oh, and look, the tribal police have contacted Nighthawk's sister. She'll be calling tomorrow morning at ten.'' Sandy looked at Nina. ''Try to get hold of Nighthawk and ask him to be here in the morning. I think he'd like the chance to talk with his sister. My treat.''

And that, she thought, wrapped up all the loose ends but one: her heart.

''Nina,'' Garrett said, ''you'll have to excuse us, but I need to yell at your boss for a few minutes about risking her lovely neck.''

Sandy looked up at him. ''Didn't you already do that?''

''No, I only told you to remind me when we got to that part of the story, and then you managed to avoid it. So I'm going to do that right now. Here or upstairs. Your choice.''

She picked upstairs, because if she burst into tears she didn't want any witnesses. It would be humiliating enough for Garrett to see it.

And she very much feared she was going to cry. She had been a blind fool for a couple of weeks now, ignoring her deepening feelings for Garrett, refusing to consider the eventual cost when he left. Focusing all her attention on the case, while her heart ran amok behind the scenes. Well, now she would get exactly what she deserved for her foolishness. If not this very day, then soon, when Garrett headed home.

Upstairs, she put on a pot of coffee and joined Garrett at the dinette. "So yell at me," she told him.

"Nah, I'm not in the mood anymore." He gave her a faint smile. "I guess you'll put your practice back together pretty quick."

She shook her head and looked away. "For some reason, I really don't care if I do or not. I've got the sourest taste in my mouth about it."

"About the way so many of your clients bailed out?"

She nodded slowly. "There isn't a one of them who wouldn't have expected me to handle their defense if they'd been accused of something, rightly or wrongly. To have them turn on me for doing the same thing for someone else makes me feel…" She hesitated, trying to find a word that adequately described the mixed sense of betrayal, disappointment and hurt—not to mention an inescapable feeling of disgust. "I guess I found out who my friends really are."

"If that's how you want to look at it."

"What do you mean?"

"Just that these people didn't so much betray you as register a protest, which they're entitled to do. It would be nice if everyone were able to adhere to high-minded moral principles, but most of us just can't. It's all well and good to say you believe in the First Amendment, but lots of folks got really sick to their stomachs when the American Civil Liberties Union defended the American Nazi Party's right to march in a Jewish suburb. The courts upheld it, but an awful lot of people couldn't escape the feeling that it was inherently wrong."

"I know. I backed the ACLU, but it wasn't easy. I choked on that one."

He smiled. "See? Well, these folks weren't thinking about constitutional rights as much as they were thinking about a truly horrible crime. Try not to take it too personally."

She sighed and nodded slowly. "I know you're right. But it's going to be a while before I feel the way I used to about the people in this county. Somebody spray-painted my front porch, someone threw a rock through my window.... I guess this isn't the kind of place I thought it was."

"There are people like that everywhere, honey. Just write them off."

Honey. Oh, how she wished he meant that! But it was just a casual endearment, and she swallowed hard against the lump in her throat.

That was when she realized that she was avoiding a confrontation that had to occur sooner or later. By evading the questions that meant the most to her, she was merely postponing the inevitable conclusion of their relationship. What could that do except draw out her agony in exchange for a few more moments of stolen bliss?

Feeling suddenly determined, she opened her mouth to say something, when Garrett forestalled her.

"You know," he said, "about those two women I was engaged to."

It was as if her heart stood stock-still. Was he about to give her all the reasons why he would never get involved again? Oh, God, that was exactly what he was leading up to! She tried to tell herself it was for the best, but the truth was that she would have jumped off a cliff without a parachute if it would have kept Garrett with her. "I know," she managed to say.

"Well... Oh, hell. You know what they say—once burned, twice shy. I swore I was never going to care about a woman again."

"I know. You told me." And this was it, she thought. It was over. He was prefacing his farewell with his reasons.

"Hell," Garrett said again, in almost impatient exclamation. "What I'm trying to say is that I've been a total ass!"

Astonished, she felt her jaw drop. "About what?" Yes, this was it. He was about to tell her that he'd been incredibly insensitive to have started a relationship with her when he had no intention of permanence, that he ought to be strung up or shot or whatever it was he would feel was suitable punishment for his transgression. Bottom line: she was being dumped.

"I knew from the start that you wouldn't consider giving up your practice here," he said. "It's your home and always has been, and I'd have to be an arrogant jerk to even suggest it. But the trouble is, I knew it was impossible, but I went and fell in love with you anyway."

Her heart began to hammer so hard that she thought it was going to explode right out of her chest. "Garrett..."

But he plunged ahead, heedless. "I thought about giving up the rangers, but...darlin', I'm sorry, but I'd be as useless as warts on a hog if I came up here, and I can't stand to be useless. It'd kill me. And I can't ask you to do what I won't do—"

"Why not?" she interrupted him.

He froze, his mouth open on a word that never emerged.

"Why not?" she repeated.

"Because you've worked so hard to build all this," he said.

"So?" She shook her head. "Just exactly what did I

build, Garrett? A practice that evaporated the very first time I took a controversial case? A safe little hiding place where I didn't have to deal with real life—until it walked up and grabbed me by the throat?"

"I think you're being a little hard on yourself, honey. Really, you invested a lot of time and effort—"

"Yes, I did. And it's gone. Just like that, it's gone. And you know what? That's fine. Because now I'm free to do any damn thing I want. I've been wondering for some time what would have happened if I'd had the guts to stay in Cheyenne. Well, actually, I've been trying not to think about it, but I've had this inescapable sense of being...cheated, I guess. Like I've missed things I really wanted to do."

Garrett's expression changed slowly, gradually shifting to one of uncertain hope. "What did you really want to do?"

"Way back when, I wanted to specialize in criminal work. The prosecutor's office didn't have any openings, which is why I went to work for my husband's firm and found myself doing family law. But I always wanted to be a criminal lawyer."

Now it seemed Garrett was the one holding his breath. Finally he released it. "Would you consider coming to Texas? I'm sure you'd find plenty of work."

Everything inside her suddenly became hushed with joy. "Come to Texas with you?"

He nodded, a smile spreading across his face. He rose and came around the table, tugging her gently to her feet. "With me," he said huskily. "As my wife. If you think you could stand living with a cop."

Her arms slipped upward to close snugly about his neck. "What I absolutely couldn't stand, Garrett, is life without you. Of course I'll come to Texas with you."

His blue eyes grew bright. "It gets hotter'n Hades in the summer, and I tend to get obsessed with the job."

"Heat sounds good after all the cold winters I've had, and I get obsessed with the job, too. We'll work it out, Garrett."

Suddenly he threw back his head and let out a loud whoop of joy. And Sandy burst into happy tears.

* * * * *

Silhouette®

INTIMATE MOMENTS™

The thrilling spin-off from the popular
FAMILY SECRETS continuity

FAMILY SECRETS

THE NEXT GENERATION

No one is alone....

Thirty years ago an illegal genetic experiment spun out of
control and led to the death of an innocent woman. Now
her six children are being hunted by a hidden enemy. Can
they trace their past and find each other—and confront
their darkest secrets—before it's too late?

Don't miss these exciting books, featuring six favorite authors:

A CRY IN THE DARK by Jenna Mills
(Silhouette Intimate Moments #1299, on sale June 2004)

IMMOVABLE OBJECTS by Marie Ferrarella
(Silhouette Intimate Moments #1305, on sale July 2004)

TRIPLE DARE by Candace Irvin
(Silhouette Intimate Moments #1311, on sale August 2004)

A TOUCH OF THE BEAST by Linda Winstead Jones
(Silhouette Intimate Moments #1317, on sale September 2004)

IN SIGHT OF THE ENEMY by Kylie Brant
(Silhouette Intimate Moments #1323, on sale October 2004)

IN DESTINY'S SHADOW by Ingrid Weaver
(Silhouette Intimate Moments #1329, on sale November 2004)

Available at your favorite retail outlet.

Silhouette Desire from *his* point of view.

BETWEEN DUTY AND DESIRE
by Leanne Banks
(Silhouette Desire #1599, on sale August 2004)

MEETING AT MIDNIGHT
by Eileen Wilks
(Silhouette Desire #1605, on sale September 2004)

LOST IN SENSATION
by Maureen Child
(Silhouette Desire #1611, on sale October 2004)

FOR SERVICES RENDERED
by Anne Marie Winston
(Silhouette Desire #1617, on sale November 2004)

Available at your favorite retail outlet.